ONLY A HEARTBEAT AWAY

A MODERN HISTORY ROMANCE

DONNA LOVITZ

Only a Heartbeat Away

ISBN: 978-1-7340842-3-8

Published in the United States of America

Email contact: donna@donnalovitz.com

Edited by Sherri Hildebrandt

Cover Design by D. Lovitz

❀ Created with Vellum

To my sister, Debbie Leabch.
A true fiery redhead.

1

"I am not speeding," Jolene Garrison snapped. A quick glance at the speedometer on her Firebird confirmed her mother was right — fifteen miles an hour over the speed limit was definitely speeding. Jolene looked at her mother from the corner of her eye and discreetly let up on the accelerator. They were almost to Watson and she could feel her anxiety grow with every passing mile that brought them closer to the small Minnesota town.

"I hope my hair looks okay," Mary Garrison commented from the passenger seat. "Do you think this new permanent makes my hair look fuzzy?"

"No, Mom. Your hair looks just fine," Jolene assured her. Her mother was on edge — she was about to meet the family of the man her daughter and Jolene's older sister, Cheryl, planned to marry.

"This being your sister's second marriage, I still can't believe they decided to have a bridal shower. I guess they do things differently in 1974. When I got married in '46, if you were married once, folks figured you had everything you needed to start a household."

Jolene sighed but didn't answer. She had already explained to her mother several times that the women of the Watson Lutheran Church thought it right to have a shower on account it was the groom's first marriage.

"The other night Cheryl sounded nervous on the phone when she spoke about Jake's mother. What do you think that's about?" Mary wrinkled her brows.

"Let us just say … Lucille can be a handful. But keep in mind, Cheryl is marrying Jake and not his mother." She reached and squeezed her mother's hand. "Don't worry. Everything is going to be fine." *As long as I keep it together when I see him.*

"Yes, of course," Mary agreed. "I'm just tired. I didn't sleep much last night. I kept thinking about the shower and the family dinner tonight at their house. Cheryl said Jake's parents' place is pretty ritzy. So, how fancy are we talking?"

"Yeah, it's a little over the top." Jolene recalled last fall when she and Cheryl had been invited to the Sugar King Farm for Thanksgiving. The Sugar King was the largest producer of sugar beets in the area and Jake's family — the Cameron's — were more than likely the wealthiest, too. Jolene found it hard to believe a farm house out in these parts could be so luxurious. She recalled the gorgeous crystal chandelier above the dining room table and the marbled floor in the foyer.

"If you don't mind, I'd like to leave right after dinner," Mary said. "The two and a half hours back to Aberdeen is a long drive and I do have to work in the morning."

"That's totally up to you." *The quicker we get out of there, the better!*

"I think it would be best for both of us." Mary gave her a knowing look. "I know you're nervous about seeing *him.*"

Stunned at the comment, Jolene silently stared ahead at the road. *Am I really that transparent?* If her mother could see through her facade, how was she ever going to fool anyone? Especially Michael Cameron? She pictured his dark, captivating eyes on her from across the table, stalking her like she was prey.

"Honey, it wasn't your fault what happened between you

and that ... Casanova," Mary paused and shook her head, "Robert and you had just split up. You were lonely and he took full advantage of the situation. Thank God, Jake is nothing like his brother."

A voice screamed in her head — *It was me who seduced him, Mother!* "Which one, Michael or Brett?" Jolene steadied her breath.

Her mother looked at her annoyed. "Michael, of course."

At the mention of his name, a vision flashed in her head of him lying naked on her bed with an irresistible grin on his handsome face. Her foot quickly hit the brake and she pulled her Firebird over to the side of the road.

"What are you doing?" Mary asked. "Watson isn't that far down the road."

"I need a cigarette."

Mary frowned. "The shower starts in twenty minutes. I don't want to be late."

"We're plenty early, Mom," Jolene said getting out of the car. She leaned against the front fender and lit a cigarette. Watching the smoke blow away in the wind, she thought about her mother. It seemed the woman had come close to piecing together what happened between her and Michael, and yet, she didn't have a clue. Mary wouldn't have known the man existed had he not shown up on her doorstep four months ago demanding to see her daughter.

"I don't know what Cheryl told you about what happened, but it was basically nothing," Jolene said after she got back in the car. "I really don't want to talk about Michael, if that's okay with you?"

When the Watson Church came into view, Jolene scanned the parking lot for her big sister's pickup and found the green Chevy parked in the front row. The only other vehicle she recognized was Jake's mother, Lucille's, red Cadillac parked a few rows behind Cheryl's truck. No one could deny the Camerons were wealthy, and it would take some adjustment for her sister to fit into their family. Cheryl wasn't the type to depend on anyone but herself. It had been two years since her first husband's fatal farm accident and she was still successfully farming and raising their young son.

When the "Rat" — formerly known as Jolene's husband, Robert — ran off with his boss's daughter, Cheryl had welcomed Jolene into her home. She made Jolene realize her marriage had ended, not her entire life. Cheryl deserved the best wedding, and if that meant returning to Watson to deal with a liar like Michael, Jolene knew she would.

In the church parking lot, Jolene smoothed her hands over her celadon colored sun dress and retrieved her and her mother's gift from the trunk. They had decided on a new blender, knowing it was something a little more fun and not exactly necessary. She carried the large, wrapped package into the fellowship hall while her mother held open the door. The room was alive with chatter and laughter from the thirty-plus women seated around decorated tables. Strings of intertwined crepe paper in mint and lilac were carefully draped from pillar to pillar around the room. White tissue bells hung between each post and above the head table in the center. Some of the women stopped their conversations to stare at Mary and Jolene.

Dori Olson, Cheryl's best friend, maneuvered around the tables to greet them.

"Hi, ladies. Welcome!" She gave Jolene a hug then smiled at Mary. "It's so nice to see you again, Mrs. Garrison."

The older woman instantly corrected her. "I go by Mary, these days."

"This place looks amazing, but where's Cheryl?" Jolene asked looking around the room.

"She's in the restroom. I think she's a bit nervous," Dori confided with a quick nod in Lucille Cameron's direction.

Jolene shrugged. "I guess things haven't changed since I left."

Mary raised a brow at her daughter.

"I'll fill you in later, Mom," Jolene quietly whispered.

4

Moments later, Cheryl came into the room and rushed to her sister and mother's side. Hugs were exchanged and they were escorted to their seats at the head table.

"I'd like you to meet my mother, Mary." Cheryl told Lucille at the table. She then turned toward her mother. "Mom, this is Jake's mother, Lucille."

Lucille smiled sweetly as her eyes swept over Mary's modest attire. "It's a pleasure to meet you."

"It's nice to meet you, too," Mary responded as the two shook hands.

Another woman came out of the kitchen and Lucille introduced her as her friend, Joan. The woman barely managed a smile before her condescending eyes turned to Jolene.

"And who is this young lady?"

"Oh, this is Cheryl's sister, Jolene, the —" Lucille paused, "what is it dear? Are you the matron of honor or maid of honor?"

"It's … maid of honor," Jolene answered, caught off-guard. She thought at this point Jake's whole family knew she was divorced.

Joan boldly surveyed Jolene for a moment before she went back into the kitchen, leaving frosty air behind her.

The shower began with introductions as each woman stood and introduced herself then revealed how she was associated with the bride. Two tedious word games were played and lunch followed shortly after.

Before they started opening the gifts, Jolene stepped outside the hall. She was dying to have a cigarette and found an area by the building where no one could see her from inside. Placing a cigarette between her lips, she found her mouth literally hurt from all the smiling. She needed a break from the niceties, and trying to remember so many names had given her a dull headache. Dori came out minutes later and turned her head from side to side apparently searching for someone or thing. Her head stopped seeing Jolene who hastily dropped her cigarette on the ground and snubbed it out with her wedged sandal.

"There you are," Dori stated when she got close enough. "They're ready to open the gifts and they need the maid of honor to record them."

"What?"

"The maid of honor documents who the gifts are from when the bride unwraps them."

Jolene blinked at her. "Really?"

"With a shower this size, it would be difficult to remember who gave what without writing it down."

"I guess I have more responsibility than I thought," Jolene said, shaking her head. "At Cheryl's first wedding we had a small shower and the only attendants were me, and Jon's cousin, Mark. I'm going to have to rely on Brett during the wedding to keep me informed on what is expected."

"Don't worry. You'll do fine. Brett and I will both be there to help you out. Other than walking out of the church together and a brief dance during the Grand March, you won't have to interact with Michael whatsoever."

Jolene was suddenly confused. "Why would I be walking out of the church or dancing with him when Brett's the best man?"

Dori's eyes got huge. "Oh, God. I thought you knew. Cheryl wasn't exactly sure why, but Jake decided to make Michael the best man."

Her words were like cold water in Jolene's face. "No, I think you're mistaken." *Cheryl wouldn't do this without saying something to me.*

"I'm so sorry I spilled the beans." Dori put her arm around her. "No one can blame you for being upset. If any man tried to take advantage of me to get revenge on my sister, I'd want to give him a knuckle sandwich, not walk around arm-in-arm with him."

Jolene nodded.

Dori smiled. "But I can't deny I'm dying to see what the

handsome horse's ass looks like in a tux," she smacked her hand to her mouth. "Michael's like pretty fruit cake that tastes like crap."

Jolene couldn't help but laugh.

"And I'm thrilled to get into that house and check it out at the rehearsal dinner. If it's anything like how you and Cheryl described, it will be an interesting experience. I've lived in this neighborhood most of my life and never once been in the Sugar King Farm house. Michael and I were in the same grade at school and in third grade we took a class field trip to his parents' farm to see the horses. But we never got to see inside the house."

Jolene was listening but her thoughts were on seeing Michael that evening at the family get-together dinner.

Dori must have noticed her distraction. "I would talk to your sister and ask her what's going on."

At the head table, Jolene wrote down the names in a notebook with an enthused smile and "oohed and awed" at most of the gifts Cheryl had received. She managed to laugh and make some comments but her thoughts kept drifting back to the conversation with Dori outside. The whole thing didn't make any sense. Surely, there was more to the story. Why would Jake ask Michael to be his best man after what he did?

THE BACKSEAT of Jolene's car was packed tightly with opened shower gifts when she and her mother left the hall for Cheryl's farm. When the road turned into gravel just outside of Watson, Jolene looked up and groaned in her rearview mirror. A funnel of dust was following behind her once-clean Firebird. *So much for washing my darn car.* Oh, well. It had been clean for the ladies who attended the shower, who cared about dinner at the Sugar King tonight. She wasn't trying to impress anyone. It didn't matter what any of the Camerons thought of her.

Mary talked about the wonderful gifts Cheryl had received

and how nice and polite everyone had been. Jolene listened half-heartedly as she gazed out at the endless rows of planted corn and sugar beets that stretched out as far as the eye could see.

The fields had been covered with a heavy blanket of snow and the road was layered thick with ice on the day she left. It had been a miracle she hadn't gone into the ditch with her eyes full of tears and the bright glare from the afternoon sun off the slippery road. It was only eleven miles to the highway, but it seemed to be a hundred that day. She remembered how maddening it was being forced to drive at a snail's pace when she wanted to push the accelerator through the floor. The only thing that had kept her going was knowing she needed to get as far away from Michael as possible.

In the end, she realized there was no one to blame but herself. Life was about choices, and she'd made a few bad ones during the past year. First she believed a cheating husband could change his ways. Then she foolishly fell in love with a womanizer who used her.

But she wasn't the same naïve woman who had left here broken hearted and disillusioned. Hitting rock bottom had caused her to be honest with herself and the rest of the world. She was the one who had let Michael into her life and playing the part of a high society wife had left her exhausted and uninspired. It had all been about Michael and the Rat, and she had finally realized it really needed to be all about her.

When her divorce finalized, she used her share of the money from the sale of their house to get a real estate license. Her plans were to move out of her mother's house as soon as she found a job in Aberdeen or Mitchell. Mary more than understood her daughter's situation, having gotten divorced from Jolene and Cheryl's father the previous year. Living with her mother was fine, but Jolene couldn't shake the feeling she'd moved back in time. It seemed her future was calling out for her to take center stage while she waited in the wings.

They started to unload the shower gifts from the trunk of

Jolene's car when Mary went inside Cheryl's farmhouse. Jolene waited until the door shut behind their mother before she quickly blurted, "Is it true Michael is going to be the best man?"

Cheryl released a sigh. "Oh, God. Dori told you." She looked down at the ground. "I was going to tell you before you left today. I swear I just found out two days ago and since then I've done everything but beg Jake to change his mind. But he keeps saying he has reconciled with Michael and he wants to start our lives off right. He believes the only way to do that is to put the past behind us."

"What do you mean, they've reconciled? Jolene set her arm load of shower gifts down into her trunk. "How can either one of you forgive him for what he did?" Her heart raced. "He lied to all of us and almost destroyed your relationship with Jake."

"I've argued the fact with Jake for days, and for some crazy reason he thinks Michael deserves another chance."

Cheryl shook her head. "I'm tired of fighting with the whole world for us to be together," she continued. "I know this isn't what you or I want, but I love Jake and I just want us to be married and to be a family."

"Maybe Dori can be the matron of honor and I'll stand up with Brett."

"Please, Jolene." Cheryl took her hand. "I want you to be my maid of honor. I promise you'll never have to be alone with Michael at any time." She paused. "Maybe this is the best way for you to show him it's over between you two?"

Both women glanced toward the house seeing Mary step outside.

Cheryl lowered her voice. "Jake said there's a chance Michael won't be there tonight. But if he is, just try and be civil to him."

Oh, great! Jolene didn't know if she was relieved or disappointed, but the thought of him not being there left her feeling somewhat deflated. She chalked it up to having psyched herself up for weeks for this dinner with plans to show him that he'd meant nothing to her.

They finished unloading the gifts but as the afternoon wound down, the uncertainty of the evening did double duty on Jolene's already soaring anxiety. Why did her heart race at the thought of seeing him again? It was this way every time he crossed her mind. Trying to regain control, she quickly reminded herself for the millionth time that he had used her. And who could dismiss the fact he may have impregnated his best friend's girlfriend. *I'll just have to be cool and ignore the dumb ass.* She didn't know which would prove more difficult: trying to disregard him or fighting the urge to slap his face.

2

The clock ticked loudly on the wall at the St. John's Recovery Center in St. Paul. Michael nervously waited with his therapist, Dr. Munson, for Dr. Hill to join them for a final meeting before he ended his drug treatment at the facility.

"Good morning, gentlemen," Dr. Hill addressed them when he came into the room. He sat down in his chair behind the desk and glanced over the report in front of him. "Mr. Cameron, it appears that you are not physically addicted to any substances. Your blood tests have all come back negative, and you have not displayed any withdrawal manifestations."

Michael silently nodded.

"But the results from your psychoanalysis that Dr. Munson performed has revealed some troubling results. It appears that while you were under the influence of Methaqualone, that you now acknowledge was ingested numerous times for recreational use, you experienced complete memory loss. During that time you attacked your brother's fiancée not once, but twice." He paused to study Michael through his thick glasses.

Michael looked down and nodded with his eyes closed. *Forgive me, God. For the life of me, I don't remember.*

"A total blackout is rare using the drug but has been documented in a small percentage of patients in the last few years." Dr. Hill raised a brow at his colleague. "With the patient's apparent memory loss how was it determined the attacks actually occurred? Were charges filed against him?"

"No. It was my understanding the woman involved didn't contact the authorities," Dr. Munson reported. "Michael's brother, Jake, was a part of his therapy and confirmed the incidents. It was after the attacks were brought to Michael's attention that he was compelled to commit himself for treatment."

"Is that the same brother whose fiancée you attacked?" His eyes went to Michael.

"Yes sir, it was," Michael solemnly answered.

"You're a fortunate man to have a brother so sympathetic of your situation." Dr. Hill leaned back in his chair. "You were lucky all around considering all the things that could have possibly happened to you. I hope you've learned using barbiturates for entertainment is a reckless and dangerous practice. And do keep in mind, it's also illegal to possess Methaqualone without a prescription. But we're not here to pass judgment on what happened. We're only here to help you get better."

Michael remembered the hurt in Jake's voice when he told him about the attacks on Cheryl. The whole thing still seemed like a hideous nightmare.

Dr. Hill pulled open his desk drawer and took out a piece of paper and clicked his ball point pen. "This is the paperwork stating you've completed the recommended therapy and are no longer under our care." He signed the document, then slid it across the desk for Dr. Munson and Michael to sign.

"Mr. Cameron, it seems you've been given a second chance," Dr. Hill said before their meeting adjourned. "I suggest you take it very seriously and clean up your life." He then placed the paper in Michael's file and the three men stood and shook hands.

Michael left the recovery facility and drove his truck across the state toward home. He had plenty of time to think about his family and how grateful he was that they promised to keep his stay at St. John's a secret. He felt incredibly lucky ... until he got onto the highway and the song "Yesterday" began to play on the radio. Hearing the lyrics in the song, a slap of remorse hit him hard. His whole world had crumbled in the past four months and it had been no one's fault but his own. He had been a fool in a blind vendetta to get revenge and lost everything — his family's respect, his best friend, and the woman he loved.

His dismissal at St. John's had been quicker than expected, and he would likely be there in time for the family get-together with Cheryl's family. A picture of Jolene's lovely face came to mind and a lump formed in his throat. How would she treat him this evening after everything that happened? *I hope she doesn't hate me!*

Jake had been careful on his weekly visits not to say anything about her. Maybe it was for the best not knowing what happened after she left. One thing was for sure; She didn't deserve to be with someone who seemed to poison everything and everyone around him.

MARY GARRISON'S jaw fell open when Cheryl turned her truck onto the blacktopped driveway of the Sugar King Farm.

"Oh, my! Is this where Jake lives?"

"Yes, Mom, it is," Cheryl answered.

Jolene had a similar reaction the first time she saw the magnificent, three story, white mansion in front of them. The fancy house and well-kept buildings hadn't been the only things that amazed her last fall.

It was also the first time she had laid eyes on Michael. She had been momentarily lost for words when they were introduced. No one had warned her he was so staggeringly attractive. When he hit on her later that day, she remembered how good it felt to have a handsome hunk show some interest in her, and how it stroked her ego to turn him down. It was during the time when she believed that she and the Rat were destined to get back together. She was still angry at herself for failing to recognize both men had been a dead end street.

Cheryl parked in front of the impressive house and Jolene swung open the passenger door. Taylor, Cheryl's seven-year-old son, immediately leaped out of the truck.

"I'm going to ask Grandpa Chet to take me down to the stables," he stated and ran to the door.

"Don't ask until we're finished with dinner," his mother ordered as she walked around her vehicle.

They rang the bell and the large wooden door opened. Brett, the youngest of the Cameron brothers, answered the door wearing a huge smile. He resembled their father, Chet, with his blonde curly hair and green eyes. Both of his older brothers took after their mother with brownish-black hair and eyes so dark it was hard to see there was a pupil.

"Hi, Brett," Taylor shouted as he came in the door.

"Hey, buddy," Brett greeted him, then rubbed his head. He cleared his throat. "Evening ladies. Please come in."

Cheryl immediately put her arm around Mary once they were inside. Her mother was wide-eyed while she took in the extravagant atmosphere around her. "Brett, this is our mother, Mary."

"Nice to meet you," Brett replied. "I can see that beauty runs in the family."

Jolene let out a giggle. He had always been full of compliments, and it didn't appear he'd changed any. She was only a year and a half older than him but his pretentious mannerisms always made him seem so much younger.

"We're having dinner on the patio. Please follow me." He turned on his heel and led the group through the luxurious house. On the way to the patio, they went through the dining room and Jolene heard her mother gasp when she saw the huge crystal chandelier above the dining room table.

Chet and Lucille stood from their chairs when the group came out the French doors onto the patio. Jake was suddenly in the doorway behind them. When he moved closer to Cheryl, Jolene saw Michael standing behind him. She took a quick inventory of him from the corner of her eye. *Take a breath, girl!* He was striking, dressed in a blue short-sleeved shirt and black dress slacks. The light-colored shirt cuffed at his biceps emphasized his muscular arms. His hair was perfectly combed and his eyes were like Jake's— deep as the night. When those eyes found hers, he nodded and she instantly averted her attention to Jake.

"Dad, this is Cheryl's mother, Mary," Jake introduced his father.

Chet reached out and shook her hand. "It's my pleasure to meet you, Mrs. Garrison."

"I would prefer you call me, Mary," she told him with a confident smile.

"Mary, it is." He smiled.

"Will your father be joining us tonight, Cheryl?" Lucille asked.

"I'm afraid not. He said he's behind with planting. But he promised to be here for the rehearsal dinner."

Lucille cocked an eyebrow at her and promptly changed the subject. "Michael, have you met Cheryl's mother?" She motioned to him to come closer.

The smile suddenly dropped from Mary's face. "Yes. We've already met." She eyed Michael suspiciously. "You're looking much better than the last time I saw you."

Jolene recalled it was last winter after Jake found out Michael was responsible for trying to sabotage his and Cheryl's relationship. The brothers had fought and Michael had two black eyes and a split lip when he came to Mary's house looking for her daughter. Jolene stayed in the house while her mother went outside with a rolling pin and threatened to call the police if he didn't leave. When he refused to go, Mary promptly made good on her threats and called the cops.

The housekeeper came out to the patio and offered refreshments. Jolene recalled her name was Irene, and that the Cameron family thought highly of her. Shortly after everyone had a glass of wine or a cocktail, Jolene took a seat around a beautifully set table. When Michael took the chair across from her, she pretended he wasn't there. Instead of acknowledging his presence, she made a comment to Cheryl on how lovely the bouquets of colorful roses were on each end of the table. Jolene was careful not to let her eyes wander across the table for most of the evening.

The sun was descending but still high above the horizon when Jolene touched her hand to her warm shoulder. Being a redhead, bright sunlight had never been her friend, so she was grateful when someone adjusted the awning behind her. She turned to say thank you and observed Michael return to his chair.

"I wouldn't want to see those pretty shoulders of yours get burned," he told her.

Really? She stared at him. *You're going to hit on me here?*

He gave her a small smile and she coolly looked away in another direction.

Brett sat on Michael's left side before Chet bowed his head and started to recite the mealtime prayer. The rest of the group chimed in and soon after the food was passed around the table. A conversation started about a gift Cheryl had received at the bridal shower.

Lucille had a smirk on her face. "I just couldn't believe Sophie Blackstone is still giving a doll with a crocheted skirt to cover toilet tissue as a gift. How many rolls of tissue does she think a person needs to cover?" Her comment got a few laughs around the table.

The food was half eaten when Chet turned his attention to Mary.

"Are you ladies staying at Cheryl's or are you heading back to Aberdeen tonight?" he asked.

"We're going home tonight. I have to work in the morning," Mary answered. "It won't be too bad of a drive at this time of the year. It doesn't get dark until almost nine."

"And what about you, Jolene?" Lucille piped up. "Jake said you were pursuing a job in real estate. Have you found any prospects?"

Michael's fork stopped moving, but he didn't look up.

"I've got a lot of prospects to explore and more are pouring in every day." She caught her mother's concerned look but didn't acknowledge.

The rest of the dinner was about Jake and Cheryl. Jolene was relieved to be left out of the spotlight. The less Michael knew about her life, the better. Throughout the entire dinner he seemed to be distant and talked very little. Something about him seemed different, but she wasn't sure what. *Don't go there!*

On the way home, she couldn't help but wonder what could've possibly happened between the brothers that would cause Jake to condone Michael's awful behavior.

Are their parents pushing them to forgive and forget?

THE MIDDAY SUN was shining brightly when Lucille stepped out from her air conditioned car into the Watson Lutheran Church parking lot. Her late arrival to her appointment at the Beauty Spot had delayed her arrival for the quilting group. She quickly reminded herself that her financial support alone was more than that of the rest of the women put together. They would just have to wait for her. She made her entrance with a confident smile toward the group of quilters.

Joan Uterman came out of the kitchen and cut her off before she reached the table. "How are the wedding plans going?" she whispered.

"Fine, as far as I know," Lucille answered politely.

"Did you know Cheryl is wearing a white wedding dress?"

"What?"

Joan turned toward Cheryl seated in the middle of the room. "She's showing everyone a sample of the lace and it looks pretty white to me."

Another quilter held the sample in her hand while she admired the lace pattern.

Lucille could see it was bright white and felt her temper flare. *Doesn't she know it isn't right for a bride to wear white when she has a child? Is she trying to embarrass all of us?*

"Excuse me. I need to get a drink of water," she told Joan and retreated into the kitchen. Lucille held onto the sides of the large sink and watched the water run from the faucet. "Our whole family is going to look foolish with her in a white dress, Jake," she said out loud.

"What did you say honey?" A voice came from behind.

"Jo ... Joan, I didn't know you were standing there," Lucille stammered but quickly recovered. "I ... I was wondering if we we're having cake."

"No. I made pies." Joan stepped next to her. "A lemon meringue and a pecan that I whipped cream ..." She stopped speaking and stared at her friend. "They don't care at all about your opinion concerning this wedding, do they?"

The splashing water in the sink and noise from the next room was enough to mask their conversation.

"Does it really show that much?" Lucille looked down into the sink.

"For God's sakes, she's marrying your son. She's going to make your whole family look foolish wearing a virginal white dress." Joan shook her head.

"I just don't know what to do. That woman has got Jake so mixed up. He'll do anything to please her." She pulled a handkerchief from her sleeve and dabbed her eyes. "She's leading him around ... like a doe in heat."

"I've heard it was like a cat house at the Langtree Farm last winter." Joan's eyes lit up.

Lucille's mouth snapped open. "Why are people saying that?"

"The word's out that her sister, Jolene, who was still married at the time, was all over Brett, at the M & M Ballroom on New Year's Eve."

That has to be the reason Michael and Brett had that awful fight last winter. Oh God. Now the whole town knows they were feuding over Cheryl's floozy sister.

"A wild streak obviously runs in the family. You know their mother is divorced, too. It sounds like the whole family is trashy."

"Yes, I'm aware."

"We better get back out there." Joan looked toward the door. "But I think you need to put the trash where it belongs." After Joan turned off the water, the two friends hugged.

Lucille went out into the commons area with a smile on her face. She dished a plate and looked around for a place to sit. The only chair left was next to Nell Thompson. *Damn!*

"Isn't that a beautiful lace pattern on Cheryl's dress?" Nell asked before Lucille got her chair pulled up to the table.

Lucille looked up into Cheryl's eyes. "I've yet to see it."

"I only have a sample in —" Cheryl was interrupted by Nell.

"This wedding is coming up so fast. I can't believe it's only two weeks away."

"Yes it is," Lucille agreed and faced Cheryl. "By the way, are your sister and mother bringing dates to the wedding?"

Cheryl stared at her future mother-in-law but didn't answer.

"The only reason I'm asking is because Chet and I were wondering who we will be sitting next to during dinner."

"I doubt either will bring a date." Cheryl shook her head.

"I'm sorry to have to ask you about it here," Lucille looked around. "But Jake doesn't say much about the wedding and you haven't let me know what's going on."

"I've been a little busy with planning the wedding and running a farm."

Joan rolled her eyes down at the end of the table urging Lucille to continue. "I worry about you both looking foolish." Lucille's eyes settled on Cheryl. "I can't understand why you thought to buy a white dress."

Cheryl's mouth dropped open and ladies went silent around the table.

"You can wear whatever you want, dear," Alma Green announced. Being the oldest parishioner in the church, she was highly respected.

"She can't wear white!" Lucille snapped. "She has a child."

Cheryl pushed out a deep breath. "The sample of lace is the only one the shop had available and it's in white. My wedding dress is ivory."

Lucille felt herself flush. "I guess if I had been included in some things, I would've known that."

"The most important thing is for the ceremony to be performed in the church," Patsy Timms, the pastor's wife, slipped into the conversation. She always made a point to keep the peace in the room. Moments later, pie was served and the women showered Joan with compliments on the perfect tartness of her lemon pie.

The women began their quilting when Nell commented, "It will be so nice for you to get some help on the farm, Cheryl. A woman shouldn't have to work as hard as you do."

All heads turned for Cheryl's reply, "Yes. Our dream has always been to farm together."

Lucille was going to say something but thought about her husband and held her tongue. Chet had talked for many years about owning the Langtree land. *Too bad the only way to get it is for Jake to marry a conniving little tramp.* She watched as Cheryl interacted with the quilting ladies. *Look at you. Fooling all these women with your sweet and innocent act. We'll see how you react when your farm becomes part of the Sugar King and we call the shots.*

"WELL, I see your real estate license number is on your application and everything seems to be filled out correctly." Bill Elliott scanned the paper from the other side of the desk. Jolene smiled when he briefly looked up at her. "The only thing that brings up any concern for me, Miss Garrison, is your lack of experience." He dropped her application down on the desk and waited for her response.

"I agree I don't have the experience, but I can assure you Mr. Elliott if you hire me, I promise to work very hard for your business. You wouldn't be disappointed. All I need is an opportunity to prove myself."

He stared for a moment rubbing his chin and appeared to be considering her application. "Well, I may be taking a risk …"

The door suddenly burst open and a tall, plump woman barged into the room. Her eyes immediately traveled over Jolene who wore a conservative navy blue business skirt with a matching jacket and a cream colored silk blouse.

"Marjorie!" he exclaimed. "What are you doing here?" He looked surprised.

"Can I have a word with you, Bill?" she blurted ignoring his question. "Privately?"

"Yes, dear." He glanced at Jolene. "Miss Garrison could you step out and give my wife and me a moment."

"Sure, by all means. I'll wait out in the hall." Jolene left the room and closed the door behind her.

Marjorie's blaring voice erupted on the other side of the thin office door. "Thank goodness, Louise tipped me off you're about to hire a young hussy like her. I won't have it."

Jolene recalled the nameplate on the receptionist's desk read, "Louise."

"But dear, she's just a kid looking for a break," Bill defended himself.

"Let her get a break from somewhere else. I don't want you

and I'm sure Linda doesn't want Jim to be working closely with anyone who looks like that."

Jim was the other partner at the agency, and Jolene assumed his wife's name had to be Linda.

Moments later, Marjorie bolted out of the office and avoided eye contact with Jolene when she passed her in the hall.

Feeling awkward, Jolene knocked on Mr. Elliott's door and was told to come inside the room.

He quickly stood from his chair. "I'm sorry. But in light of your inexperience as a Realtor, I'm afraid I'll have to pass on hiring you." I hope this won't discourage you from pursuing a career in real estate."

"I'm sorry, too." She swallowed trying to hold back her emotions. "I would've worked very hard for your agency."

Outside in the parking lot, she opened the driver's door of her car and hastily removed her jacket. She tossed it and her purse onto the passenger seat then got in the car and slammed the door. Tears welled up in her eyes as she stared at the front of the building of Elliott's Realty. She quickly blinked them back seeing someone peek through the blinds at her from inside. Knowing it was likely the battle-axe receptionist, Louise, Jolene knew there was no way she was going to let the woman see her cry. She cranked the key in the ignition then put her car in gear and stomped on the accelerator. Not looking back, she let her tires squeal on the blacktop the entire way out of the parking lot.

A block away Jolene pulled her car over to the side of the road then screamed and pounded her fist onto the steering wheel. She had spent the money for the gas and traveled the two and a half hours to Mitchell for her fourth interview in the area only to have it end without a job offer.

Once settled into a lane on Highway 37, she took a few deep breaths and was surprised when her frustration evolved into an uncontrollable fit of laughter. How could Marjorie realistically think she would chase after her husband? He was bald, over-weight and looked to be around her dad's age. *Eww!*

A few more miles down the road she rehashed the appointment and decided it had been a victory despite how strangely it had ended. Bill Elliott was about to hire her seconds before his jealous wife barged into the room. It was the closest she'd come to actually getting a job and definitely progress compared to her last interview in Pierre. She was told by the male interviewer a pretty girl like her should just find herself a husband and forget all about this nonsense of getting a job. He didn't care how high she'd scored on the test for her Realtors license or that she wore the latest business suit and conducted herself as a professional. His attitude made it more than clear that a real estate license issued to a woman carried as much weight as a gum wrapper. It all boiled down to one thing — she had to convince someone to take her seriously.

MICHAEL ENTERED Schommer's barber shop in Montevideo and was surprised to see how busy the place was on a Thursday morning. Considering Jake and Cheryl's wedding was fast approaching, he decided to stay and wait for a haircut.

Taking a seat by the window it wasn't too long before he started to think about Jolene. The way she treated him the other night hurt more than he ever imagined. She was so cold and distant. But what had he expected? He broke her heart. She had the right to treat him like he was invisible. It was what he deserved — to be non-existent. The thought left him feeling alone and completely empty. *Why couldn't I see what I had before it was too late?*

Not wanting to think about her any longer, he picked up the newspaper on the small table next to him. On the front page there was a picture of a corn field across the border in South Dakota. The rows of new corn plants were wilted and some looked completely dried up. They had received little rainfall so far this spring and it was a big concern for every farmer in the area.

He was about to read the local news when he noticed a couple pass by the window pushing a baby stroller down the sidewalk. Dropping the paper on the table, he quickly wove through the crowd and ran out the door. Outside on the sidewalk, he whistled loudly, and the man turned, a huge smile growing on his face.

"Mike! How the hell are you?" Jim Stanton stepped over to him with his hand out. The woman turned the stroller around and pushed it toward them.

"Hey, stranger." Lyla Mason was dressed in a nice pant suit, and without her heavy makeup, she looked great.

Michael was completely taken aback when Jim pulled him into a hug after they shook hands. It had been months since they'd last talked. Their friendship had reached a parting of the ways when Jim told Jolene that Michael had used her in a plot to break up Cheryl and Jake. Jim also dropped the bomb that Michael may have fathered Lyla's child, as well.

"You haven't formally been introduced to my wife." He put his arm around Lyla. "This is Mrs. James Stanton."

Michael struggled for words. "Con … congratulations," he managed to spit out. Jim turned and pushed back the canopy on the stroller. "And this is our son, James Junior."

Inside the stroller was a baby with light hair. Michael bent down to look at the infant and a flood of relief rushed through his body. The child looked like a miniature Jim lying in the stroller with the same shaped head and the distinctive Stanton dimple in his chin.

Michael took an easy breath. "He sure is cute. How old is he?"

"One month tomorrow," Jim proudly reported. "Hey if you want, why don't you stop over. We're in the new Golden View apartments on Snake Hill Road by the river." Jim reached in his pocket and took out a business card and an ink pen. He jotted down the apartment number on the card and gave it to Michael.

Turning it over in his hand, Michael saw Jim's name and telephone was on it with his father and brother's. Michael noticed the three crowns on the card and remembered he'd heard the three had formed a corporation called Triple Crown Association. Jim's dad, Fred, had apartment buildings in Montevideo and other neighboring towns.

"I'll … do that," Michael said, certain that he wouldn't. He glanced back at the barber shop and saw a man step out the door. "I better get back in there if I want my haircut. "Well, take care, you two, and congratulations again."

While the barber cut his hair, Michael's thoughts drifted to Jim and Lyla and the situation last winter. There had been a lot of women during the short period he lived with Jim but none like Lyla and her sister, Linda. Everyone knew their homelife suffered with an alcoholic mother and her violent boyfriend. The two sisters followed him and Jim around like misguided groupies, doing whatever was requested in order to hang out around the apartment. Jim was always doing Lyla while Michael let 'ludes and Linda take care of him.

It was Dr. Munson's theory that years earlier Michael had shut off his emotions after a bad break-up. When he met Jolene and started to feel again, he didn't know how to deal with his feelings. To insure he wouldn't get hurt again, he tried to prove to himself that she meant nothing and foolishly had sex with Lyla. Had he known how Jim felt about her, it would've never happened.

Michael didn't know if the doctor was right, but the most important thing he learned during his months of therapy was to take full responsibility for his actions. He no longer blamed Jim for disclosing the terrible things he'd done. His friend had been blinded by the desire to get revenge just as he'd been with Cheryl and Jake. The situation was what it was. Michael knew there was nothing he or anyone else could do about it now.

3

J olene stood on a pedestal before a ninety degree mirror and stared at the mint green dress for Cheryl's wedding. It fit her figure well and only the hem needed to be altered. The fabric crisscrossed each breast and had thin spaghetti straps with an attached cape. The cape, made of sheer chiffon, draped over the top of the dress and made it appropriate for a church wedding. It was the final fitting for the girls, and Cheryl was taking longer than expected with the seamstress down the hall. Dori came out of the dressing room wearing her bridesmaid's dress in a lilac color.

She stared at Jolene. "Well, look at you. You fill it out like Raquel Welch." Dori tugged on the straps of her dress. "I'm going to need a little help here."

Another seamstress close by nodded. "We can sew some cups into the dress. It's much more comfortable and looks better than wearing a padded bra."

"I wonder what the hold-up is with Cheryl?" Jolene asked.

"I think her dress needed more alterations," the seamstress answered.

"What could they be altering? When we were here a few weeks ago, her dress fit like a glove." Jolene walked toward the small room where Cheryl and the other seamstress were assessing the wedding dress.

"We can let it out another quarter inch, but that's it," the woman mumbled with pins tucked between her lips.

Jolene stared at her sister and wondered how she could've possibly gained a dress size in less than a month's time. Cheryl worked hard and staying in shape had never been an issue. It was even more strange that hearing the dress needed to be enlarged hadn't upset the future bride.

That's weird! Jolene watched her the rest of the appointment trying to figure out what was going on with the sudden weight gain. Maybe the stress that comes with a wedding had driven her sister to eat more.

Later that afternoon, Dori and Jolene sat at Cheryl's kitchen table while she made coffee.

"I think we should forget the coffee and have a glass of wine to celebrate our last fitting," Jolene said and went to the refrigerator.

"You girls go right ahead. I think I'll stick to coffee," Cheryl said instantly. "Taylor is going to be home from school soon. I wouldn't want him to think I just sit around and drink wine all day."

Jolene slapped the refrigerator door shut and put her hands on her hips. "Okay, Cheryl. You want to tell me what's going on?"

"What do you mean?" Cheryl asked innocently.

"Your dress needing to be let out and now you've become worried about Taylor thinking you're a drunk." The notion suddenly hit her like a ton of bricks. "Oh my God! Are you pregnant?"

Cheryl tried to hold back a smile before she turned to Dori. "I told you she'd figure it out."

Jealousy sliced through Jolene like a machete. *You shared the news with Dori and not me?*

Her sister must have read the hurt on her face. "Dori figured it out right before the shower. Jake and I weren't going to tell anyone until after the wedding. Please, Jolene. Don't tell Mom," Cheryl begged. "Jake and I made a pact we wouldn't tell anyone until after the wedding. Taylor doesn't know yet."

"So how far along are you?" Jolene asked.

"Well. That's the real shocker ...." She took a deep breath. "I've never been regular, so I went to see Dr. Morgan. He thinks I'm somewhere around four months."

Jolene felt her jaw drop. "So the baby's due in ..." she paused to calculate the time, "in October?"

Cheryl nodded. "Early October."

"And how is Jake reacting to being a father?" Jolene spit out without thinking.

"He's on cloud nine." Cheryl smiled blissfully. "We're both shocked but thrilled. But we want to keep it quiet until after the wedding." Her eyes went from her sister to her best friend. "Other than Jake and I, you two are the only other people who know about the baby. I'm counting on you both to keep it to yourself."

Both women immediately pledged to keep it a secret.

Cheryl looked up at the ceiling and rolled her eyes. "And I would die if Jake's mother found out right now. It's been hard enough dealing with her about the wedding. I just gave Joan Uterman at church the final head count for the guests for the wedding dinner a week ago, Tuesday. I had to wait for Lucille's list. A person would think with the wedding two and a half weeks away, she would've figured it out before then." She released a deep sigh.

"I don't blame you for getting upset with her," Dori shook her head.

"She was terrible yesterday at the quilting session," Cheryl continued. "She told the whole group about how I'm going to embarrass Jake and myself by wearing a white wedding dress."

"What?" Jolene asked puzzled. "Your dress is off-white. Why would she say that?"

"She saw the sample of the lace in white and assumed it was the color of the dress."

Dori released a deep breath. "I know Lucille is claiming the contrary, but I don't think she's really happy about you becoming a part of their family." She took Cheryl's hand. "You just have to keep your eye on the prize —you're marrying the man you love. Hopefully, the man upstairs will help you with his mother."

THE SMELL of dressing from stuffed pork chops filled the south end of the house on the Sugar King Farm. Michael entered the dining room and found his father and brothers seated at the table, but his mother was strangely absent. Irene, the housekeeper, stood in front of the swinging kitchen door with her arms crossed.

"Where's Mom?" he asked.

"She's still upstairs," Irene answered.

"Did you tell her we're waiting for her to come down for supper?" Chet asked.

"She told me to tell you she isn't coming down."

"Is she sick?" Chet stood up.

"I don't think so but she does seem to be upset about something," Irene told him.

Chet went out the door into the hallway, and seconds later they heard his footsteps going up the long staircase.

Irene turned to the men at the table. "Which one of you is responsible for upsetting your mother this time?" Each brother glanced at the other two and shrugged. A few minutes later, their father returned and went straight to the swinging door between the kitchen and dining room and held it open.

"Irene. Let's go ahead and eat. She's not coming down," he told her. The old woman brought in bowls of food and they recited a hurried prayer. Chet frowned at Jake after his plate was dished.

"I know the way you're looking at me, Mom's problem is my problem. Right?" he asked.

"It seems your mother went to the quilting group yesterday and is still upset." Confused glances were exchanged around the table.

"I don't know anything about it," Jake answered, and continued to cut up his pork chop.

"She said your fiancée was filling everyone in on details about the wedding before she arrived. She thinks Cheryl did that on purpose. All she wants is to be a part of the wedding."

Jake took a deep breath and let it out. "Yeah, Dad, maybe she should keep Mom more in the loop, but Cheryl's trying to keep things simple. And you know how Mom can get."

Chet nodded. "Enough said." He turned to Michael. "Did you get that entire field planted by Iversons?"

"It's all done," Michael told him.

The phone rang once and they heard Irene pick it up in the kitchen. Seconds later, she stuck her head around the door. "Chet, it was Charlie Vanders on the phone. He said to give him a call whenever you're done with dinner."

"Okay, I'll do that." A small smile came to his lips. "With the wedding coming up, I bet he wants to congratulate me about acquiring the Langtree land. He knows I've had my eye on that piece of river bottom property for a very long time."

Jake stopped eating and put down his fork. "Dad, there's something you should know."

"What's that?" Chet's amused smile remained.

"I was hoping to tell you after the wedding," Jake paused to swallow, "Cheryl and I getting married isn't going to give us her farm."

Chet cocked his head. "You're marrying the woman. Of course it will."

"No. I will own only part. There's going to be a partnership like we have."

"A partnership? With who?" Chet lunged forward in his chair. "Did she borrow against the place?"

"No, she didn't. Cheryl wants it to stay in the Langtree name. She and I are going to be in a partnership with Taylor."

Chet's mouth dropped open. "That's ridiculous. He's just a kid!" His eyes searched his son's. "Are you seriously telling me that you're going to be partners with a seven-year-old kid? Where would you get such a stupid idea?"

"I got it from you," Jake said calmly.

"What do you mean, from me?" Chet raised his voice.

"She wants to protect her son and make sure he gets his inheritance, just like you did with us boys."

Chet shook his head. "You and your brothers are grown men who helped make this farm what it is. I can't believe she talked you into something so idiotic."

"She didn't. I talked *her* into it."

There was a long silence before Chet said, "I figured you would have more loyalty to *this* family."

Brett stared down at his plate while Michael carefully watched Jake.

"Can't you look at it from her point of view?" Jake slid back in his chair. "Would you agree to let someone have complete ownership over your farm with no investment in theirs?"

Chet's eyes went cold. "I never dreamt you'd let this woman rule you like the last one did. If word gets out about this, you'll be the laughing stock of the county."

Jake raised his arm and pointed at his father. "If you wouldn't have put that damn stipulation in the contract about spouses being exempt from ownership in our own contract, I don't think we would've done any of this." His eyes flashed when he threw his napkin onto his plateful of food and jumped to his feet. He glared at his father for a moment then headed into the kitchen. The back door slammed and seconds later they heard his truck go out the driveway.

Later that evening, Michael lay and watched the curtains move slightly from the breeze coming in his open bedroom window. He'd awakened several times thinking about the conversation during dinner. It was he who'd convinced Lucille to add the stipulation into the contract about any future spouses being exempt from any assets in case of a divorce or death. He felt guilty, knowing his intent at the time hadn't been to protect the family corporation, it was to cause trouble between Jake and Cheryl. Once again he had let anger make his decisions.

He recalled during rehab when Jake told him he was still a good man despite his bad choices. Jake's encouraging words had pushed him to take responsibility for his actions. They embraced, and afterward Michael swore he'd be truthful to him for the rest of his life no matter what. It was amazing the faith the man had in him after everything he'd done to him and Cheryl. The last thing he wanted to do was go back on his word. *Should I tell him?* He decided Jake had enough on his mind with Mom, Dad and the wedding. He would tell him next week after he came home from his honeymoon. Jake didn't need any more crap from his family during the most important time of his life.

JOLENE TURNED into the driveway of her mother's small house in Aberdeen but didn't get out of her car. She flopped back in the driver's seat and closed her eyes. It had been a long drive from Sioux Falls after being in court all morning with the Rat. He and his colleagues of skilled, cut-throat divorce lawyers had convinced a judge to reduce her meager monthly alimony to the unreasonable amount of one hundred and fifty dollars. It hadn't mattered that she worked as a secretary to put him through law school or that she had helped him with all of his cases the first few years after he became a lawyer. The Rat knew dragging her back into court endless times would eventually financially exhaust her. Now that his affair with his boss's daughter, Stephanie, had evolved into a marriage proposal, he had infinite access to a free legal team. *How am I going to tell Mom I'll be contributing less for household expenses?*

Mary had been more than understanding in the beginning about her desire to become a Realtor but lately her mother made hints that perhaps it was time to rethink her career path. Jolene couldn't blame her for having doubts, because it appeared getting hired in a male-dominated profession was only a far-fetched dream. Her last job interview in Pierre had turned out to be another dead end. Jolene, and the other two applicants who both happened to be men, sat in the hallway outside the interviewer's office. The men were called in ahead of her and each interview had lasted twenty-five to thirty minutes. Her entire appointment was less than fifteen. The male interviewer was more concerned with how the weather was on her way down from Aberdeen than her qualifications as a real estate agent. It seemed he couldn't get her out of his office fast enough. She was certain she wouldn't get the job. *What was she going to do now?*

Perhaps she could get a job at Herberger's department store in Aberdeen. Maybe sell make-up or become a clerk in the ladies clothing department. She took a deep breath and slowly let it out. The thought made her feel like a complete failure, but it would pay her bills. It was bad enough her mother had paid for her maid of honor's dress. Mary was a saint, and Jolene knew she'd lived off her long enough. The only thing left to do now was — to admit defeat. She would go downtown next week and apply at Herberger's after Cheryl and Jake's wedding.

Her current employment status would make her portrayal of successful business woman much more difficult to pull off to Michael and the rest of his family. To most women it would be impossible, but she had a secret weapon. Being married to a lawyer for more than six years had taught her well how to side-step the truth in every situation.

WHEN MICHAEL CAME out of the tool shed at the Sugar King, he saw his mother rush from the garage and into the house. Curious, he jogged to the house and went inside.

"Chet, Jake! Are either of you here?" Lucille yelled loudly from the dining room.

Apparently she heard the back door shut and went into the kitchen. "Where is your father and Jake?" she demanded.

"They're out in the field working on the beet planter."

Her eyes narrowed. "You go back out in the field and tell them both I need to see them immediately."

"Somebody better have died, because neither is in the best mood. They're at each other because Jake told Dad to replace that planter last year and now it broke down. They sent me back here for some more wrenches."

Lucille took a few distressed deep breaths.

"Come, sit down." He put his arm around her. "What's going on?" He led them to the table in the corner of the kitchen.

"Cheryl Langtree is pregnant." She rubbed her forehead in her hand.

He looked at her curiously. "A person would think having a grandchild would be *good* news."

Her hand slapped the table. "I doubt the child is Jake's. She's four months along. If you remember right, she and your brother were broken up for a while last winter."

"Who told you all of this?"

"I can't say. Someone could lose their job."

"Well, I know you went out for lunch with Joan Uterman." He crossed his arms. "Are you sure she got her facts right?"

Her eyes narrowed. "She heard it straight from someone who knows someone who works in Dr. Morgan's office. Everyone's talking about what happened at the Langtree house last winter. Some people are calling it a 'cat house.'"

Michael recalled the sex with no strings attached arrangement he had with Jolene. That was the way it all had started. Unfortunately for him, it wasn't the way things had ended.

"I know you're aware of how her sister enticed Brett into taking her out on New Year's Eve," she closed her eyes, "and it all happened after Cheryl and Jake broke up. Don't you see? It could be anyone's child."

Michael searched for something he could say to calm her down. Jolene would've never told anyone about their exclusive situation and knowing Cheryl, he had no doubt the child was Jake's. She wasn't a lose woman, and he couldn't imagine her ever being unfaithful to his brother. His mother had no idea the hell he'd put his brother's future wife through. He couldn't inform her nothing had happened between Jolene and Brett without revealing his secret involvement with her.

Taking her hand, he looked into her worried eyes. "It won't work to confront Jake. You and I both know he'll do the right thing and marry her anyway. If I were you, I wouldn't let on to anyone that you know anything about her pregnancy. Just wait until after the kid's born. If it doesn't look like him, tell him then. He'll divorce her immediately."

"And if they divorce, we'll get half of her farm." Her voice rang triumphantly.

Oh boy! Dad never broke the news to her about Jake's new partnership!

"THERE HE IS," Dori whispered to Jolene. Both women turned their heads in the pew and watched Michael stroll confidently up the aisle of the Watson Lutheran Church.

The light green shirt he wore contrasted nicely against his dark, tanned face and arms. *Why does he always have to look so good?*

Reaching the group at the front of the church, he discreetly shook his head at Jake.

The wedding rehearsal was set for six o'clock and it was five minutes past the hour. Maybe it was some sort of farming issue, but what could be so important that the entire wedding party had to wait for the inconsiderate best man? Jake's eyes briefly met Cheryl's before he nodded to the pastor.

"If I could have everyone's attention. Now that everyone is here ... we can begin." The pastor seemed anxious to get started.

"Wait a minute." Lucille turned to Cheryl. "Where is your father? Isn't he going to give you away?"

Cheryl straightened in a pew where she sat with Taylor. "No," she calmly said. "Taylor is giving me away."

Jolene was startled by the news. She had assumed her father wouldn't attend the rehearsal, but she had no idea he would be a no show for the entire wedding. *I was afraid of this. He's not man enough to face any of us since Mom and he got divorced.*

"Can we proceed, Pastor?" Jake asked.

The pastor cleared his throat. "Yes." If the bride and her son," he smiled down at Taylor, "and the two bridesmaids would line up in order in the back of the church, we can begin. But first let's have the usher bring up the mother of the groom and then the mother of the bride." The usher, Chuck, a tall friend of Jake's from college, immediately got to his feet and led Lucille and Mary to the back of the church.

Jake and the groomsmen were directed by the pastor to stand at the front of the church. Jolene noticed Michael observing her several times during the rehearsal, but she pretended to be unaware. It was important not to give someone like him any encouragement. *Why did I think to wear this dress?* It was bright blue and the low-cut front bordered on sexy.

When they rehearsed walking out of the church, she barely let her fingers touch his arm the entire time. At one point, she caught a whiff of his aftershave and it triggered a memory of a romantic dinner they once had shared. *Don't go there!*

Driving to the Sugar King, Jolene listened while Cheryl told Mary, Dori and her about the phone call from the night before.

"Dad told me he was behind with planting and seeing how he already gave me away once, he wouldn't be attending. He said most folks on their second time around saved the money and get hitched at the court house."

Mary released a disgusted breath. "That sounds like him."

"So, he's not coming at all?" Jolene was amazed how well her sister was handling the news.

"He said he wasn't. Jake thought he would change his mind and asked Michael to keep an eye out for him."

"Then Billy won't be attending, either?" Jolene felt an ache in her chest knowing she could've picked up their brother on her way, had she known. "Do you think Dad will let him come on his own?"

"Billy has a farm permit that only allows him to travel within twenty miles of the farm. And you can bet Dad would never let him borrow his truck."

"I could go back and get him," Jolene offered.

Cheryl shook her head. "I thought about that, but I really doubt Dad will let him out of chores."

Dori reached and patted Cheryl's shoulder from the backseat. "I'm so sorry he's being so insensitive."

This time dinner was being served in the formal dining room. The room looked fabulous with the tall lit white candles and a huge flower arrangement of white roses and pink lilies in the center of the table. Jolene waited for most of the guests to be seated before she took a chair. She wanted to make sure not to sit anywhere close to Michael. Her plan was spoiled when she noticed a place card with her name on it next to him. Chet and Lucille sat on each end of the long mahogany table with the wedding party and rest of the guests seated between.

Taylor smiled from across the table. "Aunt Jolene, there's a *man* in the kitchen and he's cooking our food."

Jolene was surprised to learn dinner was being prepared by a professional chef, and prime rib was on the menu for the evening. Lucille had obviously gone through quite a bit of trouble to make this dinner a success. It was odd behavior when Cheryl believed the woman had deep reservations about them getting married. Maybe it was a way for Lucille to flaunt their wealth?

When everyone's glass around the table was filled with champagne, Chet raised his glass in a toast, "To Jake and Cheryl. May they have a long and happy life together."

Michael brought his glass to his mouth but before taking a swallow, he lifted his glass again at Jolene and nodded.

She squinted and shook her head. *Do you honestly think you're going to impress me?*

"How about we call a truce?" he whispered.

Her lips were close to her glass. "Sure. You don't speak to me and I won't speak to you."

He winced slightly like she had inflicted pain. "I'm sorry about what happened," he got in when someone laughed loudly at the end of the table.

"At this point, I really don't care how you feel," she quietly murmured, then turned her head to Brett and made a comment about how perfectly the prime rib was prepared.

They were enjoying their dessert — a chocolate soufflé — when Lucille focused her attention on Jolene."

"Tell us Jolene, how is the job hunt going?"

"I've been looking at some excellent opportunities."

"Oh? Where at?" Lucille wasn't going to leave it alone.

"I made quite an impression in Mitchell, but right now I'm considering a job in Aberdeen," Jolene answered in a nonchalant tone.

"That would be nice to stay closer to your mother," Lucille commented.

Jolene was thankful during the rest of the meal that neither Michael nor his mother tried to address her.

Later that night, Jolene slept in Cheryl's spare bedroom with her mother. Mary was fast asleep shortly after her head hit the pillow and she now snored loudly from the other side of the bed.

Jolene had told herself during dinner she wasn't going to give Michael another thought. Now, she lay awake in the dark going over every detail of the evening.

How dare he act so casual and carefree? He gave off the impression he was innocent of all his wrong doings. Or was he under the crazy assumption that if Jake could forgive him, everyone else would, too? Was he stupid or just that arrogant? He had definitely lived up to his reputation as a player tonight. She could kick herself for not listening to her sister in the first place. Cheryl had warned her more than once not to get involved with a man whose heart was made of stone.

THE SUN WASN'T UP in the eastern sky, but Michael could see faint streaks of pink above the horizon when he drove the farm truck to the pasture. It looked like it was going to be a nice day for Jake and Cheryl's wedding. He smiled to himself knowing he couldn't be happier for them, especially now with the baby coming.

Michael knew what he did to Cheryl was inexcusable and he wouldn't blame her for never forgiving him. Why would she, when he couldn't forgive himself? It was truly amazing she would allow someone who tormented her be the best man in her wedding. Jake and her were both incredible people and God had blessed them when they found each other.

The cattle were peacefully grazing on grass when he made his way down the fence line with a flashlight, checking for any downed posts or wires. Deer were always a problem, and more so closer to the river. While his eyes searched the grass, events of the previous evening slowly took over his thoughts. He wondered if he should've made a better effort to apologize to Jolene. It was something he wanted to do at the family get together, but the timing hadn't been right. The last thing he wanted to do was to ruin the evening for Jake or Cheryl. So he played it cool. It had been pure hell last night to sit so close and not touch her. She looked sizzling hot in that blue dress. He couldn't help but wonder if it was something she'd worn to secretly torture him. He tossed and turned for hours during the night, before deciding he had two choices: He could talk to her about what happened and risk making a scene, or he could sit back and enjoy the time with her. Either way, it was unlikely anything would change between them. She was only here for the wedding and God only knew when he'd see her again. Maybe after Jake and Cheryl's baby was born? Hopefully, there would be few family gatherings because it would be hard to see her with the new love she would eventually find.

4

"Show time in five minutes," Chuck announced to the women and Taylor. The group waited in the basement for the wedding to start.

Jolene turned to her sister who couldn't have looked any more beautiful. At Jake's request, her hair was styled simply — parted down the middle with only the ends of her long blonde locks curled and flowing at her waist. A sheer veil trimmed with a delicate Chantilly lace was secured with tiny pearl combs in her hair. The veil hung down to the middle of her back and matched the lace of her lovely Gunne Sax wedding dress. It was breathtaking, with a scooped neck and a row of pearl buttons running down the front. The sleeves were lace, embellished with the same buttons on the wide cuffs at her wrists. A satin bow, tied in the front of the A-line cut gown, did an excellent job of camouflaging the slight bump she was trying to hide.

"This is it. Are you ready?" Jolene asked, handing her sister a bouquet of purple and white tulips with soft pink roses. They followed Chuck up the basement steps and formed a line in the back of the church. The organist began to play the song "Ode to Joy," and Dori straightened her posture and adjusted her bouquet before she proceeded to walk down the aisle. When she reached the middle of the nave in the church, Jolene turned and mouthed, "Love you," to her sister before she started to follow.

Cheryl's hired hand, David Cowen, and an elderly lady Jolene presumed was his mother, both smiled when she passed their pew. The Garrisons were a small group and there were few from their side of the family. The rest of the crowd she guessed were either Camerons or friends and associates of Cheryl and Jake's.

A man sat at the end of a pew and gave Jolene an adoring smile. She remembered his name was Will Vanders. Cheryl had introduced him as the banker's son whose intentions were to open a law office in Watson. *I wonder if he ever opened his practice?*

Close to the front of the church, Jolene's eyes went to Jake and a feeling of pride filled her chest. He was a good man and madly in love with her sister. She couldn't ask for a better brother-in-law. Her attention was suddenly drawn to the man next to him. Oh my God, Michael! Dori was right. He was nothing short of spectacular in a tuxedo with his bright smile and perfectly groomed hair. His gaze held hers and she saw the longing in his scintillating eyes. Even though it made her insides melt, she commanded herself not to pay any attention. He had worn that same expression when he pledged his love to her months ago. *It's nothing but a ruse.*

The crowd got to their feet when Cheryl and Taylor came into view and the Wedding March began to play. He appeared as a miniature man in his tuxedo. Taking the first few steps, Taylor's small head moved quickly from side to side as he took inventory of the congregation. After a few encouraging words from his mother, he put on a brave face of determination and looked straight to the front of the church. There were gasps when Cheryl made her way down the aisle. Jolene could see her blue eyes were filled with unmistakable bliss when Jake and her son shook hands. The boy scooted away and took a seat next to his grandmother, while Jake and Cheryl stood before Pastor Timms with the rest of the wedding party.

Jolene thought she heard someone whimper during the vows and observed Lucille Cameron cough after Chet turned toward her. Neither Jake nor Cheryl seemed to notice because they didn't miss a word of their pledge to one another.

"You may kiss the bride," Pastor Timms announced and Jake didn't hesitate. Cheryl's face was flushed when he released her.

Irene, the Cameron's house keeper, sat behind Jake's parents wearing a joyful smile. Lucille's chin trembled as she dabbed her eyes with a lace embroidered handkerchief. She appeared to be struggling to keep the smile on her lips. On the other side of the aisle, Mary appeared delighted as she watched her grandson jump up and down in the pew. Michael and Jolene waited until Cheryl and Jake were more than half way down the aisle before they joined arms and followed.

"You look magnificent," he told her with a dazzling smile.

She smiled at the congregation on her right then turned her head back to the left and whispered, "Save your breath. I don't care what you think."

Outside, hugs, kisses and handshakes were exchanged and they soon formed a receiving line next to the bride, groom and their parents. Jolene was grateful for the steady flow of well-wishers who made it impossible for Michael to speak to her about anything other than the wedding.

MICHAEL WATCHED a young server at the Fellowship Hall refill each wine glass around the head table and knew it was his cue to make the best man's toast. He was a little nervous because he wanted his family and everyone else to know how much he loved Jake and couldn't be happier for him and Cheryl.

Rising from his chair, he cleared his throat and banged his fork against his raised glass. "I'd like to make a toast to my brother and his beautiful bride." The crowd of chattering guests immediately quieted their conversations and all attention went to the head table.

"I cannot think of two people more perfectly suited for one another." His mother's eyes subtly narrowed at his remark. "As kids, Jake and I did about everything together. He's my big brother, someone I've always looked up to. Someone who has always been there for me. And now that he's going to be a husband and a stepfather to Taylor, I'll just have to learn how to share him." A few laughs erupted in the room. Jake gave him a pleased smile. Cheryl only stared. "I'm thrilled to have Cheryl as a sister-in-law and Taylor as a nephew.

"And to Cheryl's family." He motioned with his glass to Mary and her elderly parents sitting with Lucille, Chet and Irene. His eyes went back to the head table where they settled on Jolene. "Welcome all of you to our family." He raised his glass higher and faced his brother and his bride. "To Jake and Cheryl."

"Hear, hear!" Chet's response was heard above everyone else's before the room came alive with cheers.

Some of the wedding party had already left the head table when Michael noticed Jolene's critical eyes were boring into him.

"You act like you have something to say," he said.

"It's bad enough you lie on a regular basis, but to stand up there and say all that crap to our families and everyone else you know is despicable, even for you."

"I didn't say anything I didn't mean."

"Maybe you should've told everyone how you tried to break them up." Her green eyes flashed.

"Do you really want to do this now?" he asked, looking from side to side.

Cheryl and Jake stood to leave the table when another wave of clanging glasses and howls urged them to embrace in a kiss.

"We both owe them a great deal. Can't we put our differences aside today and pretend to get along for their sakes?"

She gazed at the happy couple and slowly nodded.

"Hey, Michael," Will Vanders stood on the other side of the

table. He held out his hand and Michael shook it. He smiled at Jolene. "I know you're Cheryl's sister … Jolene, right?"

Jolene's face lit up. "I'm surprised you remembered."

Easy enough. It's printed on the program they handed everyone when they entered the church.

"I would never forget a face as pretty as yours."

Michael felt ambushed, seeing her cheeks lightly flush.

She immediately recovered. "Did you ever open that law office in Watson?"

How would she know about that?

"As a matter of a fact, I did." His eyes beamed with pride. "It's just a building down from my dad's bank."

"Well I'm so happy to hear you've achieved your goal.

Not really too hard when daddy's financing the whole thing.

Michael saw Will's mother, Helen, approach the table and smile at the group. "Will. I'm going to say goodbye to Lucille. Your father and I are ready to leave whenever you are."

"Okay, Mother," Will answered, then turned back to Michael and Jolene. "Looks like I'll see you two out at the Sugar King." He faced Jolene, "Hope you save me your first dance."

Jolene smiled. "I'll do that."

"Yeah, we'll be there in a bit," Michael told him half-heartedly.

The two Vanders walked away and Michael asked, "When did you meet him?"

"I really don't think that's any of your business." Jolene stood and grabbed her bouquet off the table in front of her.

"I guess you're right. But as far as your first dance, you're already spoken for."

Her brows furrowed.

"The Grand March is the first dance. The maid of honor's first dance is reserved for the best man."

"Hopefully, it will be the last time I ever have to come near you." She quickly spun away from the table and stormed out of the room.

It would be the best thing for both of us.

LUCILLE FINISHED as much food as she could stomach while listening to Chet and Cheryl's grandfather talk about farming in the old days. She looked at the guests around her and felt a pang of embarrassment thinking about spending the rest of the day in the shed. Never in a million years would Susan, Jake's former girlfriend — ex-fiancée! — have chosen to have part of their wedding in a shed. Some of the guests had started to leave when Lucille saw Jean Malend sitting at a table by herself. She and her husband, Ron, were good friends, and he was also the family attorney. Immediately, Lucille excused herself from the table and made a beeline for Jean.

"I'm so sorry I didn't get over here sooner." Lucille took a chair next to her.

"I certainly understand with the amount of guests you have."

Lucille released a deep breath. "You know we're continuing the wedding celebration at the Sugar King. Cheryl and Jake are going to open their wedding gifts, and later we'll finish the day with a light supper and a shed dance. It isn't exactly what I wanted, but the bride and groom insisted."

"It will work out great," Jean told her. "I'm not too old to use a portable toilet."

"Oh my God, Jean. I insist you use the facilities in the house."

"No. It will be fine."

"You know how much I love my son. I just wanted to do whatever would make him happy."

"I know how you love all three of your boys. You're such a good mother."

"Thank you." Lucille laid her hand over Jean's. "Then you can understand why I agreed to whatever they wanted for the wedding. Besides, I didn't want to upset the bride. I keep reminding myself that Jake loves her and it's a great price to pay for the Langtree land."

Jean blinked in astonishment. "What?"

"You and Ron both know how Chet's had his eyes on it for years. It being so close to the Sugar King, it's certainly an added benefit to the marriage."

Jean was silent and her eyes focused on the table in front of her.

"What is it, Jean?"

"I think you need to talk to your husband," she said slowly. "There's Ron." She shot up from her chair and gave Lucille a brisk hug. "I forgot we have to get going. My sister and her husband are coming to visit from Massachusetts. Their flight landed in Minneapolis hours ago and they should be at our house soon." She left the table and intercepted her husband a few steps away. Taking his arm, she turned him toward the door and whispered something in his ear. They smiled and waved at Lucille as they left the fellowship hall.

Chet put the last load of wedding gifts along with the box of cards in the back seat of Lucille's Cadillac. He opened the driver's door and plopped into the seat.

"We got all the money." He winked at his wife in the passenger's seat. "Should we beat it for Las Vegas?"

When she didn't laugh, he asked, "Doesn't a trip to Vegas sound like fun to you?"

She crossed her arms and demanded, "I want to know what is going on with the Langtree Farm."

"What do you mean?" He sat up straight in the seat.

"I had the strangest conversation with Jean Malend." She watched his reaction closely. "Chet, do we, or do we not, get the property now that they're married?"

His brows furrowed as he frowned. "No, we don't."

"Why not?" she burst out loudly.

"Calm down, Lu. It's because of the stupid stipulation we put in the contract for the boys."

"I don't understand." She shook her head. "They're married. Everything of hers is his."

"No. Jake pointed that fact out last week. He asked me if I would invest in something which gave ownership to our farm without any stake in my partner's property."

"Leave it to that little — witch."

"Hey! Before you go running her down, you should know it was Jake's idea to make a partnership so it stays in the Langtree name."

"There isn't any — the *boy*?" She rolled her eyes. "What are people going to say about this?"

"No one is going to say anything at all," Chet predicted. "What's there to say? Jake is married to her and now is a partner on the Langtree Farm."

"I can't believe you knew about this since last week and didn't tell me."

"I knew you felt left out of the planning of this wedding and I didn't want to upset you any further."

"I don't know if I can go home now and act like everything is fine."

"If you want your son in your life, you best put on your happiest face and give it a shot." He started the car and drove out of the parking lot.

"WHAT'S GOING on with you and Jolene?" Brett turned his head to Michael on the other side of the truck.

"What do you mean?"

"What was up with all the whispering you two had at the head table?"

Michael loosened his bow tie. "She's still angry at me for what I did. And I can't say I blame her."

"Why don't you tell her the truth about what happened? You got high and don't remember a thing."

"That's not the sort of thing I want everyone to know about." He turned his head toward the window. "I wasn't high when I used her to get back at Jake and Cheryl. I was a fool and didn't realize how I felt about her until it was too late."

"Are you still in love with her?"

Michael's head snapped back at him. "What difference does it make? She isn't going to forgive me."

"I was surprised when she knew who Will was."

"Me, too."

"I couldn't believe the way he was hustling her."

"Yeah, he was coming on strong."

Brett couldn't believe his ears. *Really?* "And that didn't bother you?"

"Don't get me wrong. I wish the best for Cheryl and Jake, but I'll be happy when this wedding is over and I won't have to see her … at least not for a while."

"Remember when Will dated Beth Akerman? Everyone but him knew the only reason she dated him was to get to you."

"I never touched her. I told her right out that Will was like a brother to me and I wasn't going to do anything to hurt him."

"Will was kinda different after that. He quit coming out to the farm as often."

"Why are you bringing all that up?" Michael sounded irritated.

"I don't know. Maybe it reminded me of the same situation."

"Not quite. Jolene isn't carrying a torch for me. Heck," he smiled, "she'd rather see me burned at the stake."

Brett smiled. *That isn't how I see it.*

Not long after the wedding gifts had been opened and a buffet supper had been consumed, the wedding party was summoned to the dance floor. Jolene looked around at the huge shed her sister said was used by the Cameron family to park all of their personal vehicles on the Sugar King Farm. *Wow!*

From the way her sister sounded, Lucille hadn't been on board in the beginning with using the shed, but the bride and groom insisted the whole event be laid back and casual. Jolene thought back to her own wedding day and remembered how the Rat's family had done most of the planning. They invited a huge list of influential people who could possibly help the Rat's career. It hadn't felt like her wedding at all. There was nothing wrong with Cheryl and Jake getting what *they* wanted.

The building was nicely decorated with crepe paper streamers and bells in white, lilac and mint. Vases filled with purple lilies, white roses and green ferns sat on each table covered with a white table cloth. A crowd was gathered on one side of the room next to a makeshift bar of wide boards supported by barrels in the corners. On the other side of the room, the band had just finished tuning up and were ready for the Grand March.

Brett and Dori had locked arms in front of her, when Jolene looked around for Michael. He was busy talking to three young women by the bar. She noticed how one beaming woman playfully ran her fingers down Michael's arm. *If they only knew what a scoundrel he was, they would run away!*

The women escorted Michael over to where the rest of the wedding party was gathered, then stood outside the designated dance floor and waved and giggled at him. When he took Jolene's hand and wrapped it around his bicep, the smiles fell from their happy faces.

The band played "This Magic Moment" while Dori and Brett began to move in front of them. Michael and Jolene followed their lead with the bride and groom close behind. Taylor was perched on Chuck's big shoulders and towered over the group at the end. The child smiled from ear to ear as the group took a lap around the dance floor. The lead singer read out each of their names as they passed by and the three women whistled and cheered when Michael's name was announced.

"I can see your fan club is still in the infancy stage," Jolene told Michael midway through their dance.

"Just a few young neighbor girls here to have a little fun." He leaned his head toward her. "You do remember what fun is, don't you?"

"Of course, I do. That was before I met you."

His smile turned into a sexy grin. "If I remember right, our little arrangement was a lot of fun, too."

Jolene's heart raced as she thought about their "sex with no strings attached" agreement. Trying to keep the images at bay she told herself it had been a dark time in her life. Her marriage had come to an end and either rejection, boredom or a combination of the two, was the reason she'd lowered herself to his level.

"I'd appreciate it if you refrain from ever mentioning that mistake in judgment to me or any other living soul again."

Before he could respond, the song ended and she immediately pulled away from him and walked off the dance floor. She looked back at Cheryl and Jake. They were staring into each other's eyes as they danced and seemed so much in love. *Will I ever have that?* A voice inside her head answered, *Not if you keep picking losers like the Rat and Michael!* She tossed her bouquet on a table and exchanged it for her clutch purse. *I need a cigarette!*

MICHAEL TOOK a few steps toward Jolene but stopped himself. *Let her go!*

The last thing he wanted to do was make a scene at Jake and Cheryl's wedding. What the hell was he thinking, bringing up their arrangement?

He reminded himself Jolene wasn't exactly an innocent young girl, and she seemed to enjoy herself as much as he did during their intimate get-togethers. His comment shouldn't have offended her as much as it had. She certainly hadn't been shy during their first night together when she ripped his clothes off and used him for what they both thought to be meaningless sex.

Of course, he knew her husband's rejection had cut deep into her self-esteem and she was on the rebound that night, but what red-blooded man wouldn't have taken full advantage of the situation? His sole intention had been to get laid by a beautiful woman without the messy emotional ties. But unfortunately, he got caught up in his own game. The way she looked in her red bra and panties was better than anything he'd ever seen in any Playboy magazine. He shook his head and decided to stop tormenting himself with thoughts of Jolene. Hours from now she would be on her merry way back to Aberdeen.

He was startled when someone tapped his shoulder. It was one of the girls who had cheered him on during the Grand March. "Would you like to dance?"

He looked one more time toward the door where Jolene had gone. Nothing seemed to matter at that moment. The woman he wanted hated his guts and there was nothing he could say or do to change things.

"Sure," he answered quietly, and took her hand. It was best he leave Jolene alone for the rest of the evening and ... forever.

BEHIND A LARGE ELM TREE, Jolene enjoyed a Virginia Slims cigarette while she watched the steady stream of guests filter in and out of the shed. She laid her head back against the tree and closed her eyes for a second. *Why do I let him get to me?*

For some unexplainable reason, seeing those women fall all over him was tougher than she thought. There was no denying she was physically attracted to him because in theory, he was what every woman wanted — tall, dark, and unbelievably handsome. It was easy to see why women swooned over him. They weren't aware that underneath those striking good looks was an incorrigible player who was incapable of feeling any real emotion or loyalty to anyone but himself. How could she have been so gullible to believe he would actually change for her?

Thank God, once the wedding was over she wouldn't have to see him for a while. The next time would be months away at Cheryl and Jake's baby's baptism.

Maybe if she hadn't bantered with him with the comment about the young women, he wouldn't have brought up their previous arrangement? She had reacted like a flustered school girl. The last thing she wanted was for him to think he had some kind of an effect over her. *I'm going to completely ignore him for the rest of the evening.*

Jolene extinguished her cigarette and fell in line behind a group of teenagers into the shed.

With plans to go in the opposite direction, her eyes discreetly scanned the room for Michael. Will Vanders jumped to his feet and beckoned her to his table where he sat with his parents.

He remained standing until she reached them. "Mom, Dad have you met, Jolene?"

"Not officially." The older woman smiled and stuck out her hand. "I know you're the bride's sister."

"Jolene, these are my parents, Charlie and Helen," he proudly told her.

Jolene smiled and shook their hands. "I'm pleased to meet you."

"Would you like to join us for a drink?" Will asked.

Knowing only a few of the guests, she readily accepted his offer. "Yes. That would be nice."

Will immediately pulled out a chair for her and asked, "What can I get you?"

"A glass of white wine would be great."

He left the table and zigzagged through the crowd to get to the bar. He wasn't gone long when Helen asked Jolene where she lived and what she did for employment.

"I live close to Aberdeen. I've just started a career in real estate."

"That sounds interesting," the older woman commented. "Do you own your own company or do you work for an agency?"

Will suddenly appeared and set a tray of drinks down.

"Did you know Jolene is in real estate?" Helen asked Will.

"Wow! A woman of today." He sounded impressed. "What agency do you work for?" he asked and took the seat next to Jolene.

"I'm new to the business, but I'm looking at an opportunity in Aberdeen."

"For which realty, Premiere or Sinclair?" Charlie joined the conversation.

Oh crap! "Sinclair," Jolene spit out then took a sip of her wine.

"Pete Jackson owns Premiere Realty but I'm unfamiliar with Sinclair." Charlie mused.

Thank you, God!

The conversation went to Will's new law office, and Jolene could see the pride in his parents' faces as they talked about their son. When their glasses were empty, Charlie turned to his wife. "I'm ready to go home, if you are?"

Helen nodded. "Yes. I'm more than ready to get out of these heels."

"I better let you three go." Jolene stood and Will laid his hand on her arm to stop her from leaving.

"We drove separately. I thought perhaps you would stay and have another drink with me."

Jolene felt Michael's stare from across the shed. "Sure, why not? The night is young."

"For *young* people." Helen chuckled. "We old folks need to get home. Nice to meet you, dear. 'Bye now!"

A few minutes after the elder Vanders left, Will went to the bar for more drinks. Once again, Jolene noticed Michael's scrutiny. *Please don't come over here.* She casually turned her attention to Will on his way back to the table.

"I was amazed to hear how fast you got your law office in operation," she commented after he sat down. "You must have a great staff behind you."

Will's smile was lukewarm. "Well, yes and no."

She tilted her head. "And that means?"

He released a labored breath. I got one great assistant and one — not so."

"What do you mean?"

"Barb is great, but Yvonne ..." he blew out a frustrated breath, "leaves a lot to be desired. Although her primary position is a secretary, her responsibilities are to answer the phone, schedule client appointments, help research cases and most importantly *keep track* of our court dates. The woman can't keep anything straight."

"Oh, no. Let me guess. You showed up late for court? Judges, tend to frown on that."

"No, I was early. Seven days, in fact."

Jolene laughed at his comment and remembered that the Rat had once shown up late for a court trial due to a scheduler's blunder. "It's best to keep an active case calendar. A place to record court dates as well as active cases that have been filed but have yet to secure a court date."

Will jerked his head. "How do you know that?"

She took a sip of her wine. "My ex was a divorce lawyer."

"Really?"

"Yeah. When we were first married, I worked at a law office as a secretary while he finished law school. I helped him pass the bar exam and then continued to help him with cases the first few years until he became an up-and-coming attorney."

"He was fortunate to have you as a wife."

"I guess he didn't see it that way. He had to leave me in order to make partner at the firm where he works in Sioux Falls."

Will's eyes rapidly blinked. "What?"

"He left me for the senior partner's daughter and one week later ... voila! He made partner."

"Oh, I see." He shook his head. "I'm so sorry to hear that."

"Oh, well." She shrugged."Obla-di, obla-da."

Will smiled. "Considering what happened, you have a great attitude about your situation. I wish I could find someone like you to work for me."

"I worked pretty hard to get my real estate license, otherwise I'd take you up on that," she laughed.

He held his chin in his hand like he was pondering something. "Dad has put me in charge of the foreclosures at the bank. I'm working with Larsen's Realty in Montevideo," he rattled out then stopped. A big smile spread across his face. "How about you coming to work for me?"

She felt her mouth drop open. "You're not serious?"

"Whatever they're going to pay you at Sinclair — I'll match it. No — I'll do better. You're going to have to relocate to Montevideo. There aren't many options for housing in Watson."

Live around here? I don't think so. "Most Realtors work off a commission. I'd … really have to think about it."

"Okay … you drive a hard bargain." He took a quick breath. "I'll pay you to be my secretary and give you a fair commission on all the foreclosure property sales you handle with Larsens."

"Are you pulling my leg?" she asked incredulously.

"I couldn't be more serious. You're exactly what I'm looking for."

Am I dreaming? Jolene smiled and held out her hand. "You've got yourself a new employee, Mr. Vanders."

"Just call me Will," he said as they shook hands.

A movement on her left made Jolene turn and see Michael seat himself in the chair next to her. "You two look pretty happy." He flashed a gorgeous smile. "What's happening over here?"

Will waved his hand at Jolene. "You are looking at the newest employee of the Vanders Law Firm."

The color left Michael's face. "What?" he croaked out.

"She's everything I'm looking for," Will announced. "A

person with law experience *and* a Realtor — a perfect combination, don't you think?"

"What about your great job in Aberdeen?" Michael's eyes nervously shifted to her.

"I guess … I'll just have to turn them down," Jolene answered with a smug smile.

"Excuse me," Michael slid out of his chair. "I need to get a drink."

"What's with him?" Will asked as Michael walked away.

Jolene shrugged her shoulders. "I have no idea."

"Now that your sister and his brother have tied the knot, maybe he views you as a sister and wants to protect you?"

Jolene feigned a carefree laugh. "I don't think so. Other than being Jake's brother, I don't really know the guy."

5

The song "These Eyes" played on the radio while Michael moved a large push broom across the shed floor. He and Brett had loaded all of the tables and chairs into the back of their trucks to bring them back to the town hall in Watson. All of the decorations were down and the bar had been dismantled and hauled out of the building. It seemed everything had returned to normal except Michael's feelings which were twisted in every direction.

Brett stepped toward him hands on his hips. "Looks like we got everything put back where it belongs."

"Yeah," Michael said quietly and bent to sweep the pile of dirt into a dustpan.

Brett looked at him strangely. "You have hardly said a word all morning. What's going on?"

"Tired, I guess."

"It wouldn't have anything to do with Will hiring Jolene, would it?"

"How did you know about that?"

"I heard her tell Cheryl and Dori." His green eyes searched Michael's. "Talk about a kick in the pants, huh?"

"More like a sucker punch to the gut."

"So now what are you going to do?"

"What can I do? I'm just going to have to find a way to accept it. Hopefully, I won't run into her too often."

"I heard her say she'll be moving to Montevideo. Avoiding her will be difficult."

Michael sighed. "Yeah, you might be right, but it will be better for both of us if I do."

Minutes later, the two brothers drove their parents' vehicles inside the shed and shut the garage doors. They went to the house for lunch and found Lucille sitting alone at the dining room table in tears.

"What's going on, Mom?" Michael asked.

"It just struck me." She wiped her eyes. "Jake isn't going to be living here anymore."

Brett rolled his eyes at Michael. "Where's Dad?"

"I thought he was with you ..."

Everyone watched Chet silently come into the room and sit at the head of the table. "It's getting pretty dry out there," he declared. "We better get some rain soon."

"Where were you all morning?" Lucille asked.

"I checked on the irrigation by Thompsons and when I was out there, Earl came out to the field."

"Oh? And what did he know?" She tucked her handkerchief into her sleeve.

"He mentioned Lloyd Jenson's farm is in foreclosure."

Her mouth dropped open. "You're not serious, are you?"

"Yes. I am." Chet shook his head. "I keep thinking about the money he donated the last few years to the Association of Growers for the refinery in Renville."

"It doesn't sound like anyone will get reimbursed any time soon," Michael cut in.

Chet nodded in agreement. "None of us thought it would take this long, that's for sure. And with the number of farmers around here who borrowed against their farms to help finance the refinery, things could get rough, especially now, if we don't get a crop."

"Hopefully, we'll get some rain soon." Lucille sounded more positive.

"There isn't any in the forecast." Chet let out a disgusted breath. "I'm going to make a trip into Watson sometime soon and talk to Charlie at the bank. I need to know what's being done to help Lloyd."

"I don't know what you're going to do about it, if it's already gone into foreclosure," Lucille told him.

"I'd like to know what happened. It's going to be a real shame to see a farm that's been in a family for generations get sold to the highest bidder."

"IT'S the job opportunity of a lifetime," Jolene informed her mother as she placed a stack of folded shirts into a suitcase on her bed. "It's beyond all of my expectations. I'll receive Realtor commissions and have a steady income as a secretary to fall back on. It's the best of both worlds."

"I don't know. For some reason it sounds too good to be true." Mary crossed her arms. She frowned and the worry lines that formed confirmed her concern. "I like the idea of you and your sister living closer to one another but I hate knowing you'll be around that gigolo brother of Jake's. I caught him watching you during the wedding."

"I noticed." She put an arm over her mother's shoulder. "I'm a big girl. You need to stop worrying about me. I'm in a different place in my life now. I will never fall victim to a predator again. From this moment on, my life is about me and no one else."

Mary smiled. "Just promise me you'll stay as far away from him as possible."

"Yes, Mother. I promise. It won't be hard, because there's no reason for me to see him." *God willing!*

"It's nice of Cheryl to let you stay at her house while she and Jake are in Duluth for their honeymoon."

"It will only be for the week. It shouldn't be too difficult to find an apartment when you work for a real estate agency. Will is going to meet me on Tuesday morning at his office in Watson and then on to Larsen's in Montevideo to introduce me to everyone at the agency. He said the owner, Donnie Larsen, is very excited to have me on board."

Mary left the room, and it didn't take Jolene long to pack up everything she owned into a few suitcases. She had only her clothes, a few photos, and a transistor radio. When she and the Rat split up neither wanted the furniture in the house so they sold it all.

Jolene sat on the bed then dropped back onto the pillow. She was finally on her way to having her own life. Her excitement grew as she thought about getting her own apartment. It would take a while but eventually she would furnish and decorate it in a welcoming contemporary style. She remembered her house in Sioux Falls and how the Rat had to approve every stick of furniture in the place. He wanted the house to exhibit a very modern and cutting edge image. Thinking about it now, it hadn't been a home at all. It had been nothing but a flashy showcase. An ideal place to entertain important clients.

In the beginning it was what she wanted, too, but achieving success was like a drug to the Rat. Just one more cocktail or dinner party with that certain client and it would be enough to send him over the edge into making partner. They never had time to visit her family or make any friends except for those who worked at the firm.

Jolene's mind drifted back to high school when she and the Rat dated. She admitted to herself that she wasn't attracted to him physically in the beginning, but he had blown her mind intellectually. He was the valedictorian of the class, the smartest boy in school and of course the most likely to succeed. When other boys couldn't talk about anything else but sex and cars, he talked about having a life plan that included her. His future had been carefully mapped out by his family at a young age. He would go on to college, law school and then on to a promising career. His family wasn't wealthy, but all had been sacrificed for their son's future. His parents were opposed to the idea of them getting married, but changed their view once it was established she would work full time to help support them. Of course, even the slightest idea of having children was severely frowned upon. Jolene remembered how tense things got between them when she had a false alarm. Knowing she was late, he accused her of selfishly trying to sabotage the plan.

Had she ever been in love with the guy? Or had she been brain washed into thinking she was? She had never experienced fireworks or felt her heart flutter with excitement from simply being near him, like she had with ... Michael. How ironic? She and Michael's relationship had been completely the opposite — purely physical and nothing else. *Would she ever find passion, love and intellect in one man?*

MILES OF DROOPING crops stretched out in the fields around Michael's truck as he and Chet drove to Watson. In many places the plants were spindly and yellow and in others the seed without moisture failed to germinate and left empty gaps in the rows.

"I didn't want to scare your Mother, but when I checked the irrigation I took a measurement of the water level in the river. I've been scratching a line on that big rock where you kids always swam."

"And?" Michael anxiously asked.

"It was down an inch. That might not seem like a lot but we need to keep an eye on it. If it keeps going down, we might be sucking mud instead of water."

"I heard on the radio there's a good chance of rain up north later this week," Michael reported.

"Let's pray it happens."

They unloaded the tables and chairs from the back of the truck at the town hall then drove down the street and parked in front of the State bank of Watson.

Michael felt his heart pound in his chest when he saw Jolene's Firebird parked in the row of cars.

Father and son got out of the truck and saw Will and Jolene step out of the door of Vander's Law Office next door to the bank.

What shitty timing!

"Hey there, Camerons," Will hollered out. He casually draped his arm around Jolene and waited for Chet and Michael to come closer. "Michael already knows, but I want to introduce my newest employee."

Chet smiled. "Well, congratulations to you, young lady. I thought I heard something about this at the wedding dance."

"Thank you," Jolene smiled but kept her eyes on Chet.

Will pulled back the cuff of his suit jacket and checked his gold wrist watch. "We better get going if we're going to make our appointment with Larsen's."

"Catch ya later," Michael answered but studied Jolene out of the corner of his eye before following his father inside the bank. He looked back through a window at Will's new, blue Chevy convertible as he backed out of the spot. Jolene looked different somehow, but he couldn't put his finger on what had changed.

Charlie Vander's secretary served coffee to Michael and Chet before she left the room.

Shortly after the dry weather had been discussed and the chit chat was over, Charlie sat back in his chair. "Well, what can I do for you, gentlemen?"

Chet took a deep breath. "We'd like to know what's being done about Lloyd Jensen's situation. I hear his farm is in fore-closure."

"Tsk, tsk." Charlie shook his head. "It's a sad deal. He got behind on his loans after his wife went through some medical issues."

"Can you stop the foreclosure? Maybe offer a lower interest rate of some kind?"

"Will is handling all the foreclosures now and the way he sounded, Lloyd declined on everything he offered."

"That doesn't seem like something Lloyd would do." Chet's brows wrinkled. "Why on earth wouldn't he jump on any offer to save his farm?"

Charlie blew out a breath. "I was just as surprised as you when Will told me. He was led to believe Lloyd wants to get out of farming."

"What about Lloyd Junior?" Chet asked. "I always thought his boy was set on taking over the family farm one day."

"I guess he changed his mind."

"That sure is strange."

It seemed Charlie knew Chet wasn't taking this news well and changed the subject.

"Did you hear Will hired your daughter-in-law's sister, Jolene? She's sure a pretty little thing. He seems to think she's a perfect fit for the law office and for helping out with the foreclosures down at Larsen's."

And no doubt perfect for him, too, Michael thought as a jealous vibe ripped through him.

Chet nodded but seemed to have his mind on other things as they finished their meeting. They were on their way home when he told Michael to turn onto County Road nine and head out to the Jensen Farm. When they drove into the farmyard, the place seemed deserted for the middle of the day. A large barn cat came to greet them when they got out of the truck. It meowed loudly as it followed them across the yard and onto the porch. Michael knocked for a while before one of Lloyd's younger sons came to the door.

He opened the door a crack. "What do you want?"

"Is your dad around?" Chet asked.

"Hang on." The boy shut the door.

A moment later Lloyd appeared. Michael could smell the liquor on his breath. "You got a lot of nerve coming here," he shouted.

Chet ignored his comment. "What's this business about you selling your farm?"

"Like you don't know. You and those Vanders. I hope you all rot in hell!"

"Lloyd, it's me, Chet Cameron."

"I know perfectly well who you are. I still own this place … at least for a while. Get off my farm or I'll call the sheriff." He slammed the door.

The two men on the porch stared at each other. "Something isn't right here," Chet said shaking his head. "But I don't want him to call the sheriff. We best be going."

Neither father nor son said anything as they drove away.

THE SUN WAS high above the horizon when Jolene left Vanders Law Office in Watson for Cheryl's farm. It had been a hectic first day trying to remember names, and learning what Will and Donnie's expectations were of her. Donnie Larsen — middle-aged and round as he was tall, was almost giddy when Will introduced them. Jolene noted he was very knowledgeable about real estate and was definitely a smooth-talking salesman. He was the type who could easily market anything he chose to sell. In the end, he seemed pleased with her credentials and surprisingly enough, didn't once mention her inexperience. *Thank you, God, for this opportunity!*

When a side road lined with trees came into view, Jolene slowed down, then turned off the main road. She drove to a secluded area where the trees were the thickest and parked her car. Taking a fast glance ahead at the road and then in her rearview mirror, she pulled her blouse out of her pencil skirt and frantically undid the buttons. Her fingers found the hooks and unfastened the tight, lacy bustier underneath her blouse.

"*Finally!*" she breathed out loud.

It was ten miles to Cheryl's house and she wasn't going to wear that thing any longer than she had to. Winding down the window, she lit a much needed cigarette and reminded herself that the breast-binding garment was a necessary evil if she was going to be taken seriously by a male dominated business world. She had worn a suit jacket during her job interviews and still caught the majority of the male interviewers staring at her breasts. For this morning's meetings she wanted her confidence and professionalism to be the only things catching her new bosses' attention.

Thank God, she didn't have to wear the bustier the next day. Will was giving her the day off to find an apartment. It seemed he hadn't noticed her new look, but she was sure the way Michael checked her out, he certainly had. She remembered Cheryl mentioning all the Camerons banked in Watson and cursed her bad luck for seeing him the very first day of her new job. Or had he gone to the bank in hopes of seeing her? But if that were the case, would he have brought his father?

BRETT CAMERON'S mind was on the cheeseburger and fries he'd ordered while he sat with his friend Roger Black in a booth at Trailways Café. The M & M ballroom in Montevideo had closed minutes ago and Brett was happy they had beaten the usual bar rush crowd to the restaurant. While they waited, Brett watched the groups of mostly younger people fill the booths and tables around them. It seemed the door opened shortly after they arrived and hadn't shut for several minutes.

"Man, did you see how drunk Jeff Simmons was tonight?" Roger asked. "He could hardly stand on the dance floor."

"He's always three sheets to the wind," Brett answered and looked up as three women entered the restaurant. Two of the girls were average-looking but the dark-haired girl in the middle with the cute face and groovy shag haircut was hard to miss.

Roger noticed too. "Wow, I think that's Karyn Pehrson. She used to hang out with my little sister, Marilyn. I haven't seen her in years." He smiled at Brett and then returned to observe her. "Sure looks like the butterfly has emerged from the cocoon."

Brett didn't respond. He was too busy watching her move confidently through the room in her tight fitting bell-bottomed jeans. Within seconds, the trio was greeted by the hostess. Brett quickly glanced around the room and noticed all the booths and tables were taken. He could see the discouraged expressions on the women's faces as they turned to leave.

"Roger," he barked. "Jump up and stop them."

"What?" his friend looked confused.

"Don't be an idiot. We've got a booth big enough for the five of us."

Roger bolted toward the door. It was noisy in the room and Brett couldn't hear what his friend was saying but he could see Karyn's surprised reaction. A beautiful smile came to her lips before they embraced in a brief hug. His friend immediately pointed in Brett's direction then escorted the group to their booth.

Brett stood up and the two other women smiled and slid in the round booth. Roger let Karyn slide in first and then he sat at the end.

"Roger, these are my friends, Jenny and Cindy." Karyn motioned to the women.

Brett cleared his throat.

"Oh, and this is my friend, Brett," Roger said.

Karyn's eyes went to Brett and lingered for a few seconds before she turned back to Roger.

"I just can't believe you recognized me. Since I came back,

everyone tells me I look so different with my shorter hair. How long has it been since we saw each other last?"

"It's got to be over two years. Where have you been hiding?" Roger smiled.

"My grandmother in St. Paul became ill shortly after I graduated from high school and I stayed with her until she died a few months ago."

"I'm so sorry to hear that," Brett got in before Roger.

Karyn gave Brett an appreciative smile. "Thanks."

A waitress came to the table and the group turned their attention to her.

"If it isn't too much trouble, could you possibly wait with our order and make at the same time as these ladies' so we all can dine together?" Brett asked.

"That could work." The waitress turned her head toward the booth next to them. "They ordered practically the same things as you two." Karyn and her friends gave their food order to the waitress and she left for the kitchen.

"So, two years in St. Paul," Roger commented. "Montevideo must seem pretty dull now."

"I took care of my grandma during the day time and took some secretarial classes at the U in the evening. I'm more than happy with the slower pace. I've been applying for jobs all over Montevideo, so who knows how long there will be a lull in the action."

Brett was going to jump into the conversation when Roger beat him to it. "Have you talked to Marilyn since you've been back?"

"Yes, I have. It sounds like your sister has her hands full with the new baby." Karyn smiled.

The two women between Brett and Karyn started their own conversation about their jobs and Brett had to listen closely to hear what Roger and Karyn were saying. When she shot — what seemed to him — an interested glance his way, he straightened his posture in the booth. *She obviously sees something she likes!*

Karyn's eyes were on Brett much of the time while they ate their food. Roger noticed too, because he subtly shook his head acknowledging his defeat. Brett was about to ask Karyn if she needed a ride home when Cindy whispered something in her ear. Cindy then sweetly declared she needed to use the ladies' room.

"I better go, too." Jenny announced and reached for her purse. "I drank way too much Coke."

Brett sprang to his feet and then with one hand behind his back, he bowed slightly and waved for them to exit the booth. "Proceed ladies."

They were gone for about a minute when Karyn asked, "Please tell me you're not *the* Brett Cameron."

Brett took in a pleased breath and smiled. "Why, yes I am." *Maybe she's heard of my reputation as a ladies man.*

"Are you from the Cameron family who bought the Iverson property?"

"Yeah. Why?"

"Nothing. Just wondering." She glanced in the direction of the restrooms. "I better go and check on what's keeping my friends." Roger stood up to let her pass then sank down in the booth to watch her walk away. Distracted with those jeans, neither man noticed she was going toward the entrance until she went out the door. They turned their heads toward each other and stared dumb-founded.

Still stunned, Brett slowly asked, "Did they just dine and dash?"

"Seems like it. It's the first time I ever heard of her doing something like that."

Brett put his hands on his hips. "What a tease. I don't care how much time it takes, I'm going to track her down and give her a piece of my mind."

6

Lucille saw Jake's truck pull into the yard from her bedroom upstairs. She yelled at Chet in the shower. "Jake's home." Her hand slid down the smooth rail, as she raced down the long staircase. She heard him talking to Irene and his brothers in the kitchen and pushed open the swinging door.

"Oh, Jake you're finally home." She rushed to him with open arms.

Brett scrunched his brows and crossed his arms.

Jake laughed as he hugged her. "With this kind of a reception, I'd swear I was gone a month, not a week."

Lucille grabbed her eldest son's arm. "Come and tell us what you did in Duluth." She led him through another swinging door.

She looked back to see Brett shake his head at Michael as the two followed them to the dining room table.

Irene came into the room with another place setting and Jake stopped the old housekeeper. "I got supper waiting for me at home. I'm just here to say I'll be here for chores tomorrow morning."

It breaks my heart to hear him call that place home. "Why don't you call Cheryl and tell her to eat with her sister and stay here with us for supper?" Lucille asked with a sweet smile.

"I'd love to take you up on that, but I don't know what my new bride would think. Besides, Jolene isn't there. I guess she found an apartment while we were gone. Cheryl asked her for dinner but she said the Vanders had invited her for dinner at their house."

Lucille saw a tiny vein bulge in Michael's forehead. "Hmm," she said. *It's best that wild girl be with someone else's son and not mine.*

Jake turned to his mother. "Tell Dad I'm back. I'll be here for chores before sunrise."

"You can tell me yourself," a voice answered from the door way. "How you doing son?" Chet asked on his way to the table.

"Great, Dad," Jake answered then stood to shake his father's hand.

"You really should stay for dinner," Lucille pleaded. "Once the ba ... by —" She clamped her mouth shut. *Oh, good Lord!*

Jake's eyes narrowed at Michael. "So that's what all the whispering was about between you and Jolene at the wedding. She told you Cheryl was pregnant and you felt the need to tell Mom."

"N ... no," Michael stammered. "That's not what happened."

"Cheryl is pregnant?" Chet's eyes bulged.

Jake released a breath. "Yes," he answered with a pleased smile. "She's expecting in late September or early October."

"That's great!" Chet shouted. "Let's celebrate!" He shook Jake's hand again but this time pumped it harder.

Brett swiftly rounded the table and shook his older brother's hand then pulled him into a hug. He released him with a few rapid pats to the back.

"Look, I'd love to stay, but she's waiting at home. How about I bring her over on Saturday night and we'll celebrate then? I've really got to get going." He gave Michael an irritated glance when he left the room.

Michael scowled at his mother.

"Did Jolene tell you her sister was pregnant at the wedding?" Chet asked him.

"No, she didn't." His angry eyes stayed on his mother.

"Well, someone better speak up and tell me how everyone found out except for me."

"I didn't know a thing about it," Brett shrugged his shoulders.

Seconds past before Lucille confessed, "I heard about it from a friend."

Chet crossed his arms. "Let me guess. Was that friend — Joan Uterman?"

"Yes," she was slow to answer. "She heard it from a friend who knows someone who works at Dr. Morgan's office."

"Why didn't you ask Jake about it?"

"Being his mother, I was waiting for him to tell me."

"Things were just getting better between those boys, and now Jake thinks Michael is talking behind his back. You better set him straight."

And while I'm at it, I'd like to ask him if the child is actually his. Her eyes went to Michael and then back to her husband. "I will."

"WAIT UP, SON," Chet called after Michael. They were on their way to the barn after breakfast. "I need to talk to you about something that's been bothering me."

Michael stopped on the sidewalk and waited for his father to catch up to him. "If it's about Cheryl being pregnant, I swear Mom told me about it, not the other way around."

"No. It's something else. I can't seem to get the Jensen family off my mind since we left their farm last week."

"Yeah, Lloyd Junior was a year behind me in high school and I remember how active he was in Future Farmers of America. I talked to him a few times after the meetings and I never met anyone so proud to be a farmer. I'm having trouble believing he doesn't want to farm their land."

"It struck me strange, too. I've laid awake for a few nights thinking about how it could've possibly happened. But I've known Charlie for years and it seemed to me, he was telling the truth." Chet scratched his chin. "I'd like you to pay Will a visit and ask him what happened."

Michael let out a groan. "Why can't you go and talk to him yourself?"

"You and Will were pretty close in high school. I think he would be more apt to tell you what happened than me."

"I don't want to go down to his fancy office and talk to that college-educated idiot." Michael crossed his arms.

"Don't try and fool me, son. You're afraid of seeing Cheryl's sister. Jake wasn't the only one who noticed you two during the wedding."

Michael let a moment go by. "You're right, Dad. I don't want to see her if I can help it."

"Can't you put your feelings aside and find out what really happened with Lloyd's family? Hell, if I'd known his wife was sick, I would've organized some sort of a fundraiser myself. It's sad to see someone lose their farm when the rest of us in the community could've done something. Every one of us owe it to the Jensens to at least find out what happened."

Damn it! "Okay, okay! If you're going to put it that way, Dad, I'll go in this morning and talk to him."

Around ten-thirty Michael peered into the window at the Vanders Law Office. He noticed a woman working behind the desk and did a double-take seeing it was Jolene. She looked totally prim with her long hair pulled back into a tight bun and wire rimmed glasses perched on her small nose. When he walked in the door, she looked up with a smile but it fell the second she saw it was him.

Here we go!

OH GOD! No! "What are *you* doing here?" Her tone poked like a pin.

"I'm ... happy to see you, too," Michael replied.

She pushed her glasses back further on her nose and pursed her lips. "What business do you have here?"

"I'd like to see your boss."

"Concerning what?" She stared into his inky eyes.

"I would like to speak with him."

"And like I asked, what does it concern?"

"That's between me and him. I just need a few minutes of his time."

Her temper began to surge with her steady rising heartbeat. She subtly turned her head from side to side and leaned across the desk. "Look," she said in a lowered voice. "If you're here to screw this up for me by telling him about the huge mistake I made with you, I'll deny..." She stopped speaking, seeing Barb, the legal secretary, come out of her office and go to the water cooler.

Jolene casually smiled. "If you'd like to see Mr. Vanders, I certainly can buzz him."

Barb kept an eye on Michael while she filled a paper cup with water. He gave her a brief smile then turned his attention back to Jolene. "Sure, I would appreciate that very much."

Jolene commanded her fingers to stop shaking when she pushed a button on the intercom.

"Yes," Will answered.

"Michael Cameron is here to see you."

"Michael?" He sounded surprised, but pleased. "Well, send him in."

Jolene watched Michael with a pounding heart while he opened the heavy oak door and went inside Will's office. When the door closed, she took a few deep breaths then slowly let them out in an effort to calm down. Maybe she was jumping to conclusions. There could be a chance Michael was here to talk to Will about something else. He had no reason to tell her boss about their arrangement, other than knowing it would ruin this opportunity for her. There certainly wasn't a reason for him to seek revenge when he had wronged her. She thought about him trying to break up his own brother's relationship with her sister. He had no integrity or loyalty even when it came to his own family. The real question was: Why wouldn't he tell Will?

Thankfully, Barb had gone back into her office just as tears started to fill Jolene's eyes. Blinking them back, she shuffled the stack of papers together in front of her. She had known from the very second Will had hired her, this scenario had the potential to play out and explode in her face. She had hoped it wouldn't have occurred before she proved herself as a motivated and dedicated employee. Her eyes blurred with tears as she sought out the newspaper on the table in the waiting area of the office. She would take it home to resume her hunt for a new job.

WILL LOOKED up from his desk and sprang to his feet. "Hey, buddy." He shook Michael's hand and motioned for him to sit in the chair in front of his desk. "So what do I owe for this unexpected pleasure?" he asked, then dropped back into his oak desk chair.

"I was hoping to get the scoop on the Jensen Farm."

Will's eyes got big. "What do you mean, scoop?"

"No one suspected the family was in a financial crisis until we saw the foreclosure sign at the end of their driveway. Dad and I talked to Charlie about it and he said you were handling all the foreclosures for the bank. We were just wondering what happened."

"It's such a dismal situation." Will pushed his hand through his fine brown hair. "I tried to work out a payment plan with them, but they were in so deep with Mrs. Jensen's medical bills, there just wasn't any way out."

"I don't know if you're aware, Lloyd Jensen was a major contributor of the Association of Growers for the refinery in Renville. None of us farmers have received any reimbursement yet, but we're told it will be sometime next year. Lloyd will be receiving a nice-sized check. Dad thought if we all got together and did some sort of benefit in the meantime, maybe we could hold off the foreclosure of their farm."

"I'd like to help but I'm afraid that would be impossible," Will's words sounded final.

"What do you mean?"

"I'm afraid we've already signed a buyer for the Jensen Farm."

"Who's buying it?"

"I really can't reveal that information at this time."

"Oh come on, Will. If I come home and tell Dad it's too late to have a benefit because someone bought the place, he's going to ask who the buyer is. It wouldn't surprise me a bit to see him down here bugging you day after day until he finds out."

Will stiffened in his chair. "You think he'd really do that?"

"You know my old man. Have you ever seen him back down?"

"The name is Paul Hansen."

"The name doesn't sound familiar. Is he from around here?"

"All I know is his name." Will ran his hand through his hair again.

"Thanks." Michael stood. "That might be enough to convince the old man to let this go."

"You let him know there's nothing anyone can do now. I tried to help the Jensen family but my hands are tied at this point."

"I'll do that." Michael walked out of the law office, disappointed his high school friend hadn't shed much light on what happened with the Jensen Farm. He casually nodded at Jolene and left.

IN THE MIDDLE of her surprisingly affordable apartment, Jolene listened to the song "Diamond Girl" on the radio she'd brought from home. She scanned the near empty space around her and sighed. Other than the old table, four chairs and bed Cheryl had graciously donated, the place was bare. They were old pieces of furniture her sister had stored in a shed after a remodel a few years prior. Jolene sat in one of the well-worn chairs and sipped on a cup of tea. She promised herself eventually she would be able to afford some new things. For now, it was going to be garage sales and thrift shops for dishes, cookware or anything else she needed.

Tomorrow was Saturday and she planned to hit as many sales as possible, but for now her mind was on what she was going to make for dinner. The thought of eating another peanut butter and jelly sandwich made her stomach churn. Her mouth suddenly watered thinking about the leg of lamb Will's mother served last week. Thankfully, Michael hadn't ruined all that for her. When he'd shown up at the law office yesterday, she was certain Will was going to fire her. She had anticipated Michael would come out of Will's office wearing a victorious smile, but instead he seemed to be contemplating something. He glanced in her direction with a discreet nod and left the building without incident.

It seemed like an eternity before Will came out of his office. When he invited her for lunch shortly after, she agreed but was dreadfully afraid the entire time it was some sort of a termination tactic.

They were seated at a table in Dell's restaurant a few doors down from the law office when Will first spoke. "Did you finish working on the appointment calendar?"

"Ye — ye — yes," she sputtered. "Everything looks great. I rescheduled all your appointments at the bank to days when you're not in court and sent a copy next door. I plan to update the schedule on a weekly basis. Hopefully, it will cut down on some of the confusion you've had in the past."

Will had a satisfied smile. "It's been only a short time and you've already improved a ton of things at the office. To let you know — Barb isn't one to give anyone a compliment and she thinks you're doing a great job."

"But?" Jolene asked over the heart beat that echoed in her ears. She anticipated the worst.

"But what?"

"Nothing. I just thought you were going to say something else."

His eyes flicked to hers for a brief second before he changed the subject to his court date the following Monday.

They were still talking about the case when she noticed he was looking at her in an appraising way. From then, it didn't take long for the topic of work to disappear from their conversation.

"I was going to ask you sooner, but I got distracted," he said with a smile. "If you're not busy on Saturday night, I was wondering if you would like to join me for dinner? I've had my mind on a steak at Rosy's Supper Club all week."

Oh, no! "A steak does sound good, but I was planning on spending the entire weekend painting my bedroom. I just can't seem to fall asleep in a room with bright white walls."

The last thing she wanted was for him to think she had romantic feelings for him. She had accepted his dinner offer during the week solely out of starvation and maybe a bout of loneliness. Cheryl was out of town for her honeymoon, and knowing Will's folks would be there, she knew it wouldn't be like a date. Besides, lamb was one of her favorite dishes and she hadn't eaten any since the last business dinner she had attended with the Rat.

While they continued to chat about her apartment, it was her turn to discreetly survey her boss. Will was attractive in a Dustin Hoffman sort of way. He could be charming at times but he generally seemed to be more on the serious side. The only thing they seemed to have in common was their desire for success. Her plan was to achieve it the old fashioned way with hard work and ingenuity. Any other way wasn't an option. She remembered the stories about a couple of secretaries at her ex-husband's firm who lost their jobs after an affair with their boss.

Jolene gave Will a final assessment when the waitress set a bowl of chicken soup in front of her. Even if she had feelings for him, she wasn't about to do anything to jeopardize her career — it was all she had at this point in her life.

MICHAEL GLANCED at the passenger seat of his truck where the box of nozzles for the sprayer sat and sighed. He had gone to Meyer's Implement for the parts and had to wait for what seemed forever for the new kid working there to find the order.

Driving past Bob's Bar, he checked his wristwatch and saw it was just after four o'clock. He chuckled when he thought about all the Friday happy hours he and Jim had spent there, drinking and picking up women. Nothing would ever be the same again with Jim married and a new father. It was impossible to turn back time. Michael gave in to nostalgia and pulled his truck around to the back and parked in his old spot behind Bob's. He'd have one drink to honor days gone by and hit the road soon after.

The familiar smell of stale beer and cigarette smoke met him at the door when he stepped inside the building. He glanced around at the throng of people surrounding the bar and recognized a few patrons, but there were many he didn't. His usual barstool next to the corner where Jim had always sat was occupied, so he found an open stool on the other end and took a seat. Jim always thought he could get his drinks quicker sitting on the corner because that was where the ice tub was located under the bar. Michael was happy to see the familiar face of Joe, the bartender, approach him from behind the bar.

"Hey, Michael. Where you been hiding?"

"Planting season. Give me a whiskey Coke," Michael replied and Joe went to work on his drink.

A ray of sunlight flashed in the mirror behind the bar when someone opened the backdoor. Michael turned to see a man in a business suit come inside and disappear into the large crowd that filled up most of the room. His head was tilted away in search of a place to sit when Michael caught another glimpse of him on his way to the bar. The man took the empty stool at the corner of the bar and Joe proceeded to make him a rum and Coke. Michael wove his head back and forth, trying to get another look at the guy, but his view was obstructed by two large men. Joe was laughing when he took a few steps away and pointed in Michael's direction. When Michael looked up into the mirror, Jim Stanton stared back at him with a big grin.

Both men rushed around the lively group between them and vigorously shook hands. "What the hell are you doing here?" Jim hollered as he patted his friend's back.

"Just thought I'd come in and have one during happy hour for old time's sake. I can't believe you're still down here keeping your barstool warm."

"My old lady is doing Tupperware parties with her mother on Friday nights. She took the baby with her to show him off to the women. I have to pick him up later so I decided to come down here and wait."

Michael snatched his drink from the bar and followed Jim through the crowd. Michael then sweet talked the gal sitting on the bar stool next to him into moving over so he could sit by Jim. She looked Michael up and down with a flirtatious smile then slowly moved.

"I see you still got the women melting in your hand," Jim murmured.

"Yeah, I wish. I only attract the ones I'm not interested in."

"That doesn't sound like the Michael Cameron I know. What gives?"

"I fell in love with a woman who doesn't feel the same way about me."

"If you're talking about that red head, buddy, I'm sorry."

"Jolene," Michael reminded him and wondered what difference it made.

"I was so pissed off knowing you had been with Lyla, I wasn't thinking straight. I should have never told Jolene about what you did in the Cities to break her sister and your brother up. Or that you may have impregnated my girlfriend." Jim's expression appeared sincere. "Lyla came clean right after and confessed that she told you we weren't a couple."

"I'm the one who messed everything up, not you." Michael swigged back a mouthful of his drink.

Jim raised his glass. "Let's make a toast to never knifing each other in the back again."

Michael nodded and smiled when their glasses clinked together.

They ordered another drink and talked about Jim's new business with his family and Jake and Cheryl getting married. Michael told him how Jolene treated him throughout the wedding and about her landing a job at Vanders Law Office and Larsen's Realty.

Jim smiled down at his drink. "Even if we hadn't met down here tonight, I was going to give you a call."

"Why?" Michael's curiosity was piqued.

"There's something at my new place I want to show you."

"What's that?"

"It's a surprise. Do you still have my card I gave you with my new number?"

"No, I threw it away," Michael admitted.

Jim reached into his wallet and retrieved a card then wrote his number on it. "Keep this one." He handed to Michael. "Give me a call and plan to come over sometime on the weekend or after five during the work day."

Michael stared at his friend wondering what he was up to.

Jim suddenly stood. "I need to go rescue my son from the hen party. Don't forget — call me!"

7

The members of the Association of Growers were nearly assembled for their monthly meeting at the Montevideo Community Building when Brett excused himself for some fresh air. It was warm in the un-air-conditioned building and he didn't want to sit inside any longer than necessary.

"I'll be back when they call the meeting to order," Brett told his father and Michael on his way outside.

Leaning against a large pillar, he felt the warm breeze ripple through his blonde curls. It hadn't been his plan to attend tonight's meeting in this heat until his father reminded him of his obligations as a partner of the Sugar King Farm.

He was about to go back inside when an old blue pickup pulled up with what looked to be three high school boys in the cab. They spun the tires on the truck and created a large cloud of dust in the dirt parking lot before they cut the engine. The boys piled out of the vehicle and headed to the front door of the building, but seeing Brett, the taller of the three smirked at the other two.

"Isn't this one of the assholes?" he asked.

Brett threw back his shoulders. "Who you calling an asshole, kid?"

"You." He stepped closer to Brett.

Just then Michael came out of the door. "They're starting the meet —" His words stopped when his eyes circled the group. "Is there a problem out here?"

"No," the tallest boy answered and the two followed him inside the hall.

"What the hell was that about?" Michael asked.

"I haven't the slightest idea," Brett shook his head. "The big one asked the other two if I was 'one of the assholes.'"

"What did he mean by that?"

"Like I said, I don't know. But that's the second time in the last few weeks a stranger has come along and acted like I wronged them somehow." Brett then told his brother about Karyn Pehrson and her odd behavior toward him.

"It's weird about those farm boys, but you ticking women off isn't anything new," Michael said with a laugh. "But we better get back in there or Dad's going to think we've wronged him."

The meeting had already started when the two Cameron brothers took their seats in the front row. Chet, the chairman of the AOG, sat in the middle of a long table in front of the room with the four other board members. Brett turned his head and watched the boys who confronted him a few rows back. It was easy to see the loathing in their eyes when they stared back. *What the hell is their problem?*

Brett thought the meeting was close to concluding when Chet asked if there was any further business to discuss.

Lloyd Jensen Junior raised his hand and stood. "I would like to make a motion we have a new election for the officers on the board of the AOG."

The boys who harassed Brett cheered and blasted out a series of sharp whistles. A loud roar of muffled conversation broke out and Chet hammered a gavel on the table to restore order.

"You are aware we've never had an actual election," Chet

informed him. "The board members are nominated and then approved by a show of hands during the January meeting each year."

"I make the motion we do it tonight, instead," Lloyd Jr. declared, and a bout of whistles erupted again.

This time, Chet appeared annoyed when he banged the gavel. "We can't do that without sending out a special letter to each member in advance." His eyes narrowed. "And most importantly, we would have to state the reason why a special election is necessary."

"I believe there's a board member with a personal agenda that isn't in the best interest of the AOG."

Chet turned and quietly whispered to each board member on both sides of him. They in turn relayed the message to the next person at the table. They all nodded back in agreement to Chet before he proceeded to address Lloyd Jr. "That is a very serious accusation, young man. But if what you're saying is true, the board, and I'm sure all of the members," he motioned his hand to the crowd, "would greatly appreciate that you reveal the identity of this person."

"You, Mr. Cameron," Lloyd Jr. answered emotionless.

Chet flinched before his mouth dropped open.

"You donated alongside of everyone else here for the refinery but you have more money to gamble with than most of us. It was your plan all along to set us up for failure."

Chet took a deep breath to compose himself. "I'm sorry your family is experiencing some financial difficulties at this time, but my family and I are not personally responsible for any of it. You can check the records and see the Sugar King Farm has wagered a great deal just like every other farm around here."

"I can't say how because I have no proof, but I want you Camerons to know, you aren't fooling anyone. You're in this for yourselves and nobody else."

Chet's eyes flashed in anger when he loudly announced, "All

those in favor of notifying the members of a new election — raise your hand and say, "Aye!"'"

Brett stared at Michael in disbelief when over half of the present members raised their hand.

WHILE JOLENE DRIED dishes at Cheryl's house, she gazed out the window at Jake and Taylor playing catch in the yard. Both she and Cheryl had a lot going on in their lives and Jolene was thankful to have some time alone with her sister. She was also grateful for the invitation to join the newly formed family for a delicious chicken dinner. Jolene had yet to find any decent pots and pans in her hunt for garage sale treasures and a peanut butter sandwich was the only thing on the menu at home. A couple of nice pots would be her first purchase after she cashed her very first check from the law office.

"I can't tell you how wonderful it is to have you around again," Cheryl told her with a fond smile.

"It sure is," Jolene agreed. "Who knew you getting married would land me my dream job."

"Oh, before I forget, I saved you this." Cheryl pulled out a newspaper from a drawer and handed it to her.

"What's this?" Jolene unfolded a copy of the Daily Montevideo Reminder. On the front page was a picture of a man riding in a convertible in the Fiesta Days Parade. Jolene took a closer look at the photo. "Is that Will?"

"Yes. It's from last month. I just thought I'd let you in on what type of a guy you're working for. Jake and I are amazed to learn how involved he has become in the community in such a short time. It states he's a financial supporter of the Kiwanis Club and the 4-H Club. He is also a member of the Knights of Columbus in Montevideo. The article goes on to say he wants to start a boys club in Montevideo and plans to run for the township board in Watson."

Jolene couldn't help feeling proud of her boss. "That must be why he's always in and out of the office so much."

"So how's work going, anyway?" Cheryl asked.

"At which place?"

"Both."

"It seems to be going great at the law office. Will has expressed he's more than satisfied with my work. But I can't really tell how good I'm doing at Larsen's. I knew when I was hired, I would be helping out with the bank foreclosures, but I didn't expect to be the listing agent for the majority of them."

"Wow!" Cheryl blinked her wide blue eyes. Donnie Larsen must have an extreme amount of confidence in you to give you so much responsibility."

"That's exactly what I'm thinking. And it puts a lot of pressure on me because I don't want to let anyone down and that includes myself."

"He must think you're the right person for the job."

"Every once in a while I have to remind myself I graduated at the top end of my Realtor's class. The percentage I'll be receiving from the commissions alone are a huge motivation for me."

"It sounds like this opportunity is exactly what you need to establish yourself as a successful Realtor."

"I'm going to give it my best shot and hope it all works out that way." *And maybe say a little prayer!*

"The reason is obvious. The Jensen family and the AOG are still upset because of me," Jake announced to his family at lunch. "I was their representative at the capital — I failed to get them a reimbursement."

At the end of the dining room table, Lucille's heart was breaking as she listened to her eldest son hold himself accountable. "Oh, Jake. No one can blame you. You were only trying to help." *He's got enough on his plate with the baby coming. He doesn't need another thing to feel bad about after he finds out it's not his child!*

Chet stopped dishing his plate. "My gut tells me it doesn't have anything to do with what happened at the meeting the other night."

"What else could it possibly be?" Jake's eyes searched his father's.

"You would think if that were the case, the members would've brought it up last fall." Chet shook his head baffled. "Governor Andersen told you right out there wasn't any money in the budget. There wasn't anything else you could've done. All of us on the board agree the AOG should've done their homework and applied for a grant from the government before we started building the refinery in the first place. We all lost money after the refinery in Chaska closed three years ago and everyone was itching to get a new plant up and running. I'm as guilty as any other member for putting the horse before the cart, but I refuse to take any responsibility for what happened with the Jensen Farm."

Michael quietly listened while he loaded his plate.

"What do you think, Michael?" Lucille asked.

"I know a person doesn't want to kick a guy when he's down, but it doesn't seem like Lloyd Jr. has any proof for his bogus accusation. Couldn't we sue him for slander?"

"Suing isn't the answer. It will only make us look bad and it certainly wouldn't regain anyone's trust," Chet told them.

"Anyone who knows you, Jake, knows you did everything you could," Brett proudly stated, then raised his fist. "If someone wants to say anything different, they're going to meet up with this."

"Enough of that talk," Chet barked out. "I've got an idea." He stared at his wife. "I never thought I'd say this, but do you think you could ask your friend Joan if she's heard anything?"

Brett smirked. "If Joan Uterman doesn't know what's going on, I think our next step should be to contact the FBI."

Chet shook his head at him. "Every one of us needs to keep our eyes and ears open until we figure out this mess."

A STRONG, steady flow of water sprayed out from the irrigation system onto a field of soybeans next to the Chippewa River. Michael checked the valves and nozzles on the entire apparatus and was pleased when everything appeared to be functioning well.

Knowing they were going to bale hay whenever he got back, he decided to take his time and go down to the river and check the water level. The grass had grown up some on the trail they used when they were kids but it was still visible enough to follow. The cool shade from the tall elm trees that canopied the river was a welcome refuge from the infernal heat of the hot sun in the field.

Happy memories of swimming came to mind as he got closer to the water's edge. Brett was younger and was always trying to keep up with him and Jake. Michael remembered a summer day when Will was with them and they decided to cross the river. It was a year when the water was higher and running faster than normal. The older three boys hopped across the line of rocks sticking out of the rushing water while Brett hesitated and stayed on the other side. Michael recalled how they teased him until he started across the slippery moss-covered stones. He was close to reaching them when he suddenly lost his balance and fell into the water. They watched in horror as his blonde head went under the water and disappeared from sight. Both he and Jake dived in and almost drowned themselves before they pulled him to the surface. Michael chuckled knowing neither Will's nor their own mother had ever found out about the incident.

He walked closer to the bank of the river and located the line his Dad had scratched onto a rock and noted the water level was down another quarter inch. *Damn!* He needed to let his father know.

When Michael arrived at the Sugar King, he came up the back steps but hesitated before going inside hearing his Dad's loud blaring voice. He quietly slipped into the back door of the kitchen and listened to Chet and Jake argue at the table in the corner of the room.

"So you think you're going over there and help them bale when we got hay bales of our own laying out in the field?"

"Dad, I'm in a partnership with my wife who is too pregnant to stay out in the scorching heat all day."

"Where's Brett?" Michael faced Irene by the sink.

"He went to town for parts on the baler. It broke down on the first round."

Michael turned around when the conversation got louder between his brother and father.

"Dad, she's my wife."

"You go over there and …"

"Dad!" Michael's voice escalated above his father's. Both Jake and Chet stopped talking and stared at him. "I'll go over with Jake and help them while you wait for Brett. When we get done over there we'll come back here and finish up."

Chet crossed his arms. "You're willing to bust your ass in this heat for nothing?"

"I'm not doing it for nothing. I'm doing it for my brother."

The combination of relief and shock was on Jake's face. "You're serious?"

"Yeah," Michael answered. "Let's get going before I change my mind."

While the afternoon sun beat down on a field east of the Langtree Farm, David, Cheryl's hired hand, drove the tractor while Michael and Jake piled bales onto the wagon. Each time they returned with a full wagon to the farm yard, David and Jake went up into the hay loft in the barn to pile bales, while Michael stayed down and loaded them onto a conveyer. His sleeveless T-shirt was completely saturated with sweat and stuck to his upper torso like a second layer of skin. He stopped momentarily to wipe the perspiration off his forehead and out of his eyes with a handkerchief then continued to move bales. The wagon was empty when he shut off the conveyer and heard a noise behind him. He turned to see Jolene slam the door on her Firebird a few yards away. She turned her head so fast, he didn't have time to see the expression on her face but he saw her look back again in his direction before she made it to the house.

How long was she watching me?

ONCE JOLENE STEPPED onto Cheryl's porch, she halted in front of the screen door and tried to catch her breath. She told herself it wasn't his sizzling, muscular body glistening in the sunlight that got her heart pumping so hard, it was simply the shock of seeing him there in the first place.

Thinking he could still be watching, she hurried inside the house and let the screen door slap shut behind her with a bang. Cheryl was by the sink snipping the ends off a mound of green beans.

"So why is *he* working here?"

"Hello, to you too."

"Sorry, I was just surprised to see Michael."

Cheryl smiled at her knowingly. "Jake said he volunteered. I told my husband we didn't need him and I could certainly drive the tractor. He said it's too hot for 'a woman in my condition' to be outside that long." The women looked out the window to see Michael and Jake drive off in Jake's truck.

"He's probably right. It must be close to ninety degrees out there. And look at you." Jolene took her sister's hands and pulled her arms apart. "I was here last week and I can't believe how much you're showing since then."

"Yeah. I'm really starting to look like I'm popping out." She laughed.

"Well, did you decide what night would work for Dori and me to come over to plan a baby shower?"

Cheryl patted her stomach. "This is my second baby. Some people may think I'm being greedy for gifts."

"You're starting to sound like Mom. What does Jake say about us giving you a baby shower?"

"He doesn't really care either way."

"Okay then. We'll have a shower right here at the farm. Let's call Dori and pick a day we can get together to plan. We need to get the ball rolling on this thing. How about Friday night?"

"You don't have any exciting plans for Friday evening?" Cheryl raised her eyebrow.

"No. I don't," Jolene answered. *You're not getting out of the shower.*

"I can't Friday evening. Taylor has a baseball game in Watson."

"Taylor's in Little League?"

"No. He's too young for that." Cheryl shook her head. "Some of the parents at church formed a team for the younger kids. Jake has been working with Taylor as often as he can."

"That's wonderful to hear they've gotten so close. We'll plan for another night to meet up with Dori."

"Thanks. Taylor is counting on me to come and watch him play. Speaking of relationships, how are you and Will doing?" Cheryl asked.

"Things are still going good. I think Barb, the legal secretary is finally warming up to me. She asked me the other day if I wanted a cup of coffee and then poured me a cup and brought it to my …"

"I'm not talking about her," Cheryl interrupted. "I'm talking about you and Will. How's that going?"

"We get along fine. I don't know what you're thinking, but there's nothing romantic brewing."

"What? Nothing? Look at you. Is he blind?" Cheryl frowned and pretended to be disappointed.

"Real funny. He did ask me out for dinner last week and I turned him down."

Cheryl stared in disbelief. "Why did you turn him down?"

"Because I want to keep my job."

"What's going out with him got to do with that?"

"I remember the secretaries who got involved with the lawyers at the Rat's office. If it was an extramarital situation, the secretary was immediately let go after the affair. And I've seen it where both parties were single, but after their romantic relationship ended, the secretary got fired because they could no longer work together."

"I can see why you want to keep things professional."

"He's attractive enough, and certainly respectful to women. I'm not saying my feelings about him couldn't change." *But he doesn't make my heart flutter at the sight of him.* A picture of Michael's sexy, sweaty body flashed in her head. *Better try and scrap that from my memory!*

I**T WAS STIFLING** hot with only a slight breeze stirring the leaves on the few trees surrounding the Chippewa County Fairgrounds. The sun was still above the horizon when Brett and Roger arrived for the tractor pull. The evening event had always been a big draw at the fair and this year the line of people waiting to get in was longer than ever.

"Look at that line. We'll never get in," Roger groaned.

"Never fear. Just stick close," Brett told him and kept walking.

They moved past the lengthy line and followed the fence to the contestants' entrance where Brett showed two passes to a large man at the gate. Brett was happy that his buddy, Dan Meyer, was competing in the event and had given them free access. Dan's dad owned and operated Meyer's Implement and the Sugar King Farm did a lot of business with them.

"Hey, Cameron!" Dan hollered from inside a group of men gathered around him. "You want to get in on wagering money for the winning tractor?"

"I bet you're talking about the tractor you're driving." Brett laughed and handed him a ten dollar bill. Brett looked at Roger. "Are you going to get in?"

"Don't let a Cameron rip you off," a voice behind Roger stated.

Brett turned and peered into the face of the tall boy who had confronted him at the AOG meeting. The same two boys he was with the other night stood on either side of him. It was easy to see all three had glassy eyes when they moved in closer to the group of men. Brett made a fist while he sized up the larger kid, trying to gage his age. He'd have to let him swing first in case he was under eighteen.

Brett stuck his chest out. "I don't know who you are, sonny boy, or what your game is, but you best keep your opinions to yourself."

"Afraid of folks finding out how your family is screwing people?"

"What the hell are you talking about?"

"Names Keith Pehrson, asshole."

"Karyn's brother?" Brett glanced at Roger and he nodded.

"Yeah, that's my sister. How do you know her?"

"I dined with her the other night." Brett's smile taunted. "Tell Karyn and her friends, Cindy and Jenny, that Brett says, 'Hi.'"

Keith's eyes narrowed before he cocked his fist and swung hard at Brett. Anticipating his move, Brett blocked his arm and punched him hard in the stomach. Keith went down on his knees and Brett twisted the younger man's arm back and secured him in a head lock.

"Tell me what's your problem," Brett demanded through gritted teeth.

"You and your rich parents," Keith panted out his answer. "Your old man convinced the farmers around here to invest into the refinery knowing," he paused for a breath, "full well it would bring them to their knees financially."

"My father didn't know that!" Brett countered. "Our family invested just like the rest."

"Yeah, you Camerons contributed just as much, but you had more money to invest. There was no threat of losing your farm."

Brett felt himself lose patience and tightened his grip. "There is no logical reason to blame us for what happened."

"Oh yeah? That's what you want everyone to believe. While your family and those fat bankers down in Watson snatch up all the land around here."

"That's bullshit, and you know it," Brett said and pushed Keith away. The younger man fell onto the ground. Brett stood above him and scanned the people huddled around. "For the record, he swung at me first." *Has everyone gone crazy?*

8

J olene was at her desk on Thursday afternoon when Barb, the legal secretary, came out of her office and went to the filing cabinet. Feeling she was being watched, Jolene looked up and caught the woman studying her.

"Do you need something, Barb?" Jolene asked.

"No. I just wanted to compliment you on the good job you did transcribing the Torgeson case."

Jolene smiled. "Thank you. You had such wonderful notes. It wasn't too difficult."

A moment went by before Barb spoke again. "I heard you tell Will a few weeks ago about the newly built apartment you found. So, have you gotten settled in yet?"

"Yes. Things are starting to fall into place. My sister gave me a dinette set and a few other things I needed. Right now, I'd love to find an affordable used couch and a chair or two."

Barb's face lit up. "You know, my mother just replaced her couch and chairs a couple of months ago. I was there the other day and the old set was still in my parents' garage. I'm sure if you can find a way to haul it away — it's yours."

Will came out of his office and caught the last of their conversation. "Haul away what?"

"A couch and chairs from her mother's garage," Jolene told him. "I wish I had access to a truck. I'd ask my new brother-in-law, but he's busier than anyone I know trying to run two farms."

A smile formed on Will's lips. "My dad has an old truck. I'm sure if I asked, he'd let me use it to help you."

"Really?" Jolene asked surprised. "You're so busy. I wouldn't want to put you out."

"Never too busy to help out a friend. We could grab dinner after we unload it at your apartment tomorrow night. How's that sound?"

"Just great!" *Very clever how he worked in a dinner date!*

IRENE BROUGHT two large platters filled with pancakes and sausage into the dining room at the Sugar King. Lucille cleared her throat and bowed her head indicating it was time to recite the mealtime prayer. Brett quickly stabbed a pancake onto his plate before he folded his hands.

Lucille looked around at her family gathered at the table. She worried about all three of her sons. Brett went out most nights and often stayed out until early morning. Michael seemed lonely and withdrawn for the past few months. He rarely went out and when he did, he always came home early. And Jake, of course, was headed for heartbreak. It was nice seeing him each morning for breakfast after chores. They could always share a family meal together even if he was living with *her*. She smiled to herself knowing it was only a matter of time before things would turn back to the way they were.

"I thought I would let everyone know I went to the quilting group yesterday and I had a talk with Joan after." Lucille took a bite of her pancake.

"And?" Chet asked.

"Well. She said the only thing she heard is a few farmers

think the AOG should find ways to help out the farmers who are in financial trouble."

"If we had known about the Jensens sooner, we would have."

"It isn't just the money, Dad," Brett spoke up. He then told his family about his night at the fair.

"Some of the farmers think the whole thing is a conspiracy with us and the Vanders family." Brett looked at his father. "The kid said you convinced the farmers, knowing they wouldn't get their money back in a plot to snatch up their land."

Jake slowly shook his head with his eyes closed. "I told you it was about me failing to get reimbursement for the AOG."

"No, it's not," Brett told him. "I think most of the members are aware there was nothing anyone could do once the governor said there was insufficient funds in the budget. It's about them thinking Dad knew what the outcome was going to be and is now somehow using it for our own personal gain."

"That preposterous!" Chet hollered from the end of the table. "Anyone who knows me, knows I wouldn't be involved in anything corrupt."

"Yes, it's crazy. But how are we going to prove it?" Michael jumped into the discussion.

"If we don't purchase any of the land. That would show everyone we're not involved in any of it," Chet answered. "But that brings us to the question: Who is this Paul Hansen who supposedly bought the Jensen property?"

"I'll find out from Jim," Michael announced. "He and his family are on top of who's buying what in the area."

Brett leaned forward in his chair. "I thought you were on the outs with him."

Michael let out a breath. "Yeah, we were, but we decided to call a truce." His voice went lower. "Since he became a new father."

Chet nodded in understanding and Lucille let out a deep sigh of relief. *Thank God, it wasn't your child. One down, one to go!*

The other two brothers silently stared at Michael.

THE NEWLY DEVELOPED area on Snake Hill Road outside of Montevideo had grown, and Michael was amazed to see how fast things had changed. During high school this whole section of land was mostly woods next to the river. Now a large apartment complex blocked most of the view of the water. The bottom apartments each had a semi-private, cement slab patio separated by wooden partitions on two sides and a roof above. He found Jim's apartment by the pool and smiled, knowing his friend always liked living close to the swimming pool to watch the girls.

Michael heard a baby crying from inside when he knocked on Jim's apartment door.

Jim opened the door holding the infant in his arms. "Hey! You decided to drop by." He waved for Michael to come inside. Michael had lived with Jim and was surprised to see the place was immaculate and smelled great.

Jim looked down at his son. "You got here just in time for this little guy's fussy time."

"He just needs to eat and he'll be fine," Lyla yelled from the kitchen. She came and took the baby from his father. "Hi Michael," she said, then turned her attention to their child. "Daddy's had you all afternoon but this is where I need to take over." She smiled and gave her husband a quick peck on the cheek.

Jim went to the fridge and got out two beers. "Would you care to join me on the patio?"

Michael was impressed with how well Lyla and Jim worked as a team with their son and their marriage. Years earlier, Jim's first marriage to the doctor's daughter in Watson had failed miserably. He was young when they had gotten married, and she had left town and moved to Portland with his first son shortly after their divorce.

They each sat on a chair by a glass-topped patio table. "So

you finally decided to come over and check the place out. What do think?"

"It's great," Michael took a swallow of his beer. "I checked the parking lot at Bob's to see if your car was there before I drove out here. Then it occurred to me I didn't know what you drive these days. In any case, I didn't mean to just barge in on you. I thought you said Lyla and her mother do Tupperware parties on Friday nights?"

"Yes. They usually do, but the lady who was hosting tonight canceled because she was sick. She likely came to her senses and decided to go to the bar, instead."

Michael laughed.

"I bet your old man is really worked up about this dry weather."

"We've got the irrigation running steady. But he's more worried about his reputation."

Jim cocked his head. *"His reputation?"*

Michael filled him in what was going on with the AOG and the farmers in the area.

"Wow! No one would ever believe your dad would do anything wrong."

"Brett got into a scuffle at the fair a couple of nights ago, but he got some information out of the kid who tried to punch him. I was wondering if you could find out some more for me?"

"Sure."

"I need to know about a guy named Paul Hansen. Will Vanders told me he's buying the Jensen property out on County Road nine."

"What do you want to know about him?"

"Where he's from. How long he's been farming. *If* he's farming. Anything you can."

"Okay. I'm on it," Jim said and glanced at his wristwatch. "Do you want to switch chairs?"

"Switch chairs? Why?"

"Because you need to be in this chair to see what I wanted to show you."

"Oh, yeah. That's right. You had something you wanted me to see."

"I'll go in and get us another beer. Sit over here and you'll have a perfect view."

Michael shrugged and sat in Jim's chair.

They were talking about Lyla's family when Michael saw a truck with furniture in the back pull up on the road alongside the end apartment on his right. A red Firebird followed the truck and turned into the parking lot.

"Here we go," Jim said when a woman got out of the car and came toward the man in the truck.

Michael felt the planet come to a screeching halt seeing the woman was Jolene.

"I thought you would be interested." Jim smiled. "I just happened to be home when the super was showing her around. I waved him over and told him to put her in that ground floor apartment instead of the one on the second floor."

"Doesn't it cost more for a ground floor apartment?"

"I told him to wave the difference and I would deal with my old man."

"Why would you do that?" Michael was skeptical.

"I thought I could keep an eye on her for you."

"Why?"

"Because I screwed things up between us and … I've known all along you're in love with her."

The man stepped up into the box of the truck and Michael's stomach clinched seeing it was Will."

"Do you know the dud who's with her?"

"Unfortunately, I do. It's her boss — Will Vanders."

"No shit. That's Will?" Jim stretched his neck to get a better look. "He's sure looks all grown up now."

Michael and Jim watched Jolene knock on the door of the next apartment. Seconds later, a man came out and helped Will carry the couch inside her new home. Once all the furniture was hauled inside, the neighbor left. Michael was relieved when Will and Jolene came out a short while later and got into the truck. It wasn't enough time for anything intimate to take place. When they drove out of the parking lot Michael noticed Jolene's head tilt back like she was laughing.

"SO WHAT DID you think of the place?" Jolene asked. She had noticed Will assessing her from across the seat when they got into his dad's truck.

"I think it's great. How much did you say the rent was?" He turned the key in the ignition.

"Around a hundred."

"Wow, that's reasonable for a new ground floor apartment." He smiled. "I was thinking if she can afford this place, I must be over paying her." He put the vehicle in gear and slowly drove away from the complex.

"No. It's proof you've hired someone who can wheel and deal. Either that, or someone who is incredibly lucky." She laughed.

They exchanged the truck for Will's car on the way to the Lenz Supper Club where he had made reservations. The waitress had just removed their salad plates from the table when she noticed Will's gray-blue eyes boldly stay on her.

"I was more than pleased yesterday how quickly Mr. Hansen agreed on the purchase price of the property out on County Road nine," she quickly stated. "I hadn't even gotten into many details when he told me he'd take it for the listing price. It really surprised me he didn't throw in a lower counter offer."

Will took a sip of his wine and nodded. "Maybe he saw what he wanted and went after it."

Knowing the comment was directed at her, she shifted it back to business. "I told Donnie I checked out the appraisal and we actually had it listed very close. This being a prime piece of farmland, I told him we should've listed it much higher. There was the possibility Mr. Hansen would've either argued it down or purchased it for what we were asking."

"Maybe that's why Mr. Hansen didn't argue. He knew he was getting a good deal."

"So you agree with Donnie on this?" She cocked her head at him.

"Well, I believe folks should be treated fairly."

She stared at him in surprise. "Excuse me. I was under the assumption we are in this to make as much money as possible."

"Look. I like your way of thinking, but you're new at this." He released a breath. "I realize you're trying to make a great impression on everyone. And I have no doubt you're a great negotiator, but in this case you've got to listen to the people with the experience."

"Okay. But I feel in my gut I could've pushed this and earned everyone on our end an impressive commission."

Will looked around at the room filled with mostly couples. "Let's not talk anymore about business." He laid his hand over hers and gently ran his thumb over her knuckles. "I just want to hear you're happy."

"Of course I'm happy," she answered, thankful to see the waitress come through the room with their entrees. She nonchalantly slid her hand away from his and sipped her wine. The rest of the dinner conversation was pleasant and uneventful while she talked about how she and Barb were getting better acquainted.

Will pulled his car in front of her apartment and she promptly thanked him for the lovely meal and for his help with the furniture. When she grabbed her doggy bag and tucked her clutch purse under her arm, he immediately got out of the car and opened her door.

"I wouldn't be a gentleman if I didn't walk you to your door."

"I left the light on by the door and it's only a few feet away," she tittered nervously. "I'm sure I can make it there on my own."

He ignored the comment and walked with her into the small patio. When she opened her purse to get out her key, he stepped closer and put his hands on her shoulders. Seeing his face move in on hers, she instinctively threw her head back. He jerked his head away and stared at her with wide eyes.

"Look, Will. You're a great guy," she said apologetically. "But the thing is: I love working for you and I wouldn't want to do anything to jeopardize my job."

He tilted his head. "What does that have to do with me kissing you?"

She pushed out a breath. "I've heard of several stories about secretaries getting personally involved with the boss and then end up losing their jobs."

"I know it's early in our relationship and I'm sorry for crossing the line, but you can rest assured I would never fire you because things didn't pan out between us romantically."

"You say that now, but when emotions get stomped on, anything can happen. Do I need to remind you my ex is a divorce attorney?"

"No. But it does explain why you're apprehensive. How about we just take things slow and see where it leads us?"

A wave of relief washed over her. "That sounds better than just jumping into something head first." Feeling awkward she stuck her key into the lock. "Good night, Will, and thanks for everything. See you on Monday."

She stepped inside and immediately pushed the door shut with her backside. A moment went by while she stood in the dark with her eyes closed. *I hope that didn't cost me my job!*

THE SETTING SUN was suspended above the horizon and hung like a ball of fire tucked into a background of clouds in crimson, peach, and gold. Michael drove with the window down in his truck and gazed at the spectacular sky. He had started the evening watching a rerun of The Mary Tyler Moore show with his parents, and then decided he had to get out of the house and go for a drive.

Ten miles northwest of the Sugar King he saw a sign next to the road and slowed down to read it. Seeing it was another Larsen's foreclosure sign he released a disgusted breath. *This is the Sorenson place — another member of the AOG.* Michael remembered how concerned old man Sorenson was about donating such a large sum of money for the refinery. Chet had convinced him it was the right thing to do for the future generations of beet farmers in the area. *Dad is going to freak out when I tell him about this.*

On his way back home, the song "Desperado" played on the radio. It was strange he'd heard the song many times but tonight the lyrics seemed soul-stirring. He couldn't help but retrace his love life in his head. He'd been with a lot of women and couldn't ignore the fact he was often drawn to the ones he couldn't have. Jolene was the only one who had been completely honest and straightforward with him. Their relationship had started out to the contrary, but it quickly evolved into something wonderful that he didn't have to fake or lie about. Loving her came easy.

He felt torn up inside knowing he had let his desire to get revenge ruin the best thing he ever had. Michael stared out over the dry fields and replayed the whole stupid mess in his head.

In confidence, Jolene had told him Cheryl was going to surprise Jake in the Cities the night before his appointment to see the governor. Realizing it was an opportunity to get back at Jake for stealing Cheryl away, he cooked up a plot with Susan, Jake's scorned ex. Using Jolene to find out Cheryl's precise departure time, he set a scheme in motion for Susan to get to Jake's hotel room first. Susan arrived as planned, but Jake refused to let her into his room. As he chatted with her in the hallway, Jake mentioned a glitch in the governor's schedule and the possibility he wouldn't get in to see him. Seizing her opportunity, Susan reminded Jake her uncle was the lieutenant governor and if he would let her in to use the phone, she would call her uncle and guarantee his appointment. Loyal to the AOG, Jake let her inside his room and while they waited for her uncle to call back, Cheryl arrived and saw Susan in Jake's room. Cheryl assumed Jake planned a romantic rendezvous with his ex and the incident ended their relationship for a brief time.

Michael figured out shortly after he was in love with Jolene, but it was too late to undo what he did to Cheryl and Jake. He was a coward and let Jake blame their mother for what happened. No one would've known any better if Jim hadn't told Cheryl and Jolene what really happened in the Cities.

As the miles passed, Michael recalled seeing Jolene and Will yesterday and felt his stomach knot. She looked very happy when they left her apartment. He being a lawyer like her ex-husband, they had a lot in common. Will was a slick negotiator and would do well as a lawyer. Michael thought about how quick Will was at forming alibis to tell their parents whenever they went out drinking in high school. Some of them were very elaborate. Suddenly, he remembered watching Will run his hand through his hair whenever he lied to Helen Vanders. He did the very same thing several times the other day in his office when Michael asked him about the Jensen foreclosure. *That lying son-of-a-bitch!* He took a few deep breaths to compose himself. Oh, my God! Jolene! *If he does one thing to hurt her, I'll kill him.*

When Michael arrived home, he moved swiftly from the shed to the house on a mission to inform his father about the Sorenson foreclosure and his suspicions about Will. He swung open the back door of the kitchen and found his mother talking to someone on the phone.

Lucille turned toward him and said, "He's here right now. I'll let you talk to him." She handed him the phone.

He cupped the receiver before he asked, "Who is it?"

She shrugged and shook her head. "It's a woman. That's all I know."

He put the phone to his ear. "Hello."

"Oh, Michael! You don't know how great it is to hear your voice."

His heart was doing somersaults. "Who is this? Jolene?"

9

"**N**o. It's Diana. Diana Iverson. Well, it's ... actually Diana Levine now."

Michael tried to speak, but no words would come out of his mouth.

"Michael, are you there?"

"Yes. I ... I'm just surprised to hear from you," he finally stammered out.

"I know. It has to be ... what? Eight years?"

"Yeah, about that."

"I don't mean to bother you. It's just I've moved back to Montevideo and I thought maybe we could get together and catch up on old times."

"You and your husband moved here?"

"No," she paused, "we're divorced."

"Oh. I'm sorry."

"Don't be. Listen, can you meet me tonight?"

His thoughts were spinning in his head. *I need time to let this sink in.* "I can't tonight. It's late and I have some business I need to take care of with my Dad. How about tomorrow at Trailways for lunch? Let's say noon?"

"Sure. That sounds great. See you then."

Hearing the dial tone, he lowered the phone in his hand and stared at it a moment before he hung it back on the cradle.

"You look like you've just seen a ghost." Lucille put her hands on his shoulders. "Who was that on the phone?"

"Diana Levine."

"Who?" his mother asked.

"Diana Iverson," he stated. He pushed open the swinging door and went through the hallway and into the den.

Lucille trailed after him. "Are you talking about your old high school girlfriend?"

"Yes, Mother. I am."

"What on earth did she want?" Lucille demanded.

"Who wanted what?" Chet asked from a leather easy chair.

Lucille turned to her husband. "Diana Iverson. That was her on the phone."

"That Iverson girl you used to date?" Chet raised his brows.

"Yeah, Dad."

"What did she want?"

"I don't know … Talk, I guess." Michael shook his head. "Dad, I think we better check on Alex. I thought he was acting a little strange when I left."

Chet's face went blank. "What do you mean? There was nothing wrong with that horse when I went down there earlier."

"I think we better go check on him."

Michael knew suggesting something was wrong with his dad's Arabian horse was a sure way to get him outside.

The older man jumped to his feet. "Don't just stand there. Let's go."

Once father and son moved far enough from the kitchen windows, Michael told his dad to slow down.

Chet quickly turned his head. "What do you mean?"

"There's nothing wrong with Alex. I just wanted to get you alone to talk."

His dad scowled at him. "Get me fired up … to talk? What the hell's wrong with you?"

When they got to the stables, Michael held the door open for his father and they went inside.

Chet went directly to Alex and pet him above his nose. "Okay. What's so important you had to make up lies to get me down here?"

"I drove up by Sorenson's and there was a foreclosure sign on their property."

"Oh, God no!" Chet sucked in a breath and closed his eyes.

"Yes. And it makes things look worse for us, seeing how you personally convinced Olaf Sorenson to donate five thousand dollars to the refinery."

Chet sank down on a wooden box outside Alex's stall. "I never dreamt we'd have to wait years for reimbursement."

"There was a Larsen Realty sign out by their mailbox. Dad, I think there's something more going on than what we think."

"What do you mean?" Chet looked up.

Michael put his hands on his hips. "I got this feeling in my gut it has something to do with Will Vanders."

"Will? Why would you think that?"

"You may think I'm crazy, but I think he lied to me that day I saw him about Jensen's foreclosure."

"What makes you think he lied?"

"Will has this nervous habit of running his hand through his hair whenever he isn't being truthful."

"You're going to accuse my best friend's son, the newest hometown hero, of doing something underhanded on a hunch?" Chet stood.

"I know it sounds far-fetched, but I can't help feel something isn't right."

"Could this feeling have anything to do with him hiring Cheryl's sister as his secretary?"

Michael sighed. "No. It doesn't."

"My advice to you is to keep your hunches to yourself until you have some sort of proof."

"I'm not stupid, Dad. I know I can't accuse him without some concrete evidence."

"I'd make damn sure it's something solid."

Michael tossed and turned in bed later that night thinking about the evening's unexpected events. Diana calling had tipped his world upside down. She was his first real girlfriend and they dated steady all through high school. They had planned to backpack through Europe after graduation and get married soon after college. Diana had accomplished two of their goals without him; backpacking and getting married to someone she met along the way.

He had no idea how he felt about seeing her again. So much had changed. He recalled how hurt and angry he had been, hearing she married a doctor and was living in Connecticut. She was the one Dr. Munson suspected had changed him into an emotional mess. Why would she call him after all these years? What were they going to talk about? Most importantly, what did she expect of him?

THE SMELL of fresh coffee brewing in Jolene's apartment made the place seem more like home. Wearing a blue flowered house coat, she dropped a cigarette and a lighter in the pocket and filled a cup with coffee. She carried the steaming liquid and a McCall's magazine outside to the patio and set them both on a small metal table. A neighbor had given her the table and two matching metal chairs. They needed to be painted, but working two jobs all week, she hadn't the energy to tackle the project this morning.

Instead, she chose to enjoy her morning coffee and cigarette while leisurely paging through her magazine. She tore out a few coupons and smiled seeing the Betsy McCall paper doll cut outs. As young girls, she and Cheryl had played with them for hours after they removed them from the magazine each month. She thought about how simple life was back then.

Her thoughts went to Will and she concluded their evening had definitely ended on a different note. Was her refusal of his kiss strictly about losing her job? Suddenly, she tried to imagine what it would've been like if she had let him kiss her. The thought made her feel ill at ease and it didn't seem to stir any real romantic excitement inside her. It was confusing. Most women wouldn't hesitate to snatch up a nice-looking man with a successful law practice. He was a real catch being so highly educated and motivated. Everyone in the Watson and Montevideo area was aware of his efforts to improve the community.

Then against her better judgement, she thought about kissing Michael and felt a whirlwind of hot desire blow through her body. She immediately told herself it was just a reaction from seeing him hot and sweaty last week at Cheryl's. Will was the complete opposite of Michael. He was a decent, honest man. She thought about his claim he would never fire her if they got romantically involved and it didn't work out. He was only starting his career and was perhaps a little naïve about how things actually worked in the real world.

The sound of a baby crying brought her back to reality and Jolene stood from her chair. Moving toward her patio entrance she looked out to the right at her neighbors across from her. A woman with dark hair paced in front of the patio trying to console a wailing baby in her arms.

For some reason, Jolene thought the woman looked familiar, but she couldn't quite place where she'd seen her before.

MICHAEL PARKED his truck in the parking lot at the Trailways Cafe and took a deep breath. Instead of getting out of his truck, he collapsed back in the seat. *This is crazy. What am I doing here?* It was strange but he felt like he was sneaking around.

He shook that thought and checked his hair in the side mirror before opening the door. On his way to the entrance of the restaurant, he looked at the vehicles parked in the lot and tried to figure out which one was Diana's. Not having a clue, he realized she was more or less a stranger to him now. He noticed his palms were wet when he pulled the door open and went inside. Within seconds, a waitress stopped him and asked if he wanted to sit at the counter or in a booth.

"I'm supposed to meet … " He stopped speaking when he saw Diana wave from a booth across the room. His heart beat faster with each step he took toward her.

"Michael!" She slid out of the booth and rushed to him with opened arms.

Wow! She looks great! And smells great too! He hugged her back. "It's good to see you, too."

She looked thinner in the face but her blonde hair was shoulder length and the same color as it was in high school. The expensive-looking blue jumpsuit she wore clung to the top half of her slim figure before it flared out in bell-bottom pant legs. It seemed she was taller until he saw the high wedged sandals on her feet.

"I was so thrilled to hear from my sister you were still in the area," she said after they sat. "I thought why not give him a call and catch up on old times."

"I was shocked when you said you moved back."

The waitress appeared and asked if they were ready to order and Michael asked her to give them a few more minutes.

"Remember that time we were in here and a fight broke out between the Olson and the Hendrickson boys?" She smiled.

Gazing into her blue eyes, he tried to recall how many times he lost himself in them. They were as alluring as he remembered.

They placed their order and started to talk about their families. Michael filled her in about the partnership he and his brothers had with their father. He also mentioned that Jon

Langtree was killed in a farming accident and Jake and Cheryl had recently gotten married and were expecting a child soon.

Her eyes lit up. "They're expecting? Wow. That's *so* great!" Michael was surprised how excited she got hearing Jake was going to be a father. The two rarely interacted in high school and his brother had been away at college the last two years he and Diana had dated.

"So why did you decide to move back here?" The question had been burning inside him.

She looked down and then back up into his eyes. "Because I realized how I screwed things up with you and me."

No kidding? "It took you eight years to figure it out?"

"After you didn't go with me to Europe, I was devastated." She stopped speaking when the waitress set down her bowl of soup and his cheeseburger and fries.

When the server was far enough from the table, Michael couldn't stop himself from asking, "So you married someone else because you were angry at me for not going to Europe?"

"I was young and impressionable, and yes, angry when I met Mark. Being a couple years older, he manipulated me into thinking you didn't love me or you would've gone with me."

Michael felt a heated rush of anger wash through his body. "I wrote immediately after to let you know what a mistake I'd made letting my parents convince me not to go. You have no idea how badly I regretted that decision," Michael defended himself. "But I never heard from you again. You had to have met Mark right away because you didn't write back. I had to hear it from your sister you were getting married. For a long time I felt like my whole world crashed. Because I loved you."

She closed her eyes and took a few breaths before opening them. "Michael, it sounds like we both made some bad decisions. I'm so sorry things ended the way they did. I really didn't expect Mark to propose in Italy."

The conversation took a pause when the ketchup didn't come out of the bottle and he rapidly shook it up and down. "Tell me," he said as he drizzled ketchup over his fries. "Why did you and Mark decide to call it quits after eight years?"

She raised her spoon and took a sip of her soup. "Our marriage was good for the first five until I found out he lied to me."

Michael stopped eating. "What did he lie about?"

She took a deep breath and let it out. "Mark found out shortly before he went to Europe that he couldn't father children. But he failed to tell me. After we got married, he convinced me to wait for three years to start a family in order to pay off some debt he accumulated from going to medical school. Even though he knew all along it wasn't possible, we tried when the three years were up and did so for another three years to get pregnant. I was angry when I found out he knew before we met about his almost nonexistent sperm count. But I never thought about getting divorced until he told me adopting a child wasn't an option for him. He said if God hadn't made it possible for him to father a child, he wasn't meant to be one. I got tired of sitting alone, night after night whenever he got called away on an emergency. I felt empty inside and I knew I had to get away and start over."

"Sorry you had to go through that," he told her sincerely.

She looked up at him through her thick lashes. "Thank you. It was a lot to deal with."

"Do you think being back here is actually starting over?"

She placed her hand on his forearm. "I think we were both too young to realize what love was about back then. I thought maybe if you still felt something for me —" her eyes locked with his, " — we could possibly give it another try as adults. That is, unless … you're involved with someone else?"

A picture of Jolene's joyful face in Will's truck flashed in his head. "No. I'm not seeing anyone. But I'm going to need some time to process all this before I give you an answer."

"Sure. I don't want to pressure you. We could take things as slow as you want." She smiled. "Whatever you decide I'll have to accept, but you need to know a part of me never stopped loving you."

LUCILLE SAT at the dining room table and felt a pang of jealousy when she read the local section of the morning paper. There was another article about Will Vanders. This time he had officially announced his candidacy for the Watson town board in November. There was no argument; the boy was ambitious, and Charlie and Helen had done a fine job of raising him.

It wasn't like her sons didn't have a strong work ethic, but Jake was busy trying to run two farms and Michael wasn't the type for public office. Brett had the personality for it but no desire to take on any extra responsibility.

She heard the back door open and shut and Michael saying something to Irene in the kitchen. A minute later he seated himself at the dining room table and poured a cup of coffee.

"Where's everyone else?" she asked.

"Jake went to the Langtree Farm for breakfast."

Such a shame. She won't even let him have a meal with his family!

"Dad and Brett should be back any time from checking the irrigation by Thompson's."

"Great. We have a moment by ourselves to talk," she said smoothly.

He eyed her suspiciously.

"I saw how nice you looked the other day when you went to town." Her tone was sugary. "I imagine you went to see Diana."

"Yeah, I did."

"So what's going on with her? Is she still married?"

"No, she's not."

"What about children?"

"What about them?"

She blew out a disgusted breath. "Does she have any?"

"No, but I know she'd like to."

"Are you and her getting back together?"

"I guess I really don't know right now." He filled her in on the basics of Diana's situation and the proposition she had put before him.

"That is quite the story," Lucille said. "The poor thing. Being lied to had to be awful."

"Yeah. It sounds like her ex-husband was a real jerk."

She was silent for a moment. "Michael, I'm not telling you what you should do, but you need to think about your situation. You're twenty-seven years old and you're not getting any younger. And as far as I know, you're not involved with anyone." She watched for his reaction. *Thank God, he didn't pick up with that tramp, Jolene.* "You and Diana were pretty serious back in the day. I just can't help but feel — she may have been the one all along."

JOLENE AND DORI sat with Cheryl at her kitchen table composing a list of guests for the baby shower.

"On the Garrison side we're thinking you and me … Mom and Grandma Thielen," Cheryl told her. "On the Cameron side —I guess only — Lucille."

"Isn't she more than enough?" Dori laughed. "But who knows maybe in two weeks when we actually have the shower, we may have to invite Diana, too."

"Who?" Jolene asked.

Cheryl pursed her lips and shook her head at Dori before she addressed her sister's question. "Diana is a girl Michael dated in high school."

"Why would you want to invite his old girlfriend?"

"She was the one who *changed* Michael," Dori reported, not picking up on Cheryl's warning.

"Changed him?" Jolene's interest was piqued. "How?"

"Well for one thing, he never dated anyone but her. He was

so in love with her ... until she broke his heart."

Jolene blinked her eyes in surprise. "I thought Michael was always the player."

"No. In high school I remember girls constantly hitting on him, but he only had eyes for her." Dori explained the story about them backpacking and Diana marrying someone she met in Europe.

If I didn't know any better, I'd feel sorry for him.

"A girlfriend told me she saw Diana in town and she looked great. She told my friend she decided to move back to Montevideo," Dori announced. "Then a couple of days ago, another friend saw her and Michael at Trailways eating lunch together. She said they were staring at each other like it was high school all over again."

"Maybe it wasn't what it looked like," Cheryl suggested.

"Oh, it was," Dori countered. "My friend said when they left she saw Michael give Diana a long, drawn out hug in the parking lot."

The news was unsettling and Jolene got up from the table to refill the wine glasses and Cheryl's coffee cup. She caught Dori and her sister raise their brows at one another when she turned from the stove.

"We best stay on task, if we're going to get done planning this shower," Dori said, and named off a few more possible guests.

On the way home, Jolene thought about Michael and Diana's reunion and concluded her reaction was strictly the result of a long day at work. What did she care if he rekindled an old relationship? If this Diana had any brains, she'd see through his bullshit and run back to Connecticut as fast as she could.

10

It was a hot, muggy afternoon under a hazy sky when Michael and Jake drove down the field road to the river in Michael's truck.

"I'm starting to hate going down here," Michael commented when the trees surrounding the river came into view. "It doesn't matter how much the water level goes down, Dad gets worked up when you give him a report. I keep telling him, 'Don't shoot the messenger,' but he ignores me."

Jake didn't appear to be listening. "How many days in the average summer do you think we swam in this river?"

"I don't know, but I remember once Irene checked us for gills."

"Do you remember the time when Will came with us, and Brett tried to tag along?"

Michael shut his truck off and sat back in the seat. "It's funny you would bring that up. I was just thinking about it when I was down here awhile ago."

"I still don't know why Will pushed Brett into the water. That dumbass."

Michael cocked his head. "From where I was standing, it looked like he slipped and the water swept him away."

Jake shook his head. "No. He made it across. Will banged his chest into him and Brett bounced backward off the rock."

"Here all this time, I was thinking Brett didn't make it." *Interesting.*

They moved through the trees then stood on the large rock where Chet had etched a line into the stone. Jake lowered a long yard stick to the water's surface below and Michael read the measurement. The water was down another quarter of an inch. It wasn't as bad as expected, but knowing it was steadily going down wasn't good news.

"Maybe it will rain with all these clouds." Jake looked up in the sky.

"A person can only hope," Michael answered. "But it's been two days of hazy weather and it hasn't rained a drop."

"I don't ever remember seeing it this dry."

"Dad said it's been awhile for him, too," Michael commented.

"Speaking of things that haven't happened in awhile," Jake paused, "Cheryl told me Diana's back in town."

"Yeah, she's back."

Jake raised his brows. "Any idea why?"

"Her and her husband split up."

"Is that right? I heard you met up with her at Trailways."

Michael busted out laughing. "Oh Lordy, Jake. You got married two months ago and now you've turned into a Nosey Nellie."

"Very funny. But what's her plan? Does she want to get back together with you?"

"Yes," he paused, "she thinks we should, and so does Mom." Michael recalled his mother's comment that Diana may have been the one.

"Well, what do *you* want?"

Michael stared down at the slow flowing water. "I really don't know. I loved her at one point, but have no idea how I feel about her now. I guess we could hang out together for a while until I figure it out."

"What about Jolene?" Jake asked.

Michael's head swung in his brother's direction. "What about her? She's with the town hero now." *Or whatever it is he's trying to portray.*

"I don't think the situation is cut and dried yet. Cheryl says she knows her sister and it doesn't sound like she's interested in him."

"That information doesn't help out a guy she despises."

"I thought before you get roped into a situation, you should explore all your options."

"I've used up all my options with Jolene."

"Do you really believe that? I keep thinking about that day at St. John's Recovery Center when you broke down just talking about her."

Michael remembered trying to choke out the words after he realized he was never going to be with her again. "I guess things couldn't be any more screwed up at this point."

Jake crossed his arms. "Oh yeah, it could. My advice is to not screw it up any worse by jumping into something when you're not absolutely sure."

It was dark despite the lights being on at the office of Larsen's Realty. There wasn't any trace of the sun behind the thick blanket of clouds outside. Jolene stopped working at her desk and stared out the window at the buildings across the street. It seemed like ever since she heard about Michael and his old, but new, girlfriend, the sun had ceased to shine. She got angry at herself for becoming so melodramatic about a situation that was no concern of hers.

One thing was for sure. It was a shock to learn that at one time, Michael Cameron had been a decent human being who treated women with respect. It sounded like this Diana had broken his heart and ruined a young man's ability to accept love for the rest of his life. How could anything be more tragically sad than that? When the phone rang, it brought her back to reality.

"Larsen's Realty. Jolene speaking. How can I help you?"

"Are you working hard?" Cheryl asked.

"I was just taking a little break. What did you need?"

"What are you doing for dinner tonight? I'm making a lasagna and I know how much you like it."

"Sure. That sounds great."

"And I'm frosting an angel food cake as we speak."

Knowing it was her favorite cake, Jolene became suspicious. "Why are you trying to be so nice to me?"

Cheryl took a quick breath. "Because you seemed so bummed out when you left here the other night."

Was I that obvious? "What are you talking about?"

"Whatever. Are you coming over for dinner?"

Knowing she had no plans for the evening made it an easy decision. "What time do you want me there?"

"Whenever you get off work, drive out."

Remembering the bustier, she told her sister, "I have to stop at my apartment and change out of my work clothes first. See you then."

Around six o'clock, Jolene was seated next to Taylor at Cheryl and Jake's dining room table.

"How are the jobs going?" Jake asked his sister-in-law after they started to eat.

"Great." Jolene scooped a portion of lasagna on her plate. "Will is really helpful and Donnie is easy to work for."

"Has anyone looked at the Sorenson place, yet?" Jake asked.

"Donnie told me we have a prospective buyer."

"Already? Wow, that was fast. Anyone from around here?"

"No. It's a guy named Larry Edwards. I guess he's from somewhere south of here."

Cheryl was putting the leftover food away, when Jolene

stepped onto the porch for a quick smoke. The sun was trying to peek out behind the clouds when she lit a cigarette and rested her head against the back of a wooden chair.

Today had been much like every day since she'd started her two jobs — very hectic. It looked like Monday wouldn't be any better with Mr. Edwards insisting on an earlier showing in the morning. She closed her eyes and let out an exhausted breath as she listened to the wind rush through the tall pines. Hearing a vehicle slow up, her eyes opened and she saw Michael's truck pull into the driveway. *Oh crap! Is he going to show up every time I come to visit?*

Michael got out of his truck and turned his head in the direction of her car parked next to Jake's truck. Jolene immediately zeroed in on him. It was strange to see him without a cowboy hat on his head. Her attention was drawn to the dressy burgundy shirt and the pair of dark blue jeans he was wearing. When he started for the house, she saw his silver belt buckle glitter in the sunlight as he walked. *He looks so good. I bet he's going on a date with her.*

He swiftly made his way to the porch and raised his fist to knock on the screen door but stopped when he saw her sitting on a chair. "Nice evening." He gave her a heart-stopping smile. "Just enough breeze."

Why do you have to be so gorgeous? She kept her smile casual. "Yes, it is."

He held up a wallet in his hand. "I thought Jake might be looking for this."

She nodded nonchalantly but was secretly checking him out. *Oh God, he was a sight!* His eyes sparkled and his bright white teeth contrasted beautifully against golden tanned skin.

He looked down and shuffled one of his shiny cowboy boots. "Well, I best give this to him." He brought his fist up again, but this time Jake swung the door open before he could knock.

"Missing this?" Michael showed him the wallet.

Jake slapped a hand on his back pocket. "I am now." He grabbed the wallet out of Michael's hand.

"I've gotta get going," Michael stated and turned to go.

"Wait a second." Jake went back inside and came out with his cowboy boots. He quickly slipped them on and walked with his brother to his truck.

Jolene went into the house but watched the two brothers from the window above the kitchen sink as she dried a plate. Jake stood by the driver's door and talked to Michael for a moment before he started his truck and left.

"He sure was dressed up tonight," Cheryl commented.

"I imagine he's going on a hot date with that old girlfriend."

"Yeah." Cheryl didn't look up from the pan she was washing. "Jake told me they're going to try and give their relationship another chance."

Jolene felt her stomach tighten. "There has to be something wrong with her if she wants to be with him."

"Dori's friend said she looked great. I guess Michael is different with her. Jake said if things return to the way they were in high school, he thinks Michael will marry her for sure."

The word "marry" weighed like brick on Jolene's chest. "I wonder what this Diana looks like."

"I remember seeing a picture of the two of them dancing in Jon's old high school yearbook," Cheryl recalled. "Let's finish these dishes and I'll go find it."

The two sisters sat at the kitchen table and paged through the yearbook from 1966. When Cheryl found the picture of Michael and Diana, it stole Jolene's breath away. The photo revealed everything she was afraid of — two attractive, starry-eyed teenagers — staring at each other with love in their eyes. Diana was an attractive girl with long blonde hair and a slim figure. Michael's handsome face appeared innocent in the picture and it hurt Jolene to see how infatuated he seemed to be with the girl in his arms. She could've sworn he looked at her the very same way.

"Jolene said a man named Larry Edwards is interested in the Sorenson place," Jake told Michael. "I asked her where the guy was from and she said south of here somewhere."

Michael got into his truck. "Do you think it's a coincidence no one knows anything about the buyers who are purchasing all the land from the foreclosures?"

Jake shook his head. "Yeah. It sure seems strange, but most of the farmers around here donated to the refinery and are in no position financially to purchase any more land."

"You are right about that," Michael turned the key in the ignition. "I better get going. I'm taking Diana to the Starlight Drive-In for 'The Great Gatsby.' Neither of us read the book in high school."

Jake's mouth opened like he was going to say something but didn't.

"I've got to stop at Jim's for a moment first." He started his truck. "See you tomorrow."

Michael backed his truck and left the Langtree Farm thinking about how cute Jolene looked with her hair in a ponytail wearing those striped shorts. She sure did fill out that yellow tank top nicely. He knew it was pointless to think about her like that, but a man could still dream, couldn't he?

He arrived at Jim's apartment and found him lounging in a reclining lawn chair on the small patio.

"Hey, buddy." Jim reached into a cooler beside his chair and pulled out a cold beer then handed it to him.

"Hey," Michael answered as he twisted the cap off his beer.

"Did you find out anything about Paul Hansen?"

Jim slowly shook his head. "It's a mystery, because no one has ever heard of him around here. Or in the southern half of the state."

"Well, you can add another name to the list: Larry Edwards. Jolene told Jake he's the guy interested in Sorenson's farm."

"I'm on it." Jim motioned at Jolene's apartment with the beer in his hand. "I don't know if she had a date or not, but she came home and changed her clothes before leaving again."

Michael smiled. "Jake forgot his wallet in my truck and she was at the Langtree Farm when I stopped earlier to give it to him."

"So then you must have noticed how hot she looked in that tank top and shorts?"

"I thought you were a happily married man?"

"I am. But I'm not dead. Last I checked, I still had a pulse." Jim's eyes ran up and down Michael. "Where are you going all dressed up?"

"Diana's back."

"Diana who?" Jim's eyes got big. "Diana Iverson?"

Michael nodded. "Diana Levine now."

Jim's chair tipped to one side and landed onto the cement when he jumped to his feet. "You're shitting me?"

"No. She got a divorce and moved back."

Jim picked up his chair and sat down. "So what happened?"

Michael took a seat in the chair across from him and related what Diana told him about her husband and how he lied.

Jim shook his head. "That's heavy, man." His eyes searched Michael's. "So, what's she expecting you to do about it?"

"She thinks we were too young when we dated in high school and we should give our relationship another try."

Jim blinked at him. "Don't you think it's a bit *presumptuous* of her?"

"What do you mean?"

"She runs off with this guy and breaks your heart and then when things don't work out between them, she runs back here and thinks you're going to pick up with her right where you two left off. That's bullshit."

"Well, I guess I didn't think about it like that."

"I'm not your mother. You do whatever you think you should, but I'd take things slow with her," Jim advised. "You were completely screwed up for a long time after she left you the last time."

I⊤ wasn'⊤ ⊤oo long after the sisters shut the cover on Jon's year-book when Jolene decided to call it a night. She drove home slowly and gazed at the western sky laid out in front of her. Only a faint, coral glimmer of the setting sun could be seen behind the overcast. It seemed the sunset matched her life — dull and uneventful. When she arrived home, she sat on the patio and nibbled on some chocolate then took a long bubble bath in hopes of lifting her mood.

Close to midnight, she fell asleep and dreamt of an evening six months ago — the most romantic night of her entire life.

Flickers of light lazily floated around the darkened party room from a mirrored disco ball in the ceiling. She and Michael sat below in the middle of the dance floor at a table set for two and sipped champagne from tall, tulip-shaped glasses. He rented the entire room and meticulously planned a catered lobster dinner for two.

Michael silently stared at her from across the table with the flames from the burning candles mirrored in his ebony eyes. The glorious sight of him caused a blaze of hot desire to sizzle through her body. When the melody from "Love Story" started to play on the juke box in the corner he leaned in and without a word, fervently kissed her. Her heart vibrated in her chest with each beat knowing she'd reached a startling epiphany — no man had ever made her feel the way he did.

11

"Where are you off to so early?" Irene asked Michael when he came into the kitchen showered and shaved.

"I'm going to town to look at some land." He grabbed his truck keys off the rack next to the door.

"Why?" She studied him with her hands on her hips. "I hope you haven't gone ass over teakettle with that girl again?"

Michael put his arm around her. "If you're talking about Diana, no, I haven't. But if I do, you'll be the first to know." He pecked a quick kiss on her cheek and went out the door.

She followed him outside and yelled from the step, "You just be careful."

Michael drove past the Langtree Farm and saw Jake's truck parked by the barn. *Poor guy runs from farm to farm just to do chores in the morning. I guess he has to keep everyone happy. Hopefully, himself too!*

He shook his head thinking about his own situation. Friday night at the movies hadn't gone so well. He should've asked someone about the plot of the "Great Gatsby" before they went to the drive-in.

They had quietly left the theater and had driven a few miles when she broke the silence. "That wasn't the ending I expected, that's for sure."

"No. Me neither."

"I hope you're not thinking it was a reflection on us." Her eyes studied him from the passenger side as she waited for his answer.

"No. It was just a movie." *With a disturbing ending!*

"Michael, I hope you know I would never let you take the blame for something I did."

"But sometimes a person takes the blame regardless."

Moving closer, she took his hand. "The only thing I can tell you is: I'm sorry." She held onto his hand the rest of the way to Watson.

For some reason it felt awkward after he parked in the driveway and the lights went out on the dashboard. His anxiety level soared when he went around the truck and opened her door.

Diana's hand found his again in the darkness as they strolled up the walk to her mother's front door. Under the porch light they turned and nervously faced each other.

"Are you coming over tomorrow night?" she asked.

He took a deep breath. "I want to take things slow and see if we can get it right this time."

She eyed him curiously. "You certainly have changed."

"What do you mean?"

"Years ago, you always made sure to book our next date."

"Yeah, I guess we all change with time."

Her tongue subtly slid over her lips. "Can a girl get a kiss goodnight?"

He took her in his arms and kissed her welcoming lips. It was easy to tell how much she wanted him from the hungriness of her mouth. His eyes closed and he tried to match her intensity, but the kiss didn't have the fire he hoped it would. *Damn movie!*

He pulled his mouth away and smiled. "I'll give you a call real soon."

"Okay. I'll be waiting."

Their conversation and the kiss drifted in and out of his thoughts for an hour after he got into bed. And now he was doing it again. He parked his truck in front of Larsen's Realty and told himself to quit thinking about her. It was important to have a clear head today.

THE SKY WAS a bright yellow from the morning sun behind a wall of murky clouds when Jolene arrived at the Sorenson property. Tilting her head to the side, she noticed the foreclosure sign at the end of the driveway was crooked. She got out of her car and immediately felt the warm sun penetrate her long-sleeved, pink blouse. It was cooler this morning but she had no doubt the temperature would rise throughout the day. If the shirt protected her from getting sunburned, it was worth the discomfort of long sleeves. Besides, it wasn't half as uncomfortable as the bustier. The smell of the baby powder she used for the heat rash the thing gave her, had totally overpowered the fragrance of her Sweet Honesty perfume.

A prepared Realtor is a successful Realtor, she told herself and retrieved a hammer from her trunk. Realtor school had stressed the importance of arriving early at the property, ready to anticipate anything. She checked her wristwatch and released a confident breath knowing Mr. Edwards wasn't expected for at least another twenty minutes. The wobbly sign moved sideways instead of further into the ground when she hit the wooden post with the hammer. It was evident the soil was hard as a rock from the drought after she struck her target several times and didn't gain any ground. Still determined, she gripped the handle of the hammer with both hands and lifted it above her head and swung hard. The head of the hammer landed squarely on the post and the sudden stop caused a vibration to go through her arms like electricity. She instantly dropped the hammer in the grass and rubbed her arms before she bent to retrieve the tool. Hearing a noise, she straightened, then did a double-take seeing Michael's red truck pull up.

He parked off the road behind her car and coolly strolled over to where she stood by the sign. "Good morning."

She wiped the sweat off her forehead and narrowed her eyes at him. "What are you doing here?"

He smiled at her. "I'm here to see you."

Jolene carefully sized him up. "What? Why?" she smirked. "Did your girlfriend dump you already?"

He cringed like she threw cold water on him. "No. But what has that got to do with anything?"

"Look. Whatever it is, I don't have time right now. I'm expecting a client shortly."

"I know. I went down to Larsen's and they told me you were here."

She felt her mouth fall open. "You went down to my job and asked where I was?"

"Yes, I did."

She couldn't believe her ears. "What in God's creation made you think to do that?"

"I told them I needed to see you about this property."

She crossed her arms in front of her. "I wondered how long it would take before you would try and ruin things for me."

"Ruin things? What do you mean? I'm a potential client."

"Did you tell them we were once lovers, too?"

A sly smile formed on his face. "Did you want me to? Maybe while I'm at it, I could go to Vanders Law Office and give good ol' Will a few pointers."

She swung to slap his face but he caught her arm.

"Miss Garrison. I'm shocked to see such unprofessional behavior," he said pretending to be surprised. His eyes fell to her chest and he dropped her arm like it burned his hand. "What the hell did you do?"

She rolled her eyes and looked up at the sky. "It's no concern of yours, whatever I do."

"You're right. But I gotta know — where did they go?'

She sighed in frustration. "Fine. "If you're referring to my breasts ... I'm wearing a bustier."

His eyebrows pinched together. "What the hell would you want to do that for?"

"You being a man, you wouldn't understand."

"Well, give me a try," he crossed his arms, "I'm just dying to find out."

She shook her head. "You have no idea what it's like to be a woman competing in a man's world for a job."

"It seems to me if you want to influence men, you wouldn't be trying to hide them." He nodded toward her chest.

"I want men to take me seriously." Her face was inches from his. "Not look at me as a sex object."

He flashed a teasing smile. "Honey, I don't believe any red-blooded American man can look at you without thinking of sex."

"Why are you such a bastard?" she shouted, folding her arms across her chest.

Seeing a newer blue pick-up drive up and park behind their vehicles, she backed away from him. "You need to leave."

He shook his head no.

Her head shifted back and forth from the man getting out of the truck to Michael. "Don't say a word. Please. Just let me do the talking."

Michael nodded, and a casually dressed, middle aged man came toward them and stuck out his hand. "Miss Garrison, I presume."

"Yes. And you must be Mr. Edwards." She shook his hand with a smile.

"You can call me Larry," he said before his eyes went to Michael. "And you are?"

"Michael, my ... my assistant," Jolene jumped in.

Michael gave her an amused smile before he shook the man's hand.

She motioned with her hands at the sign and the farm in the background. "And this is the property listed in our brochure that you inquired about."

Michael put his hands on his hips and studied the man, while Larry scanned the farm yard in the distance.

"Don't you have some work to do at the office, Michael?" Jolene tilted her head at his truck.

"No, Miss Garrison. I'm all caught up. I'm here to assist you."

She blinked a few times then faked a smile. "Well then, shall we proceed? If you want to follow us in your truck, Larry, Michael and I will take my car up to the homestead."

He went to his truck and Michael and Jolene got into her Firebird. She started the engine then turned to him.

"What the hell do you think you're doing?" She stepped on the gas and drove down the long dirt driveway.

"Like I told you, I'm a potential client." He smiled.

"If that's really what you think you are, you shouldn't be here when I'm showing the property to another client."

"Why?" Michael asked. "Are you afraid I might outbid him?"

"No. This isn't an auction. You being here is a conflict of interest." Jolene parked next to the house and blurted, "Keep your mouth shut and just nod if he says anything to you at all."

"Yes, ma'am. I'll be your silent but devoted assistant."

She glared at him then got out of the car with a smile plastered on her face.

They walked around inside the house and surprisingly, Larry only asked a few questions. Michael kept a careful eye on him but didn't say anything. Outside, they walked through some of the outbuildings and then ended the showing in the barn. It was dark inside the large building, and more so coming inside from the bright sunlight. Before Jolene's eyes adjusted fully, she stepped toward the overhead light switches when her foot made contact with something on the cement floor. She stumbled sideways but a pair of strong hands prevented her from falling. When Michael flipped the light switches on, his face was like the cat that swallowed the canary, having saved her from injury. She looked down at her snagged nylon and shook her head. Larry had his back turned and seemed oblivious to what had happened. He slowly paced around the barn and made a few comments but didn't pose any questions.

Jolene was unsure what his uninterested, quiet behavior meant. *I hope I'm not losing him.*

"The structure of this building is in remarkable shape," she said. "I think it has something to do with the steel roof and siding. The barn was roofed and sided in 1965."

He spun around. "I'll take it for the listing price — seventy-five thousand."

Jolene blinked in astonishment and Michael looked stunned.

"That's wonderful!" She rushed to Larry and rapidly shook his hand. "We can go back to the office right now and draw up the papers."

"I'm paying with a cashier's check. The money has already been transferred to the bank in Watson," he told them.

Jolene felt like she was walking on air while the three made their way to their vehicles by the house. It couldn't have been any sweeter with Michael there to witness her clinch the deal. If he only knew her last sale had gone pretty much the same way. The first line from the song "I Am Woman" jubilantly resounded in Jolene's head.

"Didn't the whole thing seem weird to you?" Michael asked her when she drove down the driveway to his truck.

"What are you talking about?"

"Him just agreeing like that without any haggling or stipulations?"

"Oh, here we go." She glowered at him. "Why can't you give me any credit for a job well done?"

"Believe me when I say I don't want to hurt your feelings. But you hardly did a thing to make that sale."

Watching Larry drive out of the driveway toward Watson, she quickly told him, "I want you out of my car." When he didn't move, she yelled, "Now!"

"Okay, okay. I'm going." He opened the door and got out. "You believe what you want. The whole thing was just too damn easy!" He slammed her car door and she drove into a curtain of dust from Larry's truck.

Michael Cameron, you're nothing but a chauvinist pig!

LUCILLE WATCHED Michael's truck drive past the house when she peered out the kitchen window. "Where's he off to so early?' she asked Irene.

"He said something about looking at some land," the old housekeeper answered.

"Really? Did he mention why?"

"No. He didn't. But I told him if it had anything to do with that Iverson girl, he best slow things down." Irene opened the refrigerator door and took out a large bowl of strawberries.

Why are you trying to discourage him? "Do you realize Michael is twenty-seven years old and isn't getting any younger?"

"That's not old. I just don't want to see him get hurt again. His whole personality changed after the last time with her." Irene sat at the table with a paring knife.

"Yes, I agree. It wasn't good what happened. But in the past few months, he's starting to act like his old self again." Lucille shook her head. "He's not so … moody and quiet anymore."

"I agree. And that's why it worries me to hear him talking about buying some land."

"I think he and Diana were both too immature the first time around and now after all this time it may work out for them. Besides, we should be happy he didn't pick up with that redheaded floozy, Jolene. You saw her at the wedding coming on to him."

Irene tilted her head. "I didn't see her come on to him. If anything, it looked like it was him trying to come on to her."

"Well, men seem to know where they can get the milk for free."

Irene ceased moving her paring knife. "I don't know about that. But don't you find it strange how his attitude started to change right about the same time she came to live in the area?"

Oh God, no! "That's just a fluke. We all need to be happy for Michael now that his true love has returned. I think both he and Diana need our support."

Lucille was about to go into the living room when a fantastic idea hit her. "I should give Diana a call and personally welcome her back."

Irene shook her head.

"Or maybe … I'll drop by some afternoon." When Irene stopped cleaning berries and stared at her, Lucille asked, "What? You don't think I should?"

"I don't want to bring up bad memories, but remember what happened when you invited Jake's ex-fiancée for Christmas?"

Lucille frowned. "Yes, but that was different. Jake led me to believe something had rekindled between the two of them. Michael and I have talked about Diana and I know he's trying to give it another chance. But you're right. A visit might be too soon. It would be best if I just call and welcome her back home."

I need to do everything I can to encourage Diana. I don't need another son wasting his life on a wild Garrison girl!

BRETT SAT in the small waiting room at Joe's Gas station and waited for the mechanics to finish the brake job on his truck. He looked up from an article in Sports Illustrated when a woman came in the room. When she seated herself a few chairs away from him, his neck cranked in her direction. It was Karyn Pehrson, in the flesh. He didn't waste any time and moved to the chair next to her. Her brown eyes got big when she realized it was him.

"Well, hello there." His tone was smooth.

"Hi," she managed to get out.

"Have you been doing anymore dining and dashing lately?"

She pursed her lips. "No. Have you been beating up any high school boys lately?"

"Only in self-defense."

"That isn't what my brother said."

"There were plenty of witnesses. Ask any of them."

"Okay. My brother can sometimes open his mouth before he thinks, but it doesn't change the fact that you Camerons are corrupt."

"Corrupt? Now that's a harsh word. Corrupt in what way?"

"Your family and those crooks at the bank in Watson are all in cahoots."

"My family doesn't have anything to do with what goes on down at the bank other than our own personal business."

"Then why did your father convince people to invest more than they should in the refinery?"

"Our family invested with all the rest. No one knew the reimbursement would take this long."

"You can say whatever you want to say. It won't make a difference. Your family is wealthy and it didn't matter as much as it meant to other folks."

"Brett, your trucks done," a mechanic in coveralls announced from the doorway.

"I'll be right there," Brett answered and then turned back to Karyn. "My father has always been the first person to come over and help any farmer who is sick or needs assistance for some reason. Ask yourself one question: what would my family get out of it if we were involved in a conspiracy with the bank? We're not purchasing the land. At this point, we can't afford to —just like everyone else."

He watched for her reaction as he got to his feet. Knowing it was unlikely she would believe him, he fought the urge to look back at her as he left the room.

THE BELLS WERE RINGING at church on Sunday morning when Michael slipped in the back door and sat down in a pew. He smiled when he saw his brother and his family a couple of rows up. Gazing at Cheryl — there was no denying it — she was pregnant. It had only been a month and a half since the wedding, and his thoughts went to his mother across the aisle. She's always been obsessed with appearances. *She'll just have to make the best of it.*

The service started when Michael scanned the crowd and did a double-take seeing Will Vanders across the aisle jiggling a baby in his arms. Michael looked around at the adoring crowd for the mother of the child. He found Will's sister, Alice, and her family down further in the pew. Michael then recalled she had a baby last year around Christmas time.

An elderly woman in the pew in front of Michael leaned toward the woman sitting next to her and loudly whispered, "There's that nice Will Vanders. He's such an upstanding young man. A real good example for the younger generation."

"And good-looking, too," the other woman whispered back. "The list of things that man is trying to do for the community is astounding. I wish my daughter would meet someone like him."

Michael released a disgusted breath. *Oh, dear Lord!*

The sermon was long and boring and Michael's thoughts drifted to the sale of the Sorenson Farm. Since the sale, he had spent hours thinking about the times his father had bought and sold farm equipment or land. He couldn't think of one transaction without some sort of a negotiation. Maybe this Edwards guy wasn't a good businessman, but if that were true, he wouldn't have that kind of cash for the Sorenson place. Michael noticed his shoes were worn somewhat and he didn't have the savoir faire of most wealthy folks.

Michael chuckled to himself about Jolene and her bustier. That thing had to be uncomfortable, especially in the heat. Good thing both places where she worked had air conditioning. By the time the sermon drew to the end, he thought it wasn't such a bad idea for her to wear the bustier and babble on about women's liberation. It could be a good way to ward off creepy guys like Will Vanders.

"Michael! Michael!"

Michael stopped next to his truck in the parking lot. Someone behind him was calling his name. *Aw, shit. Will!*

Will jogged to him. "Hey, buddy," he said and rapidly shook his hand. "I heard the good news."

Michael stared at him, confused.

"About you and Diana getting back together?"

"Oh yeah. Thanks."

"I always thought she was the one for you. Thank God, you two got back together. You were always so crazy about her."

Michael shrugged. "What can I say?"

"Remember the time in high school when we all went down to the ball field and Moose Swenson tried to hustle her. I couldn't believe how fast you took care of him with a right and then a left hook. He went down like a tower."

"Yeah, he certainly did. He later claimed it was all a misunderstanding."

Charlie Vanders beeped the horn on his Lincoln Continental and beckoned with his hand for Will to come. "I have to go, but congratulations."

Michael left the parking lot thinking about the reason behind Will's unexpected burst of happiness for him. Why did he find it hard to believe his old friend was genuinely happy for him? It almost seemed like he was relieved to hear they'd reunited. He never seemed that excited years ago about him and Diana. Was it possible Will found out about him and Jolene and now thought there was nothing standing in his way to her? It wasn't likely. Only a few people were aware of their relationship, and Jolene wouldn't have told anyone — especially her boss. There were days before Diana came back that Michael had wished it would've come out about him and Jolene. Maybe then she would've wanted to get back together to save her reputation.

Closer to home, Michael concluded he was acting like a teenager — coming up with silly scenarios and jumping to conclusions. If he was to make it work with Diana, he needed to forget about Jolene. There it was. The simple solution to his problems, yet he knew it was going to be one of the hardest things he'd ever done.

12

Done with updating a large stack of files at the law office, Jolene flopped back in her desk chair and closed her eyes. Barb had left for a dentist appointment and Will had been in his office all afternoon. When a set of warm hands started to knead her shoulders, her eyes popped open and she flung herself forward in her chair.

"You *are* tense, aren't you?" Will left his hands on the back of her chair. He had a flirty smile. "I'm sorry if I scared you."

"I didn't hear you come out of your office."

"I thought I'd take a break and see what you're up to."

"I finally finished updating all of these files."

"Well, I just got off the phone with Donnie. He's very pleased how quickly you made the Sorenson sale. He sure is proud of you."

Jolene smiled. "That's so great to hear." She let a moment pass. "He sure does things differently than how we were taught in school. But apparently it works for him."

"What do you mean?" he asked.

"He lists the property lower than I would ever think to. But he's definitely on top of what's going on in the business."

"Why do you say that?"

"Well … for instance, the new insurance release form. Donnie said most realties have their agents sign one after each sale. I guess it's something that protects their agency from injury lawsuits during the viewing of any property. It must be something new, or I would've heard about it at school."

"You don't keep a realty business going for over twenty years without staying up on the new rules," he said stepping away from her. "I need a cup of coffee. Would you like a cup?"

"Sure, but aren't I supposed to be asking you that question?" She laughed.

"It's my pleasure," he said and went over to the coffee pot. He brought two cups back with him and sat down in a chair in front of her desk. "There was one thing about the Sorenson deal that concerns me."

"What's that?"

"I just happened to be in the bank when Larry Edwards came in for his cashier's check and I congratulated him on the purchase of his new farm. But when I asked him how things went with the sale, he said you and your assistant, Michael, did a fine job." Will watched her closely.

Jolene felt her heartbeat in her throat. "I can explain," she blurted. "Michael Cameron decided he was interested in buying some land. He thought seeing I was his sister-in-law's sister, he could just drop by without an appointment. I couldn't get rid of the guy." She rolled her eyes. "When Mr. Edwards showed up, I didn't want him to think I was being unprofessional, so I told him he was my assistant. But in the end," she smiled sweetly, "his presence didn't have any effect on the sale."

"You are aware it's a conflict of interest to show two clients a property at the same time? It takes away your bargaining power."

"Yes, I am quite aware. I told my sister what happened and she assured me Jake would talk to Michael about it."

"I've known Michael since we were children. He can get a little pushy sometimes, but don't be too hard on him. I suppose he's all excited about purchasing some land to build a house. Did you know he and his old girlfriend, Diana, are back together?"

"No. I didn't," she lied. "That's nice."

He stared at a bookshelf. "Back in high school those two were inseparable. He was *so* crazy about her."

"So you say." She took a sip of her coffee.

His expression was serious when he set his cup down on her desk. "In order to keep things professional from now on, I would appreciate it if you did the rest of your showings solo."

"Believe me. It won't happen again." Her smile was wide. *I'm going to rip him a new one when I see him!*

I⊤ WAS another early Friday evening and Michael was enjoying a cold beer with Jim on his patio. Lyla and the baby were gone once again with her mother at a Tupperware Party.

"So, where are you and the love of your life off to tonight?"

"I guess her mother wants us to have dinner at her place with Diana's brother and sister and their spouses."

"Ah, that sounds serious." Jim raised his brows.

"It is what it is — dinner."

"You can go right ahead and think that, but I'll tell you what it is."

Michael gave him an annoyed look.

"When a woman has you over to meet the family, or reconnect in your case, it means you are, without a doubt, in a committed relationship."

"Where do you get these rules from?"

"I've been around, my friend."

Wanting to change the subject, Michael asked, "Have you heard anything about this Larry Edwards yet?"

"Nope," Jim answered. "Do you have any more information about him?"

"No, but I did meet him." He told Jim how effortlessly Jolene had sold the Sorenson's property to him.

"The guy had seventy-five thousand dollars in a cashier's check?" Jim seemed blown away. "He's got to be one rich son-of-a-bitch."

"Yeah. But he just didn't put me in mind of a well-to-do guy. I've never seen anyone wealthy agree so easily to a deal that size without haggling first."

"Yeah, that is odd," Jim agreed, then smiled. "Maybe he just liked the Realtor."

Michael gave him a dirty look before he swigged back his beer.

Around six-thirty, Michael pulled into Diana's mother's driveway in Watson. Everything was so different from years ago when they dated. Diana's family had lived on a farm a short distance from the Sugar King. Her father had passed away the year before high school and since then her family slowly spiraled into financial disaster and lost the farm. The Sugar King Farm had purchased the farm four years ago and had bulldozed the neglected buildings down after her mother moved into town.

Michael got out of his truck and walked past a blue Toyota and a Ford station wagon parked closer to the house. He assumed the station wagon belonged to her rigid older sister, Lenae. She still lived in the area with her husband and four or five children. The car likely belonged to Gary — her air-headed older brother.

He knocked on the door and was immediately greeted by Diana wearing a fire engine red jump suit. Her hair was pulled up on her head and she wore large, gold hoop earrings. It was evident she lived on the East Coast by the clothes she wore. Michael handed her the bouquet of roses and the bottle of wine his mother had insisted he take for dinner.

"Thank you," she said and placed a quick kiss on his lips. "Come on in."

Michael heard the sounds of children yelling and running

around as he stepped inside the house. The place was clean but a bit on the small side. He decided it was big enough for one woman and her worthless son who lived in the basement. He sat down on the couch where Gary and a woman Michael presumed was his significant other were snuggled together at the other end. Gary's hair was longer with wide side burns that looked ridiculous on his skinny face.

The woman turned her head at Michael and then said to Gary, "That's him? Wow! He's a stone cold fox."

Michael pretended he didn't hear her comment.

"Hey, Michael," Gary said. "Who thought we'd ever see you gathered with our family again?"

"Yeah," Michael answered. "Who knew?"

A large woman came out of the kitchen and made a bee-line to the couch. "It's nice to see you again, Michael." He was shocked to see it was Lenae. She had doubled in size and looked years older than she actually was.

"Yes, it's nice to see you, too." Michael conjured a smile.

"There he is," Marie Iverson, Diana's mother yelled as she shot through the room in Michael's direction.

When he sprang to his feet, she wrapped her arms around him and squeezed tighter than he expected. "Oh, how I've missed you."

Not knowing how to respond, Michael groaned out, "I ... I've missed you too!"

A boy and a girl around eight years old came skipping into the room and halted in front of Michael.

"Are you going to be our new uncle?" the girl asked.

"Why don't you kids find a place to sit at the table?" Diana interrupted. She looked at Michael and silently mouthed. "Sorry."

Michael folded his hands at the table and then noticed he was the only one. When someone passed a platter of pork chops to him he dropped his hands and put a piece of meat on his plate. He quietly ate, smiling at Diana at his side and occasionally to the row of children watching his every move across the table.

"Is your old man still farming?" Gary asked.

"Yes," Michael answered.

"So when are you boys taking over?" Gary continued his questioning.

Diana shook her head at him, but he didn't seem to take the hint to shut up.

"I really haven't got any idea," Michael replied, wondering where Gary's questioning was leading.

"Your older brother must be ... what," he threw his hands open, "thirty?"

"He's twenty-eight. What's that got to do with anything?"

"I heard you and your family are in a partnership now."

Michael looked at Diana who gave him a sheepish grin. "What's my brother's age got to do with my family's partnership?"

"I was wondering how many more years you boys are going to stay under the protection of your daddy's wing before you start farming like real men?"

Michael felt his face get hot. "That's some good advice coming from a man who lost the family far ..." He stopped when he felt Diana tightly squeeze his thigh.

Gary didn't say anymore but his loathing eyes stayed on Michael while they finished eating.

"Would anyone like dessert?" Marie asked. Diana got up and helped her mother serve the pineapple upside down cake to the group.

"Let's eat this and go for a drive," she whispered in Michael's ear after returning to her chair.

Michael smiled recalling how much they used to drive around after he got his driver's license. Most of the time they'd end up on Ridge Rock Hill or down at the river where they would make out or skinny dip. Sometimes they did both, which resulted in them losing their virginity to each other. Suddenly, he felt incredibly nervous thinking maybe it was sex she had in mind. They had kissed a few times since she'd returned but that had been the extent. It was strange to feel this way about her after making love to her countless times. She was a beautiful woman and having been married for eight years was probably more experienced in that department than she'd been back then. What was he afraid of?

"Where do you want to go?" Michael asked when he started his truck.

"I thought we could just drive around and talk like we used to."

We did a lot more than talk. "Okay. I guess we can head back toward my house."

Her face lit up. "I would love to see your parents again."

Oh, God no. I'm not ready for that. "Mom and Dad went out to a dinner party tonight," he lied. "I doubt they'll be home for hours."

"Then why don't we just go to your house and watch television if no one's there?"

"Brett's there."

She winced. "On a Friday night?"

"That guy isn't the social butterfly everyone thinks he is. Let's just drive around and talk like you wanted."

The sun was sinking behind the horizon when she moved across the seat and slipped in close to him. She looked up at him with her blue eyes and laid her head on his shoulder.

The song "Baby Blue" crept into his head. He'd often thought of her whenever it played on the radio.

"Michael, we don't have to go through all these silly preliminaries," she interrupted his thoughts. "We're two adults who were lovers for years. It's stupid to pretend."

She stroked a hand across his thigh and then slowly slid it further to his crotch.

He flinched at her unexpected bold move. She rubbed him

there for a moment until his fears, along with his will power started to rapidly disintegrate.

A large circle of dust rose in the air when he made a U-turn and headed up to Ridge Rock Hill.

"You have no idea how many times I've thought about making love to you," she told him in a low seductive voice.

"I thought about it a lot too," he answered. It seemed his truck and his eagerness were both rising as they went up the hill. They parked on the highest point of the entire area with his truck facing Jake and Cheryl's house below.

He pulled her into his arms and their lips met in a demanding hot kiss. Her fingers dived into the hair on his chest and his hand went to the nape of her neck causing their kisses to deepen very quickly. When she moved off him to unzip her pant suit and pull it down to her waist, his eyes focused on her lacy black bra. He reached around and unhooked it and she slid toward the passenger's door allowing him to move to the middle of the seat. Driven by lustful urgency, he let her lips capture his as she straddled him in the seat. *She wasn't like this years ago!*

He removed her bra and seized her small breasts, rubbing them thoroughly in his hands. A few moments later, she pulled her mouth away and sat back in the seat. She yanked her jump suit and her black lacy panties down her legs and off each foot. He unbuckled his belt and pulled down his jeans and underwear then took a condom from his wallet.

She immediately stopped him. "Do we really need that?"

He stared at her. "Are you on the pill or using a diaphragm?"

Her hand went to his arousal. "No, but there isn't a need for a condom."

You can't be serious! He caught her hand. "Look, Diana. I'm willing to give us another chance, but I'm not ready to be a father."

"What do you mean? We're twenty-seven years old. Do you realize both of our mothers had at least two children at our age?"

He swiftly pulled up his pants and slid away to the driver's door reeling in anger. *How dare she try to rope me in like this?* Without a word, he got out of the truck and hurriedly tucked his shirt in his jeans then zipped them. He leaned against the fender and took a few deep breaths before he got back into the truck and slammed the door.

"Let's call it a night," he said and didn't look at her.

Only a few words were exchanged between them while they drove to Watson. They parked in her mother's driveway and he walked her to the door. He was about to turn and leave when he saw the tears shine on her face from the porch light.

"Michael. I shouldn't have rushed you. I'm so sorry. What else can I say? There's no one else I want to start a family with but you. You have to understand — I love you."

THE YELLOW ICE ring that floated in the punch bowl hadn't exactly come out in one piece, but Jolene figured if it kept the punch cold, it served its purpose. She told herself it didn't matter because everything else for the baby shower had turned out great. The cake she had picked up from the bakery in the shape of a baby bottle was cute and the pastel decorations in pink and blue taped throughout Cheryl's living room were perfect.

Dori and Jolene stood in the kitchen and greeted the guests as they arrived, while Nell Thompson, Cheryl's neighbor, poured and served punch in the living room.

It was going to be a great day, Jolene thought when she took a deep breath without the restriction of a bustier. She piled her hair up on her head and wore a cream colored sundress dotted with a tiny purple floral print and her brown platform sandals. Dori was dressed in a white sleeveless blouse and a green print skirt. Between the flow of arriving guests, she looked down at her legs and groaned.

"Do you have any nail polish? I've got a run in my pantyhose."

"I don't, but I know where Cheryl keeps hers." Jolene opened a cupboard drawer and found a bottle of clear nail polish. "Here you go." She handed it to Dori.

"Thanks." Dori went to the window by the sink for better light. She pulled back her skirt and dabbed the hole in her nylon. "There, that should do it." She dropped her skirt and her head spun to the window. "Oh, my God!" Her big eyes went to Jolene. "You didn't seriously invite her?"

"Who are you talking about?" Jolene joined her by the sink and looked outside astonished. There in the middle of the yard stood the pretty woman from the yearbook.

Lucille opened the back door of her car and handed the attractive blonde a gift. She reached inside and retrieved another before she slammed her car door. The younger woman's head turned like she was looking the place over as the two walked to the house.

"I don't believe it." Dori's eyes were huge. "Lucille Cameron brought Diana Iverson."

Diana was dressed in a sleeveless, light blue sheath dress with a wide white collar framing the V-neck cut in the front. Jolene swallowed hard when she watched them come up the sidewalk. It had to be serious between her and Michael if his mother invited her to the baby shower.

"Hello and welcome," Dori told them as they came inside.

"Thank you," Lucille answered and turned to Diana. "This is Michael's girlfriend, Diana."

Diana smiled at Lucille and then at Dori and Jolene.

"Yes, I remember Diana from high school," Dori replied. "Do you remember me? Dori Olson? It's Dori Kensing now."

"Yes, I do. How are *you*?"

"I'm Cheryl's best friend," Dori said and turned. "This is Jolene, her sister."

The smile left Diana's face. "Jolene ... Michael's friend, Jolene?"

Oh, God. Did he tell her about us? "Yes," I know Michael," Jolene said with a smile and desperately hoped she hadn't blushed.

Lucille pursed her lips. "Of course they're friends, now that her sister is part of our family."

Nell came into the room for more punch. "Hello, Lucille. It's so nice you could join us today."

Jolene recognized a tinge of hostility in her voice.

Lucille put her arm around Diana. "You remember Michael's girlfriend, Diana. She's Marie Iverson's daughter."

"Yes, didn't you leave here right after high school and marry a doctor overseas?" Nell rattled out in her Norwegian accent.

"Yes, I left and got married, but that's over now and I'm back," Diana answered calmly.

"What happened?" Nell didn't let up. "Did he leave you?"

That's funny! Jolene looked at the smirk on Dori's face and fought the urge to laugh.

"We're about to start. So if you ladies would please go into the living room," Dori piped up.

When the group of ladies entered the room, Jolene saw Cheryl do a double-take at Diana, before her puzzled eyes came to her. Jolene shrugged with open arms.

To Jolene's surprise, Diana unexpectedly hugged Cheryl when Lucille introduced them. The gesture grated on Jolene's emotions and sent sparks of jealousy reeling through her. She pictured Michael and Diana having fun at a barbecue here at the house with Jake and Cheryl. The thought disappeared knowing her sister and Michael weren't exactly friends. But would that change after he and Diana got married?

Jolene watched Michael's old love from across the room and concluded she was even prettier in real life. Diana's slim figure and large blue eyes reminded her of Twiggy, the English model. *I wonder if either of them eat?*

Jolene stood next to the refrigerator and graciously assisted a few of the older women as they dished a plate. It was protocol for the hostesses to make sure all of the guests had gone through the luncheon buffet line during a shower before they ate. Some of the women had brought children and one little girl stalled the line with her indecisiveness. She whined and cried about the chicken salad sandwiches and some of the salads.

Her mother tried to hush her comments. "Shh! You don't have to eat any."

Jolene leaned up against the fridge and crossed her arms trying to ignore the girl's temper tantrum. Diana, who was standing in line, broke away from Lucille and put her arm around the child.

"Then how about some of this fruit salad with whipped cream?" She asked the girl. The child nodded and Diana put some on her plate. "Would you like one of these buns with peanut butter on it instead of chicken salad?" The girl smiled and nodded as Diana took a bun out of a bag at the end of the counter. Dori handed her a jar of peanut butter and a knife and within a few seconds the girl was ready to sit down and eat.

"You are so wonderful with children. Do you have any of your own?" the child's mother asked.

"No, I don't. But I'm planning on having a houseful in the future," Diana smiled.

Jolene imagined how beautiful Diana and Michael's children would be and her appetite suddenly left her.

"There's no doubt you'll be a perfect mother," Lucille said when Diana rejoined her.

The line progressed and Jolene noticed Diana didn't have more than a bird's portion of food on her plate when she went back into the living room. *Aha! I knew it.*

Jolene stood by Dori and Cheryl on the porch and graciously thanked everyone for coming when the shower ended. Nell was the last guest to go and Jolene was relieved to see her waddle to her car and drive away. The woman was good-hearted, but she never stopped interrogating people about their personal lives.

"It looks like all the clean-up is done," Cheryl stated after they went inside. "Jake and Taylor aren't going to be back for a while. Let's go have a drink on the screened-in porch. I can feel that south breeze right now."

"Sounds good to me. My children are at home with my niece," Dori said and followed the sisters to the porch.

Cheryl propped her swollen feet on the wicker coffee table and collapsed in the matching wide back chair.

While the three sipped their lemonade, Jolene smoked a cigarette and talked about all the nice gifts Cheryl had received for the baby.

"It sure was an exciting and eventful day," Dori commented. "When I saw Diana Iverson get out of Lucille's car, I couldn't believe it."

"To clarify — neither of you invited her?" Jolene asked seriously.

"I sure didn't," Dori rifled out. "You didn't, did you, Cheryl?"

"Of course not. I'm sure the credit lies with my meddling mother-in-law."

"Why would she invite her?" Jolene asked. "She's only been back a few weeks. Michael and her can't be that serious already?"

Cheryl smiled. "Don't you two remember Lucille invited Jake's ex, Susan, to Christmas dinner without his knowledge last year?"

"Yeah, that's right. Is that what you think happened today?" Jolene was careful to keep the optimism out of her voice.

"Who knows? But it wouldn't shock me to learn their relationship has escalated to the way things were," Dori said. "If I had to pick a couple from high school most likely to get married, for sure it would've been Michael and Diana. I never heard of him asking another girl out all the way through high school.

And some of the girls hit on him like you wouldn't believe. I remember Beth Akerman relentlessly chased him for months and it got real bad." Dori tapped her finger to her lips. "Let me think ... who her boyfriend was at the time." Her eyes slowly got big and her hand covered her mouth. "Oh, never mind."

"Who was it?" Cheryl demanded. "Tell me it wasn't Jake."

"No, it wasn't, Jake. I really don't want to get into it."

"Oh come on, Dori," Jolene coaxed. "You gotta tell us now."

"I think it's best for everyone involved if we just talk about something else."

"Was it Jim Stanton?" Cheryl asked.

"No. It wasn't Jim," Dori replied with a dirty look. "Don't ask me anymore."

"Think, Cheryl," Jolene told her sister. "Who else do you know who graduated with them?"

Cheryl's head rotated from Jolene to Dori. "Jake mentioned he graduated with Michael when he introduced me to him. Is it Will Vanders?"

Dori took a swallow of her lemonade but didn't answer.

"It's him," Jolene declared. "I can tell by the way she's acting."

"Now you better fill us in on the rest of the story," Cheryl told her friend.

"Okay," Dori answered. "But I don't want it to get out I'm spreading rumors about your boss." She shook her finger at Jolene. "If you breathe one word to Will I told you, I will never forgive you."

Jolene smiled and held her little finger up to Dori. "I pinky swear."

"That's okay. I'll take your word." Dori took a deep breath and let it out. "It was during our junior year and Michael and Diana had been an item for a couple of years. I guess Beth decided she was going to be with Michael and asked him out a few times. I heard he was nice and politely turned her down; explaining he was with Diana. But Beth Akerman was an attractive, spoiled, rich girl who was used to getting her way. We all knew she started dating Will because he and Michael were close friends. Will fell head over heels for her while Beth had it bad for Michael. She was constantly flirting with him but everyone said Michael ignored her attempts." Dori paused to take a swallow of her drink.

"After a while, Will got the idea it was Michael who was after Beth and confronted him. Michael denied it and Will didn't believe him. They argued but decided to set Beth up to prove Michael's story one way or another. Will invited them both to come to his house after school to hang out and have some beers because his parents were out of town. Michael got there first as planned and told Beth when she arrived that Will had been called away but he'd be back shortly. I guess the plan was, if she acted appropriately, Will would quietly slip out the hall closet where he was hiding and go out the back door and then reenter using the front door. But I guess it didn't take too long for Will to witness for himself. Beth was all over Michael even after he refused her advances several times. I think the whole thing ruined Michael and Will's friendship because they didn't hang out as much afterwards."

It took a few moments for Dori's story to sink in before anyone said anything.

"How did you find out all those details?" Jolene asked.

"Someone overheard Michael tell Jim Stanton about it one night at a party when he had a little too much to drink. They said Michael felt bad about the whole thing."

It explained why Will and Michael always acted respectable but distant toward one another. *How sad for both Will and Michael.*

13

The door opened on the big shed and Michael looked up to see Jake come inside. Michael checked his wrist-watch and noticed he was right on time as always.

"Morning," Michael yelled to him and continued to pull on his coveralls for chores.

Jake came toward him with an amused smile. "How are you doing this morning?"

Michael eyed him curiously. "Fine. Why?"

"I heard things are getting serious with you and Diana."

"Who told you that?" Michael demanded.

"Mom brought her to Cheryl's baby shower yesterday."

"Are you kidding me?" Michael's voice echoed in the tall ceiling of the shed.

"No. Cheryl said Dori and Jolene hadn't invited her so Mom must have took it upon herself to bring her."

Oh crap! I wonder what Jolene thinks now? What difference does it make? "Neither Diana or Mom said a word about it to me."

"Well, I can guarantee you, everyone in the neighborhood thinks there's a wedding coming now."

Michael swiftly unzipped his coveralls and Jake stopped him.

"Before you go in there and chew Mother out, you better sort out how you feel about the situation," Jake advised.

Michael slumped down in a chair. "Jake, you wouldn't believe it. Diana said she loves me and wants us to start a family together."

Jake's mouth fell open. "You're not serious?" It took a few seconds for Jake to digest the news. "Isn't she missing a few steps? Like dating for a while to see how you feel about each other? Or maybe getting married before having children? Believe me. Those are some huge steps that need to be taken first."

"I don't know how I feel about her," Michael admitted. "Maybe it's only out of habit, but part of me thinks I still love her, but I'm so confused. I don't want to tell her to get out of my life and regret it later."

"Tell her you need some more time. If she loves you like she claims — she'll wait for you."

The door opened and Chet and Brett burst into the room. "What's all this sitting around? This isn't a ladies aid meeting," Chet barked out. "We got chores to do."

Jake's right. He would take her to someplace quiet and nicely explain how they needed to slow things down. Michael got to his feet and zipped up before he went out the door. *Maybe time will give my heart a chance to catch up to hers.*

MONDAY DRAGGED ON FOREVER. Jolene reminded herself they were always long and this one was more so because she was exhausted. Throwing a baby shower the day before had turned out to be a lot of work.

She was ready to leave the law office when Will's blue convertible pulled up in front of the building. It had been interesting to learn about what had happened between him and Michael in high school. She felt sorry for Will, knowing he got his heart broken, and for Michael, for losing a friend. His and Diana's relationship had endured more than one might think.

"Are you all done for the day?" Will asked after he came in the door.

"Yes," she answered and took her purse out of her bottom desk drawer.

"I know you said you wanted to keep things on a professional level, but do you want to get supper tonight with me — as friends?" he asked. "It's better than eating alone."

Maybe it was because she knew what happened with Beth, Jolene thought about his offer. Why couldn't friends have dinner together? "Sure. Where do you want to go?"

His joyful expression was priceless. "How about Rosy's Supper Club?"

"That's pretty fancy for a Monday," she furrowed her brows. *I don't need to spend a big chunk of my pay check on dinner.*

"I asked you. It will be my treat."

It was like he read her mind.

He followed her to her apartment in Montevideo and waited in the car while she went inside to change her clothes. She wasn't about to sit through an entire dinner wearing the bustier. Will's eyes slowly brushed over her when she returned wearing a green and white print Diane Von Fürstenberg wrap dress. The garment hugged every curve and had been in her closet since before her divorce. She didn't want it to go out of style before she had a chance to wear it again.

They pulled into a liquor store and Jolene thought the evening was starting to look more like a date than two friends simply having dinner together.

"I can't have a steak without a glass of wine," he explained and went inside. She waited in the car wishing she hadn't worn such a nice dress.

Rosy's wasn't very busy and they were seated at a table in the back seconds after their arrival. The waitress took the bottle of Cabernet Sauvignon Will had purchased and returned with it uncorked. She poured them each a glass and left them to review the menu.

"This is nice," Will stated, and raised his glass. "Here's to good friends."

Jolene smiled and tapped her glass to his. She was about to take a sip but stopped with the glass close to her lips. *Oh God, no!*

Michael and Diana were being seated by the hostess at a table in the corner of the room. Michael had on black dress slacks with a light gray shirt and Diana was stunning in a deep blue dress that flared from the waist to the hem. They looked like a model couple in Vogue magazine.

"Is that Michael and Diana?" Will asked.

"Yes. It is."

"Maybe we should ask them to join us?" Will suggested then waited for her answer.

"I … I don't think that's a good idea. It looks like they're on a romantic date or something."

"Nonsense. The three of us hung out all the time in high school. It would be a shame not to dine together." He got up and headed for their table.

Dear God, please let them decline!

Will shook Michael's hand and nodded politely to Diana then pointed to Jolene sitting at the table. Jolene did her best to fake a smile and even managed to give them a little wave. She was relieved when Will returned to the table alone.

Thank you, God!

"They're coming right over." He smiled and took his seat.

Oh no! Jolene's heart fell at the thought of seeing them interact as a couple.

Michael pulled out a chair next to Will for Diana and she sat down.

"Well, isn't this a nice surprise?" Michael said, before taking the chair by Jolene. "Jolene, this is Diana …"

"We've already met," Jolene interrupted. "Yesterday at Cheryl's baby shower."

Michael turned his head at Diana and their eyes collided, but neither said anything.

I wonder what that's about!

"Yes. It's so nice to see you again," Diana finally answered.

"This is great the four of us can have dinner together," Will cut in.

"Yes, it sure is," Jolene said. "I hope you had fun yesterday, Diana."

"Yes, I did. Thank you."

"I think everyone enjoyed themselves." Jolene smiled and took a sip of her wine.

Michael gave Jolene an uneasy look from the corner of his eye.

What? Are you afraid I told her about us? How ironic the shoe is on the other foot!

The waitress came to the table with some menus and set another bottle of wine on the table. Apparently, Michael and Diana had also thought to bring wine.

"I'm so happy to see you two back together." Will's eyes shifted back and forth from Diana to Michael. "I always thought you were the perfect couple."

Diana smiled adoringly at Michael and put her hand over his. He returned her gesture with a pleased, but somewhat weary smile.

Everyone had ordered when Will started a conversation about the lack of rain in the area.

"I can't believe how dry things are getting around here."

"Yeah, it's definitely starting to look like this year will go down on record as a drought." Michael shook his head.

"I bet your Dad has the irrigation pumping night and day out of the river."

"Yeah. It's a full time job keeping an eye on it."

Jolene watched and listened to Michael and Will speak casually to one another. It was like nothing had happened between them. Apparently, they had let go of the past.

Dinner was served and they talked about Cheryl, Jake and the new baby.

"I'm so happy for Cheryl and Jake," Diana stated to the group. Her attention then went to Michael. "And your parents have to be ecstatic about their first grandchild."

"It's the second grandchild. Jake has a stepson, Taylor," Michael corrected her and then added, "Jolene's nephew."

Jolene smiled at his comment, but then addressed Diana. "Didn't Lucille talk about how she felt about the baby yesterday?"

Diana shrugged. "I expected she would've gone on nonstop about being a grandma, but she didn't say much about it. I remember when my sister had her first baby, my mother was on cloud nine for months. I guess everyone shows emotion differently."

Michael and Jolene's eyes instantly met. *We both know how your mother feels about my sister.*

"I'm sure everyone in both families is very excited about the baby," Michael said, then promptly changed the subject. "So how are sales going in the real estate business?" he asked Jolene.

"You witnessed it for yourself. Just great," Jolene said feeling her confidence soar.

Diana's brows crinkled slightly. It seemed she and Will were both listening closely.

Michael stayed on the subject. "I've got to hand it to you, Will. You and Donnie picked a great Realtor to represent the bank with the foreclosures. I was so impressed to see her sell the Sorenson place so quickly. Although, I do have to apologize for dropping by without an appointment. I just got excited with the prospect of purchasing some land."

"You're thinking about buying some land?" Excitement sparked in Diana's voice.

"There's a lot of it for sale in the neighborhood, that's for sure," Michael took a bite of his steak.

The smile lingered on Diana's face after she looked away and sipped her wine.

Will ran his hand through his hair. "Donnie and I are very impressed with Jolene and her amazing marketing strategies."

Jolene silently stared at her boss. *Amazing marketing strategies?*

"She's doing a phenomenal job," Will proudly added with an adoring smile.

MICHAEL AND DIANA walked out of Rosy's with Jolene and Will into the parking lot.

"I love your car, Will," Diana commented seeing his convertible. "I wondered whose it was when we drove in. It's fabulous."

"Thank you. It's a reward to myself for graduating law school and passing the bar exam." Will beamed as he opened the door for Jolene.

Are you sure Mommy and Daddy didn't buy it? "Business must be booming down at the law office," Michael blurted.

"Yes, it is," Will answered. "It was nice seeing you two. We'll have to have dinner together again sometime. Only next time — we'll plan it." He laughed and started the engine.

"Sounds great," Michael told him and opened the passenger door for Diana. "You folks have a nice evening."

"Good bye, Jolene. It was nice to see you again," Diana said and got into Michael's truck. He discreetly nodded to Jolene then went around his truck to the driver's door.

"Are they dating, or just business associates?" Diana abruptly asked as they followed Will's car out of the parking lot.

Michael glanced at her. "Far as I know, they're dating."

"Wasn't it strange how they never touched each other the entire dinner?"

You're absolutely right! He felt his mood suddenly lift but he knew to keep his emotions in check. "I guess some couples aren't that touchy-feely in public."

Her eyes stayed on him. "Did you ever date her?"

"I took her out once," he replied smoothly. "Why do you ask?"

She sucked in a breath and let it out. "Well, the reason I'm asking is that first night when I called you … you asked if I were Jolene."

Please don't go there. "Did I?" he asked, pretending to be surprised. "Oh, maybe I did. I told her to keep an eye out for any land she thought I'd be interested in."

"Oh." She sounded confused. "So you were interested in purchasing land before we got back together?"

"Being in a family corporation, we're always keeping an eye out for any available land."

She seemed to be satisfied with his answer because she removed her purse from the middle of the seat and slid in closer to him.

He looked over at her. "Seeing as how we're asking questions: How come you never mentioned anything about going to Cheryl's baby shower?"

"I figured you would've asked me about it earlier tonight when you picked me up."

He looked ahead at the road. "I guess I didn't want to start the evening off on a bad note."

"So you're upset that I went with your mother to the shower?" She stared at him.

"No. But why didn't you say anything about it?"

"I didn't mean to keep it a secret. If you remember, our date didn't end so well the other evening. You were angry and said we should call it a night. I didn't want to push you any further."

"I'm sorry, but you sprang the kid thing on me from out of the blue."

"I know, and I'm sorry, too." She took his hand in both of

hers. "We've got plenty of time to worry about that in the future."

Thank God, she's starting to come to her senses! Michael flipped his turn signal light on in Watson and she checked her wristwatch.

"It's only seven o'clock. We don't have to go straight home, do we?"

"If you don't mind, I'm ready to call it a night," he replied and turned off the highway.

"You're not angry with me again, are you?"

"No, of course not. I'm bushed. Dad had us moving irrigation all day."

She nodded.

When they pulled into the driveway, he parked and reached for the door handle.

"Wait!" She stopped him. "Before we say good night, I want you to know I meant what I said the other night." Her eyes searched his. "I do love you."

He knew she was waiting for him to say it back but the words wouldn't come out of his mouth. After an awkward moment, he said, "I'll give you a call tomorrow."

Michael drove home feeling guilty that he couldn't tell her what she wanted to hear. It had been eight years since he said those words to her, and back then he'd meant them wholeheartedly. She had been a major part of his world and now he didn't really know who she was. Would they ever be able to rekindle what they had? He would never know if he didn't try.

The entire evening had been so crazy. Who would've ever thought they'd meet up with Will and Jolene and have dinner with them? It had been hard keeping his concentration tonight with Jolene looking so hot in her green dress.

Dining with his ex-lover and her new — whatever he was — wasn't anything he wanted to do, especially with Diana, but if he was going to figure out what was going on he needed to spend as much time as possible with both of them.

Seeing Will brush his hair back when he complimented Jolene on her work only confirmed he was lying once again. Only this time, Michael had more to go on than just the hair thing. He'd been there to witness the Sorenson property sale and couldn't recall Jolene using anything remotely close to an amazing marketing strategy.

The gut feeling in the pit of his stomach was growing stronger every day. There had to be a connection between what was going on with the AOG, Will Vanders and Donnie Larsen.

Maybe it was a long shot, but he couldn't help but think Jolene was the key to the whole thing.

JOLENE KICKED off her sandals and tossed her doggy bag in the refrigerator before she sat down in a chair by the kitchen table. She carefully removed her pantyhose having ruined three pairs in the last three weeks: two on the sharp metal corners of her desk drawers and the other at the Sorenson's sale when she tripped in the barn. She remembered the look on Michael's face when the lights came on — complacent, but undeniably adorable.

God, he looked great again tonight. She thought about what happened at dinner and felt incredibly proud of herself. Not only had she gotten through spending dinner with a man who drove her crazy, she'd managed to keep it together with his beautiful girlfriend at his side.

It was evident there was something cagey about her attending the shower by the look they gave each other when it was mentioned. It irritated her to see how happy Diana got, learning Michael was looking at land. Jolene was sure it was like the baby shower. The subject had never been discussed between them. For such an involved couple, they didn't seem to communicate very well with each other.

Michael's compliment to Will about his great choice for a

Realtor had caught her totally off guard. On the day of the sale, he said it was strange the deal went down when she hadn't put any effort into it. Clearly, Michael didn't understand real estate. If he did, he'd realize a percentage of the buying population often purchased on a whim.

Will's comment about her amazing marketing strategies had been just as peculiar. It was only a week ago when he said to rely more on Donnie's experience in real estate and less on what she learned in school. Maybe Will was only trying to build her confidence. If that were the case, he and Donnie should've trusted her instincts at the time of the sale and listed the Sorenson property at the higher price she suggested. They could've made more money for Larsens and the bank. Not to mention, a larger commission for herself.

A soft, warm breeze blew through the courtyard of her apartment while Jolene enjoyed a cigarette on the patio. She positioned her feet in the other chair and listened to the shouts and laughter of children as they enjoyed the swimming pool a few yards away.

Hearing a baby cry, she rubbed out her cigarette on the cement and put it in a coffee can under her little table. She went to the edge of her patio and peered out at the neighbors to the right and saw the dark-haired woman walking around the pool with the baby in her arms. *How do I know her?*

"Hi," Jolene came closer to the woman with her hand out. "I'm Jolene Garrison and you are ...?"

The woman's eyes got big, but she shook Jolene's hand. "I ... I'm Lyla."

Jolene pointed to the unit she saw the woman come out of a few days prior. "You live in that apartment, right?"

"Yes. I do with my husband," her reply was somewhat uneasy.

"I've got this uncanny feeling I've met you before."

"Oh, really? I got a sister who looks quite a bit like me. It seems everyone knows her."

"I'm new in the area," Jolene told her. "I work at Vanders Law Firm and Larsen's Realty."

"It sounds like you're very ambitious." Lyla smiled timidly.

Jolene pointed at the baby. "With that little guy, it seems you are, too."

Lyla's smile got bigger.

"Say, I live alone and you're the first neighbor my age I've actually met." Jolene tried not to sound desperate. "I work on the weekdays, but if you'd want to come over for a cup of coffee on the weekends or maybe a badly needed glass of wine in the evening, give me a try and see if I'm home."

Lyla's mouth fell open in shock. "That would be *so* great. Thank you."

Jolene saw the woman was attractive in an edgy sort of way with her haunting dark eyes and shiny black hair.

The baby suddenly started to cry louder. "I better go now," Lyla said in apologetic tone. "I've got to give him a bath and off to bed, before I completely poop out. But I will take you up on that offer one day real soon." She turned and went off toward her apartment and yelled back, "It was nice to meet you."

"You, too," Jolene answered. She walked back to her apartment with a smile on her face thinking about what had transpired. It was great she made a connection with someone her own age, especially one who lived so close. How nice to have a neighbor to rely on or maybe even look out for her.

14

The hotdish bubbled lightly when Lucille opened the oven at the fellowship hall. It was her and Kathy Klies's week to host lunch for the quilters group. The menu consisted of a chow mein hotdish, green Jell-O with pineapple, dinner roll and a rhubarb crisp for dessert.

Lucille looked out of the partition at the women assembled around the long banquet table.

"It looks like everyone has arrived."

Kathy stood by her side. "Oh, and it looks like Cheryl made it." She smiled at Lucille. "I bet you're just thrilled to be a grandmother."

"Yes. It's exciting," Lucille said, trying to sound enthusiastic.

Kathy's eyebrows bunched slightly but she didn't say any more.

While Patsy Timms, the pastor's wife, recited the mealtime prayer, Lucille gazed at the women sitting around her at the table. Her eyes focused on Cheryl and she couldn't squelch the contempt she felt for her. *How can you deceive my son and pretend he's the father of your baby?*

"How long do you have to go before the baby comes?" Alma

asked Cheryl. Alma being the oldest parishioner in the church, she was a motherly figure to the group.

"I'm thinking around three months," Cheryl answered. "It's sure been miserable in this heat. My feet are so swollen, I can't get my cowboy boots on."

"Is your sister dating Will Vanders?" Joan Uterman butted into the conversation.

Cheryl looked annoyed. "My sister works for Will. Why do you ask?"

"Someone I know saw them out to dinner at Rosy's the other night." Joan continued her report. "She said your brother-in-law Michael and Diana Iverson were dining with them."

"How nice they could have dinner together," Cheryl answered and buttered her roll.

"My niece, Jan, works in the office at Larsen's Realty and she said your sister is handling all the foreclosures for the bank," Mary Swenson said.

"That's what I've been told." Cheryl appeared ready to end the questioning.

"Now that you're a Cameron, your family and the Vanders are like one happy family," Mary stated.

The comment gave Lucille an unsettling feeling. *There's something going on here.* "What exactly are you trying to say, Mary?"

"I got the new thread for the quilt on sale last week," Patsy Timms, the pastor's wife, interrupted the conversation.

Chet was right. It wasn't only the members of the AOG thinking some sort of a conspiracy was taking place. People were definitely talking about them. But why?

Lucille quietly worked on the quilt contemplating feasible reasons anyone had for mistrusting her family. Even though it was something she didn't want to believe, it had to stem from Jake's failure to get the reimbursement from the state. What else could it possibly be? *Poor Jake. Ever since she came into his world — his life has tumbled down hill.*

THE HOUSE WAS silent when Michael picked up the phone in the den and dialed Diana's mother's phone number. Lucille and Chet had gone out for dinner for their anniversary and Brett had left earlier for the evening.

"Hello," Diana answered the phone.

"Hey, it's me. Listen, I've got some business to take care of. I'm not going to make it over there tonight."

"What? I thought you were coming to get me and we were going to watch television at your house." Disappointment was in her voice.

"Yeah. That was the plan but I need to take care of something before Monday morning. If you want, how about we go out for dinner and dancing tomorrow night?"

"That sounds great. But couldn't I come over and help you with whatever you have to do tonight?" she anxiously asked.

Michael let out a quick breath. "No. It's something I best do by myself."

"Why are you being so secretive?"

"I'm sorry if it sounds that way to you."

"Just give me your word you're not seeing someone else." She sounded desperate.

What the heck? "What are you talking about?"

"Well, I've learned from friends that when your guy isn't leveling with you, he's likely cheating on you."

"I assure you. I'm not seeing anyone else." *Not physically.*

A moment went by before she said, "I'm sorry. I'm just taking things out on you. I've been arguing with my brother all day about what a slob he is around here." She released a deep sigh then asked what time he would pick her up the following evening.

The call ended shortly after and Michael felt guilty knowing he hadn't been completely honest. He hadn't lied about seeing someone else, but deep down, he had to admit Jolene was always on his mind. Diana would never understand how his heart raced whenever he saw her. He closed his eyes and pictured Jolene in the low-cut dress she wore at Rosy's and once again confirmed his theory.

Michael arrived at Jim's apartment building and found him in a lawn chair on the patio. Lyla pushed a baby stroller out of the apartment and parked it beside Jim.

"Hi Michael," she said and turned to Jim. "I'm going for a walk." She leaned over and pecked a kiss on her son's head and one on her husband's cheek. "He should be ready for bed in a little while." She took a few steps, then hollered back, "And make sure he doesn't get bit up by mosquitoes."

"Looks like there wasn't a Tupperware party tonight," Michael commented.

"Nope. You need a beer?" Jim opened the Styrofoam cooler next to him.

"Yeah, I'll take one," Michael said and sat on a chair. "You sure spend a lot of time out here."

"Yeah. I like the location." He gestured with his head toward the pool where two girls in skimpy bikinis were lounging on lawn chairs. "The view is great."

Michael smiled. "Do I need to remind you again, you're a married man?"

"Like I said, I'm not dead, yet," Jim answered. He opened a brief case on the glass topped patio table and handed Michael a large manila envelope stuffed full. "Here's everything you've asked for."

"How did you get it organized so fast?"

"I sweet talked the old man's secretary. She thought I was pulling her leg when I asked her to get the latest listings on every available piece of real estate in the southwestern side of the state of Minnesota. It should be enough to keep your real estate agent busy for a while. So what's your plan?"

"I'm thinking, if I spend enough time with Jolene driving around looking at real estate, eventually she'll let something slip and I'll be able to piece together what's going on with Will."

"Do you think she's involved in something corrupt?"

"My gut tells me no, but I want to know for sure." *Could Jolene's desire for success push her into doing something dishonest?*

THE SOUND of a light knock made Jolene put a marker in the Harlequin romance novel she was reading. Opening her patio door, she smiled seeing it was her neighbor.

"Can I take you up on that glass of wine?" Lyla asked with a sweet smile.

"For sure." Jolene opened the door wider. "Come on in."

"I would have called but I forgot to ask you for your phone number," Lyla apologized as she stepped into the apartment.

"It would be hard to give it to you seeing how I don't have a phone. But you'll be one of the first people to get it after the phone company hooks me up on Monday. I finally got enough money saved for one." Jolene saw Lyla look around at her scantly decorated home.

"It's a work in progress," Jolene informed her. "Make that a slow process when you're twenty-six and starting out on your own."

"Until I married my husband, I had no idea how much it cost to live."

"When I was married, I lived in a mansion that was decorated by an interior designer."

"Wow! I bet it was beautiful," Lyla exclaimed. "How long were you married?"

"Six years," Jolene pulled the cork out of a bottle of chardonnay. "The house was the opposite of beautiful in my eyes. It was way too modern and unfriendly."

"Oh, that's too bad."

"No, it isn't. I'm glad to be out of there. Everything in the whole place was about and for my ex — the Rat."

Lyla let out a giggle. "I'm sorry, but that's a funny nickname."

"Robert — the Rat. The name suits him perfectly. He's a lawyer and he screwed me out of everything."

Jolene handed her a glass of wine. "Shall we sit out on the patio?"

"Sure. That sounds good," Lyla answered and let Jolene lead the way.

"Is your husband watching your baby?"

"Yes. He's great with him. He loves being a father. A single friend of his dropped by and the two are doing the same thing as us, only they're having beer."

"Good. That doesn't make me feel like I'm the only one."

Lyla leaned forward in her chair. "What do you mean by 'the only one'?"

"The only single person without a date on a Friday night."

"So, no boyfriend?" Lyla asked.

"Nope."

"There must be someone you're interested in on the horizon?"

Jolene shook her head no and sipped her wine. "It's been almost a year since my husband and I broke up. I had a brief relationship since and got burned. Now I'm thinking maybe solitude is better than what's out there."

"That's not that long. As pretty as you are, I'm sure your prince charming will come along real soon now." Lyla smiled and took a swallow from her glass.

"I'm not going to hold my breath. The last guy was a handsome prince but he turned out to be nothing but a slimy frog." Jolene chuckled picturing Michael's face green with croaking sounds coming from his mouth.

"I didn't think my husband was the one in the beginning," Lyla said. "I thought he was like all the rest until I got to know him better. I don't know if it's because of the baby or not, but both of our lives have changed into something wonderful. Something I never imagined could happen to us."

"Oh, Lyla!" Jolene squeezed her hand. "I'm so happy for you."

"Don't lose hope, girl. That special someone is bound to turn up for you, too."

"Thanks, Lyla, but right now it seems like an impossible dream."

MICHAEL SAT ALONE at the M & M ballroom and waited for Diana to return from the ladies room. He became agitated listening to the band sing the song "Day After Day" and threw back what was left of his whiskey Coke. The tune about a lonely man finding out his love had left him, stirred up old painful memories. Like a movie reel, his mind went back to the day eight years ago on the porch of the Iverson farmhouse. He recalled the cold, unconcerned way Diana's sister informed him Diana had fallen in love and gotten married to someone else. He momentarily lost his breath as her words shot into his chest and shattered his heart. On the way home, he drove up to Ridge Rock Hill where he stayed for hours crying his eyes out and fighting off the urge to drive over the edge of the high hill.

"Sorry it took me so long," Diana said, her voice cutting into his thoughts. "The line for the restroom was out the door."

He took a deep breath. "I'm ready to get out of here if you are."

Her eyes searched his. "Is there something wrong?"

"No. I'm just thinking someplace quiet would be nice."

"Where were you thinking?" Her smile was inviting.

"We could go for a drive, I guess."

She slowly rubbed her hand over his. "Or maybe ... we could get a motel room."

Her suggestion sounded much better, and knowing he had a condom in his wallet made it something he wanted, too.

At the Viking Motel, Michael went inside and got a room while she waited in his truck. When they parked in front of the unit they rented, she whispered, "I love you, Michael."

She waited for him to repeat that phrase back to her, but he couldn't. He wanted to be truthful with her, and saying those words without knowing for sure, felt like a lie. Instead, he pulled her body close and ravished her mouth with a deep, sensual kiss. They stared at each other for a moment, panting when the kiss ended.

He flipped on the light switch after opening the door of the room. She immediately wrapped her arms around his neck and the kissing flared up with the same intensity as before.

His mouth covered hers when his hand went for the zipper on the back of her dress. She unbuttoned his shirt and soon they both stood undressed. Her body was thinner than he'd remembered in high school, and he couldn't keep his eyes off her narrow hips when they went to the bed. *There's nothing to her.*

Locked in a kiss, he ran his hand down the side her body and brought it up to claim one of her small breasts. They kissed for a few more minutes until he pulled away to put on the condom. Her eyes widened when he entered her and she released what sounded like a pleasurable gasp. When he closed his eyes and saw Jolene's face, there was no holding back. The entire thing was over faster than either of them wanted.

Damn, my stupid thoughts! "I'm sorry," he told Diana feeling guilty. "It's been a while for me."

"Don't apologize," she told him. "It was great."

They lay on the bed for a while and he stared into her blue eyes.

She brushed her fingers through the dark hair on his chest. "We could do it again if you want to."

"I'll have to go out to the truck for another condom."

"You don't need to." She smiled. "I'm not ovulating."

"You keep track?"

"Old habit from when I was trying to conceive."

He rolled toward the edge of the bed, got to his feet and pulled on his jeans. "I'll be right back." He headed out to the truck and found a package of condoms in the glove compartment. Outside he thought about how close she kept track of her cycle. The whole idea made making love to her again seem somewhat clinical. They didn't share the hot passion he did with Jolene. *Stop it! I need to quit doing this to myself.*

THE SMELL of brewing coffee welcomed Jolene when she entered the door at Larsen's Realty. At the sound of the door opening and closing, Jan, the secretary, looked up from her typewriter.

"Donnie wants to see you right away."

"He's here already?" Jolene checked her wristwatch to see if it was accurate. It was out of the ordinary to see her boss so early in the morning.

"Yes. He's leaving for the annual convention for the National Association of Realtors in Omaha, Nebraska."

Why didn't he mention it to me? I would've loved to have gone. Jolene swallowed hard, trying to hold back her emotions. The convention was a prestigious event, the perfect place to make new connections in the realty world. *Was I excluded because I'm a woman?*

Going back to her work, Jan continued to punch the keys on the typewriter at a fast, steady speed.

Jolene took a few deep breaths to calm herself. Should she confront the boss and ask why he didn't include her? She let her temper amp up her courage and decided to go into his office to get to the bottom of the issue. She straightened the collar on her pale green blouse and checked her teeth for lipstick in the small mirror in her desk drawer. A professional image was crucial if she wanted him to take her seriously. She conjured a confident smile and sprang from her chair ready for action. *You better have a good reason for not inviting me.* When her boss came out of his office with a briefcase in hand, he halted by her desk.

"There you are," he said. "I don't know if Jan told you or not, but I'm going to be leaving for the NAR convention this morning."

"That's what I've been told," Jolene's answer was to the point. "I would've loved to have tagged along."

He gave her a concerned look. "I agree. I would've *loved* to have my star Realtor attend, but I'm counting on her to help run things here during my absence."

His answer took her by surprise. "Oh." She smiled. "I wondered why you hadn't mentioned the convention."

Apparently running late, he wasted no time. "We've got a new client coming in this morning. He's interested in both farm and domestic properties with acreage and sounded very anxious to buy. Seeing as how I won't be here, I want you to clear your schedule and show him our listings as well as some of our competitors in the outlying areas. He said if we don't have anything listed that piques his interest, he would like you to be his buying agent."

"Me?" She found it hard to believe someone would want an agent to represent them without having met first.

His chubby face got rounder when he smiled. "He was here twice last week when you were at the law office and he specifically asked for you. I guess he heard from Will what a great Realtor you are."

Jolene grabbed an ink pen and a pad of paper. "What's the client's name?"

"Michael Cameron," he said.

Her head jerked up in surprise. *What the hell does he want? Someone should remind him he's got a girlfriend.*

Donnie noticed her reaction. "Do you know him?"

"Yes." She chose her words carefully. "I've met the man a few times."

"I suspect that's him now." Donnie pointed at the red truck pulling up in front of the building.

Michael came in and removed his beige cowboy hat. He looked ready for business, dressed in a navy sports jacket, white shirt and dark blue jeans. The man was close to breathtaking as he made his way across the room. He clung to a large manila envelope with one hand and stuck the other out to Donnie.

"It's nice to see you, again." Michael smiled as they shook hands.

Damn! He smells as good as he looks.

Donnie's attention went to Jolene and then back to Michael. "It sounds like you two have already met so there's no need for introductions."

"Yes, I've had the pleasure. It's nice to see you again, Miss Garrison." Michael reached out his hand and Jolene had no choice but to offer hers. The touch of his warm hand caused a flutter in the bottom of her stomach. *Oh, no!*

"I'm really anxious to hit the road and check out some properties."

"I think it would be in everyone's best interest if Miss Garrison gets your information first. That way she can narrow down the search for what you're looking for." Donnie's beady eyes darted at the large clock between the two front windows of the office. "I better get going. I'm already late." He nodded at Michael. "I leave you in good hands, Mr. Cameron."

You need to take immediate control of this situation. Jolene mustered the biggest smile possible. "Please take a seat, Mr. Cameron." He put his hat on the extra chair by her desk and sat down.

"Can I get you some coffee or something else to drink?" she offered.

His smile was kind. "Call me Michael. Coffee would be great."

"Do you need cream and sugar ... Michael?" Jolene asked

from across the room. She knew how he took his coffee but didn't want it known how well they were associated.

He gave her a blank look. "No, just black. Thank you."

Pouring them both a cup of coffee, Jolene glanced in Jan's direction and caught the middle-aged secretary gazing at Michael like he was a frosted pastry. She was dangerously nosey and anything said during the appointment had to sound legitimate.

Jolene set his cup in front of him on the desk and returned to her chair. "I'm going to need your phone number and address along with the type of real estate you're interested in. And of course, I'll need to know what your price range is."

"I'm interested in a house with outbuildings and some acreage or maybe just acreage where I can build a house. I've done some looking on my own." He handed her the manila envelope from Jim and her eyes got big.

"How much acreage are we talking?" she asked opening the envelope.

"Fifteen to maybe a few hundred acres."

She raised her brows. "That's a wide range."

"If I like the place, I'm willing to work something out."

"Hopefully, it won't take too long to narrow it down." Jolene smiled and glanced at Jan. Her typewriter was silent and her chin rested in the palm of her hand. She appeared like a starry-eyed teenager with her eyes focused on Michael. "I have no doubt we can find you the perfect piece of property," Jolene told him.

He smiled. "I'm ready to start searching."

"Well then, I think we're about ready," she announced and shoved a file filled with listings and his envelope inside her open satchel.

"Do we drive my truck or your car?" he asked.

"My car," she said, putting the strap of her bag over her shoulder and grabbing her purse.

Jan was watching out the window when they got into

Jolene's Firebird. Remaining as calm as possible, Jolene backed her car out of the parking spot and started down the street.

A safe distance from the building, she pulled into an alley and put her car in park. She glared over at Michael in the passenger's seat. "Alright! You can cut the charade." Her heart thumped in her chest. "What do you want from me?"

"With any luck, to find a house or some land to build on."

"*Really*? And you expect me to believe that?"

His expression was serious. "Why wouldn't you?"

It took a moment before the idea sunk in her head. *He wants a place for him and her.*

"I don't know what you think is happening, but I'm interested in purchasing some land," Michael reinforced his intentions.

"If what you're saying is true, I have one question: why pick me when there are other agencies and agents in the area?"

"After Will expressed how he felt about your work, why wouldn't I want the best Realtor around?"

Knowing Will had laid it on a little thick, Jolene instantly felt foolish. *He could be telling the truth.* "Of course. I'm sorry."

"So can we clean the slate and work together?" His smile seemed sincere.

She looked into his dark, scintillating eyes. "Yes. I believe we can." *If I can control the way I feel about you …*

15

In the warm morning air, Brett gazed at Michael. They were both shirtless and soaked with sweat from pounding stakes into the ground.

Brett nudged Michael with his elbow. "Why is it we're sweating our asses off and those two are standing over there in the shade?"

"It's this way every year. I can't believe it took you this long to figure it out," Michael told him. "Dad and Earl Thompson get all the credit for the set-up for the Watson Lutheran Church bazaar and we do all the work."

They were close to finishing with the last tent when Brett saw two young women from church approach with armloads of salads. Michael reached for his faded sleeveless shirt and slipped it on, while Brett proudly threw back his shoulders. He casually tipped his cowboy hat, "Morning, ladies."

The women turned and whispered to each other as they passed by, but took another glimpse over their shoulders at them before going into the fellowship hall.

Michael handed Brett the sledge hammer. "Looks like everyone is starting to arrive. You finish this up. I'm going home to take a shower."

"If you leave, how am I supposed to get home and get cleaned up?"

"Take Dad's truck. I gotta get going. I have to pick up Diana."

"I haven't heard you talk about her lately. How are things going with you two?"

"Fine." Michael's tone was emotionless.

"It doesn't sound like you're overly excited about it," Brett commented.

Michael shook his head. "I don't really want to talk about it. Tell Dad I'll be back later."

Brett went back to pounding in the last stake but stopped when someone blocked the bright sunlight.

"I had no idea you helped out with this."

Brett couldn't believe his eyes. It was Karyn Pehrson. She looked lovely in a white sundress and sandals. Her dark shagged hair shone in the sunlight and her smooth tan skin was irresistibly inviting.

"What are you doing here?" he asked.

"Helping my grandmother deliver food for the luncheon."

"Karyn!" an older gray-haired woman yelled. "Stop dawdling and get that salad in the fridge inside the hall. The whipped cream is going to melt."

"Sounds like you're getting bossed around today, too."

She looked back at the woman and then to Brett. "Yeah, I better get in there."

"Hey. I'm going home for a quick shower, but I'll be back. Maybe we can get some lunch together later?"

Her brown eyes swept over him. "Sure." She smiled. "I'll see you later."

Yes! She said yes! This day is looking better already.

DESPITE THE GLOOMY sight of rolled corn leaves in the fields, Michael enjoyed the peaceful drive to the Sugar King without

Brett. He needed time alone to process what happened at the motel the other night with Diana without his brother asking annoying questions.

For some reason the sex didn't have the sizzle or excitement he had hoped for or remembered. It was troubling because for years after she left, he replayed their intimate encounters thousands of times in his head. Each time they were more wonderful than the last. Could it be sex then was something to be explored when they were kids and sneaking away to do it was half of the fun? Or was it great because he had nothing to compare it to?

His mind skipped through all the women in between and went straight to that first phenomenal night with Jolene. Even though her intentions were to use him, it had been the most erotic night of his life. She had this alluring quality that was genuine and sexy as hell.

Stop it, you idiot! It's not going to do you any good to hash over what happened. If he truly wanted to give his and Diana's relationship a shot, he had to stop thinking about Jolene that way. It wasn't fair to Diana. Most importantly, lusting after a woman who despised the ground he walked on would only break his heart once again in the end.

Lucille walked around the church yard and inspected each tent to see if it was ready for the bazaar. Seeing a line of men carrying benches from the church basement to the bingo tent, she checked her wrist watch. It was almost time for the bazaar to start. When Nell Thompson waddled over to her wearing a smug smile, Lucille let out an irritated sigh.

"I think everything out here is coming along good," Nell told her. "Earl has recruited some referees for this afternoon in case something happens like it did last year." Her insensitive statement shocked like a cow prodder, knowing last year Michael and

Brett had gotten into a fist fight over Cheryl in front of the congregation and the rest of the community.

"I'm sure we won't have any trouble like last year," Lucille assured her.

"Who knows? You still have two sons who aren't married yet."

Lucille ignored her comment and walked away toward the fellowship hall to check on the food for the luncheon. Nell huffed and puffed as she trailed after her into the building.

Cheryl was with several other women when Lucille and Nell entered the kitchen.

"You shouldn't be on your feet," Nell immediately barked out.

"I'm fine," Cheryl said, and continued to fill a bowl with potato salad.

"Where's Taylor?" Nell asked.

"Jake is running the dunk tank this year and Taylor is going to be his assistant." Cheryl had a pleased, radiant smile. "Taylor wore his swim trunks so they could try it out before the crowd gets here."

"That should keep *them* out of trouble." Nell glanced in Lucille's direction.

Lucille's eyes fell on her pregnant daughter-in-law. *That fist fight would've never happened last year if it hadn't been for you.* Lucille recalled how embarrassed she was watching her sons brawl over a woman who had been teasing all three of them. *That baby best come soon, so I can finally get you as far away from my family as possible.*

JOLENE SAT out on the patio with her coffee and a newspaper the neighbor next door had given her after he'd read it. She jumped when her newly installed phone rang from inside her apartment.

"Hello," she answered expecting it to be Cheryl.

"Hi there. How are you this morning?" Will's voice came on the line.

He must have gotten my phone number at work. "Good," she answered.

"Great. What are your plans for the day?"

Be careful how you answer. "I don't really have too much going on. Why?"

"How about getting out and having a little fun today?"

"What do you mean?"

"Why don't you and I go down to the Watson Lutheran church bazaar? It used to be one of my favorite events of the summer when I was a kid."

Jolene had already told Cheryl she would come down to the bazaar for lunch. It would be less awkward if she was with someone instead of looking like a lonely outsider walking around by herself. Will was her boss and her friend. Who cared if two friends hung out together?

"Sure. That's sounds good. Do you want to meet down there?"

"No. I'll come pick you up. Let's say in about an hour?"

"I'll be ready. See you then. 'Bye."

According to Cheryl, the Camerons coordinated the bazaar and did a good share of the work to make it possible. Knowing Michael and likely Diana would be there, Jolene decided to step it up and look a little nicer than normal. She wondered what Michael thought the other night when he and Diana joined her and Will for dinner. *Was he jealous?*

Dressed in a lilac-colored sundress and gold sandals, she pulled her long red hair in a French twist and fastened it with a curved comb and bobby pins. She wound a finger around a thin tendril of hair in front of each ear and sprayed them with hairspray to keep a relaxed hanging curl. Searching through her jewelry box, she found a pair of gold earrings that dangled and glittered and put them on. Finishing with a dab of perfume on her wrists she looked up in the mirror and liked what she saw. Being a new business woman, it was important to look good whenever she was out and about in the community.

Exactly one hour after Will called there was a knock on Jolene's apartment door. She answered the door and saw Will's mouth drop open in surprise.

"Wow! You look ... just perfect."

Perfect? "Perfect for what?"

"Perfect for a bazaar." He laughed and slowly pulled his eyes away from her. "Are you ready to go?"

"Yes." She slung the chain strap of her small gold purse over her shoulder and went out the door.

Jolene heard the song "Paper Roses" blasting out from somewhere when Will slowed his convertible down to turn into the Watson Church parking lot. Brett, with Taylor's help, wired speakers outside the fellowship hall in order to have music from the local country station. The boy proudly told Jolene that Uncle Brett said he couldn't have done it without his help.

The crowd was bigger than Jolene had expected when they walked across the lawn to the village of tents set up near the fellowship hall.

"Wow! Cheryl didn't tell me how many people attended this bazaar." Jolene looked from side to side. "Is it like this every year?"

"I can't tell you," Will answered as he followed her into the sea of people in the church yard. "I haven't been to one of these since high school, but I don't remember this big of a crowd."

Seeing Cheryl standing with Nell and a few older women by the food table, Jolene meandered through the throng of people to her sister. Will followed, turning and smiling at the crowd of people close by.

"Hey. You made it," Cheryl exclaimed. "You look so pretty today." Her eyes went to the man standing next to her sister. "Hello, Will."

Will nodded. "Always a pleasure to see you, Cheryl."

"And a pleasant surprise to see you," she answered giving Jolene a discreet wink.

"Do so many people always come to this?" Jolene asked looking around.

"I have to say, this is the biggest crowd I can remember," Cheryl said with certainty.

"The fist fight last year may have helped with attendance this year," Nell jumped into the conversation.

Jolene and Will exchanged a curious look.

"What fist fight?" Jolene asked.

"Michael and Brett got into it after the food table got tipped over. They were fighting over Cheryl," Nell volunteered.

"Is that right?" Will asked in an exuberant voice. "I wish I'd have been here."

Cheryl shrugged. "What can I say?"

I'll have to ask her for the details later. Jolene could tell by her expression the topic made her sister uncomfortable and immediately changed the subject. "Where are Jake and Taylor with the dunk tank?"

"Over there." Cheryl pointed to a tent yards away. "You better go check it out. Taylor ran over here three times asking where you were."

Jake was trying to sell tickets and round up more dunk tank volunteers when Taylor spotted Jolene and ran to her.

"You're finally here!" he announced. "Aunt Jolene are you going to get dunked?"

Jolene laughed. "No, I'm afraid that kinda thing isn't for me."

Taylor eyed Will. "Are you going to try it?"

Will smiled down at him. "I didn't bring my swim trunks, so I'll have to pass."

Taylor's face lit up and he shouted, "Uncle Michael!" He turned and ran over to his uncle and Diana who were making their way toward them.

Diana smiled and bent at her waist. "You must be Taylor."

Taylor looked up at her strangely. "Yeah. Who are you?"

"I'm Diana." She looked at Michael. "I'm your Uncle Michael's, girlfriend."

Taylor furrowed his brows and snapped his head in Jolene and Will's direction. Seconds later, he ran to Jake who was trying to convince a young man in the crowd to volunteer for the dunk tank.

Seeing Michael, Jake immediately announced to the group of young people gathered, "If my brother will show you how it's done, can we count on you to take a turn after him?" He smiled. When no one replied, Jake asked, "Where's your support for the church?"

"Well, if he does it first," a young man finally answered.

Michael came closer to Jake. "Oh come on, Jake. I don't want to walk around in wet clothes all day."

Will came closer to the two Cameron brothers. "Where can a guy find a phone? I forgot I was supposed to make an important call this morning."

"There's one in the fellowship hall," Jake told him. "As long as it isn't long distance, no one will care if you use it."

"I'll be right back," he told Jolene before he walked away.

"What's this?" Michael asked when Jake handed him a bag.

"A swimsuit and a T-shirt."

"And where the hell am I supposed to change? I'm not using a portable toilet."

"Use the restroom in the fellowship hall," Jake told him.

Diana stood with her mouth slightly open, seemingly lost for words when Michael walked past her to change into the swimsuit.

Jolene decided to jump on the opportunity and rushed over to Jake. "How does this work to get him dunked?"

Jake gave her a devious grin. "You get three balls for a buck."

Jolene smiled back at him. "Give me two dollars' worth."

Jake laughed loudly and turned to the crowd. "In case this lovely lady doesn't hit the mark, who wants to buy some balls?"

"Don't you have any faith in women, Jake?" Jolene asked

playfully, and put her hands on her hips. She pretended to be slightly offended knowing that putting on some sort of show would boost Jake's sales. The crowd roared and howled at Jolene's comment and she couldn't help laughing with them. Feeling like someone was staring at her, she turned around and saw Diana leaned up against a tree with her arms crossed. She was yards away, but Jolene could see her disgusted eyes throwing daggers in her direction. *What's your problem?*

A FEW WOMEN were in the kitchen doing dishes when Michael came in the door of the fellowship hall to change his clothes. The partition was open and he nodded to them as he walked past. He was about to go in the restroom when he heard Will's low muffled voice coming from the office farther down the hall. The door was open a crack and Michael stepped closer to hear what Will was saying.

"Yeah, it's just packed down here. I've never seen it like this. It's a perfect day to introduce Miss Jolene Garrison to the community. It's about time everyone got to know the woman in charge."

What the hell does he mean by that?

Will was silent for a few seconds as he listened to whomever was on the line.

"Yes. Just do whatever it takes to get them down here. And do it as soon as possible. We don't want to miss this opportunity."

Michael didn't wait around to hear him hang up and hurried into the restroom. He waited a few seconds then opened the door a crack. Will strolled past the restrooms and down the hallway whistling like he was on top of the world.

Dressed in the swim trunks and T-shirt, Michael left the restroom and once again walked past the kitchen. The women stopped what they were doing and curiously watched him go for the door.

You owe me big time for this, Jake!

Michael swallowed hard and ignored the stares and pointing fingers once he stepped outside. His focus was straight ahead when he navigated through the herd of people with his hairy muscular legs and bare feet moving as swiftly as possible to the dunk tank.

He heard Jolene laugh when the group of people in front of him parted like the Red Sea did for Moses. Diana shook her head in disapproval when Michael glanced at her. It was clear this was something that didn't make her happy. Will wasn't anywhere in sight and Michael wondered where he'd gone since making the phone call.

Jake looked away to hide a smirk then proceeded to work the crowd. "This lady gets six tries and if she doesn't make it, it's up to the next person. So step right up and try your luck. "

Michael noticed Jolene's taunting green eyes and her mischievous smile when she turned to face him. Seeing her teasing expression played on his emotions. She looked so tempting with her hair up and wearing such a pretty dress. He felt her eyes on him when he climbed the ladder and sat on the small seat above the water tank. When her eyes found his, the whole world suddenly disappeared and the only thing he could focus on was her. The noises from the on-lookers and Jake's voice were muffled in the background as he stared at the beautiful woman in front of him. The only thing he could hear was his heart beating loudly in his head. *How can I stop myself from loving you?*

Everything was moving in slow motion when Jolene wound her hand back and threw the first ball at the round yellow and red target. When the ball hit the backdrop with a hard thud, it brought Michael back to reality.

The crowd groaned at her miss, but Jolene didn't let it discourage her as she grabbed the second ball and fired it as hard as she could. It, too, missed the mark. When her third ball failed to hit the target, Michael stuck his thumbs in his ears and wiggled his fingers back and forth before he playfully stuck out his tongue. The spectators "oohed" together in a low rumble seeing him mock her and Jolene play into it by narrowing her eyes at him. She gave Michael a hard look that was sexy as hell and took the fourth ball into her hands. An evil smile was on her face when she straightened and drew back her arm. She released the ball and a second later, Michael felt the seat drop from underneath him. Loud cheers blasted out from the crowd and Michael fell into the cool water thankful the cold temperature would reverse the uncontrollable physical effect Jolene Garrison had on him.

Jolene had disappeared and Jake was busy taking money from the long line of participants when Michael climbed out of the tank. It seemed his and Jolene's performance had piqued a lot of interest and there were several groups waiting to take part in the fun.

Diana rushed over to him. "I can't believe you agreed to do that."

"I wanted to help Jake out," he told her.

"But why with her?" she asked.

"Did you want to do it instead?" he asked, knowing the answer. Diana wasn't the type who liked being the center of attention.

"No. I'm not like *her*." She pointed to Jolene and Will not far into the crowd. A man was talking to Jolene with a camera dangling on his chest and another was writing things down in a notebook. Will stood by her side smiling and nodding his head. He must have been arranging another interview with the newspaper when he was on the phone.

Will suddenly stepped away for the photographer to take a picture of Jolene by herself.

Michael wondered why Will would call the reporters to do a story on Jolene and not himself? *The woman in charge. In charge of what?*

"I've got to change my clothes," Michael told Diana. "Wait for me here. I'll be right back."

Hurrying into the fellowship hall, he rushed to the rest room knowing he needed to change his clothes as fast as possible. *I've got to hear what that reporter is asking Jolene.*

JOLENE BOWED to the applauding crowd after Michael fell into the dunk tank. While she smiled at the swarm of people, her eyes searched for her boss, but didn't have any luck in finding him. Stepping into the crowd, she didn't get too far before seeing Will weave through the mass of people with two men at his side. Jolene noticed one man had a camera.

"Here she is," Will declared and wrapped an arm around her. "This is the woman I was telling you about." Will quickly stepped away and the man with the camera snapped a picture of Jolene with a blank stare.

Jolene was astonished. "What's this all about?"

"Jolene Garrison, this is Steve Livingston from the Montevideo Daily Reminder. He's here to interview you, the newest, most successful business woman in the area."

"Really? He's here to interview me and not you?" Jolene found that hard to believe.

"We certainly are interested in your story," Steve answered.

The photographer stepped closer. "How about a nice smile this time for the camera?"

Seeing the man take her picture, a crowd started to gather around them.

"Let me get a few more shots, Miss Garrison," the photographer said. "Could you turn to your left?" He took a few more pictures before Steve started the interview.

"Will was telling us how you're an essential part of his law office in Watson as well as Larsen's Realty in Montevideo." Steve waited for her response with the tip of his ink pen firmly pressed on the notebook in his hand.

"I … I don't know if I'm essential, but I'm doing the best I can for both businesses."

"She's just being modest," Will broke in to help her. "She's the lady in charge of most of our real estate transactions these days."

He ran a hand through his hair. "Donnie Larsen and I are very fortunate to have found someone with the organizational and people skills this woman has demonstrated," he continued. "Her astounding professional expertise has lead us in a totally new direction. You can check it out yourself, her numbers are the best in the area for agricultural sales."

While Jolene answered more questions, she thought about what a selfless man Will Vanders was. Not only had he given her an opportunity to prove herself when so many other men refused, now he was giving her a spot in the limelight with him. He left no doubt he was very pleased and excited about her work. Having his support made her feel incredibly grateful. It was sweet of him to exaggerate like he did about her. He may have laid it on a little thick, but too much good publicity never hurt anyone.

AT NOON, Brett stood outside the ticket booth by the food table and scanned the crowd. He checked his wristwatch and sighed. It looked like Karyn had stood him up once again. When he felt someone tap his shoulder from behind, he spun around and lost himself in a set of big brown eyes.

"You made it," he finally managed to say.

Karyn smiled. "Yes. You still want to get some lunch?"

Wow! You're so pretty. He forced his eyes away from her. "Sure. I've worked up an appetite after setting up all those tents."

They went through the lunch line and were seated at a picnic table when Brett noticed Nell Thompson watching them closely.

Back off old woman! Find someone else to gossip about! "So, how's the job hunting going?" Brett asked ignoring Nell's intrusive stare.

"I'm surprised you remembered."

"I wouldn't forget a thing about you," he said with a smile.

She smiled shyly and blinked her eyes. "I got a job at the Record and Title Office a couple of weeks ago."

"Good for you. That sounds like an interesting job."

"It is, I guess," she said with a shrug. "So you work for your Dad?"

"I'm in a partnership with him and my two brothers."

"You must all get along well."

Brett thought about her comment. "Yeah, I suppose we do, most of the time."

"I don't think I could work with either of my brothers. My older brother, Ken, thinks he knows everything, and you've met my younger one, Keith. His mouth always seems to get him in trouble with me and everyone else."

Brett smiled knowingly. "When you're dealing with your own family, it can get on your nerves. I find myself wanting to get away once in a while. Usually I go for a horse ride or go somewhere for a drive in my truck."

"I love horses." Her brown eyes widened. "How many do you have?"

"Me, myself? Two."

"Really? What are their names?"

"Milo and Eddy. They're both quarter horses." An idea struck him. "Would you like to go riding sometime?"

"Sure. That sounds like fun. I used to ride a lot at home before I went to stay with my grandmother. We had two horses, Ole and ..."

"Let me guess. Lena?" he interrupted.

She smiled. "No, Ingrid."

He laughed. "I would've never guessed that."

"While I was gone one of the horses bit my brother and he talked my dad into getting rid of them." Her smile fell. "I really do miss them."

"Then we'll have to go riding one of these …" he stopped talking seeing her brother, Keith, push through the lunch line and stomp toward them.

She leaned toward Brett and quickly whispered. "I'll call *you*."

"Karyn! What the hell are you doing sitting with this asshole?"

Brett got to his feet but before he could round the picnic table, Nell Thompson stepped in front of him. Her hand clutched the handle of a small cast iron frying pan.

"Just a minute, young man!" Her words thick with her Norwegian accent rang out and stopped the conversation at the tables around them. "We'll have no trouble here today."

He pointed to Karyn. "That's my sister and she needs to get away from him."

Nell's gray eyes stared him down. "The only one who needs to go is you." She raised the frying pan and shook it. "You get going or I'm going to use this!"

Brett recognized Karyn's grandmother as she approached the table. "Karyn, your brother's right. I don't think your parents would approve of you associating with a Cameron."

What the hell? The crowd around them murmured and continued to stare. Brett could see Karyn's cheeks were flushed.

"Yes, Ma'am," Karyn answered and faced Brett. "I better get going. But remember what I said."

Brett watched the old woman loop an arm through her granddaughter's and escort her through the crowd. Her brother walked on the other side of them with his head rapidly shaking back and forth while he spoke to them. At one point, Karyn looked back and Brett thought he saw her wink at him. *Are my eyes playing tricks?*

SHORTLY AFTER JOLENE finished her interview with the newspaper crew, she went into the fellowship hall to find her sister. Cheryl was never going to believe what happened with the reporter. Jolene excitedly searched the room for her sister and was told by the three ladies washing dishes that Cheryl was either in the restroom or somewhere outside. Jolene walked swiftly toward the restroom when the door opened and Diana stepped into the hallway.

"Oh hi, Diana. Is my sister in there?"

"No, she isn't."

"Well, I'll check outside then." Jolene turned to leave but stopped halfway down the hall hearing Diana call after her.

"Jolene! Can I have a word with you?"

Turning to face her, Jolene asked, "What do you need?"

Diana stepped closer. "I just thought you and I should talk."

"About what?"

"Michael." She took a deep breath and eyed Jolene accusingly.

Did he finally tell you we were lovers? Just spit it out! "What about him?"

"I just wanted you to know he and I have been together since ninth grade."

Why are you telling me this? "And?"

"And there's been more girls than you could ever imagine who have looked at him with desire and lust in their eyes."

"Is that right? So what has that got to do with me?"

Diana's eyes narrowed. "You had that look on your face out there by the dunk tank."

"What the hell are you saying?" Jolene felt her heart start to race. "All I did was help my brother-in-law drum up some prospects for the dunk tank. I have no idea what you're talking about."

"You're lying. I see the way you look at him," Diana accused.

"You think I don't notice the way you're always flirting with him every chance you get?"

You've gone far enough. "Be honest with me. Is it the way I look at him that you're worried about … or the way he looks at me?"

Diana's eyes narrowed at the remark before her hand came up and slapped Jolene's face.

Crack!

Oh my God! She actually hit me! Jolene cupped her cheek, reeling in shock. "Are you crazy?"

"Many women have tried, but he'll always be mine!" Her high-pitched voice screeched in the hallway. "You just stay away from him!" Diana turned and strutted down the hallway.

Catching her breath, Jolene bolted toward her, fighting with thoughts of knocking her down onto the floor. *It would feel so damn good — Whoa girl! What am I doing? What about my big break? I can't jeopardize it.* Think of the damage it would do if people found out she got into a fight at the fellowship hall over Michael Cameron. All the good publicity from the interview would be moot.

Jolene tried to recall what happened at the dunk tank. It had all been a game, hadn't it? She thought about the playful way he stuck his tongue out at her. Had she looked back with lust in her eyes? *Maybe?* It wasn't completely her fault. If he hadn't looked so vulnerable sitting there on the bench like a little boy who was being punished …. *Damn him for being so incredibly good looking!*

Michael leaned against a tent post and waited for Diana. The crowd had thinned and he was wondering what was taking her so long. He guessed the line for the restroom was likely the problem. *Women. What do they do in there?* He thought about his mother and how she had always kept everyone waiting when they went to church. His father rarely said anything to her after she lashed out at him one Sunday. Witnessing the incident, he and his brothers all figured asking a woman what was taking her so long in the bathroom wasn't a wise thing to do. *Thank God, I got my driver's license and started driving myself.*

Seeing Diana step out the door of the fellowship hall, Michael noticed she seemed to be in a hurry as she headed in his direction. Her cheeks were red and she appeared to have her mind on something as she got closer.

"Are you okay?" he asked. "You look flushed."

"I'm fine. Just a long line in there."

Michael put his arm around her slender frame. "I think we should get you something cool to drink." He led her to a stand close by and ordered a glass of lemonade. They were waiting for her drink when he saw Jolene come out of the fellowship hall. She briefly met his gaze with an uneasy expression on her rosy face then looked away. It had to be hotter than hell in that fellowship hall. He thought it strange, remembering it was cool in the new building when he changed his clothes. Jolene swiftly moved on through the crowd to the luncheon area where Cheryl stood, then whispered in her ear. Both sisters immediately glanced in his direction.

"Michael." Diana's voice interrupted his thoughts. "I'm not feeling good. I think we should go home."

"Okay. If you're sick, we should go." He dropped his arm to her waist and guided her across the lawn toward the parking lot.

A few miles out of Watson, the cold air blew out of the air conditioner in Michael's truck. He glanced over at Diana in the passenger seat.

"Your face isn't red anymore. How are you feeling?" he asked.

She let out a deep breath and slid over close to him. "That heat must have got to me. I'm feeling much better now."

He looked her over again when her hand slid across his thigh. "You sure recovered fast."

"Yes. I guess all I needed was to cool down. But now I'm thinking heating up wouldn't be a bad idea either." She smiled and blinked her eyes. "Why don't we head up to Ridge Rock Hill? Remember how many times we slipped away in the middle of the afternoon when we were kids?"

"I got a better idea," he answered. "How about we go to the Sugar King? There isn't a soul home right now."

A big smile bloomed on her face. "That does sound better."

Michael unlocked the back door into the kitchen at the Sugar King and pushed the door open. He stepped back and waved his hand. "After you."

The door had barely closed behind them when she exclaimed, "This brings back so many memories. Hardly anything has changed."

"You better take another look. The cupboards have been redone since you were here last and my mother replaces the curtains every other year." He pointed to the window. "I think she hired someone to make those."

"They're lovely. I love the white and yellow lace."

He ignored her comment and pulled her into his arms. "Have you forgotten why we came here?" he smiled and kissed her.

Diana said little as she followed him through the door into the hallway. At the bottom of the long staircase she turned and declared, "I love this place. It's so stately and magnificent."

He smiled and took her hand. "It does make a statement, that's for sure."

"I'd love to live here."

"I hate to tell you, it's not what you think it is. It can get on your nerves with the family all caught up in your business."

"I'm not talking right now." He followed her into the sitting room where she sat down on the beige love seat in front of the fireplace. "This is so beautiful."

"It's pretty, but Mom's the only one who comes in here. The rest of us are too afraid we'll get something dirty."

"Oh Michael, your mother isn't that anal." She pulled his hand down and he sat by her.

He looked at her with raised brows. "You believe what you want. She likes everything just so."

This time she ignored his comment. "Just think a minute here, Michael. Your parents are in their fifties and they won't live forever. Jake is married now and living somewhere else. You've said Brett isn't dating anyone, but that could quickly change." Her eyes focused on his. "You don't need to find a place to buy. It's all waiting right here for you to claim it."

He let out a funny laugh. "Don't you think Brett and Jake will have something to say about me getting this place? Even if things would end up that way, I don't think it's going to happen overnight."

"I agree. So don't you think we should just rent an apartment somewhere in Montevideo? Or maybe we could move in here right after we get married?"

He felt the blood drain from his face. *Married? First time I heard anything about getting married or living together since she came back!*

"That way we can make this our home. Maybe Brett will buy a smaller farm around here."

Wow!

"Sounds like you've done some thinking about this." He blew out a breath. "I don't want to rain on your parade, but the whole thing sounds like a long shot. And living with Mom and Dad after I get married has never been something I've wanted to do. I think I'm going to continue to look for a place of my own."

"In that case, consider renting something for now. It would be silly to keep looking for land when you plan to live here. We don't need Jolene or any other real estate agent to find us an apartment. We can do that all by ourselves. I have all the time in the world to look."

He didn't comment and stared at the unlit fireplace in front of him. The whole conversation made him feel like the air was being sucked out of him. Why did he feel that way?

It wasn't the first time he heard her mention getting married.

He remembered back in high school they had talked about it often. He knew he should set her straight and remind her things had changed. This relationship was new; he wasn't in the same place as in high school, but how was he going to say something without hurting her?

Regardless of what the future held for them, he had to convince her he wanted to continue looking for land. It was the only way he was going to find out what was going on with the foreclosures. He was surer than ever that Will was up to something after hearing him on the phone in the fellowship hall.

"I'm not going to put all my eggs in one basket. I want to keep looking for land. I need to have a few options open."

She let out a sigh. "I hope your Realtor has time for you. I'm sure after her picture comes out in the paper, she'll likely be too busy to make you a priority."

"I have an appointment with her on Tuesday."

Diana watched him closely. "Well then, why don't I go with you two? I'd love to see some of these farms."

Oh God, no! I need to get Jolene alone and talking and with you there — that won't happen. "I don't want any distractions when I'm talking business. I need to do this alone."

Diana opened her mouth to respond when they heard the kitchen door open.

Seconds later they heard Brett's voice. "Michael. Are you here?"

Why the hell is he home? Michael looked at Diana and shrugged. "We're in here," he finally answered. Brett was at the end of the hallway when Michael whispered to Diana, "So much for our romantic afternoon."

16

Jolene was living on cloud nine after Will stopped by Larsen's with two copies of the morning paper. He read the article out loud to both her and Donnie at her desk. At one point, Jolene thought her bosses were more excited than she was. *I couldn't ask for two better guys to work for.*

"It was a real stroke of luck when I saw Steve standing in the crowd covering the bazaar," Will said after he finished reading. "He just interviewed me last month and I told him he had to meet you."

"I just can't believe all those great things you said about me. I do so appreciate all your support." Jolene's now moist eyes found Donnie. "Both of you."

"Hey, I got a great idea. Why don't we go out and celebrate tonight?" Will asked.

Donnie shook his head. "I can't tonight. My son's got baseball practice and I'm helping out the new coach."

Jolene smiled sheepishly. "And I told Cheryl I'd come over for dinner tonight."

"In that case," Donnie interrupted. "You should take off early today. You've certainly earned it."

"For what? Smiling for the camera?" she joked.

"No. For doing an outstanding job for the agency," Donnie answered. "Marcy said the phone has been ringing off the hook all morning."

Anything more than two calls is 'ringing off the hook' for that girl. Jolene looked toward the corner of the room at Marcy's empty desk. It was ten-thirty and Donnie's niece was on her third break of the morning. She had been hired two weeks ago as the new receptionist, but her main responsibility was to open the realty office. Jolene wasn't going to be the one to tell the boss his newest employee had been late almost every morning or that she hid the key under the flower pot by the door.

Driving by Jack and Jill grocery, Jolene remembered Cheryl wanted her to pick up a couple things for her. She readily agreed knowing her sister was now seven months pregnant and very uncomfortable the last few weeks in the heat.

Jolene strolled down the cleaning products aisle and grabbed a bottle of Joy dish soap. An older woman a few feet away did a double take.

"Are you Jolene Garrison, the Realtor?"

Jolene was shocked. "Yes, I am."

"I read about you in the paper. You are as *pretty* as your picture."

Jolene felt herself blush. "Thank you."

A young teller watched Jolene set the bottle of dish soap and can of coffee on the counter before she started to gush. "Oh my gosh! You're the woman that was in the paper this morning!"

Jolene smiled and laid some money on the counter. This small town sure does like its celebrities. *Is that what I am now?*

Dori's car was up by the house at Cheryl's when Jolene drove in the driveway and parked. Taylor and Stevie, Dori's eldest son, were playing catch in the front yard while her younger son, Sam, stood close by and screamed that it was his turn to throw the ball.

Jolene waved to the boys before she knocked on the screen door and went inside the house with her bag of groceries. Seeing no one in the kitchen, she walked through the house and followed voices to the back porch.

Dori looked up when she saw Jolene and exclaimed, "There she is. The future business woman of the year."

Jolene couldn't help but smile and play along. "The sky's the limit now."

"Grab yourself a glass of ice tea in the fridge," Cheryl told her.

When Jolene returned to the porch with her drink, she sat next to Dori on the wicker love seat.

"You're early. What gives?" Cheryl asked.

"Donnie said I could leave early. He said I deserved it for working so hard for the agency." Jolene noticed the paper was lying on the coffee table and opened to her picture. "I see you two have read the article. Tell me what you think."

"It's sure nice to know the *woman in charge*," Dori said and chuckled.

"I thought it was great, but interesting." Cheryl smiled.

"What do you mean?" Jolene quickly asked.

"I know you've been busting your behind, but he made it sound like you are basically running both places."

"Yeah. Will did stretch the truth some. But I think he was as excited as me. I've been working hard and the way I look at it, too much good publicity can't be a bad thing."

"Speaking of good publicity," Cheryl told her, "Jake wanted me to thank you once again for getting the crowd going at the dunk tank. I guess John Kleis said it was the most they'd ever made on ticket sales."

"Tell him it was my pleasure," Jolene said. *Until that witch ruined everything!*

"I still can't believe Michael agreed to do it, but I think it was my husband's plan all along to get one of his brothers to volunteer. Jake said your performance was perfectly executed and he knew Michael was having fun with it, too."

"Did Michael bring Diana?" Dori asked.

The sisters glanced at one another. "Yes. He did," Jolene slowly answered.

Dori's suspicious eyes flitted back and forth to each woman. "Okay, ladies. Anyone care to tell me what happened?"

Dori's mouth hung open after Jolene told her the story. "She actually slapped your face?"

Jolene nodded. "She sure took me by surprise. I really hadn't expected it from her."

"This must be something new for Diana. In high school she never had to worry about other girls because Michael only had eyes for her." Dori shook her head. "She must view you as some sort of a threat."

"A threat? Why do you think that?" Jolene asked.

"Oh come on, Jolene." Dori shook her head. "Michael couldn't keep his eyes off you at the wedding."

"That was over two months ago and during the meantime the love of his life returned."

"Okay, Miss Quiet Thing sitting in the chair," Dori turned her attention to Cheryl. "What does your husband think? I know you two must have discussed this before."

Cheryl sighed. "I don't know if Jake would want me to say."

"Come on, Cheryl. This is your sister we're talking about here," Dori coaxed.

"Okay ..." Concern grew on her face. "This is just Jake's opinion, not mine. He believes Michael has turned his life around."

"And what about Jolene?" Dori sounded anxious.

"He thinks Michael's really trying to work it out with Diana but he's ..." she paused and stared at her sister, "really in love with you."

Jolene felt her insides turn to Jell-O before the words shot out of her mouth. "There's — no way — he feels that way!" Her eyes stayed on Cheryl. "You saw how he held Diana and escorted her away yesterday. I'll bet you both she told him what happened in the fellowship hall. And you better believe he's going to chew my ass about it tomorrow. Oh crap! With everything going on today, I forgot all about showing him around tomorrow!"

Dori crossed her arms. "I wouldn't worry about him chewing you out."

"What do you mean?" Jolene asked.

"Diana isn't going to say anything to him about what happened." Dori slowly shook her head. "What would she say? 'I accused your Realtor of giving you the eye and she straightened me out by saying it was you who has the wandering eye?'"

Jolene smirked at Dori's speculation. "Having learned firsthand how she really is, I wouldn't put it past her to tell him it was my fault somehow."

"Well. I'm not saying that couldn't happen, but I can guarantee she didn't tell him the truth about what was said." Dori sat back on the love seat.

Questions burned inside Jolene's head. Normally, she would value Jake's opinion, but not on this. He had to be either naïve or insane to believe the man who tried to break him and his wife up had actually changed. And even if he was right, and Michael was still in love with her, what difference would it make? Could she ever forgive or trust him for using her in his plot to break up Cheryl and Jake?

"Anyone ready for some more tea?" Jolene stood.

She took a long, deep breath in the kitchen. *Could Michael still be in love with me?* Jolene dropped more ice cubes in each glass and thought about the first time he said he loved her.

It was after she and Brett had gone out on New Year's Eve and Michael found out. At the time, she wondered why it upset him, because their relationship was supposed to be a sex-with-no ties arrangement. Michael did cool down learning it was a platonic date, but the excitement from the ordeal had sparked some great make-up sex. The details of that day suddenly popped into her mind ...

Bang, bang, bang!

Jolene's head sprung up from the bed.

"What the hell was that?" Michael demanded.

They heard another series of loud hammering before she exclaimed, "Someone's at the door!"

"It better not be my brother or I'm going to kill him."

"I'll go see who it is." She threw on her robe before she left the room.

She glanced out the window in the kitchen and almost passed out seeing her ex's car parked in the driveway. In a panic, she ran back into the bedroom.

It's Robert!" she shouted.

"Who?"

"My husband, Robert. Just stay in here and I'll see what he wants."

Jolene hurried into the kitchen but stopped to pull her robe closer around her neck and tightened the sash before she opened the door.

"What are you doing here?" She asked through the screen door.

"You're still in your bathrobe at this hour? I heard you were devastated, but I didn't think you were the type to fall apart."

"What do you want?" she asked.

"I want you to sign these divorce papers." He held up a manila envelope. "Are you going to let me in? It's cold out here."

"No. And I'm not going to make it easy for you and her to be together. I'll sign them when I'm good and ready."

"You'll sign them or I'll take that car sitting in the driveway."

"You wouldn't dare!"

"Wouldn't I? I found your extra set of keys in the safe. And I brought one of the interns to drive it home in case you decided to be difficult."

She looked out and saw the same young man who delivered her divorce papers weeks earlier, sitting in his car. "Don't touch my car!" she shouted. *How can you be like this after everything we've been through together?*

"Who's going to stop me?" Robert sneered.

"I will," Michael said calmly and stood next to her. His shirt was unbuttoned and hung open.

Robert pulled his head back from the screen, but was arrogant enough to ask, "And who the hell are you?" His eyes stayed on Michael's toned abs before they took inventory of his height and broad shoulders.

"I'm the one who's with your wife now. It's sure nice to meet the fool who let her go. Thank you, by the way."

"Stay out of this, wise guy. This has *nothing* to do with you ..."

"Michael Cameron," he answered and put his arm around Jolene.

"Well, then Michael, like I was saying, this is nothing that concerns you. If you lay one hand on me, I'll sue you so fast your head will spin." He had a smug smile.

"Well, Bob, if you touch that car, I'm going to rip your arms off, and then I guess you can go ahead and do whatever you want after that."

"The name's, *Robert*, and *why* are you involving yourself in our personal affairs?" The contempt in his voice was confirmed by the narrowing of his eyes.

"Because you're an asshole who's threatening the woman I love."

Oh my God. I love you, too. She stared at Michael. *You're my knight in shining armor!*

Robert's mouth gaped but he immediately collected himself.

"I'm leaving these papers on the porch. And when you come to your senses, Jolene, sign them and drop them in the mail. So, we — " he looked at Michael, "all can get on with our lives." Robert left the porch in a hurry and hopped into his green Mercury Grand Marquis. He quickly backed his car but took a moment to glower at her and Michael before he stepped on the gas to go forward. He displayed some sort of temper tantrum when he spun the tires in the snow on the way out of the driveway.

"I think he really believed what you said." Jolene laughed.

"Why wouldn't he? I meant it."

"Even the part about me being the woman you love?" Her heart pounded wildly while she waited for his answer.

"You're going to make me say it again, aren't you?"

"Oh, yes. I am."

"Okay … I love you, Jolene Avery," he told her.

She reached her arms around him and looked up into his eyes. "I love you too, Michael Cameron …"

"What are you doing in there?" Cheryl's voice snapped Jolene back into reality.

"Coming!" Jolene hollered back from the kitchen. "I'm filling the ice trays."

It would be interesting to see if Michael showed up tomorrow. If Diana had told him the truth about what happened there was no way she would allow him to continue to retain her as his real estate agent.

PULLING off his coveralls in a hurry, Michael left the shed seconds after chores. He rushed to the house knowing he had exactly forty-five minutes to clean up and be in Montevideo to meet Jolene. In less than twenty, he had showered and shaved and was dressed in a short-sleeved blue shirt with dark blue jeans. Irene handed him a Thermos filled with ice water and he was out the door. Earlier, he heard the weather man say it was going to be the second hottest day of the year and he wanted to be prepared for a long day in a hot car. He speeded most of the way to Montevideo and stepped through the door at Larsen's at five minutes past nine o'clock.

Jolene looked up at him in surprise. "Oh there you are. I thought maybe you changed your mind about today."

He shook his head. "Not even the heat could keep me away."

"Oh yeah. I heard it's going to be a hot one today." She stood from her desk and his eyes traveled over her white long sleeved shirt and mint green skirt.

When he noticed she'd worn the bustier, he chuckled inside thinking her long sleeves protected her arms from sunburn and the bustier shielded her breasts from ogling men. *I guess a gal can never be too careful.*

"I'm hoping to find you something today that both you and your fiancée will like." She stretched her neck and looked around him at the door. "Will she be joining us today?"

He cautioned himself to keep his temper in check. "If you're referring to my girlfriend, no, she won't be joining us."

"Oh, sorry. My mistake." She grabbed her purse and satchel. "Okay then, shall we?" He nodded with a smile and held the door open for her.

Outside, he got his Thermos from his truck and jumped into the passenger seat of her car.

"What's in the Thermos?" she asked.

"Just some ice water if we need it."

"You *are* prepared for the day."

"Yeah. I guess I am," he answered.

They had looked at two farms a few miles out of Montevideo and he pretended to find things about each that didn't suit his needs. They drove a few miles northwest of Watson when she pulled into a long dirt driveway that led to a farmstead tucked into a grove of mature cottonwood and evergreen trees.

Jolene parked her car in front of the house. "As you can see by the sign when we drove in, this is one of our listings. The property has one hundred and twenty acres of land and the homestead is listed as well-maintained."

Large elm and overhanging willow trees framed a tannish-colored brick farmhouse. The trim around the windows of the two story was painted bright red and the yard was enclosed by a white picket fence.

Michael got out of the car and immediately felt the coolness of the shaded yard and noticed how lush and green everything appeared. It sure wasn't something he expected to see during a drought year. There were places on the fence where thick ivy vines grew over and climbed onto the brick walls of the house. They opened the gate and walked through an arched wooden trellis covered with purple clematis.

"This is *so* pretty. Does Diana like flowers?"

He shrugged. "I really can't tell you."

She cocked her head seeming to be surprised by his answer, but continued to the house.

His eyes were drawn to the bright yellow and purple pansies that filled the flower boxes beneath the arched windows as they neared the front door. It, too, was arched and painted red with a small stained-glass window in an ivy pattern toward the top of the door.

Michael guessed the floor was some type of granite when they stepped inside the nice sized foyer. A built in wooden bench sat against one wall and a long closet filled the wall on the opposite side.

Jolene sucked in a breath when she saw the spacious living room with a cozy sunken area around a magnificent brick fireplace on the far wall. "Donnie told me the elderly couple who lived here built this place. The man farmed some, but was a brick layer. I guess their son comes here almost every day to take care of the flowers."

Michael nodded in understanding. "I figured by the amount of brick, it had to be someone in the masonry business who built it."

"There is so much detail in everything." She pointed to the wooden book shelves built into the wall. He noticed her gape when they reached the kitchen. It was all brick on one side of the room where a stove, sink and refrigerator sat. On the other side of the room there was a breakfast nook with a small built in table. The quaint space was filled with bright sunlight from the windows surrounding it on three sides. To the left was a dining room with a long maple table and chairs for six people.

"I wonder why they left the table and chairs?" she asked running her hand over the smooth looking tabletop.

"I would say it was built to fit this dining room," he said, and flipped on a switch. A chandelier made of metal ivy leaves lit the room and they saw the built-in wine rack in the dining room wall.

She rushed over to it. "Oh, Michael. This place is perfect." Her green eyes were lit with excitement and he remembered they got that way whenever they made love.

He instantly shook that thought and blurted, "Close to it, so far, but I like a bathroom off the kitchen like we got at home."

Jolene went back into the kitchen and opened a door next to an outside door. Inside was an enormous pantry with several shelves.

"You could easily remodel half of this into a bathroom with a sink and stool and perhaps even a smaller shower," she told him.

Damn it! She's right! He nodded.

There was another door and she opened it. "Stairs. This must go to the cellar."

He stood next to her. "Let's check it out." When she didn't move he smiled and asked, "Are you afraid of the dark?"

"No. I'm wearing heels and I just don't want to fall on those small stairs."

"I'll go first and you can take my hand. I'll catch you like I did in the barn at Sorenson's."

She smiled and it appeared sincere. "Thank you, by the way."

He smiled back but quickly said, "You know the Sorenson farm was in the family for five or six generations."

"You can't help someone who won't let you. Will said Mr. Sorenson refused any help from the bank."

"That's really strange. Olaf Sorenson told people the bank in Watson didn't offer to help him in any way."

She shrugged and waved her hand. "After you."

He pulled a chain on his left and a light went on above them. When he took her hand, her green eyes shot to his, but then she looked down at her feet. Cool air came up to greet them as they carefully made their way down the cement steps to the bottom. Michael was surprised to see the floor was also cement and things were cleaned up well. One side of the room was lined with shelves where canned goods had likely been stored.

"Wow!" she exclaimed. "It's so neat and tidy down here. I was expecting lots of cobwebs and maybe a few dead frogs."

He busted out laughing. "Yeah, I guess you never know what to expect in some of these houses." It was then he noticed their hands were still joined. She nervously glanced at him out of the corner of her eye and casually pulled her hand away.

"We didn't tour the upstairs yet. Shall we continue?" He thought she was blushing when she abruptly turned and headed for the stairs. He followed her closely watching her sexy backside sway back and forth as she climbed the steps in front of him. Suddenly he felt himself get aroused. *Oh God, no!*

They went through the kitchen and living room but she stopped by the staircase going up to the second level of the house. "I'll follow you."

He smiled and wondered if she saw him looking at her.

At the top of the stairs, rays from the sun gleamed from the window at the end of the hallway onto the shiny wooden floor. There were two smaller bedrooms on one side of the hall and a bathroom and the master bedroom on the other.

The first bedroom was painted blue and Michael was surprised to see a set of wooden bunk beds along the wall. They looked very heavy, too large to get out of the small bedroom door.

"More furniture. I should tell Donnie we need to list this place as partially furnished."

"I think those were made or put together right in this room," he said. "There's no way someone could get the beds out the door unless they took them apart."

"This would be a great room for two boys." She opened the closet door. "I've seen firsthand how good your fiancée," she put her hand to her mouth. "Sorry. I mean, *girlfriend*, is with chil-dren. I can envision a set of twin boys sharing this room."

His head swung to her. *What the hell?*

Smiling, she went out of the room and he trailed her into the next bedroom. The room was painted a sunny yellow with a large walk-in closet.

"And this is definitely a girl's bedroom or maybe a nursery." She grinned. "It's large enough for two girls don't you think?"

"Why are you talking about filling the rooms with children?"

"I heard Diana say at Cheryl's baby shower she's planning on having a houseful of children in the future. I thought it an important selling point."

He shook his head. "That sounds like Diana." Not wanting to continue discussing his girlfriend, he went across the hall and stuck his head in the doorway of the bathroom. "You gotta see this tub," he hollered to her, but she was right behind him.

"Oh, wow!" she exclaimed over his shoulder at the claw-footed brass tub. "You could get two people in there."

He turned his head and smiled at her.

"Or four children," she quickly added before moving on to the master bedroom.

When he heard her catch her breath again, he went to see what surprise the master bedroom had to offer. Instantly, he was taken aback at the large hand carved bed under a row of three small stained glass windows. The sun reflected through the glass and cast flecks of violet, green and gold light through the bare bed springs and onto the well-polished wood floor.

"Isn't it just beautiful?" she exclaimed with her hands pressed to her chest.

It is! He didn't respond knowing it would give away how much he liked the place.

They went out a set of French doors downstairs and continued their tour in the backyard. Michael took note of the swinging lawn chair made for two sitting on the brick patio and the tire swing that hung from one of the tall elm trees shading a large portion of the lawn. He had to agree with his Realtor. This place had a profound family atmosphere.

There was a paved walkway going from the backyard through a row of hedges to a remarkably clean tool shed. The building was perfect in size but he pretended it was too small. If she knew he thought the place was extraordinary, she would expect him to make an offer. He had to maximize their time together.

"I was thinking of raising a few beef cattle and maybe a couple of horses." He scanned the shed and surrounding area. "I don't think this property will work for that."

"So, is it on to the next place?" she asked. "If you want to keep viewing places in this heat, I'm willing to keep going."

"Yes. I'm rather anxious to find a place," he said pretending to be enthusiastic about their search.

Hours later, they finished viewing three more properties and Michael didn't have to fake his dislike for them. Most had aging buildings that hadn't been kept up or only a small amount of acreage. The last farm of the day had been twenty miles off the main road on a back road that didn't get much traffic.

A mile or so down the deserted road, she started a conversation about the bazaar.

"Did you and Diana enjoy the bazaar?" she asked and glanced at him in the passenger seat.

"Yes we did, until she became ill from the heat."

"Oh? I wondered what the problem was. I saw you two leave in a hurry."

"Yes. It must have been like an oven in that fellowship hall."

When she didn't comment any further, he decided to test the water on another subject.

"I read the article about you in the newspaper. I wonder how they knew you were down at the bazaar?"

"I can thank Will for that. Will recognized Steve Livingston at the bazaar and told him all about me — a woman in the working world."

"Is that what Will told you?"

"Yes." She scrunched her brows. "Why would I doubt him?"

"I know you trust Will and aren't going to believe me, but I heard him on the phone when I went to change my clothes in the fellowship hall. He was talking to someone about getting the press there so the whole community could meet 'the woman in charge.'"

"That's a lie, Michael, and you know it," she said, with her eyes flashing.

"All I know is what I heard. If you don't believe me why don't you call up that Livingston guy and ask him?"

She sucked in a disgusted breath. "You better believe I'm going to."

"And when you do it, don't tip Will off or he'll have another lie prepared."

"You just can't accept the fact I'm doing a good job and that I'm working for a decent man." Her eyes narrowed. "The thing I think is really crappy is the way you act like Will's friend and yet you talk behind his back. You're nothing but a hypocrite."

"I'm not sure what kind of guy Will is. But I do think he's up to something."

He put his hand over the vent in front of him. The air conditioner was barely keeping up and the rising temperature gauge on the dash showed the car was starting to overheat.

"You might want to shut the air off. It looks like your temperature gauge is rising."

"What?" She looked down and groaned and switched off the air. "Oh, great. It was going to be a long drive and now without air conditioning it's going to be pure hell."

Knowing he had pushed her far enough, Michael gazed out at the parched fields as they drove past. Another quarter mile down the road, the car made a strange noise.

"Damn it. I got no power!" Jolene yelled and steered the car to the side of the road. Steam was puffing out from under the hood when she shut off the vehicle. They both got out and she swiftly went to the front of the car and reached down in front of the hood.

"Don't touch it!" he shouted and pulled her away from the car.

"What do you think you're doing?" She twisted out of his grip.

"You've got to let it cool down first or you'll get burned."

She stood back and crossed her arms in front of her. "And how long is that going to take?"

"I don't know," he said and got his thermos from the backseat. "Just give it a little while." He unscrewed the cup on the Thermos and poured some water in it. He took a big swallow and then offered it to her. "Want some?"

"No, thank you." Her voice bordered on sarcastic.

He saw her cheeks were bright pink and a line of sweat was running down the side of her face. "Suit yourself." *Crazy woman!*

She sat inside the scorching hot car with the driver's door open while he looked around for some kind of shade. Seeing nothing but fields around them, he decided to see if the car had cooled enough and pressed the hood latch. He threw open the hood and pulled back when a fair amount of steam rolled out into the air. He'd have to give it a while before he opened the radiator cap. Stepping away from the heat of the engine, his attention was drawn to Jolene in the car. Her head was hanging down and it appeared she was having difficulty breathing.

"Jolene!" He rushed to her side. "What's wrong?"

"I'm okay. I'm just finding it a little … hard to breathe … that's all."

Michael got the thermos from the backseat. "Here take a drink."

His right hand pressed her back when he brought the cup to her lips. She took a small sip, but gasped afterwards.

"Do you have asthma or something?" he urgently asked.

She shook her head no.

"Then what is it?" he stared at her.

"Help me out of this car and … turn around."

He looked at her strangely but did what she said. When he heard her fall against the car he turned to see she had her blouse undone.

That damn bra! "That thing is squeezing you to death!" He plunged his hand in his jean pocket for his knife. "Here! Let me cut it off you."

"No," she panted. "It cost … twenty … dollars."

"Then tell me how to get it off you!"

"H … hooks." She started reaching for the front of the bra.

Pushing her hands aside, he fumbled with a set of six small hooks but managed to get them unfastened. When the garment fell to the sides of her breasts, he couldn't help but stare. *Oh sweet, lord!* She pulled her white blouse around herself and sank down onto the driver's seat. When he gave her the cup of water this time she was able to drink and breathe at the same time.

"Take a good drink," he said. "As soon as that radiator is cool enough we're going to pour what's left in the thermos into it." She nodded and he went to the front of the car.

Taking a folded blue bandana handkerchief out of his back pocket, he used it to protect his hand when he opened the radiator cap. He was relieved to see only a minimal amount of steam erupt and a small amount of water boil out the opening. *It must be cooling down.*

"How are you doing?" Michael asked after he returned to her. He gently rubbed her back and then caught himself and dropped his hand.

"Just fine now." Her eyes flicked to his. "Do you think you can get my car running?"

"I think if we give it a little while, we could try starting it. If we don't cool it down enough before pouring cold water in the radiator, it could crack your engine block."

A half hour later, he slowly started to add the water to the radiator. Within a few minutes she turned the key and the engine fired up. He smiled at her in the driver's seat after he shut the hood and she flashed a triumphant smile back.

They drove for a few miles when she broke the silence. "You're not going to tell anyone about what happened back there?"

"You have my word. I won't."

"Thank you. I appreciate it." She glanced at him. "If you wouldn't have gotten me so worked up about Will, I probably wouldn't have had that attack." She was quiet for a few moments. "Whatever happened between you two needs to be left in the past."

"I don't have a personal vendetta against Will. All I have is a feeling in my gut something isn't right. You've got to trust me on this. I know you're dedicated to Will and Donnie, but you need to keep your eyes and ears open to protect yourself."

"You're the last person who should speak about trust."

"I know I deserved that comment." He looked down at the floor and then over at her. "But I'm not that person anymore."

Her eyes briefly met his. "Do you want to know what I think?"

"Sure, tell me."

"I think you're not as happy with your relationship with Diana as you pretend to be." She stared out at the road ahead. "And for some reason you can't stand to see me, or a wonderful man like Will, succeed." She slowly wagged her head. "It sounds like jealousy to me."

He took a deep breath to hold back his anger. It irritated him that she of all people had figured out that things between him and Diana were strained. He then recalled Will's conversation on the phone in the fellowship hall. *Could I be wrong and he called the press only to boost Jolene's confidence?*

17

Michael's truck was the only vehicle parked in front of Larsen's Realty when Jolene pulled up to the front of the building. She waited for what seemed an eternity for him to get out of her car. It was obvious he was taking his time when he finally reached into the back seat for the empty thermos.

His hand was on the door handle when he said, "I'd like to resume our search for land."

"Is that what you're calling it?"

He cocked his head. "What do you mean?"

She gazed at him unblinking. "Do you think I'm stupid?"

He cocked his head. "I don't think you're stupid. Why are you asking me something like that?"

"Because every parcel we look at you seem to have a problem with. And you don't waste an opportunity to talk about the fore-closures or how devious the men are that I'm working for."

"I'm just a little particular, that's all. I thought seeing how you were the one who sold the land, you'd be interested in the history of it."

"Until you can narrow your search, I'll no longer be your agent."

"Okay. Fair enough. I'll try and figure out what I'm looking for." He opened the door and stepped out of the car. "And if I were you, I'd get this car to a mechanic. It shouldn't have over heated like it did. Try Joe's in Montevideo."

"Thanks. I'll do that."

The door had barely shut behind him when she threw her car into reverse and stepped hard on the gas. *It's bad enough he saw my breasts, now he thinks I'm incapable of maintaining a car.*

Later in the shower at her apartment, Jolene's thoughts drifted to the brick layer's charming house. That visit had been like a dream. It was like she and Michael were a couple viewing the place for themselves. She remembered how her stomach fluttered when he took her hand and held it as they descended all the way down the cellar steps. Her heart pounded recalling the playful grin on his face after her comment that two people could share the tub. But without a doubt, the most memorable image of the day was the terror in his big eyes when she couldn't catch her breath. Was it her imagination how he lovingly rubbed her back? *Don't be an idiot and think it was something. It wasn't!*

Maybe she had been influenced by Cheryl's comment that Jake believed Michael was in love with her. The Rat had often stated that the power of suggestion was huge in a jury case. Was there some kind of subconscious reason behind the comments she made regarding Diana? Some had been justified, but telling Michael he and Diana weren't happy had crossed the line. *What was I thinking?* Even if she thought Diana was pushing him into something, what did it matter to her?

It had cooled off some when Jolene stepped out onto the patio and lit a cigarette. She needed to stop thinking about Michael and figure out how to get her car to the mechanic and still get to work in the morning. It would be ideal to drop off the car first thing at the repair shop before it opened. Knowing Cheryl wasn't doing chores anymore, perhaps she could meet at Joe's and give her a ride to work.

When she heard voices and a door shut at the neighbors, an

idea struck. Why make her very pregnant sister drive out when maybe she could get her neighbor, Lyla, to give her a lift to the gas station a few minutes away?

Jolene went back into her apartment and dressed in a pair of blue gingham pedal pushers and a sleeveless white blouse. She made her way down the sidewalk to her neighbor's door and knocked. It was only a few seconds before the door opened and a man stood holding Lyla's baby in his arms.

"Jim?" Jolene blinked a few times seeing Jim Stanton. *What the heck?* "What are you doing here?"

"I ... um ... live here," he answered. "I guess you've met my son." He wiggled the baby's arm to make him wave.

Lyla poked her head around Jim's shoulder. Her brown eyes popped open. "Jolene!"

"So you're Mrs. Stanton?" Jolene asked more as a statement than a question.

"Y... Yes," Lyla finally got out. "I was going to say something but you never ..."

"It's so nice to make your *honest* acquaintance," Jolene interrupted. "I must be going. Good evening." She started to walk away, but stopped and turned back. "Oh, and do say 'hi' to Michael for me."

THE AIR HAD COOLED some but the sun was still high above the horizon when Brett pulled his truck and trailer down a deserted field road and parked by a row of trees. He took a deep breath and told himself to be cool. He didn't want to blow things with Karyn. She was funny and attractive and the first girl he'd met in a long time who held his interest. It had shocked him earlier to hear her voice on the line when Irene told him he had a phone call. He never expected Karyn would keep her word and actually call. They made a plan to rendezvous at seven o'clock to go horseback riding.

He saw a line of dust rising behind a moving vehicle on the road to his left but he wasn't sure what Karyn drove. Seeing an orange hatchback slow down as it approached, he knew it had to be her and got out of his truck.

"Hey," she said and slammed the car door behind her.

She looks so good! His eyes went to the bright yellow halter top tied around her neck and waist. He was happy to see she had been smart enough to wear jeans. Riding a horse with shorts on wasn't a smart idea, especially in the heat.

"I can't believe you're really here," he blurted without thinking. "I mean, I'm glad you followed through and came."

"Of course. Why would I change my mind?"

"I don't know. Maybe because your family hates me?"

"Don't worry about them. My parents are at a church meeting and my brother went out with some neighbor kids." She smiled but it quickly fell. "I hope you didn't mention to anyone we're going riding."

"Nope. Not a soul." He grinned. "It's our little secret. Shall we get started?"

She followed him to the back of the trailer where he put the ramp down and a horse stepped out.

"He's beautiful!" Karyn exclaimed and rushed over to the animal. "Hey, boy." She hung on to his halter and petted his nose. "What's his name?"

"Eddy," Brett answered and led his second horse down the ramp.

"You are such a handsome fellow, aren't you Eddy?" She continued to stroke the horse.

"This one's name is Milo. He's a bit of a free spirit. So I'll ride him."

In no time they were headed down the edge of the field talking and laughing about what happened with her brother and grandmother at the bazaar.

"I didn't want to make a scene, otherwise I would have told my brother where to stick his temper."

Brett busted out laughing at her comment. She had a fun personality and was easy to talk to. As they rode he could see the sun reflect in her big brown eyes, and he lost himself for a moment. *God, she's pretty!* He pulled his eyes away and cautioned himself to be careful. *Slow the truck down!*

"I think we better stop and let these horses get a drink," he told her when they reached the river. They dismounted and he retrieved a canteen of water for them from his saddle bag.

While the horses drank from the river, Brett and Karyn stepped over to some knee high rocks next to the water and sat down. He looked down the river and noticed how the setting sun shimmered on the moving water like a blanket of diamonds. It was a nice evening and he was sitting close to a beautiful girl. What more could a guy ask for?

When she leaned over and kissed him, he knew the answer to his question.

He returned her kiss but pulled his head back seconds later in disbelief.

A big smile was on her face. "I've wanted to do that ever since I saw you at Trailways."

His mouth fell open. "You can't be serious. You stuck me with the bill."

"Yeah, I did." She looked down for a second. "But it was after I found out you were a Cameron."

He sighed. "That name used to command respect. Now I'm almost afraid to go out by myself at night. But you wait. It will all come out in the end that my family had nothing to do with the foreclosures at the bank."

"For some strange reason, I believe you," she said. "But until that day, I would really like to keep whatever we've got going on a secret."

"I give you my word. There's no way I will tell anyone." He kissed her sweet lips again but this time in a more thorough, passionate way to reinforce his vow of secrecy.

It was getting dark when they got back to their vehicles.

Karyn shone her car headlights on the trailer while Brett quickly loaded the horses. He slammed the door of the trailer and went to her open driver's window.

"There's going to be another AOG meeting on Thursday evening. I'm hoping it will shed some light on what's going on with folks in the area. It would be great if you and I could go on a real date."

She smiled. "Don't sell yourself short. I had a fun time tonight."

Yes! "Me too."

"See you on Monday night? Same time?" she asked.

"Hell or high water couldn't keep me away." He dipped his head and their lips met for a heated, unhurried goodbye kiss.

"Good night." She waved and drove away with a satisfied smile on her face.

Brett got into his truck feeling incredibly fortunate to have met a girl like Karyn who wasn't afraid to be herself. Hearing she believed him about his family and the foreclosures was like winning a million dollars. Nearing home, he relived that first kiss. He couldn't ever remember kissing a girl who had excited him so much and eased his mind at the same time.

SHORTLY AFTER BREAKFAST Michael went to the shed to do a feed inventory. He located his clip board and a pen and headed for the barn. Seconds later, he heard someone come in the barn door and saw Jake walk toward him.

"Can I have a word with you?"

"Sure. What do you have on your mind?" Michael asked without looking up.

"What the hell are you thinking, spying on Jolene?"

"What are you talking about?" Michael lowered the clipboard.

Jake put his hands on his hips. "She called Cheryl last night, upset. I guess she went over to her neighbor's apartment and found out her new friend, Lyla, is Jim Stanton's wife. No one is stupid enough to think that's just a coincidence."

Shit! "I had nothing to do with that."

"Oh come on. You and Jim were constantly spying on Cheryl last year. Why should I believe you aren't doing the same thing with Jolene?" Jake's eyes flashed.

"Look. I knew about it, but I never asked Jim to put her in that apartment. He came up with it on his own. If you don't believe me, just ask him."

"And here I thought you were really changing."

Michael felt a quick jab in his chest. "I have changed. You've got to believe me!"

"Cheryl told Jolene to dismiss you as a client. She's worried you may go off the deep end and attack her."

"So, Cheryl told Jolene what I did?" *Oh, God please no!*

"No, she didn't." Jake's eyes bored into his. "But she wanted to."

"Please, Jake. You have to believe me. The only reason I asked her to be my Realtor is to figure out what's going on with the foreclosures."

"Damn it, Michael." Jake shook his head. "Why can't you be truthful about anything?"

He's right! "Okay. I'm going to be completely honest," he paused and took a deep breath. "I'm in love with Jolene." *Oh Lord, I said it out loud!*

Jake gave him an approving smile. "It's about time you admitted it. Do you think she feels the same way about you?"

"I don't know, but it doesn't stop me from wanting to protect her. I really think Will and Donnie are going to end up hurting her somehow."

"Do I have your word you're not spying on Jolene because you're jealous of her and Will working together?" Jake crossed his arms.

"I'd be lying if I told you it didn't bug the hell out of me. But

I'm telling you the truth. I'm not using Jim or his wife to spy on her. Just give me some time and I'll prove it to you."

"My wife's going to kick me in the ass, but for some odd reason — I believe you." Jake's eyes stayed on him. "Now, what are you going to do about Diana?"

"I really don't know." Michael looked down at the floor. "But until I do, can you please keep this conversation to yourself? And I mean completely to yourself, and not a word to your wife?"

"You got it." Jake smiled. "Believe it or not, I once was in a similar situation."

It looked like every member from the AOG was in attendance when the Cameron family stepped inside the Montevideo Community Building. When the room went instantly silent, Michael noticed the disgusted stares and the low whispering from some of the farmers. He knew it wasn't going to be a pleasant situation but this was worse than expected. What was once a group of people who stood together to help one another had turned into a jealous, vengeful mob.

Chet took his place in the front of the room with the four other board members. All eyes were on the group as they leaned toward each other. Michael watched his father nod in agreement and soon after John Klies stood from his chair.

"We the officers of the board agree," John's eyes went to Chet, "that I will be acting chairman this evening, so I bring this meeting to order." He banged the gavel on the table. "We have three very important items on the agenda tonight. The first will be to establish if any of the accusations that have been directed at the Cameron Corporation are warranted. The second will be if Chet Cameron is to remain or be removed from the board." A cheer came from the back of the room and John banged the gavel once again. "This is to be a fair and unbiased procedure so if everyone would please refrain from any outbursts. The third item on the agenda will be to vote in a new chairman if it's found necessary. Two members of the AOG whose farms have gone into foreclosure will be testifying and Chet Cameron will speak on his own behalf."

The first man to testify was Olaf Sorenson. The old man's eyes slowly combed over Lucille and the boys in the first row before they focused on Chet, before he sat in a chair in the front of the room.

"I've always been in support of the refinery fund," Olaf stated. "But when we needed more money to get started on the project, Chet Cameron urged me and everyone else to donate more. He said he was going to do the same and he did. I guess it didn't dawn on me that Chet had the money to do so, but I didn't. I went ahead and donated more after Chet assured me we would all get our money back soon. When his kid went to the capital and couldn't get our money back, things took a tumble downhill for me. The bank offered no help and I couldn't keep up on my bills," he said, then sucked in a painful breath, "and I lost my farm. I wouldn't have blamed Chet or his kid if the man at the bank hadn't brought it to my attention that there had to be a rat in the wood pile." A bout of whispering simmered from the crowd.

John Klies immediately hit the gavel on the table twice. "Let's keep order here." He turned to Olaf. "Who was the man at the bank and what did he tell you?"

"It was the banker's kid. Will."

Michael felt his blood pressure rise hearing Will's name. His brothers and mother instantly made eye contact with each other.

Olaf continued, "He didn't exactly say Chet set us all up. He said we should be paying attention to whoever convinced us to put our necks out in the first place. He told me that person, or persons, are likely getting paid off by someone. Then I find out my farm was sold to one of those big corporate farmers, Paul

Bradford." The room erupted with gasps and the crowd was immediately calmed by the gavel of the acting chairman.

That's impossible! I was there. Jolene sold it to Larry Edwards!

John turned to Chet. "Chet, this is your opportunity to question Olaf."

Chet cleared his throat. "Olaf, why didn't the bank offer to help you?"

"The kid claimed his hands were tied. He said the bank hired a woman to be in charge of both the foreclosures and selling the properties and it wasn't her policy to give anyone help." Olaf narrowed his eyes at Chet. "I found out that woman is related to you, Chet."

Oh God. Jolene! Was she set up or a part of Will and Donnie's scheme?

Chet's face turned pale when blaring conversation exploded all around and someone in the back shouted, "Kick that asshole out of the AOG!"

This time John Klies motioned to two farmers and they went to the back of the room in an effort to keep order.

When most in the room had calmed down, Olaf was dismissed and John called Lloyd Jensen Senior to testify.

Michael was surprised to see Lloyd appeared to be sober. He looked shaven and wore a clean shirt with jeans. Soon into his testimony, he affirmed Olaf's statement that Will had said basically the same thing to him.

"Do you know who purchased your farm?" John asked when Lloyd finished speaking.

"I sure do. I checked at the title company yesterday. It was that same fellow who bought Olaf's place — Paul Bradford."

The room came alive with loud chatter.

What the hell? Michael started to breathe hard. *Will said it was Paul Hansen!*

Chet's eyes met Michael's and he knew his father was thinking the same thing he was — Will had told a bold faced lie!

"Chet, do you have any questions for Lloyd?" John asked after his gavel hit the table and the crowd quieted.

"No, I do not, but I would like to address the members."

John nodded and Chet stood and took a long labored breath before he spoke. "I've always been a believer if a man thinks he's been wronged he best say something, so I cannot take offense to what Lloyd or Olaf have said here tonight. They are good men who felt they got the short end of the stick. I agree they both deserved better than what they got. The only thing I had hoped for tonight was for them and the rest of the members of the AOG to see through the gossip and hearsay and get to the truth of this situation." He paused and scanned the group in front of him. "But it doesn't look like it's going to happen tonight. So I want to set the record straight and say I do not know Mr. Paul Bradford. I have never met the man and everyone here can rest assured I have never done his bidding nor have any intentions of doing so."

"That said, those of you who actually know me, know the success of this group is very important to me. I can't think of anything I want more than what's best for all the hard-working farmers in this room. So if my position of chairman puts a wedge between the members, I will gracefully step down from the board of the Association of Growers. I thank you all for letting me serve you for these past two years." Chet stepped away from the table and took a seat in the first row with his family.

The room fell silent and Michael was in complete awe of his father. He didn't appear to be angry about the accusations. It seemed he was more concerned about his accusers than himself. There was no doubt he was a virtuous man.

John Klies was voted in as chairman minutes later, and the meeting progressed to the business part of the agenda. The stares and whispers had lessoned some during the rest of the meeting but things were far from normal. No one flagged Chet down to talk to him and no one seemed to notice when the Cameron family quietly left with the majority of the members when the meeting adjourned.

It was clear Chet Cameron, a founding member, was no longer the man everyone went to when there was a problem or one of the last to leave the building after a meeting.

18

There wasn't a cloud in the morning sky when Jolene arrived at the realty office. She was amazed when she tried the door and found it unlocked and the lights on in the building. It was astonishing to learn Marcy had actually arrived on time to open the office. Perhaps the girl was finally taking the responsibilities of the job seriously.

Jolene's eyes went to Marcy's desk and didn't see her or smell any aroma in the room from brewing coffee. Assuming she had arrived and was in the restroom, Jolene proceeded to the opposite side of the room and set her satchel and her purse down on her desk. Minutes passed when Jolene gave up on Marcy and decided to make some coffee. She was filling the pot with water from the dispenser when Donnie came out of his office. He had his head down like he was deep in thought but stopped in his tracks when he saw her.

"Oh, you're ... here already?"

Jolene smiled. "Good morning. I got here a few minutes ago. I'm surprised to see you here so early."

"I have a few things to attend to this morning." His eyes nervously moved about the room. "Where's Marcy?"

"I thought she was in the restroom and now I'm thinking she

hasn't arrived yet." She noticed his agitation. "Is there anything I can help you with?"

"No," he said forcefully but then his voice softened, "I'm sorry. Will is going to be here soon. If Marcy ever gets here have her send him in."

"I'll do that," she answered and watched him return to his office.

The outside door suddenly burst open and Marcy raced inside. "Sorry about being late. My car wouldn't start."

A list of Marcy's many excuses went through Jolene's head. *Over slept, road was closed, her friend was sick, her cat got out and ran away ... now her car wouldn't start.*

Marcy's eyebrows scrunched. "How did you get in the building?"

"Your uncle opened up today," Jolene said and tried not to laugh when the girl's mouth dropped open like an old oven door.

"Donnie said when Will gets here, you should send him to his office." Jolene looked out the window and saw Will's blue convertible pull up in front of the building. *I wonder what's going on why they're both here so early in the morning.*

Will came in the door without the usual bounce in his step and immediately headed toward Donnie's office.

He was about to open the door when Jolene cleared her throat and yelled, "Good morning, Will."

His head snapped in her direction and he gave her a quick but somewhat guarded smile. "Good morning." He went inside the office but a short while later poked his head out and held the door open with his hand.

"Jolene. Could we have a word with you?"

"Sure," Jolene stood. Her gut told her something big was going to happen.

"Sit down," Donnie instructed from behind the desk. Will pulled up another chair and sat beside her.

"What's going on?" she asked with growing anticipation.

"Something happened at the AOG meeting last night that impacts us here and at the law office," Will said in a sober voice.

Jolene wondered what the possible connection could be as she waited for him to continue.

"It seems Chet Cameron stepped down as chairman because of some vicious rumors he was involved in purposely setting up some of the AOG members for failure."

"Why would Chet do something like that?"

"I'll just spell it out for you," Will said. "The farmers believe the Cameron Corporation convinced some of the members of the AOG to invest more than they should've in order to set them up in foreclosure. The rumor is ..." He glanced toward Donnie, "Chet and his boys were working together with you in secret in order to sell the land to some big corporate farmer named Paul Bradford."

"That's ridiculous. We all know I did no such thing," Jolene defended herself.

"Yes *we* in this office know but unfortunately the people around here don't. So sadly it looks like we're both going to have to," Will paused and ran his hand through his hair, "lay you off for a while until this all blows over."

"What?" Jolene couldn't believe her ears. "You need to tell everyone I have no connection business-wise with the Cameron family. I think the worst thing I could do is run and hide. I need to stay in the public eye to try and prove my innocence."

"Look, Jolene. The bottom line is that neither Donnie or I can afford any bad publicity right now." He reached for her hand and held it. "You're a wonderful secretary and Realtor. There's no question in either of our minds you were ... and will always be ... the perfect employee for the jobs we gave you. But right now we need to let a little time go by for things to cool down. Think of it as a mini vacation."

"How long are we talking?" she asked.

"I'd say a few weeks, maybe a month." He shrugged and looked at Donnie who nodded.

"We both care a lot about you and we're going to try and compensate your wages at the law office. But don't take it personally if we don't associate with you during the time being. We need to regain the community's trust before we can be seen together in public again."

Too stunned and overwhelmed to know how to respond, Jolene numbly nodded in agreement. *Oh God! How could this happen?*

IT WAS quiet around the breakfast table when the telephone rang in the kitchen of the Sugar King Farm.

Irene pushed open the swinging door. "Jake, you have a phone call."

Jake wiped his mouth with his napkin and went into the kitchen. Lucille decided it was the perfect time to pose the question that had haunted her since leaving the AOG meeting the previous night.

"Doesn't anyone besides me see that Cheryl's sister, is behind all of this?" She asked in a hushed voice. When no one responded she felt her temper spark. "She had to have gotten paid off by that corporate farmer and for whatever reason she decided to rope us in with her."

"I don't think that's true, Mother." Michael finally spoke. Will told me right to my face it was Paul Hansen, not Paul Bradford, who purchased Lloyd Jensen's property. And I was with Jolene when she sold the Sorenson property to a guy named Larry Edwards."

"Did you see this Larry Edwards actually sign the contract? You know whatever you saw could've been all staged."

Jake came into the room. "What is all staged?"

"Michael said he was with your sister-in-law when she sold the Sorenson farm to Larry Edwards, but I think it was staged somehow." Lucille folded her arms and sat back in her chair.

"I don't know but that was Cheryl on the phone." All eyes went to Jake. "Jolene called and was crying hysterically to her because Will and Donnie laid her off. I guess it was on account of all the bad publicity started about her." Jake shook his head. "It seems to me, she wouldn't be all that upset if she were getting paid off somehow."

Michael glared at his mother. "Despite what you think of her, Jolene isn't a dishonest person."

Lucille shook her head. "Why are you boys so easily manipulated when it comes to women?"

"That's enough, Lu. None of us know what really happened," Chet said. "We've just got to have faith and patience that the truth will come out. I agree with Michael that Will is involved, but how does a guy call out his best friend's son without having it all blow up in his face?"

Lucille closed her eyes and thought about Will and his parents, Helen and Charlie. The Camerons and the Vanders had been close friends for at least twenty-five years. She recalled all the things the boys were involved in at school and all the fun dinner parties and traveling they did together with them and Ron and Jean Maland. *Oh, God no!* Would things between them and the Malands change, too? Lucille suddenly felt sick to her stomach wondering how her life would be until this issue was solved. Who would she associate with? Would she be able to show her face in the beauty shop or at the quilting group? *Oh Jake! You have no idea what marrying that woman is going to cost this family.*

CUTTING the engine by the barn, Michael hopped off the tractor and unwound a long reel of hose. He was washing the manure and mud off the box of the front end loader when Jake came out of the barn with a new sprayer head in his hand.

Michael shut off the water valve. "I thought you went home

for supper and Brett was bringing that out."

Jake shrugged. "I guess he had something to do and took off for town a few minutes ago. He said he had something important to check out."

"There's something going on with that kid." Michael shook his head. "Lately he's been taking a lot of drives at night and he's always so vague about where he's going. Part of me is worried about him."

Jake crossed his arms and stared out into the field. "This whole thing just keeps getting uglier. I went into town yesterday with Taylor to get a new filter for the irrigation and Al Swanson and his son were at Meyer's Implement. The kid knows Taylor and he started to say something to him when Al called him to his side. Whatever it was Al told the boy, he refused to talk to Taylor and he stared at me the rest of the time like I was Satan himself."

"I guess all of us are going to have to get used to some shit slinging until the truth is brought to light." Michael started to unscrew the sprayer head but stopped. "How's Jolene doing?"

"Why don't you go over there and find out for yourself?"

"I thought it best to stay away from her for a while until I find out if she's telling the truth. If she's in on this scheme with Will, I can't be around her. I might just wring her neck for bringing our family down with her."

"Cheryl's been over to Jolene's twice trying to talk to her." Jake shook his head. "She still believes it wasn't Will or Donnie's fault."

"Well then, who does she think is to blame?"

"Dad's. For convincing the farmers to invest more money than they could afford. And she honestly believes the title company got things mixed up because she saw Larry Edwards sign the purchase agreement herself."

Michael put his hands on his hips. "Did anyone tell her it's a pretty far-fetched theory to think a title company screwed up?"

"Yeah, Cheryl told her, but Jolene is confused and so panic-stricken about never being able to find a job around here that she's thinking about going back to Aberdeen."

"Don't let her go now. Will and Donnie will blame the whole thing on her and say she got paid off instead of them. Someone needs to tell her that would be playing right into their hands."

"You wanna give it a try? Cheryl said she's thinking about leaving tomorrow."

"I'll get cleaned up and head over there now," Michael said and started to wrap up the hose. "Ah shit! I told Diana I would come over right after dinner." His eyes went to Jake's. "I was going to end it with her tonight."

"Sounds like you've made your decision."

"Yes. And it doesn't have anything to do with my feelings for Jolene." He blew out a breath. "Eight years ago I loved Diana more than I could ever put into words. When she left, I let hurt and anger rule me. It seemed like everyone was out to screw me over and deep down I hated myself. Thank God, therapy made me see I had choices and I chose to forgive her. When she came back, I needed to find out for sure if there was the slightest chance we were still in love with each other. I tried hard to rekindle my feelings for her and found we were only trying to recreate the past. There's nothing left but the memories, and she needs to realize that, too."

"I guess waiting one more night to deal with your past isn't going to make a difference either way," Jake took the hose from Michael's hand. "Right now, you need to worry about your future and the rest of the family's — and make sure Jolene doesn't leave."

WHEN THE PHONE rang in Jolene's apartment for the third time in twenty minutes, she looked at her watch and debated if she should answer. Knowing her mother was supposed to call whenever she got off work, she picked up the receiver.

"Hello."

"Get out of town, traitor!" a cold voice screamed on the other end.

Jolene's heart hammered in her chest when she slammed the phone down on its cradle to disconnect the call. She then picked up the receiver and tossed it down onto her kitchen counter. The dial tone blared as she held her head in her hands and cried. *I just can't believe this is happening!*

The prank phone calls had started two days ago around two-thirty in the morning and she'd left the phone off the hook since. Several times she heard the operator's voice come on and instruct whoever was there to hang up the phone. Jolene would comply until the next phone call then hang up and leave it off the hook afterwards.

She slumped down into a kitchen chair and looked around at her apartment. It had been so much fun searching for things to make this place her home. All the garage sales had given her something to do on the weekends and she ended up meeting a few of her neighbors in the process. It made her sad gazing at the pillows Cheryl had sewn for her. They really looked great with the couch and chairs she got from Barb's folks. Maybe Cheryl would take the pillows and dinette set back, but what was she going to do with the rest of her furniture?

Jolene went back into her bedroom telling herself if she was going to leave in the morning, she better keep packing. She was trying to get all of her shoes into a large box when she heard the doorbell ring and decided not to answer. The last few nights someone had been ringing her door bell in the evenings but each time she looked out the window no one was there. Cheryl never rang the bell and always knocked in a certain sequence. When the bell kept ringing she stomped out of the bedroom and into the living room determined to catch whoever and give them a heated piece of her mind. When the bell didn't stop, a tiny ray of hope shone inside her thinking it could possibly be Will. She flung open the door and her temper instantly reignited seeing Michael.

"What do you want?" Her tone was razor sharp.

His mouth fell open like he was in shock. "I … I've come to see you."

She jammed her hands on her hips. "Why? To come and gloat I got laid off because of your corrupt family?"

"No." He blinked his dark eyes. "I haven't come to gloat and my family isn't corrupt."

"Oh yeah? Then why am I being persecuted because my sister married your brother?"

"Do you think I could come in and we could discuss this?"

"Suit yourself." She moved out of the way and caught a glimpse of herself in the mirror by the door. Black mascara was smeared under her eyes and her hair was disheveled like it hadn't been combed in days. Which may have been the case because she couldn't remember.

When he stepped inside, he immediately removed his cowboy hat. She noticed him take inventory of the cardboard boxes scattered throughout her apartment.

"Looks like you're moving out. Where are you headed?"

"If you must know, back to Aberdeen."

"Tell me what moving's going to solve?"

"So I can get as far away from here as possible. Away from the continuous prank calls and people ringing my door bell at all hours of the night."

His eyes went to the phone receiver laying on the counter. "So you believe my father is to blame for all this trouble you're having?"

She sucked in a deep breath. "Yes, I do."

"And your sister agrees with that?"

"No. She said it's the most ridiculous thing she's ever heard. She believes Chet to be an honest man."

"And you obviously don't."

"I don't know if he's honest or not. All I know is that I'm

guilty by association."

"Don't you think there could be another explanation for your troubles?"

"Like what?"

"Did you ever call that news reporter and ask if Will just happened to find him at the bazaar?" He waited for her answer.

"As a matter of fact, I did. He said someone called him but he never got the guy's name. I asked him right out if it was Will, and he said he was sure it wasn't."

"Okay, that confirms the conversation I overheard at the fellowship hall. Will was telling someone to call the press and get them down there because the world needed to meet the woman in charge."

"So what if he did call? Why is it so hard for you to believe Will could be proud of me? It doesn't prove anything."

"It proves Will and Donnie set you up."

She narrowed her eyes. "And why would they do that?"

"Because Will was handling all the foreclosures and Larsen's was selling the property. They both played their part in a deal with Paul Bradford. Will offered no help to the farmers making sure the land would be available and Donnie had you sell it at an exceptionally low price that was negotiated prior. I'm sure it also included a nice pay-off of some sort for both of them. They hired you because you're new to the area and the realty business. They knew you wouldn't ask a lot of questions. It was their plan all along to blame you for getting paid off and not themselves for selling out to the big corporate farmer because you're the *woman in charge*."

She shut her eyes briefly and shook her head. "I find one thing wrong with your crazy theory."

"What's that?"

Her eyes opened. "I saw Larry Edwards sign the purchase agreement and I signed it right after he did."

He looked down at his feet and then back up at her. "Paul Bradford's name is on record down at the title company. It was brought up at the AOG meeting that Paul Bradford's name was on both of the titles of Lloyd Jensen and Olaf Sorenson's sold properties. Brett went down to the title office and confirmed it."

She released a big breath. "Cheryl told me the same thing, but I think there's been a mistake somehow. Someone down at the title company must be getting paid off by Bradford. I promised I wouldn't go to either office until everything cools down but I wish I could get my hands on that purchase agreement. It would prove who the land was sold to and that Will, Donnie and I are all innocent. But even if I had it, I couldn't show it to anyone. It's a confidential document or Donnie would've already cleaned up this whole mess."

"Where is it?"

"Donnie keeps all of the final documents in a locked cabinet in his office."

"Do you have a key to the realty office?"

"No, I don't. Even if I did, I wouldn't go down there behind Donnie's back and break into his files. That would be what I call *criminal behavior*." She checked her wristwatch. *Don't give him any ideas!* "I think you better go. I need to keep packing."

"Instead you're going to tuck your tail between your legs and run off. Don't you think that's exactly what Will and Donnie want you to do? Leave the area so they can blame everything on you?"

She glared at him. "I'm not going to wait around here and be harassed night and day. I feel like I'm in prison."

"Then prove your case to me before you leave. Let's go down there tonight so you can show me you sold it to Edwards and not Bradford."

"I would love to do that, but I don't need to add breaking and entering to my list of offenses. I think my reputation has been tarnished enough."

"What if I get a guy to help us who knows how to get into buildings and locked cabinets?"

"I would still say *no*. It's too risky."

"I'll tell everyone I forced you if we get caught."

She crossed her arms and shook her head.

"*Damn it*, Jolene." His eyes flashed. "I love you! I need to believe you!"

His words struck like lightning, sudden and startling, and it took a few moments for the shockwaves to settle. She took a deep, much needed breath and slowly asked, "What about Diana?" Her body vibrated with each powerful heartbeat and it seemed like minutes, not seconds before he replied.

"I was going to break it off with her tonight," he said. "When Jake said you were leaving town, I couldn't bear to let you go so I came here. I can't lose you again."

That was all she needed to hear. She couldn't stop herself and rushed into his strong arms. Neither of them spoke as his loving embrace told her everything she needed to know. It soothed and reassured her that their love for each other was more powerful than her fears. He held her tightly for a moment with her head nestled under his chin, but her lips were drawn to his, and as he claimed her mouth, it quickly escalated into an uncontrollably brazen kiss.

It had been a long time coming and neither of them held anything back. The only thing her mind could comprehend was how badly she wanted and needed him. There was no other man who even came close to making her feel this way.

He raised his head after the kiss and she could see the love in his glowing eyes. "I never stopped loving you," he said.

"No matter how hard I've tried not to — neither did I," she admitted.

A tear rolled down her cheek and he gently wiped it away with his fingers before his lips found hers again. This time the kiss was slow but deliberate and revealed his unquenchable desire and unyielding love for her.

When his lips left hers, she pressed her head onto his chest and listened to his rapid heartbeat, certain she would never let him slip away again.

19

It was getting dark inside the cab of Brett's truck when he stared through the windshield at the setting sun. He could still see a remnant of faint orange behind the horizon but there was no sign of Karyn or her car. A list of feasible scenarios ran rampant in his head as he waited for her. Something maybe went wrong with her car. Or there could've been a change in her family's plans and she couldn't get away without someone noticing. Maybe someone in her family found out and forbade her to go? The list of possibilities ended with a heavy, sinking feeling. Perhaps she lost faith in him and decided he and his family were lying about being involved with the big corporate farmer. *Please don't let it be the case!*

Karyn had been his one ray of sunshine through all of this. He envisioned her smiling at him with the setting sun in her lovely eyes. Just being around her made everything he was going through more tolerable. She was smart, sweet and surprisingly supportive of his claim his family was being framed.

He slowly turned the key in the ignition and the song "Seasons in the Sun" started to play on the radio. The sad lyrics made him sigh before he put his truck in gear and started down the dirt road.

In the middle of the song Brett pounded his fist onto the steering wheel. *Life really stinks!* Roger, who also lived with his parents, told him he was welcome to come visit anytime, but he preferred they avoided going anywhere together. His friend was tired of getting into a fist fight everywhere they went.

At home it was hard to watch his family suffer from the effects of the rumors. His father pretended like none of it bothered him and assured the rest of the family it all would pass. Mother supported her husband's optimism with her own during the day, but late at night when she thought everyone was asleep he sometimes heard her crying. Jake and his new family had been snubbed at a few businesses in town and also at some of Taylor's softball games at church. Michael kept a stiff upper lip and didn't want to talk about their predicament. He seemed to be a different person lately; quiet and lost in thought most of the time.

Seeing the yard lights from the Sugar King Farm shine in the distance, Brett said a fast and heartfelt prayer. *Dear Lord, please don't let Karyn lose faith in me!*

"You want me to what?" Jim asked Michael from across Jolene's kitchen table.

Michael repeated, "I want you to help us break into Larsen's Realty Office."

"We wouldn't be actually breaking in because I know where they hide the key," Jolene chimed in.

That's my girl! Michael smiled.

Jim wrinkled his brows. "Let me get this straight. They fired you and now you want me to help you break back in there so you can prove to him," he nodded at Michael, "that you didn't sell out to the corporate dude."

Jolene gave him a sheepish grin. "Yeah, that just about sums it up."

"She believes Will Vanders and Donnie Larsen didn't set her up for the fall on this. I want to prove to her they did," Michael smiled at his friend. "You were the best at breaking into any teacher's desk for the answers to every test in high school. Can't you help us out?"

Jim frowned. "But I wasn't a husband and a father or a prominent businessman in the community when I was in high school."

"I told her if we get caught, I'll take all the blame and tell the cops I acted on my own. I'll tell them I forced you, too," Michael coaxed. "These days it won't be too hard to convince the people in this town that a Cameron committed a crime."

Jim blew out a quick breath. "Okay. Fine. I'm in. I just hope the next time I see you, it won't be on visiting day at the prison."

The street in front of Larsen's Realty had two lights on each end and one located directly in front of the main entrance of the office. Michael drove his truck around the block and then pulled into the alley and parked in the lot behind the building.

"We'll go directly to Donnie's office as soon as we get inside," Michael said to his accomplices and pulled out two flashlights from the glove compartment. He gave one to Jim. "After you get the cabinet open, I want you to go out and stand by the side of the building and keep a look out." He handed Jim a walkie-talkie and took another one out of the bag for himself. "Set it on channel nineteen."

Dressed in dark denim jeans and a black long-sleeved T-shirt, Jolene quickly tipped the flower pot by the door of the main entrance to one side and retrieved the key from underneath. The street light shined down on them and she didn't have any trouble seeing the keyhole of the lock. When she pushed the door open, a bell tinkled above them and they stepped inside. Her eyes found her old desk in the dark office and a wave of sadness washed over her. Oddly, there were a few files and a framed picture on top. Maybe Marcy was using it for some reason. Michael shined his flashlight and she led the group into Donnie's office. When they located the cabinet, Jolene was surprised when Jim pulled out a shim from his pocket and went to work on the lock.

A confident smile flashed on his face when the lock clicked and he opened the drawer. "I'll be outside. Don't take too long." He switched on his flashlight and went out the office door.

Jolene's fingers swiftly crawled over the long row of files looking for the Edwards tab.

Where is it? Not seeing it she started her search again.

"Go to B for Bradford," Michael suggested.

She frowned but then smiled deciding it was time to prove her point and show him it wasn't there. Seeing the name Bradford on a tab she sucked in a quick breath and her head sprang up. She nervously stared into Michael's knowing eyes. Her heart started to thump hard when she pulled the file out and flipped open the cover. Licking her finger, she turned over the pages of the contract to get to the last page and her entire body froze. *That can't be!*

There in blue ink was Paul Bradford's signature on a line as the purchaser and directly across the page on the line for the selling agent was — Jolene Garrison. She rapidly blinked knowing it wasn't forged; it was her own signature. *But how did they do that?"*

She was dizzy with shock. "That's my signature … but I swear Michael, I never sold it to him!"

"Let's take the file and go," he said.

"They're going to notice it gone," she told him. "They'll suspect me."

"Who cares? It's not like he's planning on giving you your old job back. Let's go!"

Her body felt numb as she shut the file cabinet and they swiftly made their way out of the office. When she passed by her old desk the light from the flashlight flicked across a gold name plate. She picked it up and read a man's name —John Hughs. *They hired a new guy?*

They only had made it a few blocks away from the realty office when Jolene felt her stomach start to move.

"Pull over!" she shouted. "I'm going to throw up!"

Michael laid on the brakes then opened his door and helped her to the side of the truck. She folded over and quickly got rid of the peanut butter sandwich she had for dinner. He handed her his handkerchief and she wiped her mouth.

"Oh, Michael," she sobbed. "What am I going to do? Even if I move away, I'll never be able to sell real estate without worrying this will come back to haunt me!"

He held her shoulders and looked into her eyes. "I promise you. One way or another, we'll figure this out."

AT THE GOLDEN View apartment building, Jolene noticed Michael parked in the shadows of the parking lot away from the security light. He stepped out of his door and helped her out of the truck.

"Well, it certainly has been a memorable evening. One that I'll never have any recollection of in court," Jim said from across the hood. "I bid you two goodnight." He walked away in the direction of his apartment.

When Jolene sniffled and wiped the tears from her cheeks, Michael wrapped an arm around her.

"You need to eat something and go to bed. Things will look better in the morning."

"I really don't think it will change anything, Michael. And I'm way too tired and upset to eat anything."

"How about I fix you something while you take a nice long shower?"

She shook her head. "I'm afraid I don't have anything you could make. I've been hiding in my apartment for over a week."

He checked his wristwatch. "No grocery stores are open at this time of night." Taking a few steps away from her door, he turned his head. "The lights are still on over at Jim's. I'll run over there and see what he'll give me. You go in and take a shower." He sprinted away and she went inside.

Jolene headed for the shower and tried to relax under the hot spray. Stepping out and wrapping herself in a towel, she dried her long hair with a towel then combed it and slipped on a blue silk robe over her matching night gown. Coming out of the bathroom, she was surprised to hear her radio play and smell a delicious aroma filling the apartment. Michael had his back to her stirring something in a pot on the stove when she came into the kitchen. On the table there were two bowls with spoons and a cup with a tea bag inside it. An opened package of saltine crackers sat on one side of the table next to a plate of what looked to be chocolate chip cookies.

He apparently sensed she was behind him because he turned around and quickly pulled out a chair for her by the table.

"I found some tea in the cupboard," he said pushing in her chair. "I figured you would like some to settle your stomach." He grabbed the handle of the tea kettle on the stove and carefully filled her cup with hot steaming water.

"Thank you." She began to steep her tea bag. "Whatever you've got cooking sure smells wonderful."

"I'm not actually cooking. I'm warming up some potato soup Lyla made. She poured some in this pot and told me to return it with her plate."

"That was very kind of her to send over soup and cookies."

"She also wanted me to tell you how sorry she is about what happened to you."

Jolene nodded, not wanting to rehash the subject.

Michael proudly poured soup in each of their bowls and took a chair next to her.

"Mmm … this is great," he said after eating a spoonful. "Who knew Lyla was such a great cook?"

Jolene agreed and continued to eat but her mind and eyes kept going back to the file laying on the counter. Their bowls were empty and the plate of cookies was half gone when he told her to sit and finish her tea while he cleared the table.

Seconds after he wiped the table, he plopped the file down in front of her. "I want you to think back real hard and tell me when and how Donnie got you to sign that."

She opened the file to the last page and stared at her signature. "That's the strangest part. I just don't remember signing it." The document blurred with her tears. "Please, Michael. You've got to believe me. I've been racking my brain trying to figure it out."

He grabbed a couple of tissues from a box on the counter then pulled a chair up close by her. Staring into her eyes, he draped his arm around her. "I do believe you." He wiped the tear from her cheek with a tissue.

"I'm so angry and embarrassed that I let Will and Donnie use me like they did. How stupid could I be?"

"You're not stupid. You're a newcomer at the real estate game. You only did what they told you to do." He shrugged. "I would've done the same thing."

She gave him a weak smile. "That doesn't change the fact I was the fool who signed forms I don't remember signing. I keep asking myself why I wouldn't have questioned signing a document if I didn't know … " The answer struck her hard like a bullet to the chest. *Those damn insurance forms!*

"What is it?" he blurted.

"Oh, Michael! I figured it out!" She sprang from her chair and started to pace by the kitchen table.

He stood up waiting to hear what she had to say.

"Each time I made a sale, Donnie had me sign what he claimed was an insurance form. I never heard about it in Realty classes so I questioned him the first time. He said it was something new that had recently become standard procedure."

Her eyes met his. "Now thinking about the whole thing, it

did look similar to a purchase agreement, but I felt okay signing it because there was only one line at the bottom of the page where I signed." Jolene continued to pace then suddenly stopped and faced Michael. "Donnie has a typewriter in his office and he must have filled in the rest and then had Bradford sign it at another time." She suddenly felt at ease knowing how it happened but the feeling didn't last long. "Oh Michael. I'm still going to have to leave town. No one's going to believe I didn't know what I was doing ..." she paused trying to keep the quiver out of her voice, "I was the lady in charge."

He took her hands in his. "That's the absolute worst thing you can do." His face lit up and he smiled. "I've got it. Why don't you move out to Cheryl and Jake's for a while?"

"I don't think the newlyweds who are soon to be parents again would want me to stay there."

"Then come out and stay at the Sugar King."

She let out a small laugh. "That would really enforce the theory I'm part of a conspiracy with your family. And the way your mother is to Cheryl, I'm sure she would welcome me with open arms. I better get out of town."

"Please!" There was panic in his eyes as they frantically searched hers. "You can't go. I love you."

The pulsing beat of the song "Temptation Eyes" played on the radio as his lips devoured hers in a kiss that sent shivers down her spine. Overtaken by her own hungry need for him, she wrapped her arms around his neck and eagerly matched the fire of his demanding kiss. The taste of his mouth was sweet and intoxicating, further igniting her desire. He lifted his head and stared at her with his dark, captivating eyes. Those eyes were beautiful, but tonight the love-light in them drew her in like a helpless moth to a burning flame.

They kissed during their entire stumbling trip across the apartment into her bedroom, where they halted by her bed to stop and frantically clawed the clothes off each other. His chest was heaving when he threw off his shirt and hastily helped her remove her robe. She heard him suck in a sharp breath when she dropped the straps of her nightgown off her shoulders and let the satiny garment slip down her curves to the floor. He pulled her back into his arms and slid his silky tongue into her mouth while his hand found a breast that he gently squeezed, making her body tingle with raw desire.

His eyes glistened as he pulled back to gaze into her face. "I will never love another woman the way I love you," he breathed.

His mouth reclaimed hers while his warm hands roved their way up her bare back caressing her skin with his strong fingers. Each loving touch confirmed how badly he wanted her. When his lips traveled across her jawline, she felt a quiver in her lower midsection from the warmth of his hot breath on her ear. She ran her hands through his thick hair as his lips traveled down her neck to her breasts. With a moan, they fell together onto the bed where he pressed his hand on the back of her head as their tongues entwined.

The only sound in the room seemed to be her own heart beat as he pulled her on top of him. He had a pleased expression as he watched her reach a fast and furious release. Her long red hair fell around them when he pulled her face down to his for a passion-infused kiss. He rolled them over and seconds later cried out with his own sheer pleasure as he finished.

Twining his arms around her, he held her tightly as he caught his breath and stared down into her eyes. "I love you, Jolene, more than you will ever know."

"I love you, too," she answered in a whisper as she lost herself in his gaze. *So much it scares me ....*

THE SOFT PINK glow from the rising sun was barely visible outside when Michael reached for his wristwatch on the night-stand in Jolene's bedroom. It was five o'clock, and if he left within the next half hour he'd be on time for chores, but that was the furthest thing from his mind.

Lying beside him was the woman he adored, and making love to her again was the only thing he could comprehend. Remembering, there was no doubt last night had been the best night of his life. Not only had he gotten back together with Jolene and made love to her, he had proven that Will and Donnie had set her up.

Jolene suddenly rolled over and threw her arm across his chest. His eyes swept over the beauty in his arms. *Thank you God, for a second chance with her!* He ran a lock of her silky red hair through his fingers before he let it fall onto the soft skin of her shoulder. She shivered before her sleepy green eyes fluttered open.

"Good morning," she said with a dreamy smile. Her fingers stroked his cheek and then touched his lips before she dropped her hand onto his chest.

He kissed her softly. "Good morning."

"I suppose you have to go home and do chores."

He smiled. "I'm willing to take a chance they won't fire me if I'm late." He cupped her face and kissed her deeper.

She eagerly returned his kiss but then stopped and pulled her face back. "Michael, I love you, and there's nothing I want more than to start over with you."

"You have no idea how much I've wanted to hear those words." He covered her mouth with his in a warm passionate kiss.

When the kiss was over, she pressed her hand to his chest. "You do believe me that what happened with Donnie and Will wasn't my fault, right?"

"Of course I do," he said with a smile. "I love *and* trust you."

"That's just it. I believe if we want to make our relationship work, we need to be as honest as possible with each other. Don't you agree?"

"Yes, I do." He wrinkled his brows. "What are you getting at?"

"I've asked Cheryl several times what happened between the two of you, but she never really addresses the question." Her eyes carefully searched his.

He felt a gut-wrenching pain in his stomach hearing her words. *Oh God, no!*

"Like I said, if our relationship is going to work, I need to know the truth."

He looked away at the window and she squeezed his bicep.

"Please, Michael, tell me what happened." When he didn't answer she sat up, holding the sheets over her breasts. "Look, you can tell me anything. Nothing's going to change how I feel about you."

He slowly pulled himself into a sitting position. "I'm afraid there's no guarantee of that." He briefly closed his eyes and felt her take his hand.

"Please, Michael," she begged. "Just tell me. If we're going to be together, I need to know."

Keeping his eyes focused on the quilt in front of him, he tried to regain his composure. There was no way he could explain the horrible things he'd done without her hating him, but he had to try.

"Before I start, you need to know how deeply ashamed I am. I have never forgiven myself for what I did."

She silently nodded.

He looked up at the ceiling. "Other than Jake and Cheryl and the doctors, no one has any idea what happened. Before I come out and say it, I want you to know what has taken place since it happened." He paused to take a needed breath. "When you came back for Jake and Cheryl's wedding, I had just completed a stay at St. John's Recovery Center in St. Paul."

Her mouth fell open slightly. "For drugs?"

"Methaqualone. Most people just call them 'ludes."

"Were you addicted to them?"

"No, not physically, but I was a fool who used them for kicks and to relax. I didn't realize for a few people they cause memory loss. And unfortunately … I was one of those people."

She stared at him with wide eyes but didn't say anything.

"You've got to believe me when I say I will never take any drugs again."

She put her arm around him. "Of course, I believe you. But what happened with Cheryl?"

Please God help her to understand! He took a ragged breath. "I don't remember, but I …" He swallowed hard, but kept his eyes on hers. "Apparently tried to … rape her … twice." His heart beat at double time as he waited for her reaction.

Her hand went to her mouth as she sucked in a long sharp breath. In a fraction of a second he watched her expression change from confusion to disgust as her eyes narrowed. She flung back the covers and jumped out of bed. "You can't be serious?" Her tone was clearly judgmental.

A tear rolled down his cheek. "Sadly, I am."

The cold dead look in her eyes confirmed how she felt. "I can see being high and doing something once and not knowing it, but *twice*? Come on, Michael it's a far-fetched story. Tell me, how many other women have you attacked?"

"None that I'm aware of."

She hung her head and stared at the floor. "You need to get dressed and leave."

"Please, Jolene. I love you." He got out of bed and held her shoulders. "I swear I didn't know what happened until I went through therapy."

She swung out of his grip. "Don't you dare touch me! You're nothing but an animal." Her green eyes flashed. "I could never be with a man who tried to rape someone. Especially one who tried to rape my own sister. Get out!" she yelled and ran out of the room.

His heart felt like it could break as he picked up his clothes and put them on, but he didn't regret telling her. It was strange, but he felt like a huge weight had been lifted off his shoulders.

She was sitting by the kitchen table with her head buried in her hands when he came out of the bedroom.

Clutching his cowboy hat, he stepped closer to her.

She dropped her hands and he could see her eyes were red and filled with tears. She quickly looked away like she couldn't stand the sight of him. "Please, Michael … just leave!"

"I will. But before I go …" He choked back his tears. "I want you to know I was lost for a long time. But you found me and made me see what love really is. I am so grateful, and I will always love you. My only hope is that you'll find it in your heart to forgive me."

She clamped her eyes shut and shook her head no.

He went out the door quietly closing it behind himself. *Please Lord! Make her change her mind!*

A STEADY FLOW of rocks from the dirt road rolled and ricocheted beneath Jolene's car as she pressed her foot firmly down on the accelerator. Going around a curve, she felt the car swerve and it scared her enough to make her let up on the gas. Getting to Cheryl's farm a few minutes later wasn't going to change a thing.

When Michael left she picked up the phone and started to dial her sister's number but then just left it off the hook. It would be easier for Cheryl to deny the truth on the phone than it would be if she was confronted face to face. *Why hadn't she trusted me enough to tell me what happened between them? And why would she ever allow me to be with him after what happened to her?*

Jolene sniffled and wiped her tears with a wad of tissue in her hand. It was hard to fathom her whole world had crumbled in a little over a week. Not only had her bosses framed her for something dishonest and unethical, the man she loved confessed he had attempted to rape her sister. The betrayal she felt from Will and Donnie stabbed like a knife in the back. Learning about what Michael did, the blade cruelly pierced her heart as well. But the thing that hurt most of all was her sister's failure to disclose what happened between her and that monster. Cheryl's disloyalty had twisted the knife in her heart and had definitely crossed a line in their relationship.

Jolene knocked and pulled the screen door open before anyone answered inside the house at Cheryl's. Steam was rising from the pots on the stove and a row of canning jars were lined up on the counter. Most were filled with peach halves and syrup. Cheryl turned and smiled with a paring knife in one hand and a scalded peach in the other. The apron she wore stood out like a tent and covered only the front of her midsection.

"Oh, Thank God! I tried to call you. I was worried you'd left for Aberdeen." She quickly dried her hands in a towel and wrapped her arms around Jolene.

It was hard to believe the woman had gotten bigger since the last time they were together.

"Where are Taylor and Jake?" Jolene blurted.

"They went to the Sugar King. Why?"

"I need to talk to you about something important,"

"Okay. But if you don't mind, could it wait just a bit. If I don't get those peaches covered with syrup in the next few minutes they'll turn brown." Cheryl turned toward the sink. "Help yourself to a cup of coffee. It's still hot. I can't tell you how happy I am you decided to stay…" Her face was serious when she turned back to Jolene. "You're going to stay, right? Or are you here to say goodbye? You know you can always stay here."

Jolene shrugged. "I don't know what I'm going to do right now. She took a cup from the cupboard and filled it with coffee. Thoughts spun through her head as she anxiously sat at the table waiting for her sister to finish. Minutes later, each jar was filled and covered with the syrup mixture and placed into a canner on the stove. Cheryl covered them with water then turned on the burner before she took a seat at the table.

She immediately started the conversation. "I was so worried about you. I was going to drive to your apartment this morning but Jake made me promise I wouldn't go into town anymore by myself. He said he and Taylor were going into town for parts later and he was going to check on you, then."

When Jolene didn't respond, Cheryl's head tilted as she curiously looked her over. "What's going on with you? What was so important you wanted to discuss?"

Jolene's anger suddenly gave way to the hurt she felt inside and her eyes filled with tears. "I always thought we cared about each other and told each other everything."

"Of course I care about you," Cheryl's brows wrinkled. "And I do tell you everything."

"If that's true, then why did you let me go out with a man who attacked you — twice?"

Cheryl gasped and slapped her hand to her mouth, but removed it to cover Jolene's hand. "Michael must have told you." She slowly shook her head. "I … I'm so sorry. You don't know how many times I wanted to tell you … but I was too afraid."

Jolene pulled her hand away. "So afraid you would put me in danger?"

"He told me he would kill me if I ever said anything to anyone." Cheryl's eyes searched hers.

Jolene flinched. "Oh my God! He actually threatened to kill you?"

"Yes, he did," she swallowed, "he held a knife to my throat." She let out a painful whimper before she pulled herself out of her chair. Taking a box of tissues from the counter, she put them on the table between them. She plopped back into her chair and started to sob."

A wave of guilt rushed over Jolene, knowing she'd been so consumed in her own anger she had forgotten about the trauma her sister had obviously gone through. Seeing Cheryl like this was totally out of character. She was always a fighter, and to see her so distraught was nothing less than heartbreaking.

Jolene slid her chair closer and wrapped an arm around her sister.

"I know this must be painful, but could you tell me what prevented him from actually raping you?"

Cheryl wiped her eyes. "The first time, Chet had fallen off a horse and the ambulance sped by here and interrupted him. The second time, Jake arrived and they got into a fight. Michael threatened Jake with the knife, too."

"Why didn't you or Jake press charges and have him arrested?"

"Jake believes it would've destroyed his family if we had."

Jolene found it difficult to accept her sister's reasoning. "So you two pretended all this time nothing happened? My God! Jake had him as best man in your wedding. You both have to be insane!"

"Jake has forgiven Michael. He believes his brother was so angry and high he was a completely different person. He believes it so much, he went to see Michael several times while he was in the recovery center. Jake helped him face up to what he did and the two are now closer than they've been in years."

Jolene took a few seconds to absorb what her sister was telling her. "Have *you* forgiven him?"

Cheryl looked down at her cup. "No, I can't say that I have," she said. "According to Jake, Michael has told him several times he would like to apologize to me, but I've told Jake to tell him no. I don't know if I'll ever be ready to hear what he has to say."

"Why didn't you tell me? I would've understood. And I certainly wouldn't have gotten involved with a dangerous man like him."

"If you remember, I begged you to stay away from him. I was going to tell you while you were living here, but during that time Jake and I broke up. The fear of not having Jake to protect me from Michael was overwhelming. I was scared if I told you and you confronted Michael, he might slip off the edge and make good on his threats. I had to think of Taylor."

It was hard to imagine the man who tenderly made love to her hours ago was the same man who had viciously attacked her sister. Was it the drugs, or could Michael possibly have dual personalities?

Jolene knew whatever the explanation, it made no difference. This time she was done with Michael Cameron for good.

20

"Hey blister! Nice of you to show up after the work's done!" Brett hollered at Michael when he stepped into the large shed. Chet, Brett, Jake and Taylor turned and watched Michael grab his coveralls off the hook.

"I had some business to attend to." Michael looked away as he pulled the coveralls over his clothes. He knew his eyes were red from crying and he didn't need anyone asking why.

Chet watched Michael for a moment before he looked down at Taylor. "Young man, I got something to show you down at the stables. He spun around and faced Brett. "I want you to go out to the field over by Thompsons and check on the irrigation."

"It was fine yesterday when I looked," Brett whined before he caught Jake's head motioning toward the door. A knowing look came over his face. "But I guess it won't hurt to check it again today." Brett grabbed the keys to the old farm truck and followed Chet and Taylor out the door.

When the door closed Jake immediately asked, "So what happened last night with Jolene?"

"If you're asking if I proved to her Will and Donnie set her up, I did," Michael said. He proceeded to give Jake the run down on breaking into the realty office and Jolene's reaction to the signed purchase agreement.

"I hope you persuaded her to stay."

"I had her convinced to stay last night, but this morning ..." he took a ragged breath, "everything went to shit."

Jake scrunched his brows. "Whadya mean, went to shit?"

Michael's eyes blurred with tears. "She wanted to know what happened between me and Cheryl last summer. And I told her the truth."

Jake's eyes popped. "How did she react?"

"She wanted to know how many other women I've attacked then went on to call me an animal and kicked me out." Michael pulled out a bandana handkerchief from his coveralls and wiped his eyes.

"It's a lot to take in. I'd give her some time," Jake assured.

"I don't think time is going to help anything. She said she could never be with a man who attacked a woman, let alone her own sister." He sucked in a sniffle. "I love her, Jake, but that doesn't change a thing."

Jake gripped his shoulder. "I'm so proud of you. No matter what happens — you did the right thing." He pulled Michael into a hug and patted his back.

Michael managed a weak smile. "I know, but it doesn't make it hurt any less."

RUMMAGING through her cupboards for food, Jolene decided it was time to either go to the grocery store or give into starvation. She knew most folks would be off to work at nine o'clock in the morning making it the best time to go into Jack and Jill's Grocery Store.

Dressed in a pair of denim shorts and a green sleeveless blouse, she combed her hair into a high ponytail and slipped her feet into a pair of wedged sandals. She was about to go out the door when she suddenly lost her nerve and thought about wearing a floppy hat and sunglasses. Shaking her head in the mirror, she smiled knowing it was time to stop hiding. She needed to get out there and face the big bad world to show everyone Will and Donnie were to blame, not her. *You're a big girl. What's the worst thing that can happen to you?*

She confidently pulled the door open and then screamed as loud as her lungs allowed. On her front door step lay a dead rat with a pink ribbon tied around its neck.

Seconds later, Lyla came running around the patio. "Are you all right?" she asked panting and then looked down. "Oh good, Lord. Who would've done such a sick thing?"

Still staring at the rat, no words would come out of Jolene's mouth. Her eyes went to the broken egg shells on the ground. Someone had thrown eggs at her apartment and delivered the dead animal during the night.

Lyla stepped over the rodent and shells and escorted her back into her living room. "Oh, honey." Her words were soothing as she stroked Jolene's back. "You can't take any of this to heart. It was likely some spoiled kids trying to get a rise out of you."

"I need to leave here right now," Jolene said, staring mindlessly at the doorway.

"Where will you go?" Lyla asked.

"Back to Aberdeen to stay with my mother."

"Wouldn't that be like admitting you sold out to that corporate guy?" Lyla asked. "My husband told me all about it."

"I don't care. I can't take any more of this. It's like I'm in jail here. I'm so low on groceries, I literally have nothing left to eat."

"Michael told us you're the strongest woman he knows. Don't let those assholes, I mean your former bosses, win now. Stay here and fight. Isn't there any place you could stay here in the area until the truth comes out?"

"The only place is my sister's and she's about to give birth soon. I don't want to barge in on her."

"How about you come over to my apartment and I'll make you a nice cup of coffee and something to eat? We'll call the super and have him wash off the eggs and get rid of the critter."

Jolene was taken aback by Lyla's kindness.

"You would do that for me?"

"Of course. We women have to stick together." She smiled and winked.

Jolene was enjoying her bacon and eggs when Lyla filled her a cup of fresh brewed coffee.

"I do want to clear the air about something." Lyla sat down at the table across from her. "I admit I knew who you were but I swear I wasn't spying on you. But I can't say the same for my husband. He was keeping an eye on you. And for the record, Michael didn't ask him to. My only motive was I wanted to be your friend."

"You've been a great friend," Jolene smiled. "And a great cook, too. That soup you sent with Michael the other night was fabulous."

"Glad I could help," she said. "So what are you going to do now?"

"I suppose finish packing and go to my mother's." The thought of living at her mother's small house made her feel claustrophobic.

"You don't think your sister will let you stay at her place?"

"She has offered plenty of times, but I don't want to be in the way."

"When I first had my baby I would have given anything to have another set of hands to help out."

"I don't know anything about babies. How much help could I possibly be?"

"You know how to do laundry and cook some, don't you?"

"Of course," Jolene answered.

"Well then, that would be a huge help. Why don't you give her a call?" She pointed at the phone on the counter.

Lyla was right. Jolene wasn't working and Cheryl had done so much for her last year when her marriage ended. It was time to return the favor. But most importantly, sticking around the area would help reinforce her innocence. Why let men like Will and Donnie get away with what they did?

It was the third evening in a row that Brett and Michael had stayed home to watch television with their parents. Brett felt like he was stuck in an episode of the "Twilight Zone" and time was going backwards. It seemed he was still in high school as he looked around at his brother on the couch and his parents each sitting in a leather easy chair.

Soon after the ten o'clock news, Chet and Lucille declared it was time for them to go to bed. They had just left the room when Brett got up off the floor and switched the channel to the "Tonight Show" with Johnny Carson. Michael gave him a dirty look.

"Turn it back to channel four," he told him. "There's a John Wayne movie I want to watch tonight."

"But Paul McCartney is supposed to be on tonight."

"Who gives a shit? We're watching 'True Grit.'"

"Come on! We've seen that movie at least a half a dozen times."

"Do you want to flip a coin?" Michael asked and Brett nodded.

"Sure. I'll take heads." Brett watched his brother toss the coin in the air and catch it. When Michael moved his hand and it showed tails, Brett demanded to see the coin. It seemed each time they flipped a coin his brother generally won the toss.

"Why aren't you hanging out at Iversons?" Brett growled at him.

Michael looked down. "I've been wanting to talk to Diana all week but she went to the Cities a couple of days ago to help her cousin out with her wedding plans. Why are you here again tonight?"

"I can't go anywhere without getting into a fist fight trying to defend our family's honor."

"You were running plenty a week ago. Where the hell were you going?"

It appeared he and Karyn were over and it wasn't going to make a difference if he told the whole world about her.

"I was hanging out with Karyn Pherson."

"That cute little brunette?"

"Yeah, but don't say anything. Apparently her parents convinced her the rumors about us were true. It really hurt when she stood me up the other night."

Michael slowly shook his head. "You never know what women are going to do." His tone was pensive but he didn't elaborate.

Brett went fishing for more information. "I'm glad Jolene has decided to stay with Jake and Cheryl and not leave town. Seeing that dead rat must have really freaked her out."

"Yeah, I can't imagine how scared she was. I'd like to beat the crap out of the dumbass who put it on her step."

Brett looked up from the floor. "Jake said he doesn't know if it will do any good, but she's planning on testifying at the next AOG meeting. At least she'll stay until then." When Michael didn't answer he asked, "You still love her, don't you?"

Michael continued to ignore his questioning and got up off the couch. "Go watch your show. I'm going to bed." He left the room and Brett instantly hopped into his spot. *There's more than one way to get what you want!*

THINKING about how to break it off with Diana, Michael nicked a spot on his chin with his razor and winced in the mirror. When he finished shaving, he stuck a small piece of toilet tissue on the cut to stop the bleeding.

His eyes traveled over the row of dress and western shirts when he opened the closet door in his bedroom. What did a man wear to break up with a woman? It was easier to think about the insignificant details than it was to focus on telling Diana he didn't love her. He knew it was the right thing to do, but that didn't make the situation any less difficult. How was she going to react? Would she yell, cry or maybe throw things at him? He pictured her blue eyes filled with tears and instantly felt sick to his stomach remembering how it felt to get left behind.

Sinking down on the edge of the bed, he closed his eyes and thought about how she had ripped out his heart and taken it with her when she left.

But he couldn't blame everything on her. He learned during his stay at St. John's it was his fault for what happened after she married someone else. For years, he let himself fall into a spiral of self-destructive behavior by using his hurt and anger to justify using women for sex and nothing more. Some guys haled him a hero for it, but deep down he knew he had been nothing but a pathetic coward. He had let the fear of getting emotionally close to anyone ruin eight years of his life.

He thought about how things ended with Jolene and blinked back the tears that instantly formed in his eyes. No other woman had mattered until he fell in love with her. It had been Jolene who had freed him of his own chains. *I know I don't deserve it, God, but please give me another chance with her!*

He finished getting dressed and was going down the long staircase when he heard the telephone ring downstairs.

"Michael!" Lucille yelled coming into the hallway from the kitchen. Seeing him on the stair landing she lowered her voice. "You've got a phone call. It's Diana, and she sure sounds excited about something."

"Thanks. I'll take it in the den," he told her knowing the rest of the family were in the dining room.

"Hello," he answered and heard his mother hang up.

"Oh, I'm so happy I caught you before you left." Diana's voice held an exuberant tone. "I'm so excited! I've found the perfect apartment for us. Meet me at the Fiesta Apartments on Third Street."

What the devil? "I don't understand. When did we discuss looking for apartments?"

"Don't you remember?" She sounded confused. "We talked about it that afternoon after we left the bazaar."

A pang of guilt shot through him, knowing he was partly responsible for this turn of events. He should've set her straight the moment she mentioned living together. "Okay ... I'll meet you there."

Terminating their relationship was definitely getting more complicated as time went by and he knew without a doubt that he needed to end it now.

IN THE QUIET of her bedroom at Cheryl's, Jolene woke early and stared at the other side of the bed. She envisioned Michael lying there in the morning light and started to cry. Why couldn't he be the man of her dreams instead of the mixed-up mess he was?

Her mind replayed the conversation the previous evening with Cheryl and Jake when Taylor went outside after dinner.

"Where's he off to in such a hurry?" Jolene asked hearing the screen door slam behind her nephew.

"Out to check his traps. Jake showed him how to catch gophers," Cheryl answered as she filled their cups with coffee. "They get a fair price for them at the township meetings." She smiled at Jake. "My husband told him a story about how he and Michael saved enough money one year to pay for a new baseball bat and a glove. Now, Taylor has his sights set on a new bat."

"Michael and I had a lot of fun that summer, and we learned how to work together." Jake smiled. "Who knows? Maybe that's the reason we ended up being partners."

Jolene looked down at her cup, appalled by how he could talk so fondly of his brother. How could he casually overlook the fact the man had attacked his wife? She had to know how her brother-in-law could forgive him for such an unspeakable act.

"Jake, I appreciate you and Cheryl letting me stay here, but I can't pretend to like how you two seem to be about Michael. I can't believe how you can just ignore the fact he tried to attack your wife — twice?"

Jake's dark eyes bored into hers. "It took more strength than I ever imagined."

"So you bought the whole story that he was using drugs?" Jolene blurted.

"I know you think you know Michael, but you don't. I shared a childhood with him and I could usually tell when he wasn't being truthful. Cheryl and I were both in the room when he found out about the attacks. I knew right then, he didn't have any idea about what happened."

"You're going on a hunch that he wasn't aware of what he was doing when he attacked my sister?"

Cheryl took a deep breath and let it out slowly.

"I was there at St. John's." Jake's eyes flashed. "He cried his heart out because he was so confused and ashamed about what happened."

Jolene looked at her sister. "Do you think you'll ever be able to forgive him?"

"I told you, I don't know," Cheryl said with her gaze inside her cup.

Jake stared at Jolene. "What about you? I know he loves you. Can you find it in your heart to forgive him?"

"All I know is … I can't be with someone I don't trust." Jolene grabbed her cigarettes from the counter and went out the door.

She thought about the discussion with Jake and Cheryl most of the night and had awakened thinking about a man who had already let her down twice. *Only a fool would try it three times!*

MICHAEL SAW Marie Iverson's car parked in front of the Fiesta Apartment building. He parked his truck next to it knowing Diana didn't have a car and likely borrowed her mother's.

He went inside a set of glass doors into an entryway and was about to push the office button when he saw Diana and her mother through another set of glass doors. *Oh, good Lord! She brought Marie!*

Another woman pushed open the door. "Welcome, Mr. Cameron," she told him with a pleasant smile. "I'm Jan Evans. My husband, George, and I are the superintendents of this building."

Diana's smiling face beamed with sheer joy when she grabbed his arm. "Michael, you've got to see the apartment. It's a two bedroom on the first floor. It's totally perfect for us."

"We have laundry downstairs and there's a garbage shoot located on each floor," Jan informed the group as she led them to an apartment door around the corner. She retrieved a key from her pocket and unlocked the door.

Michael felt suddenly helpless. He wanted to stop the whole thing right then and there but it wasn't how he wanted to end things with Diana. Taking a deep breath, he let her escort him inside the apartment. The room was painted a pale yellow and a multi-colored light fixture hung above an area he assumed was the dining room.

Diana stepped to her left and swung open a set of doors. "Look at these closets, Michael. They're huge!"

When he didn't respond, Jan started her spiel on why the place was a steal of a deal.

"An older resident lived here since the building was built

and she kept the place in mint condition. The appliances are spotless." She rushed to the stove and opened the oven door and it was clean as stated. "The refrigerator was replaced just last year."

Michael gave her a slight nod, doing his best to appear interested.

Diana's face lit up. "Come see the master bedroom. It's got big closets like these and there's a large window."

Michael followed her down the hallway and she pointed to a room on the way. "That room will be perfect for the nursery, but wait till you see how big our bedroom is."

Hearing the word nursery, Michael felt a tightness in his chest.

Diana opened the door and swiftly pulled him into the master bedroom where she spun around with open arms. "Isn't this great?"

"Yeah."

Her brows wrinkled. "Is there something wrong?"

He was searching for words when they heard Jan and Marie chatting in the hallway. The women abruptly stopped their conversation when they entered the bedroom.

Jan must have sensed something was amiss and immediately said, "How about I give you and your fiancée some time to talk about this alone. But don't wait too long. First floor apartments go fast. And at a hundred dollars a month, it won't be available long."

Seconds after Jan left the room Michael turned to Marie. "If you don't mind, I would really like to talk to Diana alone. If you want to take your car and go, I'll bring her home."

"Sure. That would be fine with me." Marie started for the door but halted. "Oh, I almost forgot." She rushed to Michael with open arms. "Welcome to the family." She gave him a kiss on the cheek and a big hug before she exited the room.

Hearing the front door of the apartment close, Michael ground out, "Why did you tell them we were engaged?"

"My mother wasn't on board with the idea of us living together. To make her happy, I mentioned we were talking about getting married. She must have assumed we were engaged. She was the one who told Jan."

"Diana, I care a lot about you," he said as calmly as he could. "And I want you to know I would never do anything to intentionally hurt you, but I can't … I can't do this anymore."

"What? Pretend we're engaged? I promise to straighten it out with my mother as soon as I get home."

He closed his eyes briefly to keep his thoughts straight. "No. I can't keep pretending that I love you." His heart hammered in his chest.

She flinched like she had touched an electric wire. "You don't love me? I don't believe you." Her eyes frantically searched his.

"I'm telling you the truth, and I'm very sorry. I know I should've told you sooner."

"I don't understand. Were you faking it all those years in high school?"

"No, I wasn't. I loved you with my whole heart back then."

"Are you doing this to me as some sort of punishment for marrying Mark?"

"It has nothing to do with what happened. It's me. I want to be honest with myself and you. I just don't feel the same way about you anymore."

"Seeing as how we're being honest with one another, I need to know … are you in love with Jolene?"

He took a quick breath and let it out. "Yes."

She looked away with a pained expression. "I knew it," she whispered softly. "I saw how you looked at her at the bazaar. It was the same way you used to look at me." A mischievous smile came to her lips. "Now I don't feel so bad for putting that dead rat on her step."

Michael couldn't believe his ears. "*You* did that?"

Her smile then turned undeniably wicked. "I knew when you canceled our date the other night you were going to be with her.

So I went to her apartment and found your truck in the parking lot. I waited for hours," she paused and sucked in a breath, "but you never came out. A few days later I heard how folks wanted her gone because she sold out to the corporate farmer. I thought I'd just give her a little push to leave."

"Why would you do such a mean, disgusting thing?" He felt his face burn with rage.

"I wanted you to be the father of my baby and she was ruining all my plans. Tell me, are you two a couple now?"

Michael looked down. "Unfortunately, no."

Diana chuckled. "History does repeat itself."

Michael was confused. "What do you mean?"

"Have you ever wondered why I was so easily led astray by Mark?"

He stared at her for a moment, not sure if he wanted to know.

She smiled. "He was a great lover. You — at best — were adequate."

His mouth dropped open in shock. "We were young and you were my first and only. How good did you expect me to be?" he demanded. "And if I was so bad, why did you come back here?"

"My sister heard from a few women in town that you turned out to be some kind of monumental lover." Her eyes held his gaze. "I always thought about the beautiful babies you and I could've had. So, I thought why not come back to see if the rumors were true? Once I saw you, I prayed things would return to the way they were between us. I wanted so badly for you to be the father of my children."

"Have you ever considered what *I* wanted? I was willing to give you a second chance but it sounds like you were only in it to use me."

"If you had wanted to get married, I wouldn't have turned you down. But I guess it wasn't how things turned out."

"Thank God they didn't. Who would want to spend the rest of their life with a cold, heartless woman like you?"

Her eyes narrowed.

"Find another poor sap to knock you up." He flipped his cowboy hat on his head. "And while you're at it — find your own ride home." Michael then marched out of the apartment feeling relieved. He had dodged a fatal bullet that had been aimed at his heart.

21

I t was after nine in the morning when Brett stepped into the Record and Title Office and made his way up the stairs. Behind a long half wall with a countertop, he could see Karyn working at her desk. Her head was down and she appeared to be reading something. When he cleared his throat, she yanked her head up and looked at him in surprise.

Two older women in the office sat at their desks but didn't attempt to make a move.

Karyn shot up from her chair and walked to the counter. "Can I help you?"

"Yes," Brett answered casually. "I was corresponding with someone about some land and I haven't heard anything from that person in quite a while. I was wondering if you could tell me if the land is still for sale or did someone else register the title?"

She quickly glanced over at the woman in the corner and then winked at him. "Can you give me the name of the possible land owner or tell me the land coordinates?"

He smiled. "I sure can. I wrote them down." He handed her a piece of paper on which he had printed, "Did your family find out about us or have you decided to end things with me?"

She squinted at the note. "Yes, I think you have the first part right here, but not the second. Just let me check the files." She walked over to a long file cabinet and pretended to search and then came back. "No one has registered that parcel, so I believe your land is still available. Let me see those coordinates again just to make sure."

He gave her the note and she discreetly wrote something on it with a pen in her hand.

"They do look correct." She slid the note back in his direction and he read, "'Family knows. Riding to work with aunt in corner.'"

"Well, thank you," Brett told her. "I'm really happy to hear the property is still for sale. Hopefully, I can reconnect with the owner soon and work something out." He smiled again seeing her cheeks turn slightly pink.

"Is there anything else I can help you with?" she asked, blinking.

"No. Thank you. You've answered all my questions. Have a good day, now." He left the office and practically felt himself float down the stairs. *Life is good!*

MICHAEL WAS WALKING down a darkened hallway when he heard what sounded like a woman weeping on the other side of a closed door. He tried to open the door but when he turned the knob back and forth, he found the door was locked. When her cries grew more forceful he threw his shoulder into the door to break it open. After a few tries the door burst open and he saw a woman lying on a bed. Her hair covered most of her face and she was tied to a brass headboard with baler twine.

"Who tied you to this bed?" he demanded and reached into his pocket for a knife to cut her free.

She turned her tear soaked face toward him and he saw it was Cheryl. "It was you!" she lashed out. "You did this to me!"

Just then he noticed Jake and Jolene standing by the door with their eyes filled with total repulsion.

"It isn't what it looks like," Michael tried to defend himself, but a roaring noise drowned out his words.

"Michael!" Chet's voice boomed outside in the hall. "Michael wake up!"

Realizing he'd been dreaming, Michael shook his head but was confused he could still hear the blaring sound from his nightmare.

"Get up!" Michael heard his father's voice again and felt the covers being ripped off him.

Michael sprang into a sitting position and winced from the bright glare of a flash light in his face. "What's going on?"

Chet pulled his arm. "Come on! There's a storm coming! Your mother and Brett are headed for the basement."

Michael frantically grabbed his pants hanging over a chair and followed his father out of his room and down the long stairs. The downstairs of the house lit up several times with multiple flashes of lightning outside as they made their way to the basement door off the kitchen.

Down in the basement, Brett held a flash light with his arm around Lucille.

She had a blanket wrapped around her shoulders. "Thank God, you two finally got down here."

Chet popped open a small basement window. "By the sound, it has to be a tornado coming."

Lucille lit a candle and Brett fiddled with the buttons on a radio trying to find a weather station. Finally he picked up an announcer's voice.

"A mile-long severe storm cell has crossed the county line from Yellow Medicine into Chippewa County. It looks like it's going to miss Montevideo but is moving northeast toward Watson. Anyone in the area should take shelter immediately."

"Unfortunately, that's us," Chet said. "All we can do is pray now."

The family huddled together as they heard the roar outside rev to a spine-chilling howl.

THE SCENE out the kitchen window reminded Jolene of pictures she'd seen in high school of a tropical island after a cyclone. Clusters of pine needles, twigs, and bits of leaves were plastered onto the muddy ground and everywhere else in the yard. Thank God, none of the buildings had blown down on Cheryl's farm but a number of trees in the yard had met their demise. Jolene sighed looking at her red Firebird. It was splattered with the grimy debris and a large elm branch was sprawled across its smashed windshield. She knew it would be days before her insurance man would come out to assess the damage because the phone wasn't working to call him. Cheryl was making her nervous as she paced the kitchen floor behind her.

"I should be out there helping Jake find the cows, not Taylor," she stated and continued to pace.

"Not in your condition," Jolene answered with certainty. "Where's your hired hand, David?"

Cheryl let out a big breath. "Chet and Michael toured the neighborhood and stopped here at sunrise this morning with a report. Cowen's yard is full of downed trees. David said he'd be here as soon as he could get out of his driveway."

"How much damage did the Sugar King get?" Jolene asked turning away from the window.

"They had a couple of trees down in the yard. But it sounded like not as much as we did," Cheryl said, and finally stopped to plop down into a chair.

Jolene refilled their cups with coffee and joined her sister at the kitchen table. When a vehicle pulled in moments later, she got up and went to the window expecting to see David. She was surprised to see Michael get out of his truck and start for the house. *I wonder what he wants?* He took a few steps but stopped momentarily to gaze at her destroyed windshield.

"It's Michael," Jolene announced to Cheryl and went to the door.

He raised his hand to knock then blinked, perhaps surprised to see her standing on the other side of the screen door.

"Why are *you* here?" she demanded.

He dropped his hand and his eyes narrowed. "I'm here to help my brother."

"Then why are you here instead of out in the field some-where with him?"

He shook his head. "Well, I thought instead of wasting time searching for him on five hundred acres, I'd just ask his wife where he was going to start his search for the cattle."

Jolene felt herself blush. *How presumptuous of me.* "Okay. Give me a moment, I'll ask her."

She went over to the kitchen counter where Cheryl stood, apparently listening to their conversation. "Jake was going to start in the field behind the barn and work northeast."

Jolene returned to the screen door and began to relate the information in her best professional voice, "She said that Jake was going ..."

"Aahh!" Cheryl wailed painfully from inside.

Michael's eyes popped open wide before he ripped open the door and followed Jolene into the kitchen. Cheryl was hunched over with her head down clutching onto the counter. Her head suddenly snapped up. "Oh, my God!" she cried out hysterically. "My water broke!"

Seeing liquid soak into Cheryl's light-blue pant legs, Jolene completely froze.

Michael leapt to Cheryl's side and took her arm. "Get some towels!" He looked down at the floor and his eyes got big. "Bath towels!"

"Bath towels?" Jolene finally responded. "For what?"

"Just get them!" he ordered.

Cheryl gave her a quick nod and Jolene rushed down the hallway to the bathroom.

Michael took two of the towels and handed them to Cheryl. She unfolded them and placed them between her legs. He held onto her forearm and turned to Jolene. "You bring those other towels and take her arm. We need to get her into my truck and to the hospital."

Jolene couldn't move. Everything was moving too fast and she felt suddenly dizzy.

"Come on, Jolene," he coaxed. "Cheryl needs you."

Hearing his words, Jolene took in a breath and went to her sister's side. They hadn't gone three steps when Cheryl halted and gasped with what Jolene assumed was a contraction.

"Ooh!" she squeezed Jolene's arm. "No. We're not going to ... make it!" Cheryl frantically got out. "I can feel the baby. It's coming now!"

Jolene and Michael's eyes met before he took charge again. "Let's get her to the living room and onto the couch."

In the living room, Michael laid his hand on Cheryl's shoulder. "Just hold on. I'll go and find Jake."

Cheryl was about to answer when she doubled up in pain. She moaned and they both knew she was having another contraction. "No," she got out afterwards shaking her head. "There isn't time. This baby's coming, and I mean fast!"

Jolene panicked at the thought of being left alone. "Please Michael, I don't know a thing about childbirth. For God's sake! You can't leave now."

"I'm not a doctor!" Michael threw his arms open. "I have no idea what to do."

"It can't be that much different than the hundreds of animals you've seen give birth!" Jolene rattled out.

"She's right," Cheryl broke in. The desperation was clear in her voice. "Please Michael! There's no time. Help us through this."

"Okay," he swallowed hard. "Tell me what to do."

"Go wash your hands," she panted and he left for the bathroom.

"Jolene, help me off with these slacks."

They removed her slacks and placed a towel over Cheryl's bottom half. Jolene was sitting on the coffee table by her sister's head when Michael returned.

When Cheryl had another contraction he looked beneath the towel and his expression was profound when he looked up at them. Cheryl's screams lessoned but she still was pushing hard.

Michael laid his hand on her stomach, "I know it's strange to compare you to a cow but you and I both know you don't wrench the calf puller unless the cow's in a contraction. I know you must want to push, but stop and rest until the next contraction comes."

Cheryl's face was wet with sweat. "Okay… I'll try." She closed her eyes and laid her head back.

Less than two minutes later, Cheryl gritted her teeth and squeezed the pillow in her hand and cried out in pain. Jolene held her other hand and winced from her sister's strong grip.

"Push!" Michael shouted and moved his arms forward holding a towel. "I can almost see its whole head. One more push and you'll have it. Come on, Cheryl, push!"

With a loud groan, she pushed. A few seconds went by and Jolene heard a baby's sharp cry.

Michael's mouth hung open as he looked down at what he held. "Oh my … God! It's a girl and she's beautiful!"

Inside the towel, a baby was moving and flinging her tiny arms in the air.

Jolene smiled at her sister. "You have a daughter! I have a niece!"

"And so do I," Michael added. He wrapped the towel around the infant and set the baby in her mother's outstretched arms.

Cheryl's face was glowing as she looked down into the child's eyes. "Hey you," she said softly and held her small fingers. "You weren't supposed to be here until next month.

Nothing like just dropping by." They all had tears in their eyes but laughed at the comment.

"She looks like Jake," Jolene said.

"No denying that. The hair Taylor had was so blonde you couldn't see it. Her hair is dark like his," Cheryl stroked the top of her head then unwrapped the towel to survey the infant. "Ten fingers. Ten toes." Her eyes went to the umbilical cord. "I remember Nell Thompson talking about when women delivered their babies at home with the help of a mid-wife. She told me how they cut the cord."

Jolene noticed Michael flinch at the word "cut."

"There's a bottle of rubbing alcohol in the medicine cabinet in the bathroom. Take it into the kitchen, Michael, and pour it over the sharpest knife you can find." She turned to Jolene. "You know where I keep the string in the drawer in the kitchen. Cut two pieces of string about ten inches long and bring them in here."

Both Michael and Jolene did as they were told and returned to the living room.

"Michael, you need to tie the cord very tight a few inches from her belly," Cheryl instructed. He wrapped the string around the cord twice before tying it snugly. "Now tie another string a couple of inches away from where you tied the first. When you have it tied tightly, cut the cord in the middle."

Jolene watched as he carefully cut the cord and was impressed how level-headed Michael was through the whole thing. *I could never be so calm!*

Cheryl blew out a big breath. "Now, someone needs to go and get Nell. She'll know what to do next." She smiled. "And if you see my husband, you might want to let him know he has a daughter."

"If you gals think you'll be okay, I'll go find him after I get Nell."

"We'll be fine now, Michael." Tears were in Cheryl's eyes. "Thank you."

Smiling at the tiny bundle, he left. Jolene covered Cheryl and the baby with a blanket and sat close to them. The sights and sounds from the miracle that just happened were still spinning in her head. She stopped herself from thinking about what would've happened if Michael hadn't showed up. *Thank God he was here. There's no way I could've done it on my own!*

"Hurry up, woman!" Chet anxiously yelled to Lucille. "Get in!" He was waiting in his truck in the driveway with the engine running.

She shut the back door and leisurely came down the steps.

Once inside the truck, she asked her husband, "What's the big rush to get to the hospital? They're more than likely still checking Cheryl and the baby over."

His green eyes stared at her. "Aren't you the least bit excited to see your granddaughter?"

"Of course I am."

"Michael told me Cheryl and her sister both think she looks like Jake," Chet said when they turned onto the road.

Lucille put on her best smile and looked out the passenger window. *They're already planting the seed in everyone's head the baby resembles Jake. How clever!*

Chet suddenly chuckled.

"What's so funny?" she asked.

"Michael was always the most squeamish of the boys when it came to blood. It's amusing to think he was the one to deliver the baby."

"I can't imagine what went on in his head."

"He knew what he had to do and he faced it like a man." Chet had a beaming smile. "I've never been more proud of him."

"I guess he really didn't have a choice."

Lucille cringed seeing Nell and Earl sitting next to Jake in the waiting room of the hospital. Her son stood with a relieved smile seeing them come into the room.

Chet immediately stuck out his hand. "Congratulations, son." They shook hands and gave each other a hug which ended with Chet patting his son's back. Jake stepped away from his father and pulled his mother into his arms.

"Congratulations, Grandma."

She stiffened at his comment.

"Wait until you see her, Mom. She's a little angel."

"I ... I'm sure she is," Lucille answered.

"She's cute as a bug's ear and very alert," Nell piped up. "I was expecting the worse when Michael came flying in the driveway and told me he delivered the baby. I was so thankful when I saw for myself that Cheryl and the baby were okay."

"Yes. That was quite a story Michael told Chet and me," Lucille said primly.

Two men in white coats came out of a set of double doors and made a bee-line to Jake.

"Mr. Cameron?" one man inquired.

"Yes," Jake practically jumped out of his chair.

"I'm Dr. Spencer and this is Dr. Andrews. I'm the obstetrician who examined your wife. I'm happy to inform you she's doing just fine." Jake let out a relieved breath. "And my little girl?" he rifled out.

So sad! He still believes the child is his.

Dr. Andrews smiled. "I've examined her thoroughly and I'm very pleased to say she is a perfectly healthy six-pound, one-ounce baby girl. But we would like her and her mother to stay in the hospital for a few days for observation."

"Oh, God! Thank you, doctors!" Jake vigorously shook each of their hands. "When can I see them?"

"You all can follow us. The rest of your family will have to wait a few minutes. We're getting her settled into a room in the maternity ward."

Lucille watched Jake go through the doors then sat down.

Nell immediately started talking about the old days when she assisted a midwife with several births in the neighborhood. Perhaps either uninterested or uncomfortable, Chet and Earl started a conversation about the drought and the value of an irrigation system.

When an attendant came to get the group, Nell and Earl said they would leave and let the family have some time alone. Lucille was more than happy to get away from Nell's constant chatter.

In Cheryl's room, they found Jake standing close to her bedside holding a snugly wrapped baby in a pink blanket.

He smiled at Cheryl then tilted the bundle in his arms and pulled the blanket from the infant's face. "We are thrilled to introduce the newest member of the family, Michelle Marie Cameron."

Seeing the child, Lucille gasped and stepped back with her hand over her mouth. *Oh good, Lord! She's the spitting image of Jake!*

"What's wrong, Mom?" Jake asked.

"I can't believe it!" Lucille rushed to the baby. "She looks exactly like you did as a newborn."

"You would know that better than anyone," Jake smiled. "Would you like to hold her?"

"Yes." Lucille was still stunned at the resemblance, but snapped back into reality. "I certainly would." She held her hands open and demanded, "Hand over my granddaughter!"

Chet smiled at his wife and then at the baby. "She sure is a little cutie."

Lucille stared down into Michelle's face and gently stroked her soft cheek. *At last I have a girl! Thank you, God!*

JOLENE STARED through the windshield of Jake's truck at the outside of the Montevideo Community Building.

"Are you sure you're ready for this?" he asked. "The members of the AOG are a pretty tough audience."

"I guess I'm as ready as I'll ever be," she answered. "They need to know I was never involved in a scheme to sell out to Paul Bradford and neither was your family."

Jake held the door and she took a deep breath to steady her nerves before crossing over the threshold. Their entrance instantly spurred a wave of curious stares from the crowd of farmers seated throughout the room. Jolene saw Chet and Lucille along with their two other sons, seated in the first row. Jake tapped Jolene's elbow and motioned for her to go up the side where there were two empty chairs alongside Michael. Most of the eyes in the room were glued on them as they made their way to the front and took a seat.

Jolene slid her purse under her chair and pretended the attention she was getting had no effect on her. Michael turned his head and gave her a supportive smile and then reclined back in his chair. His enticing aftershave wafted in the air and messed with her nerves as it heightened her awareness of how close he was.

Jake rose from his chair and went to the front of the room where a group of men Jolene assumed were board members sat at a long table. She watched her brother-in-law say something to the man in the middle then turn briefly at her. The man nodded then wrote something down and handed him a piece of paper. Jake then returned to his chair next to Jolene and showed her the paper.

"This is the agenda for tonight's meeting. Right after they're done with the treasury report, the chairman, John Klies," he pointed to the man he spoke to, "will introduce you and then you'll be able to address the members."

Jolene nodded. *Please, dear Lord. Let them believe me!* She jumped slightly when the meeting began with a bang of the gavel on the table.

Michael noticed her flinch and discreetly patted her arm. "Just relax. You can do this."

At the end of the treasury report, Jolene could feel her heartbeat vibrate through her entire body when John Klies stood with his eyes on her and then on the group in front of him.

"A Miss Jolene Garrison would like to address the AOG members at this time."

The room exploded into a clamor of conversation from every corner.

John Klies rapped the gavel three times on table to get order. "Please, people. Can't we be civil enough to let this young woman speak?" The room quieted.

Jolene stood and went to the front of the room.

"I know most of you know who I am," she began. "I was the real estate agent who sold some of the farm foreclosure properties in your area."

Someone in the back yelled, "You're a cold-hearted bitch."

John hit the gavel hard on the table top and stood up. "No more of that! At least be respectful enough to hear her out." He nodded for her to proceed.

Jolene started again. "I was unknowingly led to believe by my employer, Will Vanders, that the State Bank of Watson was doing everything possible to keep the farms in the area from going into foreclosure." Murmurs in the crowd prompted her to pause. "But as you all know, that wasn't the case. My other employer, Donnie Larsen of Larsen's Realty, had me sign what I was told was an insurance form. But it was actually a purchase agreement he filled in later with the corporate farmer, Paul Bradford."

She heard a few gasps and whispers, but continued. "I was under the impression I was selling the foreclosed farms to private farmers such as yourselves, but as we've all learned, that wasn't the case. It's obvious someone got paid off by Paul Bradford, but it wasn't me." She paused and took a deep breath. Jolene's eyes swept over the front row. "It was Will Vanders and

Donnie Larsen. The Cameron family had nothing to do with any of it."

The room burst into loud debate when a man in the middle of the crowd stood up. John brought everyone to order then motioned to the man to speak.

"May I address Miss Garrison?"

"Is it okay if young Lloyd Jensen asks you some questions?" John asked Jolene.

Her eyes shot to Michael and Jake. "I suppose it would be fine," she answered.

Lloyd cleared his throat. "If the Camerons weren't involved in any part of it, why would Will Vanders indicate they were?" Heads in the room rotated to her.

"I think it was to keep everyone off his trail," Jolene answered and saw a few people in the crowd nod.

"And the other thing," Lloyd continued, "how stupid could you be to sign a form and not know what you were signing?" The noise level flared but went back down to hear her response.

"I ... I believed my employer when he said it was an insurance form."

"Don't you Realtors go to school and get some sort of license?"

"Yes. I do have a Realtor's license."

"Do you really think anyone actually believes a licensed Realtor would be so dumb? There's no way you're telling the truth." Lloyd nodded his head to the people around him and they mimicked his actions.

Jolene suddenly felt deflated. *Oh no! This isn't going in the right direction.*

Michael stood. "May I say something?" The crowd and his family turned their attention to him.

What are you doing?

John nodded for him to go ahead.

"For the record, Miss Garrison is one of the most intelligent and honest women I know." His tender eyes fell on her.

You don't know how much it means to hear you say that!

"But it takes intelligence *and* experience to know precisely what you're doing with most things in this world. I believe Will Vanders and Donnie Larsen specifically hired Miss Garrison with intentions of using her inexperience as a way to sell our farms to outside corporations."

"They could've done that on their own. They didn't need her," Lloyd Junior spouted.

Michael sucked in a breath. "Yes, they could've, but they didn't want any blood on their hands. If folks suspected they were paid off, their businesses would've been ruined, and they would've been run out of town. They had to find other people to take the fall and unfortunately ... that was Miss Garrison and my family."

"That doesn't prove anything. Her sister is married to your brother." Lloyd nudged his head at Jake. "You Camerons and her are family." His eyes narrowed. "You're all in it together."

The sound of a heavy door opening and two men stepping inside took Jolene's and everyone else's attention to the back of the room. She blinked twice, unsure of her own eyes, seeing the man she'd sold the Sorenson property to a few months ago. Larry Edwards looked timidly at the crowd of curious people who stared. Jim Stanton stood next to him, wearing a nice suit and a big smile.

"This guy has something to say," Jim shouted then grabbed Larry's arm and escorted him toward the table of board members."

John Klies got to his feet. "And who is this man?"

"He should tell you," Jim answered and looked at Larry. "Go ahead, tell them what you told me."

Larry looked apprehensive. "My name is Larry Edwards." His eyes found Jolene. "I was the one who Miss Garrison thought she was selling the Sorenson property to." A low roar ignited in the crowd.

John banged the gavel. "Let this man continue," he ordered.

"At the time of the sale, I was an employee for Mr. Paul Brad-ford. I was told by my boss that a deal had already been worked out for the land. All I had to do was go to the property location and pretend to buy it."

"And why would you have to do that?" John took over the interrogation.

"My boss learned from Will Vanders that some of the farmers in the area were facing some financial difficulties due to funding the refinery in Renville. Will gave him a list of properties and promised him the land would be available, and the two worked out a deal with Donnie Larsen for prime farmland at bargain prices. When this little lady came onto the scene," he waved his hand at Jolene, "all the land prices had already been negotiated. She never knew what was going on."

"Was the Cameron family involved in any of their dealings?" John asked.

"No, sir." He turned his head to Jim. "I never heard of the name until this fellow here mentioned it this morning."

"Well, thank you Mr. Edwards for shedding light on this subject for the AOG," John said loudly over the audience's excited buzz. He smiled proudly at Chet in the front row. "I think we've all heard enough to clear the Cameron family and Miss Garrison of any wrong doings. As acting chairman," he shouted, "I motion Chet Cameron be reinstated as chairman and this meeting be adjourned. All those in favor, say, aye!"

"Aye!" The crowd shouted unanimously. A dark-haired girl came from somewhere in the crowd and hugged Brett.

Michael rushed to Jolene and wrapped his arms around her. "Are you alright?" he whispered in her ear.

"Now I am," she answered and found herself not wanting to let him go. Maybe it was out of gratitude knowing he tried to defend her. He slowly pulled away and she watched him shake his father's and brothers' hands with a huge smile that enhanced his gorgeous face.

She had been quick to dispose of him after finding out what

happened between him and Cheryl. The whole thing had been too horrible to comprehend and it had been so easy to condemn him without thinking it through.

Yet, he took her word and believed in her innocence even after seeing her name written on a contract. They both had done something to hurt people without realizing it. He had forgiven her. Could she possibly find it in her heart to forgive him?

22

Jolene sat on the porch in the morning sunlight yawning uncontrollably. Sweet little Michelle had awakened every two to three hours during the night with hungry cries that kept everyone in the house awake with her. Jolene loved her niece, but was relieved knowing it had been her last night at Cheryl and Jake's. Her suitcases were packed and sitting in the foyer and Black's Auto Body Shop had promised to deliver her repaired car to her apartment sometime in the afternoon. All she needed was for Jake to return from chores at the Sugar King and take her into town. Cheryl offered, but Jolene knew her sister was busy enough with a newborn and told her she would wait for Jake.

Thoughts about the future drifted in and out of her head as she waited. Should she go back to Aberdeen and stay with her mother until she found a job? Or maybe go to Sioux Falls to try and make it as a Realtor there?

Jake's truck finally pulled into the driveway and Jolene put out her cigarette. She was surprised to see Michael's truck drive in seconds later and park alongside of Jake's. Both brothers casually came up the walk to the house.

"So how's everyone doing this morning?" Jake asked her as he stepped onto the porch.

"Taylor tried watching cartoons but he fell asleep on the couch," Jolene answered. "And Cheryl was feeding Michelle when I came out here."

"You two stay right here. I'll be right back," Jake told them and went inside.

Jolene's attention went to Michael. "What brings you here?"

"I heard you need a ride into town. And Jake being so busy, I told him I'd be more than happy to take you."

"That's very kind." She tried to squelch the elated tone in her voice. "But I wouldn't want to bother you."

"Oh, no bother. I was hoping it would give us a chance to talk." He sounded hopeful.

"Talk about what?" she asked.

Before he could answer, the door opened and Cheryl and Jake came out of the house.

"She's fast asleep," Cheryl reported and retreated to one of the wooden chairs on the porch. "Come sit down, Jolene and Michael. Jake and I have something we'd like to ask you two."

Jolene took the other chair and Michael sat on the deck rail.

Jake stood next to Cheryl and squeezed her hand. "Before we ask you, there's something that needs to be said." He looked down at his wife.

It took a moment for Cheryl to start. "I was terribly traumatized after what happened last summer."

Michael dropped his head in his hands.

"But with the help of time, my husband's insight, and the arrival of our daughter, I'm seeing things in a different light." She stood from her chair and went to Michael with her hand extended.

His hands fell at his sides as she lifted his chin with her fingertips. There were tears in his eyes as he gazed up at her.

"I know now it was the drugs that made you attack me. And I forgive you, Michael."

He took a ragged breath. "I know … I don't deserve it, but thank you." She softly patted his shoulder.

Jake nodded approvingly at his wife and brother before his eyes met Jolene's.

Oh my God! They made it look so easy.

Cheryl went back to her chair and Jake hugged her before she sat down.

"Now that we've got that behind us." His eyes went back and forth from Michael and Jolene. "How would you two like to be godparents to Michelle?"

"I'd be delighted to be her godmother," Jolene answered.

"I would be honored," Michael replied a beat later and shook Jake's hand.

"Then it's final. Baptism is on Sunday in Watson." Jake smiled at Jolene. "You'll have to stick around until then."

A wounded look flashed on Michael's face but he looked away.

"Yes. I guess I'll have to." Her answer sounded weak.

MICHAEL AND JOLENE were a mile down the road when he finally got the courage to ask, "Are you leaving the area after the baptism?"

"That's my plan," she answered. "I don't think anyone around here will hire me now."

"I think you underestimate the people in this area. Most appreciate honesty above anything else."

"That may be true, but I don't see Larsen's hiring me back anytime soon."

"There's always Spencer's Realty in Montevideo or maybe … you should consider starting your own real estate business."

She cocked her head. "You really think so?"

"Why not?" He smiled. "You're an intelligent, hard-working woman."

"Thanks for the vote of confidence, but it takes money to start a business."

"Well, I'm not saying the Watson Bank, but you could apply for a loan."

"I guess I never thought about it," she said.

"Sometimes a person doesn't see things until someone else points them out."

She was quiet for a few seconds. "I heard about you and Diana breaking up. I'm sorry."

"What are *you* sorry for?" He glanced at her. "She wanted to get married, but her real agenda was having a baby. All I was to her was a possible sperm donor."

Her green eyes widened. "I guess she did like to talk quite a bit about babies."

He blew out a breath. "She wasn't the sweet thing she was back in high school. That's for sure. I don't know of very many women who would actually touch a dead rat to make a point."

Jolene's mouth fell open and her eyes narrowed. "She was the one who put that gross creature on my step?"

"She saw my truck at your apartment that night after we broke into Larsen's. She heard how angry folks were about you supposedly getting paid off by a corporate farmer and took it upon herself to give you a visual incentive to leave."

Her eyes stared at the dash in obvious disbelief. "I should have decked her when I had the chance."

His head spun to her. "What?"

"That day at the bazaar in the fellowship hall. She accused me of flirting with you with lust and desire in my eyes."

Michael recalled seeing Jolene in her print dress throwing the ball. Her hair was up and she was breathtakingly beautiful. *I was the one doing the flirting.*

"It wasn't so bad until she slapped my face," Jolene continued.

He slammed on the brakes and faced her. "She struck you?"

"Yes. But I may have thrown a little gas on the fire," she added a little sheepishly.

He put the truck in park. "What do you mean?"

"I told her she should be more worried about how *you* look at *me*."

"Wow! I didn't realize I was so obvious," he felt himself blush.

A smile bloomed on her face but it quickly faded. "Michael, I've been terribly unfair to you."

"How's that?"

"When you told me about what happened with Cheryl, I was immediately filled with horror and disgust. It seemed you were talking in a tunnel far away and my ears were only hearing bits and pieces of what you were saying." She covered his hand with hers. "I was foolish to instantly sever my feelings for you and not even consider you may have been telling the truth." Her suddenly teary eyes searched his. "But you ... you never questioned my innocence. You believed me when everyone else wanted to run me out of town."

"That's because ... I love you."

"I love you, too," she said breathlessly and slid across the seat. Their lips came together in a sweet but wonderfully passionate kiss.

Kissing her back, the longing he had for her went through his body in a rush of razor sharp desire.

Beep! Beep! Beep! A horn startled them from behind the truck. Michael quickly looked around Jolene's head into the rear view mirror. A car was idling behind them and the man driving was waving his arms up in the air. Realizing they were parked in the middle of the road, Michael pulled the truck to the edge and waved him through.

Jolene giggled. "I've heard of a heart-stopping kiss, but not a traffic-stopping one."

He laughed with her. "I think we better get to your apartment."

Rubbing his bicep, she laid her head on his shoulder and they took off down the road. It felt wonderful having her so close to him. Her perfume was intoxicating and undeniably arousing. He couldn't remember a time in his life when he wanted a woman so much. *God, help me, convince her to stay!*

Arriving at Jolene's apartment building, they carried her suitcases across the parking lot and into her darkened apartment. Her luggage barely touched the floor in the entry way before their hungry mouths found each other's. He was thrilled when she took his hand and led him toward the bedroom with a tantalizing smile.

She glanced back at him and suddenly sucked in a sharp breath. Michael cranked his head over his shoulder and his blood ran cold. There in the semi-darkness stood Will Vanders with a shotgun raised in their direction.

Michael instinctively stepped in front of Jolene.

Will flipped on the lights and it was shocking to see his frazzled appearance. He looked exhausted with his matted hair and unshaven face. His suit was wrinkled and the tie he wore was stained and hung loosely around his neck.

"Well, isn't this romantic." He smiled with bloodshot eyes. "You people should really lock your doors."

Michael immediately recognized the shotgun as one belonging to Will's father, Charlie. They had used it a few times for pheasant hunting when they were kids. "What are you doing with that shotgun, Will?"

"Giving myself some leverage." He smiled smugly and waved the shotgun barrel to the right. "Step out from behind him, Jolene." When she didn't move, he screamed, "Now!" She shuddered then moved away. "Both of you, sit on the couch."

Michael sat down but continued to glare at him. "What the hell do you want with us?"

"Shut up!" he ordered. "I'm the one running the show here, not you." His eyes swept over Michael. "It must be a little hard to take, me being the one calling the shots. But I guess we're not in high school anymore, and there isn't a group of idol-izing guys hanging around or a harem of women chasing you."

"If this is about Beth Ackerman, you know I never ..."

"I said, shut up!" He raised the shotgun.

Michael took a deep breath and nervously pushed it out. *Don't work him into doing anything stupid!*

"You Cameron boys always thought you were in control of every situation. It sure was amusing to see how unglued you and Jake got after I pushed Brett off the rock down at the river." He chuckled. "The whiny smart ass deserved it."

Jake was right. Will had pushed him!

His eyes traveled to the other side of the couch. "Just look at her. She's a pretty sight, isn't she, Michael? I knew at Jake's wedding you had feelings for her and hiring her was nothing less than genius." Will smiled. "Not only did I have someone to pin selling out to Bradford on, I had the woman you wanted at my disposal and a sure way to tarnish your family's shining reputation. Her sister being married to your brother made it easy for folks to connect the dots."

Will's expression turned remorseful. "In my head, the ulti-mate prize was going to be her falling in love with me so I could take her away from you. I wanted you to feel the pain I did in high school when I was stuck in your shadow. She was green enough for Donnie and me to take advantage of, but I didn't count on her actually being in love with you." He sighed deeply. "Oh well, I guess a person can't win them all."

Jolene's chest was heaving as she ground out, "You haven't won a thing and you're insane to think I would ever fall for you."

"Maybe it was a little crazy, but sometimes people can surprise you. Who would've imagined you two would break into a business and steal a file? Or that you'd actually find Larry Edwards?"

Her eyes got big, but she didn't say anything.

"By the way, where is that file?" His head turned from side to side like he expected to see it lying about the apartment.

When neither answered, he pointed the shotgun at Michael. "Tell me, Jolene! Or live with the consequences."

The color left her face.

"What's the plan, Will?" Michael fired out. "Kill us for the file and face murder charges instead of simply being discredited by the town?"

"There's also the matter of *my* family's reputation. If there's no file, it's her word against both Donnie and me."

Michael shook his head. "Maybe you should've considered your family's reputation when you decided to sell out to Bradford."

"No more delays." He raised the weapon again. "Where's the file?"

"Do you even know how to use that old pump shotgun?" Michael asked. "If I remember right, you had a helluva time hitting anything with it."

Boom! The shotgun went off and Jolene let out a blood-chilling scream. There on the floor was a deep blackened hole with bits of carpet and wood chips scattered around it. Before Will could reload, Michael jumped from the couch and pulled the shot gun out of his hands.

"Give it up, Will. Everyone is wise to what you did. No one's going to believe you."

Will backed up and proudly announced, "My father will never believe I did anything wrong. He will *always* stand behind me."

"Just so you know, we gave the file to the AOG after Larry Edwards confirmed he was the one Jolene sold the property to."

Will spun away for the door and swung it wide open. He poked his head outside and looked from side to side before he ran in the direction of the parking lot.

Jolene rushed to Michael and burst into tears. He carefully set the shot gun down on the couch before he drew her close.

"It's over now," he assured. "He has no reason to come back here."

"I really thought he was going to kill us."

"I did too, for a moment." *Thank God he's always been a coward!*

DURING THE MEALTIME PRAYER, Michael scanned the people seated around the dining room table at the Langtree Farm. Jake proudly held the spot at the head of the table with Cheryl at his right and Taylor on his left. Sitting next to Taylor, Brett sat with his chair positioned close to Karyn's on his left. Irene was seated next and the old housekeeper sure looked different with her hair done and wearing a nice dress.

Michael's eyes went to Mary, Jolene and Cheryl's mother, who sat between her daughters. He winked at Jolene next to him then turned his head and smiled at his mother on his right. Lucille was holding baby Michelle with her pleased eyes on her husband at the end of the table.

"Thank you, Lord, for bringing us together for Michelle's baptism and for keeping everyone safe during the fire this week," Jake added at the end of the prayer.

"Amen!" Michael joined in with the rest at the table.

"I'm so thankful the pastor at Immanuel Lutheran let us have the baptism at his church," Cheryl commented with a grateful smile.

"I still can't figure out what went through that boy's head to make him want to burn down the Watson Lutheran Church," Lucille shook her head. "I can't imagine what Helen and Charlie are going through."

"No one knows if it was an accident or Will was attempting suicide," Jake reported. "I guess he'd been hiding in the bell tower ever since Charlie told him he couldn't condone what he did to the community. Will was lucky they got him out of the church alive."

"I heard Donnie Larsen and his family left town in the middle of the night," Brett informed the group.

"Greed is a terrible thing, especially when you let it get the best of you," Chet said from his end of the table. "It led those two fools into taking advantage of a lot of good people." His eyes went to Jolene. "What are your plans now, young lady?"

Her head briefly swung to her mother before she turned to Michael. "Someone pointed out a few opportunities I hadn't thought of before, so I'm thinking maybe I'll stick around here for a while." Michael found her hand and lovingly squeezed it. She smiled at him and then at the people around the table. "It's strange, but after what I've been through, I somehow feel ... like I belong here."

Michael smiled seeing his father's approving nod. *What can I say, Dad? I love her.*

"How much longer do I have to wear this blindfold?" Jolene asked Michael from the passenger seat in his truck.

"Hang on." He laughed. "We're almost there."

Feeling him brake then turn and stop shortly after, she wondered where they were. She reached up to take off the blindfold and he caught her hand.

"Please. Don't take it off, yet. Just give me a few more minutes."

She heard him open his driver's door and shut it before he opened hers seconds later. Taking her hand, he helped her out of the truck.

"Now just a few more steps forward."

She could feel the wind blow her hair away from her face and smell some type of fresh cut grass wafting in the air. *Maybe hay?* She did as he instructed, totally intrigued by where he was taking her.

"Okay. You can take it off now."

Pulling the blindfold away, she blinked at the bright red and white "For Sale" sign in front of her. A sticker with the word "Sold" in big letters was sprawled diagonally across it from corner to corner. She raised her head, then recognized the farm in the distance.

"Isn't this the farm we looked at last month? The one with the darling brick house?"

"Yes, this is it." He shook his head at the sign with concern. "Looks like someone must have bought it."

She stared at him for a brief moment. "So, why are we here?"

"I guess I wanted to see how you felt about the place."

"I don't think it matters now." She suddenly remembered the listing was about to expire and looked at the bottom of the sign. It didn't have a realty listed. "Someone likely dealt with the son and purchased it without a Realtor. I would assume they got a better deal without having to pay a commission."

He nodded in agreement. "It sure looks that way."

"So, were you interested in this property?"

"Yes."

"I thought you said the tool shed was too small and it wasn't right for beef cattle or horses."

He looked down. "I lied."

She narrowed her brows confused. "Why did you lie?"

His eyes met hers. "It was the only way I could spend more time with you. I knew Will and Donnie were up to something. I was hoping if you and I spent some time together, you would let something slip about them."

"So you thought I was in on their shenanigans?"

"I couldn't imagine you were part of any dishonest scheme, but I had to make sure."

"That's why you gave me all those history lessons on the generations of farmers who previously owned the land."

"Yes. I was hoping you would see they were taken advantage of by Will and Donnie."

She looked down. "The whole time I was thinking you were jealous of Will."

"I was, for a while." He smiled. "It looked like you two were an item."

A big smile broke out on her face. "Really?" she teased. "Michael Cameron, jealous?"

"Yeah, I was. Weren't you the least bit jealous of Diana and me?"

"Okay. I admit I was." She slipped her arms around his waist. "But it appears I was victorious in the end."

He pulled her close and turned them in the direction of the house. "So do you still think the place is perfect like you said on the day we toured it?"

"Of course I do, but there's nothing to think about now. I'm unemployed and the place has been sold. What about you? Do you regret not buying it?"

He pulled a keyring out of his pocket and dangled a gold colored key with his fingers. "No, I don't."

Jolene felt her mouth drop open wide. "You?" She rapidly blinked at him. "You bought this place?"

"Yes. I did." His eyes circled the area and then went back to her. "I know you loved it as much as I do. I can't imagine being here a day without you." Reaching into his pocket, he retrieved a small, black velvet box.

Oh, my God! She felt the air leave her body when he dropped to one knee.

When he opened the lid the sun caught a diamond inside and sent dazzling rays of rainbow colors in every direction. She gasped at the sight with both hands on her mouth.

"I love you, Jolene." His eyes sparkled. "Will you be my wife?"

Is this really happening? "Yes!" she finally got out. "Yes! I'll marry you!" Rushing to him, she held his beautiful face with her hands and laid a crushing kiss on his luscious lips. His eyes never left hers as he got to his feet. He took her hand and tenderly kissed it before he slipped the ring on her finger. A second later, two strong arms wrapped around her waist and she felt her feet leave the ground. Squeezing her tight, he twirled them around in a circle then let her body slide down until their lips met in an electrifying kiss.

"Let's go home," he told her after the kiss was over. He pointed to the house.

She smiled and nodded, knowing it was true. She was finally home.

The End

I hope you enjoyed reading this book as much as I did writing Jolene and Michael's story. If so, please help me on my writing journey and post a review at:
https://www.amazon.com/dp/1734084235

Without reviews, my books are unnoticed by book sellers and it makes it hard for readers to find me.

ABOUT THE AUTHOR

Donna Lovitz grew up near Clear Lake, Minnesota, but considers tiny nearby Palmer her real home town. Her parents owned and operated the only bar and restaurant there, so she spent her early years meeting and observing a variety of interesting people. She married the love of her life, Rick Lovitz, and lived in Sauk Rapids, Minnesota, for 33 years before moving to Lake George, Minnesota, where they currently reside.

Along with writing, Donna enjoys snowshoeing, ice fishing and gardening, and has also added wine making to her lists of interests. Though winters in the Northland can be long, Donna doesn't mind. The calm beauty and serenity in the forest where she lives often kindle her creative spirit, and the nature around her home inspires her writing adventures.

Donna is a member of Romance Writers of America and has had articles published in the St. Cloud Times and poetry published in the literary journal "St. Cloud Unabridged." She is also a prolific creator of slogans and has won several contests for her creations.

Only a Heartbeat Away is the third book of the the Heartbeat Series. Heartbeat of Desire is the first and Revenge in a Heartbeat is the second book. The books in the Heartbeat Series center around a wealthy family of sugar beet farmers in Central Minnesota.

It has always been a dream of Donna's to write romance novels, and now she is making that dream a reality.

If you would like to know more about Donna, visit her website at: http://www.donnalovitz.com or visit her on Facebook at: http://www.facebook.com/donnalovitz

Other books by Donna Lovitz

Ryley — A Christmas Romance

(Book #1 of the Heartbeat Series)
Heartbeat of Desire — A Modern History Romance

(Book #2 of the Heartbeat Series)
Revenge in a Heartbeat — A Modern History Romance

ACKNOWLEDGMENTS

I am grateful to everyone who has helped and encouraged me on my writing journey. I am especially thankful to all of my readers. Your support motivates me to do what I love — write!

A special thank you to Katie Schlomann for critiquing this book — your help was invaluable. I would also like to thank my proofreaders whose help was a crucial part of getting this book ready for publication. Finally, I would like to thank all of the members of the Northern Lights Writers, a Minnesota chapter of Romance Writers of America.

Made in the USA
Monee, IL
08 December 2021

84223189R00184